PRAISE FOR THE NOVELS
OF ANNE O'BRIEN

The King's Concubine

"*The King's Concubine* is a delicious and satisfying Cinderella story, following the rise of Alice Perrers from powerless naivety to the pinnacle of the realm as the mistress of Edward III. Anne O'Brien brings Alice's story to life with vivid details and glorious writing that will please any fan of historical fiction."   —Gillian Bagwell, author of *The September Queen*

Queen Defiant

"*Queen Defiant* lives up to its title as Anne O'Brien, with sensual lyricism, gifts readers with the lesser-known story of Eleanor of Aquitaine before Henry Plantagenet swept her away to immortality. Married to the monk-king of France, Louis II, Eleanor fights Louis, the Church, and the French nobility to go on crusade to Jerusalem, where she finds unexpected sexual fulfillment before a much younger Henry pursues and wins her to an even greater love. We are more familiar with her tumultuous story as England's great queen, but O'Brien brings us the equally fascinating tale of Eleanor's little-known earlier years, the years that gave her an enduring defiance and strength that she would need for the rest of her life."
     —Jeane Westin, author of *His Last Letter* and *The Virgin's Daughters*

"Passionate and romantic . . . *Queen Defiant* is another fascinating look at the early life of Eleanor of Aquitaine. O'Brien's Eleanor is a fine tribute to the woman that she was historically: complex, ambitious, intelligent, and alluring. Eleanor of Aquitaine would be proud."
                                   —Examiner.com (Pittsburgh)

"Eleanor is the picture of defiance, and her bold, fiery voice is the strongest asset of this successful historical."   —*Publishers Weekly*

continued . . .

"The reader is taken on a roller-coaster ride through Eleanor's emotions and her story, and you just cannot help but fall in love with this passionate heroine. . . . O'Brien brings Eleanor, Louis, Henry, Aquitaine, and Paris to life with her writing, and it is a gripping story [that] the reader will find hard to put down. . . . This is a wonderful romp through Eleanor's life."
—The Anne Boleyn Files

"Anne O'Brien provides a fresh perspective [on Eleanor's life] . . . engaging."
—Genre Go Round Reviews

The Virgin Widow

"Packed with royal intrigue and stunning reversals of fortune, *The Virgin Widow* is a thrilling romance drawn from history, beautifully told. Anne O'Brien's spirited and courageous heroine, Lady Anne Neville, a traitor's daughter and future Queen of England, vividly narrates her incredible journey through treachery and heartbreak into the arms of the man she loves—the last Plantagenet King of England, Richard III."
—Sandra Worth, award-winning author of *Pale Rose of England*

"O'Brien pulls us by our heartstrings through the power struggles between the House of York and Lancaster, telling the story through the seemingly hopeless love of Anne Neville for the man who would become Richard III . . . a little-known story that you will never forget."
—Jeane Westin

"*The Virgin Widow* is a novel so engrossing that I couldn't put it down. Anne Neville comes to full and glorious life on these pages—a courageous woman of her own time, timeless in her appeal to readers."
—Kate Emerson, author of
Secrets of the Tudor Court: At the King's Pleasure

"Anne O'Brien's *The Virgin Widow* takes the reader on a compelling journey through medieval history and the heart of Anne Neville, a pawn and power in Plantagenet England. The vibrant characters, especially the narrator heroine, leap off the page. O'Brien weaves love, lust, tragedy, and triumph into a rich historical tapestry to treasure."

—Karen Harper, national bestselling author of
Mistress Shakespeare and *The Irish Princess*

"*The Virgin Widow* is the finest portrayal of Anne Neville in historical fiction. It gives a flattering portrayal of Anne, a historically accurate view of this tumultuous time in England, and great romance and drama. O'Brien's first venture into novels on historical figures gets two thumbs up."

—Examiner.com (Pittsburgh), included in the
Best Ten Historical Novels of 2010

"O'Brien has excellent control over the historical material and a rich sense of characterization, making for a fascinating and surprisingly female-focused look at one of the most turbulent periods of English history."

—*Publishers Weekly*

"A strong tale filled with intrigue, a deep understanding of historical events, and a far more sympathetic portrait of Richard III than Shakespeare's that will fascinate readers."

—*Romantic Times*

"If you need a good book for holiday reading or for relaxing with in the garden on a sunny day, you just cannot go wrong with this one. All of the right ingredients: romance, intrigue, betrayal, glamour, history, murder . . . brilliant!"

—The Anne Boleyn Files

"With this winning novel, Anne O'Brien has joined the exclusive club of excellent historical novelists."

—*Sunday Express* (UK)

Other Novels by Anne O'Brien

Queen Defiant
The Virgin Widow

THE KING'S
CONCUBINE

A NOVEL OF ALICE PERRERS

Anne O'Brien

 NEW AMERICAN LIBRARY

NEW AMERICAN LIBRARY
Published by New American Library, a division of
Penguin Group (USA) Inc., 375 Hudson Street,
New York, New York 10014, USA
Penguin Group (Canada), 90 Eglinton Avenue East, Suite 700, Toronto,
Ontario M4P 2Y3, Canada (a division of Pearson Penguin Canada Inc.)
Penguin Books Ltd., 80 Strand, London WC2R 0RL, England
Penguin Ireland, 25 St. Stephen's Green, Dublin 2,
Ireland (a division of Penguin Books Ltd.)
Penguin Group (Australia), 250 Camberwell Road, Camberwell, Victoria 3124,
Australia (a division of Pearson Australia Group Pty. Ltd.)
Penguin Books India Pvt. Ltd., 11 Community Center, Panchsheel Park,
New Delhi - 110 017, India
Penguin Group (NZ), 67 Apollo Drive, Rosedale, Auckland 0632,
New Zealand (a division of Pearson New Zealand Ltd.)
Penguin Books (South Africa) (Pty.) Ltd., 24 Sturdee Avenue,
Rosebank, Johannesburg 2196, South Africa

Penguin Books Ltd., Registered Offices:
80 Strand, London WC2R 0RL, England

First published by New American Library,
a division of Penguin Group (USA) Inc.

First American Printing, June 2012
10 9 8 7 6 5 4 3 2 1

 REGISTERED TRADEMARK—MARCA REGISTRADA

Library of Congress Cataloging-in-Publication Data:

O'Brien, Anne, 1949–
  The king's concubine: a novel of Alice Perrers/Anne O'Brien.
    p. cm
  ISBN 978-0-451-23680-7
  1. Perrers, Alice, ca. 1348–1400—Fiction. 2. Ladies-in-waiting—Great Britain—Fiction. 3. Edward III, King of England, 1312–1377—Fiction. 4. Great Britain—Kings and rulers—Paramours—Fiction. 5. Mistresses—Great Britain—Fiction. I. Title.
  PR6115.B7355K56 2012
  823'.92—dc23   2011048198

Set in Simoncini Garamond
Designed by Alissa Amell

Printed in the United States of America

ALWAYS LEARNING   PEARSON

For George,
who managed to live comfortably for a year with both me and Alice
Perrers. As ever, with love and thanks.

Acknowledgments

All my thanks:

To my agent Jane Judd, who appreciated the possibility of Alice Perrers as an unconventional heroine. Her advice and support, as always, are beyond price.

To Jennifer Unter, my "agent over the pond," who continues to support me and my historical heroines.

To Ellen Edwards and her exceptional team at NAL. Their guidance and commitment were invaluable in enabling the real Alice Perrers to emerge from infamy.

To Helen Bowden and all at Orphans Press who come to my rescue and continue to create masterpieces out of my genealogy and maps.

To Phia McBarnet, who patiently introduced me to the benefits of social media and set my foot on the steep learning curve.

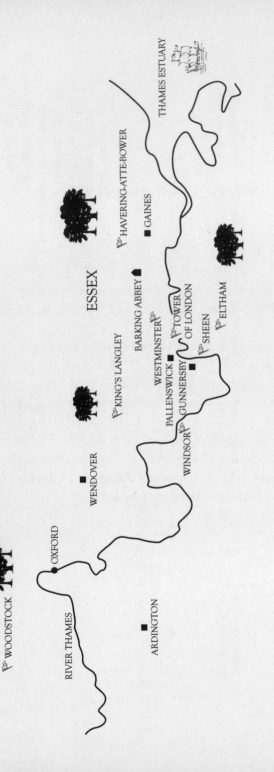

ROYAL PALACES
ALICE'S MANORS
ROYAL FORESTS

THAMES ESTUARY

HAVERING-ATTE-BOWER

GAINES

ESSEX

ELTHAM

KING'S LANGLEY

BARKING ABBEY

WESTMINSTER

TOWER
OF LONDON

SHEEN

PALLENSWICK

GUNNERSBY

WINDSOR

WENDOVER

OXFORD

ARDINGTON

WOODSTOCK

RIVER THAMES

Royal Palaces &
Alice's Manors

Descencants of Edward III (simplified)

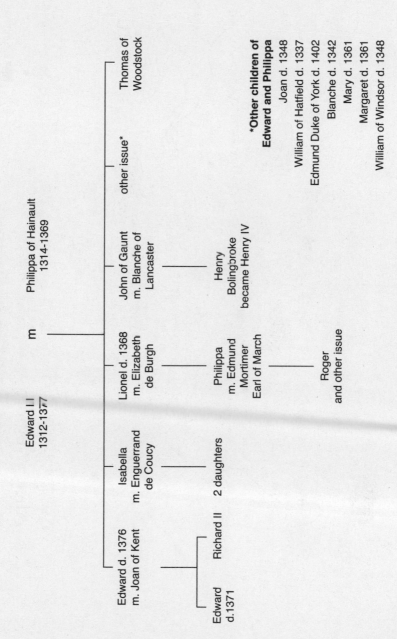

Edward III
1312-1377

m

Philippa of Hainault
1314-1369

Edward d. 1376
m. Joan of Kent

Isabella
m. Enguerrand
de Coucy

Lionel d. 1368
m. Elizabeth
de Burgh

John of Gaunt
m. Blanche of
Lancaster

other issue*

Thomas of
Woodstock

Richard II

2 daughters

Philippa
m. Edmund
Mortimer
Earl of March

Henry
Bolingbroke
became Henry IV

Edward
d.1371

Roger
and other issue

***Other children of
Edward and Philippa**

Joan d. 1348

William of Hatfield d. 1337

Edmund Duke of York d. 1402

Blanche d. 1342

Mary d. 1361

Margaret d. 1361

William of Windsor d. 1348

"There was . . . in England a shameless woman and wanton harlot called Ales Peres, of base kindred . . . being neither beautiful or fair, she knew how to cover these defects with her flattering tongue. . . ."

—A historical relation of certain passages
about the end of King Edward III and of his death

"It is not fitting that all the keys should hang from the belt of one woman."

—Thomas Brinton, Bishop of Rochester

". . . no one dared to go against her . . ."

—Thomas Walsingham, a monk of St. Albans

Prologue

"*T*oday you will be my Lady of the Sun," King Edward says as he approaches to settle me into my chariot. "My Queen of Ceremonies."

And not before time!

I *don't* say the words, of course—I am, after all, a woman of perception—but I think them. I have waited too many years for this acclaim. Twelve years as Edward's whore.

"Thank you, my lord," I murmur, curtsying deeply, my smile as sweet as honey.

I sit, a cloak of shimmering gold tissue spread around me to show a lining of scarlet taffeta. My gown is red, lined with white silk and edged in ermine: Edward's colors, royal fur fit for a queen. Over all glitters a myriad of precious stones refracting the light: rubies as red as blood, sapphires dark and mysterious, strange beryls capable of destroying the power of poison. Everyone knows that I wear Queen Philippa's jewels.

I sit at my ease, alone in my preeminence, my hands loose in my bejeweled lap. This is my right!

I look around to see if I might catch sight of the black scowl of the Princess Joan. No sign of her, my sworn enemy. She'll be tucked away in her chamber at Kennington, ill-wishing me. Joan the Fair. Joan the Fat! An adversary to be wary of, with the sensitivity and morals of a feral cat in heat.

My gaze slides to Edward as he mounts his stallion, and my smile softens. He is tall and strong and good to look on. What a pair we make, he and I. The years have not yet pressed too heavily on him, while I am in my prime. An ugly woman, by all accounts, but not without talent.

I am Alice. Royal Concubine. Edward's beloved Lady of the Sun . . .

Ah . . . ! I blink as a swooping pigeon smashes the scene in my mind, flinging reality back at me with cruel exactitude. Sitting in my orchard, far from Court and my King, I am forced to accept the truth. How low have I fallen. I am caged in impotent loneliness, like Edward's long-dead lion, powerless, isolated, stripped of everything I had made for myself.

I am nothing. Alice Perrers is no more.

Chapter One

*W*here do I start? It's difficult to know. My beginnings as I recall them were not moments marked by joy or happiness. So I will start with what I do recall. My very first memory.

I was a child, still far too young to have much understanding of who or what I was, kneeling with the sisters in the great Abbey church of St. Mary's. It was the eighth day of December and the air so cold it hurt my lungs as I breathed it in. The stone paving was rough beneath my knees, but even then I knew better than to shuffle. The statue on its plinth in the Lady Chapel was clothed in a new blue gown, her veil and wimple made from costly silk, startlingly white in the dark shadows. The nuns sang the office of Compline, and 'round the feet of the statue a pool of candles had been lit. The light flickered over the deep blue folds so that the figure appeared to move, to breathe.

"Who is she?" I asked, voice too loud. I was still very ignorant.

Sister Goda, novice mistress when there were novices to teach, hushed me. "The Blessed Virgin."

"What is she called?"

"She is the Blessed Virgin Mary."

"Is this a special day?"

"It is the feast of the Immaculate Conception. Now, hush!"

It meant nothing to me then, but I fell in love with her. The Blessed

Mary's face was fair, her eyes downcast; there was a little smile on her painted lips, and her hands were raised as if to beckon me forward. But what took my eye was the crown of stars that had been placed for the occasion on her brow. The gold gleamed in the candlelight; the jewels reflected the flames in their depths. And I was dazzled. After the service, when the nuns had filed out, I stood before her, my feet small in the shimmer of candles.

"Come away, Alice." Sister Goda took my arm, not gently.

I was stubborn and planted my feet.

"Come on!"

"Why does she wear a crown of stars?" I asked.

"Because she is the Queen of Heaven. Now will you . . ."

The sharp slap on my arm made me obey; yet still I reached up, although I was too small to touch it, and smiled.

"I would like a crown like that."

My second memory followed fast on my first. Despite the late hour, Sister Goda, small and frail but with a strong right arm, struck my hand with a leather strap until my skin was red and blistered. Punishment for the sin of vanity and covetousness, she hissed. Who was I to look at a crown and desire it for myself? Who was I to approach the Blessed Virgin, the Queen of Heaven? I was of less importance than the pigeons that found their way into the high reaches of the chancel. I would not eat for the whole of the next day. I would rise and go to bed with an empty belly. I would learn humility. And as my belly growled and my hand hurt, I learned, and not for the last time, that it was not in the nature of women to get what they desired.

"You are a bad child!" Sister Goda stated unequivocally.

I lay awake until the Abbey bell summoned us at two of the clock for Matins. I did not weep. I think I must have accepted her judgment on me. Or I was too young to understand its implications.

And my third memory?

Ah! Vanity! Sister Goda failed to beat it out of me. She eyed me dispassionately over some misdemeanor that I cannot now recall.

"What a trial you are to me, girl! And most probably a bastard, born out of holy wedlock. An ugly one at that. I see no redeeming features in you, even though you are undoubtedly a creature of God's creation."

So I was ugly and a bastard. At twelve years old, I wasn't sure which was the worse of the two. Was I ugly? Forbidden as we were the owner-ship of a looking glass in the Abbey—such an item was far too venal and precious to be owned by a nun—which of the sisters had never peered into a bowl of still water to catch an image? Or sought a dis-torted reflection in one of the polished silver ewers used in the Abbey church? I did the same and saw what Sister Goda saw.

That night I looked into my basin of icy water before my candle was doused. The reflection shimmered, but it was enough. My hair, close-cut against my skull, to deter lice as much as vanity, was dark and coarse and straight. My eyes were as dark as sloes, like empty holes eaten in cloth by the moth. As for the rest: My cheeks were hollow, my nose prominent, my mouth large. Even accepting the rippling flaws in the reflection, I was no beauty. I was old enough and female enough to understand, and be hurt by the knowledge. Horrified by my heavy brows, black as smudges of charcoal, I dropped my candle in the water, obliterating the image.

Lonely in the dark of my cold, narrow cell, the walls pressing in on me in my solitary existence, I wept. The dark, and being alone, fright-ened me.

As for the rest of my young days, all merged into a gray lumpen pottage of misery and resentment, stirred and salted by Sister Goda's admoni-tions.

"You were late again for Matins, Alice. Don't think I didn't see you slinking into the church like the sly child you are!" Yes, I was late.

"Alice, your veil is a disgrace in the sight of God. Have you dragged it across the floor?" No, I had not, but against every good intention my veil collected burrs and fingerprints and ash from the hearth.

"Why can you not remember the simplest of texts, Alice? Your mind is as empty as a beggar's purse." No, not empty, but engaged with something of more moment. Perhaps the soft fur of the Abbey cat as it curled against my feet in a patch of sunlight.

"Alice, you must walk with more elegance. Why do you persist in this ungodly slouch?" My growing limbs were ignorant of elegance.

"A vocation is given to us by God as a blessing," Mother Sybil, our Abbess, admonished the sinners in her care from her seat of authority every morning in the Chapter House. "A vocation is a blessing that allows us to worship God through prayer, and through good works to the poor in our midst. We must honor our vocation and submit to the Rules of Saint Benedict, our most revered founder."

Mother Abbess was quick with a scourge against those who did not submit. I remember its bite well. And that of her tongue. I felt the lash of both when, determined to be on my knees at Sister Goda's side *before* the bell for Compline was silenced, I failed to shut away the Abbey's red chickens against the predations of the fox. The result next morning for the hens was obvious and bloody. So was the skin on my back, in righteous punishment, Mother Abbess informed me as she wielded the scourge in the name of Saint Benedict. It did not seem to me to be fair that by observing one rule I had broken another. Unwise as I was in my youth, before I had learned the wisdom of concealing my thoughts, I said so. Mother Sybil's arm rose and fell with even more weight.

I was set to collect up the poor ravaged bodies. Not that the flesh went to waste. The nuns ate chicken with their bread at noon the following day as they listened to the reading of the parable of the Good Samaritan. My plate saw nothing but bread, and that a day old. Why should I benefit from my sins?

A vocation? God most assuredly had not given me a vocation, if that meant to accept, obey, and be grateful for my lot in life. And yet I knew no other life; nor would I. When I reached my fifteenth year, so I was informed by Sister Goda, I would take my vows and, no longer a novice, be clothed as a nun, thus a seamless transition from one form of servitude to another. I would be a nun forever, until God called me to the heavenly comfort of His bosom—or to answer for my sins. Beginning in my fifteenth year I would not be permitted to speak, except for an hour after the noon meal, when I would be allowed to converse on serious matters. It seemed to me little better than perpetual silence.

Silent for the rest of my life, except for the singing of the offices.

Holy Mother save me! Was this all I could hope for? It was not my choice to take the veil. How could I bear it? It was beyond my understanding that any woman would choose this life enclosed behind walls, the windows shuttered, the doors locked. Why would any woman choose this degree of imprisonment rather than taste the freedom of life outside?

To my mind there was only one door that might open and offer me an escape.

"Who is my father?" I asked Sister Goda. If I had a father, surely he would not be deaf to my entreaties.

"God is your Father." Sister Goda's flat response discouraged me from pursuing the matter as she turned the page of a psalter. "Now if you will pay attention, my child, we have here a passage to study. . . ."

"But who is my father *here*—out *there*!" I gestured toward the window that allowed the noise of the town to encroach, its inhabitants gathering vociferously for market.

The novice mistress looked at me, faintly puzzled. "I don't know, Alice, and that's the truth." She clicked her tongue against her teeth as she always did when short of an explanation. "They said that when you were brought here, there was a purse of gold coins." She shook her head, her veil hanging as limp as a shroud around her seamed face. "But it's not important. Now if we can . . ." She shuffled across the room to search in the depths of a coffer for some dusty manuscript.

But it was important! A purse of gold? Suddenly it was very important. I knew nothing other than that I was Alice. Alice—with no family, no dowry. Unlike more fortunate sisters, no one came to visit me at Easter or Christmas. No one brought me gifts. When I took the veil, there would be no one to hold a celebration for me to mark my elevation. Even my habit would be passed down to me from some dead nun who, if fate smiled on me, resembled me in height and girth; if not, my new garment would enclose me in a vast pavilion of cloth, or exhibit my ankles to the world.

Resentment bloomed in me at the enormity of it. *Why?* The question beat against my mind. *Who is my father? What have I done to deserve to be so thoroughly abandoned?* It hurt my heart.

"Who brought me here, Sister Goda?" I persisted.

"I don't recall. How would I?" She was brusque. "You were left in the Abbey porch, I believe. Sister Agnes brought you in—but she's been dead these last five years. As far as I know, there is no trace of your parentage. At that time it was not uncommon for unwanted infants to be abandoned at a church door, what with the plague. . . . Although it was always said that . . ."

"What was said?"

Sister Goda looked down at the old parchment. "Sister Agnes always said it was not what it seemed. . . ."

"*What* wasn't?"

Sister Goda clapped her hands sharply, her gaze once more narrowing on my face. "Mother Abbess said that Sister Agnes was mistaken. She was very old and not always clear in her head. Mother Abbess says you're most likely the child of some laborer—a maker of tiles—got on a whore of a tavern slut without the blessing of marriage. Now—enough of this! Set your mind on higher things. Let us repeat the paternoster in the very best Latin. No slurring of your consonants."

So I *was* a bastard.

As I duly mouthed the words of the paternoster, my mind remained fixed on my parentage or lack of it, and what Sister Agnes might or might not have said about it. I was just one of many unwanted infants and should be grateful that I had not been left to die. But it did not quite ring true, did it? If I was the child of a tavern whore, my parents from the lowest of the common stock, why had I been taken in and given any teaching? Why was I not set to work as one of the conversa, the lay sisters, employed to undertake the heavy toil on the Abbey's lands or in the kitchens and bake house? True, I was clothed in the most worn garments passed down from the sick and the dead. I was treated with no care or affection; yet I was taught to read and even to write, however poorly I attended to the lessons.

It was meant that I would become a nun. Not a lay sister.

"Sister Goda . . ." I tried again.

"I have nothing to tell you," she snapped. "There *is* nothing to tell! You will learn this Latin text!" Sister Goda, crippled with painful limbs, used her cane across my knuckles but without any real force.

Perhaps she had already decided I was a lost cause. "You will stay here until you do! Why do you resist? What else is there for you? Thank God on your knees every day that you are not forced to find your bread in the gutters of London. And by what means I can only guess!" There was no disguising the revulsion that filled her spare frame as she considered the lot of such women. Her voice fell to a harsh whisper. "Do you want to be a whore? A fallen woman?"

I lifted a shoulder in what was undoubtedly vulgar insolence. "I am not made to be a nun," I stated with misguided courage.

"What choice do you have? Where would you go? Who would take you in?"

I had no answer. But as Sister Goda's cane thwacked like a thunderclap on the wooden desk, indignation burned hot in my mind, firing the only thought that remained to me: *If you do not help yourself, Alice, for certain no one else will.*

Even then I had a sharp precocity. Product, no doubt, of a wily laborer who tumbled a sluttish tavern whore after a surfeit of sour ale.

An Event. An Occasion. A disturbance to ruffle the surface of our rigid, rule-bound days. A visitor—a high-blooded lady—came to stay at the Abbey. This was not out of the way, of course. We had frequent visitors to stay for one night or more, ladies of means who came to ease their souls through prayer, or to restore their peace of mind, retiring for a little while from the world. Or a flighty woman placed with us, so it was said, by a husband who was departing overseas and might not trust his wife to live discreetly, and alone, in his absence. Their sojourn with us was usually brief, making little impact on the ordering of our days other than to give us another mouth to feed and another bundle of laundry to wash.

Ah, but this visitor was different. We knew it the moment that her entourage—there could be no other word for it—rattled in fine style into the courtyard of Mother Abbess's private accommodations. She was also expected. Was not the whole company of sisters marshaled to welcome her, Mother Abbess to the fore? And what a spectacle. A magnificent traveling litter swayed to a halt, marvelous with swags and gilded leather curtains and the softest of soft cushions, the whole pulled by a team of six gleaming horses. Minions and outriders filled the space. And so much luggage in an accompanying wagon to be unloaded. I had never seen such wealth in one place. A heraldic device stamped the curtains of the litter, but I did not then have the knowledge to recognize it. A frisson of excitement moved through our ranks, of overt curiosity, causing the edges of veils to flutter as if in a breeze. Eyes were no longer demurely downcast.

Jeweled fingers emerged; the curtains were twitched back in a grand gesture.

Well! Blessed Virgin!

The sight stopped my breath as a lady, aided by her tire-woman, stepped from her palanquin. There she stood, shaking out her silk damask skirts—a hint of deep patterned blue, of silver thread and luxuriant fur—and smoothing the folds of her mantle, the jewels on her fingers afire with a rainbow of light. She was not a young woman, but nor was she old, and she was breathtakingly beautiful. I could see nothing of her figure, shrouded as she was in the heavy cloak despite the warmth of the summer day, nor of her hair that was hidden beneath a crispinette and black veil, but I could see her face. It was a perfect oval of fair skin and striking features, and she was lovely. Her eyes, framed by the fine linen and undulating silk, were large and lustrous, the color of new beech leaves.

"My lady." Mother Abbess glided forward, smooth as a skater over ice. "We are honored."

We curtsied, a rustle of starched linen and woolen cloth, like a flock of dusty-feathered rooks. The lady nodded sharply, looking around her, and at us, without expression. Since her lips were pressed together into a line as thin as the ale we drank, I did not think she was pleased to be here. Her eyes might glow, but like the stars they held no warmth.

Mother Abbess folded her hands at her waist. "Will your stay with us be of long duration?"

"It is undecided." The lady's reply was short but uttered in the most melodious of voices. "I trust you have more than a cell to offer me in this place?"

Which proved my suspicions. She was not a willing guest. I watched in appreciation as the lady withdrew her attention from Mother Abbess—whose nose thinned and bosom swelled—and gave it all to the unpacking of her property. From one of the wagons bounded a trio of little dogs that yapped and capered around her skirts. A hawk on a traveling perch eyed us balefully. And an animal such as I had never seen, all bright eyes and poking fingers, the color of a horse chestnut, with a ruff around its face and a long tail, bounded from the litter. Complete with a gold collar and chain, it leapt and clung to the bodice of the lady's servant, who submitted with resignation.

I could not look away. I was transfixed, entirely seduced by worldly glory, whilst the creature both charmed and repelled me in equal measure.

"I have rooms for you in my own accommodations," Mother Abbess was explaining as the dogs sniffed around her skirts. "Anything we can do to make your stay one of solace and comfort at this sad time, my lady . . ."

Was she then a widow, with her dark veil and cloak? Had she perhaps come to us to spend some quiet time in prayer and contemplation to honor her dead husband? But here being unpacked were a lute and coffers that could only contain clothes. The lady clicked her fingers to hurry her servants along. She did not show evidence of mourning other than her outer garments; nor did she seem aware of the honor of being given rooms within the Abbess's private lodging, out of bounds to all nuns except for Sister Matilda, Mother Abbess's Chaplain. Who was this woman who traveled with such authority and self-consequence? Who had dared to show Mother Abbess so little respect?

Mother Abbess's face continued to preserve a formidably glittering smile. "I will send refreshment to you, my lady."

"Immediately, if you will."

"We eat dinner at midday. . . ."

"I will eat in the privacy of my rooms."

"Of course, my lady. And if you require anything . . ."

"Yes. I need a maidservant, a woman to undertake basic tasks for me. I need someone young and capable." She fixed Mother Abbess with a stare that brooked no dissent.

"Indeed, my lady. I will send one of our conversa to you. . . ."

Without warning the exotic creature, held inexpertly by the tire-woman, squirmed and bit and escaped to dart through the nuns with harsh cries, snatching at skirts. The nuns flinched as one, their cries in counterpoint. The lapdogs barked and gave chase. And as the animal scurried past me, I *knew*!

Do it!

An opportunity. A twist of fate.

Do it!

Stooping smartly as the tormented creature skittered past, I snatched at the trailing end of its chain so that the animal came to a screaming, chattering halt at my feet, its sharp teeth very visible. I gave them no thought. Before it could struggle for release, I had lifted it into my arms. Light, fragile boned, its fur incredibly soft, it curled its fingers into my veil and held on.

I felt my face flush as a taut silence fell and all eyes turned on me. Should I have regretted my boldness? I did not. Not even when I discovered that the lady was perusing me as if I were a fat carp in the market. I tried a curtsy, unfortunately graceless, my arms full of shrieking fury.

"Well!" the lady remarked, her lips at last curved into the semblance of a smile, although her eyes remained sharply cool. "How enterprising of you." And the smile widened into one of blinding charm, sparkling like ice on a puddle on a winter's morn. "This girl . . . She'll do."

"My lady . . . !" remonstrated Mother Abbess, frowning at me. "One of our conversa would be far more . . ."

"I think not." And, raising her hand in an imperious gesture as if the matter were decided, she said, "Come with me, girl. Keep hold of the Barbary. . . ."

And so I followed her, my mouth dry, belly churning with a strange mix of shock and excitement. I was to become a maidservant. To fetch and carry and perform menial tasks for a woman who had chosen *me*. For only a short time, it was true, but I had recognized a chance to be noticed. To be *different*. And I had seized it by the scruff of its gilded neck. But not for long. As soon as I had stepped into the rooms set aside for our guest, the creature squirmed from my hold and scampered up the embroidered hangings of the great bed, to worry at the damask with sharp teeth. I remained where I was, ignorant of my tasks for this ostentatious person who began to divest herself of her cloak and veil.

"Take these!" she ordered.

Holding out a pair of embroidered gauntlets, she dropped them to the floor, anticipating that I would retrieve them. Her veil and wimple followed in similar fashion, carelessly discarded with no thought for the expensive cloth. I scurried to obey. Thus I had my first lesson as a lady's waiting woman.

I could not take my eyes from her.

At close quarters, her beauty was even more remarkable. Without the veil, her hair, neatly plaited and pinned over her ears, glowed a soft red-gold in the dim room, the same rich color of the pelt of the fox cub I had seen cast on the midden in the town. As for her skin, pale and translucent, it had a pearl-like hue, soft as the pearls on Mother Abbess's rosary. Her features could not have been more perfect if she had been a revered statue of Our Lady. I simply stood in silence and admired. Ungainly, inept, unattractive as I knew myself to be, I was in awe of this beauty.

The lady let the cloak fall into my arms, and I stood holding the weight of sumptuous cloth, not knowing what else to do. She gave me no direction, and the sheer arrogance of her demeanor forbade me to ask.

"God's Bones!" she remarked with casual blasphemy that impressed me. "Do I have to tolerate these drab accommodations? I wager it's worse than a dungeon in the Tower." She pointed to me to place the cloak on the bed. "It's mean enough to make me repent!" Picking up a jewel casket, she opened it and trilled a laugh that was not entirely pleasant. "I suppose to you, girl, this is beyond luxury. I suppose you have never slept in a bed such as this—nor ever will. . . ."

"Yes, madam. No, madam. If it pleases you—how should I address you?"

The lady crowed and addressed her tire-woman, who smirked knowingly.

"She does not know who I am! But then, why should a novice in this backwater of a nunnery know me? But by God! She will within a twelvemonth; I swear it! The whole country will know of me!" The viciousness of the tone was incongruous, stridently at odds with her beauty. "You will call me 'my lady,'" she said as she tossed the box onto the bed and approached me to finger my veil with obvious distaste, pulling its folds into some sort of order. "I am Joan, Countess of Kent. For now, at least. Soon I will be wife to Prince Edward. The future King of England."

I knew nothing of her. What I did know was that *I* had been chosen. She had chosen me to serve her. I think pride touched my heart.

Mistakenly, as it turned out.

I became a willing slave to Countess Joan. The Fair Maid of Kent whose grace and beauty were, she informed me, a matter for renown throughout the land. When she needed me, she rang a little silver bell that had a remarkable carrying quality. It rang with great frequency. The Countess's tire-woman, Lady Marian, a distant and impecunious cousin of Fair Joan, seemed to find every excuse to be absent when the need arose.

"Take this gown and brush the hem—so much dust. And treat it with care."

I brushed. I was very careful.

"Fetch lavender—you do have lavender in your herb garden, I presume? Find some for my furs. I'll not wear them again for some months. . . ."

I ravaged Sister Margery's herb patch for lavender, risking the sharp edge of the Infirmarian's tongue.

"Take that infernal monkey"—for so I learned it to be—"outside. Its chatter makes my head ache. And water. I need a basin of water. Hot water—not cold like last time. And when you've done that, bring me ink. And a pen."

My reply to everything: "Yes, my lady."

Countess Joan was an exacting mistress. If she was in mourning for her dead husband—he had been dead a mere few weeks, she informed me—I saw no evidence of it: Her attendance at the offices of the day was shockingly infrequent. But I never minded the summons of her bell. A window into the exhilarating world of the royal Court had been unlatched and flung wide for me to see and wonder at. How would I not enjoy the attention she gave me, even though she never addressed me except to issue orders? She called me "girl" when she called me anything at all, but I was not dismayed. If I made myself indispensible to her, what further doors might she not unlock . . . ?

"Comb out my hair," she ordered me.

So I did, loosening the plaited ropes of red-gold to free them of tangles with an ivory comb that I wished were mine.

"Careful, girl!" She struck out, catching my hand with her nails, hard enough to draw blood. "My head aches even without your clumsy efforts!"

Countess Joan's head frequently ached. I learned to move smartly out of range, but as often as she repelled me she lured me back with one astonishing revelation after another. And the most awe-inspiring to my naive gaze?

The Countess Joan bathed!

It was a ceremony. Lady Marian folded a freshly laundered chemise over her arm; I held a towel of coarse linen. And Countess Joan? She stripped off all her clothes without modesty. For a moment, embarrassed shock crept over my skin, as if I too were unclothed. I had had no exposure to nakedness. No nun removed her undershift—it was one of the first lessons taught to me. A nun slept in her chemise, washed beneath it with a cloth and a bowl of water, would die in it. Nakedness was a sin in the eyes of God. Countess Joan had no such inhibitions. Gloriously naked, she stepped into her tub of scented water, while I simply gaped as I waited to hand her the linen when her washing was complete.

"Now what's wrong, girl?" she asked with obvious amusement at my expense. "Have you never seen a woman in the flesh before? No, I don't suppose you have, living with these old crones." She laughed aloud, an appealing sound that made me want to smile, until I read the lines of malice in her face. "You'll not have seen a man either, I wager." She yawned prettily in the heat, stretching her arms so that her breasts rose above the surface of the scented water. "Both my husbands were good to look at in the flesh, were they not, Marian?"

"You have been married twice, my lady?" Aghast at my impudence, still I asked.

"I have. And at the same time!" She glanced up at me, intent on mischief. "What do you think of that?"

"That it is a sin!" I replied, unforgivably outspoken.

Her finely carved nostrils narrowed on an intake of breath. "Do you judge me, then?"

"No, my lady. How should I?"

"How indeed. You know nothing about it." Her voice had become brittle. "But many do. And I'll not tolerate their interference. . . ."

"My lady . . ." Marian admonished.

"I know, I know." The Countess's prettiness vanished beneath a grimace. "I should not speak of it. And I will not. Wash my hair for me, girl."

I did, of course.

Wrapped in a chamber robe with her damp hair loose over her shoulders, Countess Joan delved into one of her coffers, removed a looking glass, and stepped to the light from the window to inspect her features. She smiled at what she saw. Why would she not? I simply stared at the object, with its silver frame and gleaming surface, until the Countess looked up, haughty, sensing my gaze.

"What is it? What are you looking at?"

I shook my head.

"I have no more need of you for now." She cast the shining object onto the bed. "Come back after Compline." But my fingers itched to touch it. . . .

"Your looking glass, my lady . . ."

"Well?"

"May I look?" I asked.

Her brows rose in perfect arcs. "If you wish."

I took it from where it lay—and looked. A reflection that was more honest than anything I had seen in my water bowl looked back at me. Then without a word—for I could not find any to utter—I gently placed the glass facedown on the bed.

"Do you like your countenance?" Countess Joan inquired, enjoying my discomfort.

"No!" I managed through dry lips. My image in the water was no less than truth, and here it was proved beyond doubt. The dark, depthless eyes, like night water under a moonless sky. Even darker brows, so well marked as if drawn in ink by a clumsy hand. The strong jaw. The dominant nose and wide mouth. All so . . . so *forceful*! It was a blessing that my hair was covered. I was a grub, a worm, nothing compared with this red-gold, pale-skinned beauty who smiled at her empty victory over me. I was ugly.

"What did you expect?" the Countess asked.

"I don't know," I managed.

"You expected to see some semblance of attraction that might make a man turn his head, didn't you? Of course you did. What woman doesn't? Much can be forgiven a woman who is beautiful. But an ill-favored one? Such is not to be tolerated."

How cruel an indictment, stated without passion, without any thought for my feelings. And in that precise moment, when she tilted her chin in evident satisfaction, I saw the truth in her face. She was of a mind to be deliberately cruel.

"What a malformed little creature you are! I wonder why I bother to indulge you?"

Thus was the Countess doubly spiteful, rubbing salt in my wounds with callous indifference. As my heart fell with the weight of the evidence against me, I knew beyond doubt why she had chosen me— chosen me before all others—to wait on her. I had had no part in the choosing. It had nothing to do with the antics of her perverse monkey, or my own foolish attempt to catch her attention, or my labors to be a good maidservant. She had chosen me because I was ugly, while in stark contrast, this educated, sophisticated, highly polished Court beauty would shine like a warning beacon lit for all to wonder at on a hilltop. I was the perfect foil: too unlovely, too gauche, too ignorant to pose any threat to the splendor that was Joan of Kent.

"Leave me!" she ordered in a sudden blast of ill humor. "I find you repellent!"

I might have fled in a burst of emotional tears, but I did not. At least she had noticed me!

What did I think of this woman who stepped so heedlessly into my life and left so lasting an impression? Sometimes I despised her, for her beautiful face masked a heart of stone. And yet I found myself admiring her ambition, her determination to get her own way. Sometimes she was in the mood to talk, not caring what she said.

"I'm here only to curry favor!" she announced, glaring through her window at the enclosing walls of the Abbey, half-shrouded in a relentless downpour of rain.

"Whose favor do you need, my lady?" I asked, because it was expected of me.

"The King. The Queen," she snapped. "They don't want it—they'll put obstacles in my way—but I'll have him yet! The Prince, dolt!" She flung up her hands in exasperation, causing the monkey to cower. "It's time he was wed and got himself an heir. Am I not fertile? Do you know how many children I have carried? Of course you don't. Five. Three sons, two daughters. *I* can give the Prince heirs. The King wants his precious son to marry a rich heiress from the Low Countries. The Queen doesn't approve of *me*. We'll need a papal dispensation, since we are second cousins—but that should not be impossible if enough gold exchanges hands."

"Why would the Queen disapprove?" I asked. I had no finesse in those days. "Is not your husband dead, my lady?"

Her mouth shut like a trap and she would say no more except: "I'll get my own way; you'll see. I'll be a princess yet."

How could I not be fascinated? And yes, I coveted her possessions. A package was delivered to her from London.

"Open it," she ordered.

I unrolled the leather to find a set of jeweled buttons clustered in the palms of my hands. A fire in each heart: sapphires set in gold.

"Don't touch them." Impossibly wayward, she snatched them from me. "Do you know what they cost me? More than two hundred pounds. They're not for such as you!"

I think, weighing the good against the bad, I truly detested her.

"I am leaving," the Countess announced after three weeks. The most exciting, the most exhilarating three weeks of my life.

"Yes, my lady." I had already seen the preparations—the litter had returned, the escort at this very moment cluttering up the courtyard—and I was sorry.

"God's Wounds! I'll be glad to rid myself of these stultifying walls. I could die here and no one would be any the wiser!"

I knew that too.

"You have been useful to me." The Countess sat in the high-backed chair in her bedchamber, her feet neatly together in gilded leather shoes on a little stool, while the business of repacking her accoutrements went on around her.

"Yes, my lady."

"I daresay you've learned something, other than your usual diet of prayer and confession."

"Yes, my lady," I replied quite seriously. "I have learned to curtsy." She insisted on it every time I entered the room. "And to mend your pens."

She took me by surprise, and I was not fast enough. Leaning forward, Countess Joan suddenly struck out with careless, casual violence, for no reason that I could see other than savage temper, bringing her hand to my cheek with an echoing slap. I staggered, catching my breath and my balance.

"Don't be impertinent, girl!"

"But I was not. . . ."

Nor was I. Countess Joan spent an inordinate length of time in correspondence, and I had learned to mend a quill with great skill. The communication intrigued me—letters sent off every week to names I did not know. To courtiers, for the most part. Once to King Edward himself. More than one to Queen Philippa. And to the Prince—enough letters to keep the Abbey courier in work traveling back and forth to Westminster, and Sister Matilda's tongue clicking at the expense. I could do little more than write a series of crabbed marks, but Joan's hand moved over the parchment with speed and accuracy. She had a talent for it and saw a need to keep in touch with the world she had withdrawn from, weaving a web of intricate connections to tie those she knew to her will. Now, that I did admire, both her unexpected skill and the use she made of it.

As if she had not struck me, the Countess rose to her feet. "I suppose I should reward you. Take this. You'll find more use for it than I."

I accepted the illuminated Book of Hours, astounded at the generosity, except that it was given with no spirit of gratitude. The giving of the gift meant nothing to her. She did not want it, she had done with this place, and she would forget us as soon as her palanquin passed between the stone posts of the Abbey gatehouse.

"Take this box and carry the Barbary." The animal was pushed into my arms. "I'll be at Windsor tomorrow and then we'll see. . . ."

So this was to be the end of it—but there was one piece of knowledge I wanted from her. I had thought of this long and hard. If I did not ask now . . .

"My lady . . ."

"I haven't time." She was already walking through the doorway.

"What gives a woman . . ." I thought about the word I wanted. "What gives a woman power?" The word did not express exactly what I wanted to know—but it was the best I could do.

She stopped, turned slowly, laughing softly, but her face was writ with a mockery so vivid that I flushed at my temerity.

"Alice. It is Alice, isn't it?" she asked. It was the first time she had addressed me by my name. "Power? What would a creature such as you know of true power? What would you do with it, even if it came to you?" The disdain for my naïveté was cruel in its sleek elegance.

"I mean . . . the power to determine my own path in life."

"So! Is that what you seek?" She allowed me a complacent little smile. And I saw that beneath her carelessness ran a far deeper emotion. She actually despised me, as perhaps she despised all creatures of low birth. "You'll not get power, my dear. That is, if you mean rank. Unless you can rise above your station and become Abbess of this place." Her voice purred in derision. "You'll not do it."

Resentment flared in me at the ridicule, but I hid it well. "Still, I would know."

"Then I'll give you an answer. Since you have no breeding—beauty, then. But *your* looks will get you nowhere. There is only one way." Her smile vanished and I thought she gave my question some weight of consideration. "Knowledge."

"How can knowledge be power?"

"It can. It can if what you know is of importance to someone else."

"But what would I learn in a convent that is of value to anyone?"

"I've no idea. How would I?" Her arch stare was pitying. "But beggars, my dear, cannot choose."

And in her eyes I was most assuredly a beggar. What could I learn at the Abbey? The thin cloth of my learning was spread before me, meager in its extent and depth. To read. To dig roots in the garden. To make simples in the Infirmary. To polish the silver vessels in the Abbey church.

"What would I do with such knowledge?" I asked in despair, as if I had listed my meager accomplishments aloud. How I loathed her in that moment of self-knowledge.

"How would I know that? But I would say this: It is important for a woman to have the duplicity to make good use of whatever gifts she might have, however valueless they might seem. Do you have that?"

Duplicity? Did I possess it? I had no idea. I shook my head.

"Guile! Cunning! Scheming!" she snapped, as if my ignorance were an affront. "Do you understand?" The Countess retraced her steps to murmur in my ear as if it were a kindness. "You have to have the inner strength to pursue your goal, and not care how many enemies you make along the road. It is not easy. I have made enemies all my life, but on the day I wed the Prince they will be as chaff before the wind. I will laugh in their faces and care not what they say of me. Would you be willing to do that? I doubt it." The mockery of concern came swiftly to an end. "Set your mind to it, girl. All you have before you is your life in this cold tomb, until the day they clothe you in your death habit and sew you into your shroud."

"No!" The terrible image drove me to cry out as if I had been pricked on the arm with one of Countess Joan's well-sharpened pens. "Take me with you!" I pleaded. "I have served you well. I would serve you again, at Court." I almost snatched at her gold-embroidered sleeve.

"I think not." She did not even bother to look at me.

"But I would escape from here." I had never said it aloud before, never put it into words. How despairing it sounded. How hopeless, but in that moment I was overwhelmed by the enormity of all that I lacked, and all that I might become if I could only encompass it.

"Escape? And how would you live?" An echo of Sister Goda's words that were like a knife against my heart. "Without resources you would need a husband. Unless you would be a whore. A chancy life, short and brutish. Not one I would recommend. Better to be a nun." She strode from the room, out into the courtyard, where she settled herself in her litter, and as I reached to deposit the monkey on the cushions and close the curtains, my services for her complete, I heard her final condemnation. "You'll never be anything of value in life. So turn your mind from it." Then with a glinting smile she clicked her fingers at her tire-woman. "Give her the Barbary, Marian. I expect it will give her some distraction—and I begin to find it a nuisance. . . ."

And the creature was thrust out of the litter, back into my arms.

Indignation rose hot and slick in my throat. I considered mimicking the gesture I had seen the louts in the town employ when challenged by their elders and betters, graphic and disgracefully expressive in its lewdness, and would have done so if Sister Goda's eye had not fallen on me. As it was, I curtsied in a fine parody of deference, clutching the monkey—that scrabbled and fussed with no notion of its abandonment—to my flat chest.

Thus in a cloud of dust Countess Joan was gone with her dogs and hawk and all her unsettling influences. It was as if she had never set her pretty feet on the cold convent paving for even an hour, much less three weeks. It was like the end of a dream with the coming of day, when the light shatters the bright pictures. Fair Joan was gone to snare her prince at Westminster and I would never meet her again.

I would soon forget her. She meant as little to me as I to her.

But I did not forget! Countess Joan had applied a flame to my imagination. When it burned so fiercely that it was almost a physical hurt, I wished with all my heart I could quench it, but the fire never left me, and still it smolders, even today, when I have achieved more than I could ever have dreamed of. The venal hand of ambition had fallen on me, grasping my shoulder with a death grip of lethal strength, and refused to release me.

I am worth more than this, I determined as I knelt with the sisters at Compline. *I will be of value! I will make something of my life!*

I lost the Book of Hours, of course. Its value was far too great for such a creature as I was. It was taken from me. As for the monkey, Mother Abbess ordered it to be taken to the Infirmary and locked in a cellar. I never saw it again.

Considering its propensity to bite, I was not sorry.

Chapter Two

My crude, impassioned plea to persuade Countess Joan to be the instrument of my escape from the Abbey had, I was compelled to admit, failed miserably. When I achieved it, it was not by my own instigation. It came as a lightning bolt from heaven.

"Put this on. And this. Take this. Be at the Abbey gate in half an hour."

The garments were thrust into my arms by Sister Matilda, Mother Abbess's chaplain.

"Why, Sister?"

"Do as you're told!"

I had been given a thin woolen kirtle, its color unrecognizable from much washing, and a long sleeveless overgown in a dense brown, reminiscent of the sludge that collected on the riverbank after stormy weather. It too had seen better days on someone else's back, and was far too short, exhibiting, as I had feared, my ankles. As I scratched indelicately, a more immediate fear bloomed. I had inherited the fleas as well as the garments. A hood of an indeterminate gray completed the whole.

But why? Was I being sent on an errand? Anticipation shivered over my skin. Even if it was for only an hour, I felt the excitement of escape. The days of my transformation from novice to nun loomed, like the noxious, overflowing contents of the town drain after heavy rainfall.

"Where am I going?" I asked the wagon master to whom I was directed, a dour man with a bad head cold and an overpowering smell of rancid wool. Sister Faith, keeper of the Abbey gate, had done nothing but point in his direction and close the door against me. The soft snick of the latch, with me on the outside, was far sweeter than any singing of the Angelus.

"Where I'm instructed to take you," he growled, spitting into a gutter already swimming with filth and detritus from the day's market dealings.

"And where is that?" I stood beside a wagon loaded with bales of wool to be transported to London.

"To the house of Janyn Perrers."

"Who is he?"

"A man of means." The wagon master hawked and spat. "On the backs of those who have nothing."

"What does that mean?"

"Pawnbroker. Moneylender." He sneered. "Bloodsuckers to a man. Leeches who'll drain you dry."

"Is he English?" The name did not seem so.

"A foreign bastard! From Lombardy! All grasping buggers are from Lombardy."

"And where does he live?"

"London."

He sniffed and spat again. He was a man of few words and no manners, but at least I now knew more than I had. So this was not an errand of an hour's duration, but something quite different. Anticipation blazed into exhilaration, racing through me like the fever that had laid the Abbey low the previous year.

"Pull me up, then," I ordered.

"Tha's a feisty moppet, and no mistake!" he said, but he grasped my hand in his enormous one and hauled me up onto the bales, where I settled myself as well as I could.

"Why?" I asked when the oxen lumbered forward. The wagon master grunted, head cocked. "Why am I going to this man's house? Does he know I am coming?"

He shrugged. "Is tha' to ask questions all the road to London?"

"But I want to know . . . !" Happiness tingled through me, to my fingertips.

"God help th'man who weds you, mistress. . . ."

"I'm not going to be married! I have it on authority that no one will have me."

"And why's that, then?"

"Too ugly!"

"God help you, mistress. A man don't need to look too often at the wench he weds."

I did not care. I tossed my head. *London!* "If I wed, my husband will look at me."

"Feisty!"

He cracked his whip over the heads of the oxen to end the conversation, leaving me to try to fill in the spaces. To my mind there was only one possible reason for my joining the household of this Janyn Perrers, moneylender: to work as a maidservant. My services had been bought. Enough gold had changed hands to encourage Mother Abbess to part with her impoverished novice, who would bring nothing of fame or monetary value to the Abbey. As the wagon jolted and swayed, I imagined the request that had been made.

A strong, hardworking, biddable girl to help run the house.

I hoped Mother Abbess had not perjured herself.

I twitched and shuffled, impatient with every slow step of the oxen. "What is London like?" I asked.

The wagon master swigged ale from a leather bottle as if he did not hear. I sighed and gave up. I did not care. I was going to *London.* The name bubbled through my blood as I clung to the lumbering wagon. Freedom was as sweet and heady as fine wine.

The noisome, overcrowded squalor of London shocked me. The environs of Barking Abbey, bustling as they might be on market day, had not prepared me for the crowds, the perpetual racket, the stench of humanity packed so close together. But equally the city fascinated me: I did not know where to look next. At close-set houses in streets barely wider than the wagon, where upper stories leaned drunkenly to embrace one another, blocking out the sky. At shop frontages that displayed the wares, at women who paraded in bright colors. At scruffy urchins and bold prostitutes who carried on a different business in the rank courts and passageways. It was a new world, both frightening and seductive: I stared and gawped, as naive as any child from the country.

"Here's where you get off."

The wagon lurched and I was set down, directed by a filthy finger that pointed at my destination, a narrow house taking up no space at all, but rising above my head in three stories. I picked my way through the mess of offal and waste in the gutters to the door. Was this the one? It did not seem to be the house of a man of means. I knocked.

A woman, far taller than I, thin as a willow lath with her hair scraped into a pair of metallic cylindrical cauls on either side of her gaunt face, as if she were encased in a cage, opened it. "Well?"

"Is this the house of Janyn Perrers?"

"What's it to you?"

Her gaze flicked over me, briefly. She made to close the door. Forsooth, I could not blame her: I saw myself through her eyes. My borrowed overgown had collected a multitude of creases and any amount of woolen fiber. I was not an attractive object. But this was where I had been sent, where I was expected. I would not have the door shut in my face.

"I have been sent!" I said, slapping my palm boldly against the wood.

"What do you want?"

"I am Alice," I said, remembering, at last, to curtsy.

"If you're begging, I'll take my brush to you. . . ."

"I'm sent by the nuns at the Abbey," I stated with a confidence I did not feel.

The revulsion in her stare deepened, and the woman's lips twisted like a hank of rope. "So you're the girl. Are you the best they could manage?" She flapped her hand when I opened my mouth to reply that yes, I supposed I was the best they could offer, since I was the only novice. "Never mind. You're here now, so we'll make the best of it. But in future you'll use the door at the back beside the privy."

And that was that.

I had become part of a new household.

And what an uneasy household it was. Even I, with no experience of such, was aware of the tensions from the moment I set my feet over the threshold.

Janyn Perrers: master of the house, pawnbroker, moneylender, and bloodsucker. His appearance did not suggest a rapacious man, but then, as I rapidly learned, it was not his word that was the law within his four walls. Tall and stooped, with not an ounce of spare flesh on his frame, and a foreign slur to his English usage, he spoke only when he had to, and then not greatly. In his business dealings he was unnervingly painstaking. Totally absorbed, he lived and breathed the acquisition and lending at extortionate rates of gold and silver coin. His face might have been kindly, if not for the deep grooves and hollow cheeks more reminiscent of a death's head. His hair, or lack of, some few greasy wisps around his neck, gave him the appearance of a well-polished egg when he removed his felt cap. That was rare, as if he regretted his loss. I could not guess his age, but he seemed very old to me, with his uneven gait and faded eyes. His fingers were always stained with ink, his mouth too when he forgot and chewed his pen.

He nodded to me when I served supper, placing the dishes carefully on the table before him: It was the only sign that he noted a new addition to his household. This was the man who now employed me and would govern my future.

The power in the house rested on the shoulders of Damiata Perrers, the sister, who had made my lack of welcome patently clear. The Signora. There was no kindness in her face. She was the strength, the firm grip on the reins, the imposer of punishment on those who displeased her. Nothing happened within that house without her knowledge or permission.

There was a boy to haul and carry and clean the privy, a lad who said little and thought less. He led a miserable existence, but his face was closed to any offers of communication. He gobbled his food with filthy fingers and bolted back to his own pursuits in the nether regions of the house. I didn't learn his name.

Then there was Master William Greseley, who was and was not of the household, since he spread his services farther afield, an interesting man who attracted my attention but ignored me with a remarkable determination. He was a clerk, a clever individual with black hair and brows, sharp features much like a rat, and a pale face as if he never saw the light of day, a man with as little emotion about him as one of the flounders brought home by Signora Damiata on market day. He ate and slept and noted down the business of the day. Ink might stain Master Perrers's fingers, but I swore that it ran in Master Greseley's veins. He wrote a fine hand and could guide a quill up and down the columns of figures, counting with impressive acumen. He disregarded me to the same extent that he was deaf to the vermin that scuttled across the floor of the room in which he kept the books and ledgers of money lent and reclaimed. I did not like him. There was a coldness to him that I found unpalatable.

And then there was me. The maidservant who undertook all the work not assigned to the boy. And some that was.

Thus my first introduction to the Perrers family. And since it was a good score of miles from Barking Abbey, it was not beyond my tolerance.

"God help th'man who weds you, mistress . . . !"

"I'm not going to be married!"

My vigorous assertion returned to mock me. Within a sennight I found myself exchanging vows at the church door.

Given the tone of her language, Signora Damiata was as astonished as I, and brutally forthright when I was summoned to join brother and sister in the parlor at the rear of the house, where, by the expression on the lady's face, Master Perrers had just broken the news of his intent.

"Blessed Mary! Why marry?" she demanded. "You have a son, an heir, learning the family business in Lombardy. I keep your house. You want a wife at your age?" Her accent grew stronger, the syllables hissing over one another.

"I wish it." Master Perrers continued leafing through the pages of a small ledger he had taken from his pocket.

"Then choose a daughter of one of our merchant families. A girl with a dowry and a family with some standing. Jesu! Are you not listening?" She raised her fists as if she might strike him. "This one is not a suitable wife for a man of your importance."

Did I think that he did not rule the roost? On this occasion I could not have been more mistaken. He looked briefly at me. "I will have her. I will wed her. That is the end of the matter."

I, of course, was not asked. I stood in this three-cornered dialogue yet not a part of it, the bone squabbled over by two dogs. Except that Master Perrers did not squabble. He simply stated his intention until his sister closed her mouth and let it be. So I was wed in the soiled skirts in which I chopped the onions and gutted the fish. Clearly there was no money earmarked to be spent on a new wife. Sullen and resentful, shocked into silence, certainly no joyful bride, I complied because I must. I was joined in matrimony with Janyn Perrers on the steps of the church, with witnesses to attest the deed. Signora Damiata, grim faced and silent; Master Greseley, because he was available, with no expression at all. A few words muttered over us by a bored priest in an empty ritual, and I was a wife.

There was little to show for it.

No celebration, no festivity, no recognition of my change in position in the household. Not even a cup of ale and a bride cake. It was, I realized, nothing more than a business agreement, and since I had brought nothing to it, there was no need to celebrate it. All I recall was the rain soaking through my hood as we stood and exchanged vows and the shrill cries of lads who fought amongst themselves for the handful of coin that Master Perrers scattered as a reluctant sign of his goodwill. Oh, and I recall Master Perrers's fingers gripping hard on mine, the only reality in this ceremony that was not at all real to me.

Was it better than being a Bride of Christ? Was marriage better than servitude? To my mind there was little difference. After the ceremony I was directed to sweep down the cobwebs that festooned the storerooms in the cellar. I took out my bad temper with my brush, making the spiders run for cover.

There was no cover for me. Where would I run?

And beneath my anger was a lurking fear, for the night, my wedding night, was ominously close, and Master Perrers was no handsome lover.

The Signora came to my room that was hardly bigger than a large coffer, tucked high under the eaves, and gestured with a scowl. In a shift and bare feet I followed her down the stairs. Opening the door to my husband's bedchamber, she thrust me inside, still without a word, and closed it at my back. I stood just within, not daring to move. My throat was so dry I could barely swallow. Apprehension was a rock in my belly, and fear of my ignorance filled me to the brim. I did not want to be here. I did not want this. I could not imagine why Master Perrers would want me, plain and unfinished and undowered as I was. Silence closed 'round me—except for a persistent scratching like a mouse trapped behind the plastered wall.

In that moment I was a coward. I admit it. I closed my eyes.

Still nothing.

So I squinted, only to find my gaze resting on the large bed with its dust-laden hangings to shut out the night air. Holy Virgin! To preserve intimacy for the couple enclosed within. Closing my eyes again, I prayed for deliverance.

What, exactly, would he want me to do?

"You can open your eyes now. She's gone."

There was humor in the accented voice. I obeyed and there was Janyn, in a chamber robe of astonishingly virulent yellow ocher that encased him from neck to bony ankles, seated at a table covered with piles of documents and heaped scrolls. At his right hand was a leather purse spilling out strips of wood, and another smaller pouch containing silver coin. And to his left a branch of good-quality candles that lit the atmosphere with gold as the dust motes danced. But it was the pungent aroma—of dust and parchment and vellum, and perhaps the ink that he had been stirring—that made my nose wrinkle. Intuitively I knew that it was the smell of careful record keeping and of wealth. It almost dispelled my fear.

"Come in. Come nearer to the fire."

I took a step, warily. At least he was not about to leap on me quite yet. There was no flesh in sight on either of us.

"Here." He stretched toward the coffer at his side and scooped up the folds of a mantle. "You'll be cold. Take it. It's yours."

Unlike Countess Joan's cynical offerings, this was the first gift I had ever had, given honestly. I wrapped the luxurious woolen length 'round my shoulders, marveling at the quality of its weaving, its softness and warm russet coloring, wishing I had a pair of shoes. He must have seen me shuffling on the cold boards.

"Put these on!"

A pair of leather shoes of an incongruous red was pushed across the floor toward me. The shoes were enormous, but soft and warm from his own feet as I slid mine in with a sigh of pleasure.

"Are you a virgin?" he asked conversationally.

My pleasure dissipated like mist in morning sun, my blood running as icily cold as my feet, and I shivered. A goose walking over my grave. I did not want this old man to touch me. The last thing I wanted was to share a bed with him and have him fumble against my naked flesh with his ink-stained fingers, their untrimmed nails scraping and scratching.

"Yes," I managed, hoping my abhorrence was not obvious, but Master Perrers was watching me with narrowed eyes. How could it not be obvious? I felt my face flame with humiliation.

"Of course you are," my husband said with a laconic nod. "Let me tell you something that might take that anxious look from your face. I'll not trouble you. It's many a year since I've found comfort in a woman." I had never heard him string so many words together.

"Then why did you wed me?" I asked.

Since I had nothing else to give, I had thought it must be a desire for young flesh in his bed. So if not that . . . Master Perrers looked at me as if one of his ledgers had spoken. Then he grunted in what could have been amusement.

"Someone to tend my bones in old age, my dear. A wife to shut my sister up from nagging me to wed a merchant's daughter whose family would demand a weighty settlement."

Ah . . . ! I sighed. I had asked for the truth, had I not? I would nurse him and demand nothing in return. It was not flattering.

"Marriage will give you security," he continued as if he read my thoughts. And then: "Have you a young lover in mind?"

"No!" Such directness startled me. "Well, not yet. I don't know any young men."

He chuckled. "Good. Then we shall rub along well enough, I expect. When you do know a young man you can set your fancy on, let me know. I'll make provision for you when I am dead," he remarked.

He went back to his writing. I stood and watched, not knowing what to do or say now that he had told me what he did not want from me. Should I leave? His gnarled hand with its thick fingers moved up and down the columns, rows of figures growing from his pen, columns of marks in heavy black ink spreading from top to bottom. They intrigued me. The minutes passed. The fire settled. Well, I couldn't stand here forever.

"What do I do now, Master Perrers?"

He looked up as if surprised that I was still there. "Do you wish to sleep?"

"No."

"I suppose we must do something. Let me . . ." He peered at me with his pale eyes. "Pour two cups of ale and sit there."

I poured and took the stool he pushed in my direction.

"You can write?"

"Yes."

With Joan's contemptuous advice in mind, I had applied myself to my lessons with more fervor, enough to cause Sister Goda to offer a rosary to Saint Jude Thaddeus, a saint with a fine reputation for pursuing desperate causes, in gratitude for this holy miracle. I could now write with a fair hand.

"The convents are good for something. . . . Can you write and tally numbers?"

"No."

"Then you will learn! There." He reversed the ledger and pushed it toward me across the table. "Copy that list there. I'll watch you. Do it."

I sat, inveterate curiosity getting the better of me.

"What are those?" I asked. I pointed at the leather purse as I picked up one of his pens and began to mend the end with a sharp blade he kept for the purpose. Countess Joan had done me one favor.

"Tally sticks."

"What do they do? What are the notches for?"

"They record income, debts paid, and debts owed," he informed me, watching me to ensure I didn't destroy his pen. "The wood is split down the middle, each party to the deal keeping half. They must match."

"Clever," I observed, picking up one of the tallies to inspect it. It was beautifully made out of a hazel twig, and the sole purpose to record ownership of money.

"Never mind those. Write the figures!"

And I did, under his eye for the first five minutes, and then he left me to it, satisfied.

We passed the strangest night. My blood settled to a quiet hum of pleasure as the figures grew to record a vast accumulation of gold coin, and when we had finished the record of the accounts of the week, my husband instructed me to get into the vast bed and go to sleep. I fell into it, and into sleep to the sound of the scratching pen. Did my husband join me when his work was done? I think he did not. The bed linen was not disturbed, and nor was my shift, arranged neatly from chin to ankles, decorous as that of any virgin nun.

It was not what I expected, but it could have been much worse.

I awoke abruptly to silence. It was still very early, I presumed, and dark because the bed curtains had been drawn around me. When I peeped out it was to see that the fire had burned itself out, the cups and ledgers tidied away, and the room was empty. I was at a loss, my role spectacularly unclear. Sitting back against the pillows, reluctant to leave the warmth of the bed, I looked at my hands, turning them, seeing the unfortunate results of proximity to icy cold water, hot dishes, grimy tasks. They were now the hands of Mistress Perrers. I gasped in a moment of grim humor. Was I now mistress of the household? If I was, I would have to usurp Signora Damiata's domain. I tried to imagine myself walking into the parlor and informing the Signora what I might wish to eat, the length of cloth I might wish to purchase to fashion a new gown. And then I imagined her response.

I dared not!

But it is your right!

Undeniably! Tomorrow, perhaps. Next week, even. But not right at this moment. My sense of self-preservation was always keen. And so I redirected my thoughts to a matter of more immediacy. What would I say to Master Perrers this morning? How would I address him? Was I truly his wife if I was still a virgin?

With nothing better to do, I wrapped myself in my new mantle, returned to my own room, and dressed as the maidservant I still seemed to be, before descending the stairs to the kitchen to start the tasks for the new day. The fire would have to be laid, the oven heated. If I walked quickly and quietly through the house, I would not draw attention to myself from any quarter. Such was my plan, except that my clumsy shoes clattered on the stair, and a voice called out.

"Alice."

I considered bolting, as if I had not heard.

"Come here, Alice. Close the door."

I gripped hard on my courage. Had he not been kind last night? I redirected my footsteps, and there my husband of less than twenty-four hours sat behind his desk, head bent over his ledgers, pen in hand, in the room where he dealt with the endless stream of borrowers. It was no different from any other morning when I might bring him ale and bread. I curtsied. Habits were very difficult to break.

He looked up. "Did you sleep well?"

"No, sir."

"Too much excitement, I expect." I might have suspected him of laughing at me, but there was no change of expression on his dolorous features. He held out a small leather pouch, the strings pulled tight. I looked at it—and then at him.

"Take it."

"Do you wish me to purchase something for you, sir?"

"It is yours." Since I still did not move, he placed it on the desk and pushed it across the wood toward me.

"Mine . . . ?"

It contained coin. And far more, as I could estimate, than was due to me as a maidservant. Planting his elbows on the desk, folding his hands and resting his chin on them, Janyn Perrers regarded me gravely, speaking slowly, as if I might be lacking in wit.

"It is a bride gift, Alice. A morning gift. Is that not the custom in this country?"

"I don't know." How would I?

"It is, if you will, a gift in recompense for the bride's virginity."

I frowned. "I don't qualify for it, then. You did not want mine."

"The fault was mine, not yours. You have earned a bride gift by tolerating the whims and weaknesses of an old man." I think my cheeks were as scarlet as the seals on the documents before him, so astonished was I that he would thank me. I regretted that my words had seemed so judgmental of him. "Take it, Alice. You look bewildered." At last what might have been a smile touched his mouth.

"I am, sir. I have done nothing to make me worthy of such a gift."

"You are my wife and we will keep the custom."

"Yes, sir." I curtsied.

"One thing . . ." He brushed the end of his quill pen uneasily over the mess of scrolls and lists. "It would please me if you would not talk about . . ."

"About our night together," I supplied for him, compassion stirred by his gentleness. "That is between you and me, sir."

"And our future nights . . ."

"I will not speak of them either." After all, who would I tell?

"Thank you. If you would now fetch me ale. And tell the Signora that I will be going out in an hour. . . ."

"Yes, sir." So. Much as normal.

"And it will please me if you will call me Janyn."

"Yes, sir."

I stood in the whitewashed passage outside the door and leaned back against the wall as if my legs needed the support. The purse was not a light one. It moved in my fingers, coins sliding with a comforting chink as I weighed it in my hand. I had never seen so much money all in one place in the whole of my life. And it was mine. Whatever I was or was not, I was no longer a penniless novice.

But what was I? It seemed I was neither flesh nor fowl. Here I stood in a house that was not mine, a wife but a virgin, with the knowledge that my marriage vows would make absolutely no difference to my role in the household. I would wager the whole of my sudden windfall on it. Signora Damiata would never retreat before my authority. I would never sit at the foot of the table.

The scuff of leather against stone came to my ears and made me look up.

I was not the only one occupying the narrow space. Detaching himself from a similar stance, farther along in the shadows, Master Greseley walked softly toward me. Since there was an air of secrecy about him—of complicity almost—I hid the pouch within the folds of my skirt. Within an arm's length of me he stopped and leaned his narrow shoulder blades on the wall beside me, arms folded across his chest, staring at the opposite plasterwork in a manner that was neither companionable nor hostile. Here was a man adept through long practice at masking his intentions. As for his thoughts—they were buried so deep beneath his impassivity that it would take an earthquake to dislodge them.

"You weren't going to hide it under your pillow, were you?" he inquired in a low voice.

"Hide what?" I replied, clutching the purse tightly.

"The morning gift he's just given you."

"How do you . . . ?"

"Of course I know. Who keeps the books in this household? It was no clever guesswork." A sharp glance slid in my direction before fixing on the wall again. "I would hazard that the sum was payment for something that was never bought."

Annoyance sharpened my tongue. I would not be intimidated by a *clerk.* "That is entirely between Master Perrers and myself."

"Of course it is." How smoothly unpleasant he was. Like mutton fat floating on water after the roasting pans had been scoured.

"And nothing to do with you."

He bowed his head. "Absolutely nothing. I am here only to give you some good advice."

Turning my head, I looked directly at him. "Why?"

He did not return my regard. "I have no idea."

"That makes no sense."

"No. It doesn't. It's against all my tenets of business practice. But even so . . . Let's just say that I am drawn to advise you."

I thought about this. Why not? There was no compulsion to accept it. "So what is your advice?"

"I've already told you. Don't hide the money under your pillow or anywhere else in this house. She'll find it."

"Who?" Although I knew the answer well enough.

"The Signora. She has a nose for it, as keen as any mouse finding the cheese safe stored in a cupboard. And when she sniffs it out, *you'll* not see it again."

I thought about this as well. "I thought she didn't know."

"Is that what Janyn told you?"

"Well—not exactly." But the implication had been there.

"Of course she does. Nothing happens in this place without her knowledge. She knows you have money, and she doesn't agree. Any profits are the inheritance of her nephew."

The absent heir, learning the business in Lombardy. I could well believe it. "Since you're keen to offer advice, what can I do? Short of digging a hole in the garden . . ."

"Which she'd find . . ."

"A cranny in the eaves?"

"She'd find that too."

"So?" I was beginning to be irritated with his smug assumption of knowledge.

"Give it to me."

Which promptly dispersed my irritation. I laughed, disbelieving. "Do you take me for a fool?"

"I take you for a sensible woman. Give it to me." He actually held out his hand, palm up. His fingers were blotched with ink.

"I will not."

He sighed as if his patience were strained. "Give it to me and I'll use it to make you a rich woman."

"Why would you?"

"Listen to me, Mistress Alice!" I was right about the patience. His voice fell to a low hiss on the syllables of my name. "What keeps its value and lasts forever?"

"Gold."

"No."

"It does!"

"Gold can be stolen—and then you have nothing."

"Jewels, then."

"Same argument. Think about it!"

"Then since you are so clever . . ."

"Land!" The clerk's beady eyes gleamed. "Property. That's the way to do it. It's a generous purse he gave you. Give it to me and I will buy you property."

For a moment I listened to him, seduced by the glitter in his gaze that was now holding mine. His nose almost twitched with the prospect. And then sense took hold. "But I cannot look after property! What would I do with it?"

"You don't have to *look after it*. There are ways and means. Give me your morning gift and I will show you how it's done."

Well! It deserved some consideration. . . . "What would you ask in return?" I asked sharply.

"An excellent question. I knew you had the makings of a business-woman. I'll let you know. But it will not be too great a price."

I looked at him. What a cold fish he was. "Why are you doing this?"

"I think you have possibilities."

"As a landowner?"

"Why not?"

I didn't have a reply. I stood in silence, the coins in my hand seemingly growing heavier by the moment. I tossed the little bag and caught it.

"We don't have all day!" Greseley's admonition broke into my thoughts. "That's my offer. Take it or leave it. But if you think to keep it safe within these walls, then it will be gone before the end of the week."

"And I should trust you."

"Yes."

Would I trust him? Trust had not figured highly in my life, but this strange man with his love for figures and documents, seals and agreements, had sought me out and made me this most tempting of offers. Should I hand over to him all I owned in the world? It was a risk. A huge risk. A gamble when I did not even know what the odds were. The arguments, conflicting, destructive of one another, rattled back and forth in my brain.

Say no. Keep it for yourself. Hide it where no one can find it.

Take the risk! Become an owner of property.

He'll take it and keep it for himself.

Trust him!

I can't!

Why not?

My exchange of views came to an abrupt halt when the clerk pushed himself upright and began to walk away. "Don't say I didn't warn you!"

And there was the final blast of the voice in my head. *You can't do this on your own, Alice, but Greseley can. This clever little louse has the knowledge. Learn from him! Use him to your own advantage!*

Well, I would. "Stop!" I shouted.

He did, but did not return. He stood there, his back to me, waiting. "I'll do it!" I called.

He spun on his heel to face me again. "Clever girl!"

"How long will it take?"

"A few days."

I held up the pouch. Hesitated. Then dropped it into his outstretched palm. I was still wondering if I was an idiot.

"If you rob me . . ." I remarked.

"Yes, Mistress Perrers?"

It caused me to laugh softly. It was the first time I had been addressed as such.

"If you rob me," I whispered, "I advise you to employ a taster before you eat or drink in this house."

"There'll be no need, mistress." From his bland smugness, he thought I was making empty threats. I was not so sure. A good dose of wolfsbane masked by a cup of warmed ale would take out the strongest man. I would not care to be robbed.

The purse vanished into Greseley's sleeve, and Greseley vanished along the corridor.

Would I live to regret this business dealing that I had just leaped into? All I knew was that it created a strange, turbulent euphoria that swept through me from my crown to my ill-shod feet.

At some time in the following day, my room was searched. It was not done with any degree of discretion or finesse, but a rough tumbling of my pallet and bedcovers, a riffling through the coffer that contained a spare shift and a pair of stockings. For the rest of the day Signora Damiata stomped about her business. The look she cast me was not friendly.

I know you have it! I'll get my hands on it, you mark my words.

Greseley frowned, his spiky brows meeting over his unprepossessing nose. Janyn did not notice. Meanwhile, I preserved a perfectly bland insouciance.

Fool! Idiot girl! I berated myself with increasing fury over the following days. *A sensible woman, he called you. A businesswoman. And you let yourself be gulled. He knew how to dupe you, to wind you 'round his grubby fingers!*

By God he did! By the end of the week I knew I had seen the last of my morning gift. Greseley was elusive, exchanging not one word with me and avoiding my attempts to catch his eye. And when my impatience overcame my discretion . . . "What have you done with . . ." I hissed in his ear as he slid onto a stool to break his fast.

"Pass the jug of ale, if you please, mistress," was all I got. With one gulp he emptied his cup, crammed bread into his mouth, and left the room before I could pester him further.

"Stir this pot," Signora Damiata ordered, handing over a spoon.

So there was no chance of my hunting him down, and later that day he was sent into the city on business that kept him away overnight.

How could I have been so ingenuous as to trust a man I barely knew? I had lost it. I had lost it all! I would never see one of those coins again, and my misery festered, even though I was kept hopping from morning to night. My mind began to linger on the effect of a large spoonful of wolfsbane on the scrawny frame of the clerk.

And then Greseley returned. Well, he wouldn't get away with ignoring me this time. Was he suffering from guilt? If he was, it did nothing to impair his appetite, as he chomped his way through slices of beef and half a flat bread, completely undisturbed by my scowling at him across the board.

"We need to talk," I whispered, nudging him between his shoulder blades when I smacked a dish of herring in front of him.

His answering stare was cold and clear and without expression.

"Careful, girl!" snapped the Signora. "That dish! We're not made of money!"

Greseley continued to eat with relish, but as I cleared the dishes, he produced a roll of a document from the breast of his tunic, like a coney magicked from the sleeve of a second-rate jongleur, and tapped it against his fingertips before sliding it into an empty jug standing on the hearth, out of the Signora's line of sight. It was not out of mine. My fingers itched to take it. I could sense it, like a burning brand below my heart.

At last. The kitchen was empty: Janyn closed the door on himself and his ledgers, the Signora climbed the stair to her chamber, and I took the scroll from its hiding place and carried it to my room. Unrolling it carefully, I read the black script. No easy task! The legal words meant nothing to me, the phrases hard on my understanding, the script small and close written. But there was no doubting it. He had done what he had promised. There was my name: Alice Perrers. I was the owner of property in Gracechurch Street in the city of London.

I held it in my hands, staring at it as if it might vanish if I looked away. Mine. It was mine. But what was it? And more important, what did I do with it?

I ran Greseley to ground early the next morning with his feet up on a trestle and a pot of ale beside him.

"It's all very well—but what am I expected to do with it?"

He looked at me as if I were stupid. "Nothing but enjoy the profits, mistress."

"I don't understand."

"I doesn't matter whether you do or not. It's yours."

He was watching me closely, as if to test my reaction. I did not see why he should, so I said what I wanted to say.

"It does matter." And in that moment it struck home how much it meant to me. "It matters to me more than you'll ever know." I glowered. "You won't patronize me, Master Greseley. You will explain it all to me, and then I will understand. The property is mine and I want to know how it works."

He laughed. He actually laughed, a harsh bark of noise.

"Now what?"

"I knew I was right."

"About what?"

"*You*, Mistress Perrers. Sit down! And don't argue! I'm about to give you your first lesson."

So I did, and Greseley explained to me the brilliance for a woman in my position of the legal device of "enfeoffment to use." "The property is yours; it remains yours," he explained. "But you allow others to administer it for you—for a fee, of course. You must choose wisely—a man with an interest in the property so that he will administer it well. Do you understand?" I nodded. "You grant that man legal rights over the land, but you retain de facto control. See? You remain in ultimate ownership but need do nothing in the day-to-day running of it."

"And can I make the agreement between us as long or as short as I wish?"

"Yes."

"And I suppose I need a man of law to oversee this for me?"

"It would be wise."

"What is it—this property that I now own, but do not own?"

"Living accommodations—with shops below."

What else did I need to ask? "Was there any money left over from the transaction?"

"You don't miss much, do you?" He tipped out the contents of the purse at his belt and pushed across the board a small number of coins.

"You said I needed a man of law." He regarded me without expression. "I suppose you would be my man of law."

"I certainly could. Next time, we will work in partnership."

"Will there be a next time?"

"Oh, I think so." I thought the slide of his glance had a depth of craftiness.

"Is that good or bad—to work in partnership?"

Greseley's pointed nose sniffed at my ignorance. He knew I could not work alone. But it seemed good to me. What strides I had made. I was a wife of sorts, even if I spent my nights checking Janyn's tally sticks and columns of figures, and now I was a property owner. A little ripple of pleasure brushed along the skin of my forearms as the idea engaged my mind and my emotions. I liked it. And in my first deliberate business transaction I pushed the coins back toward Greseley.

"This is my . . . What is the word? Retainer? You are now my man of law, Master Greseley."

"I am indeed, Mistress Perrers."

The coins were swept into his purse with alacrity.

And where did I keep the evidence of my ownership? I kept it hidden on my person between shift and overgown, tied with a cord, except when I took it out and touched it, running my fingers over the words that made it all official. There it was for my future. Security. Permanence. The words were like warm hands around mine on a winter's day.

I did not dislike Greseley as much as I once had.

Plague returned. The same dread pestilence that had struck without mercy just before my birth came creeping stealthily into London. It was the only gossip to be had in the streets, the market, the alehouses. It was different this time, so they said in whispers. The plague of children, they called it, striking cruelly at infants but not the hale and hearty who had reached adult years.

But the pestilence, stepping over our threshold, proved to be a chancy creature.

Of us all it was Janyn who was struck down. He drew aside the sleeve of his tunic to reveal the dread whirls of red spots as we gathered for dinner on an ordinary day. We stared at the signs as if we could not believe in their existence. The meal was abandoned. Without a word Janyn walked up the stairs and shut himself in his chamber. Terror, rank and loathsome, set its claws into the Perrers household.

The boy disappeared overnight. Greseley found work in other parts of London. Mistress Damiata fled with disgraceful speed to stay with her cousin, whose house was uncontaminated. Who nursed Janyn? I did. I was his wife, even if he had never touched me unless his calloused fingers grazed mine when he pointed out a mistake in my copying. I owed him at least this final service.

From that first red-and-purple pattern on his arms there was no recovery.

I bathed his face and body, holding my breath at the stench of putrefying flesh. I racked my brains for anything Sister Margery had said of her experiences of the pestilence. It was not much but I acted on it, flinging the windows of Janyn's chamber wide to allow the escape of the corrupt air. For my own safety I washed my hands and face in vinegar, and ate bread soaked in Janyn's best wine—how Signora Damiata would have ranted at the waste—but for Janyn nothing halted the terrifying onset. The empty house echoed around me, the only sound the harsh breathing from my stricken husband and the approaching footsteps of death.

Was I afraid for myself?

I was, but if the horror of the vile swellings could pass from Janyn to me, the damage was already done. If the pestilence had the ability to hop across the desk where we sat to keep the ledgers, then I was already doomed. I would stay and weather the storm.

A note appeared under the bedchamber door. I watched it slide slowly, from my position slumped on a stool from sheer exhaustion as Janyn labored with increasingly distressed breaths. The fever had him in its thrall. Stepping softly to the door, listening to someone walking quietly away, I picked up the note and unfolded the single page, curiosity over-

coming my weariness. Ha! No mystery after all. I recognized Greseley's script with ease, and the content was written as a clerk might write
a legal treatise. I sank back to the stool to read.

*When you are a widow you have legal right to a dower—one-third of
the income of your husband's estate. You will not get it.*

*You have by law forty days in which to vacate the house: for the good
of the heir—her nephew—who will take his inheritance. You will be
evicted within the day.*

*As your legal man, my advice: Take what you can. It is your right. You
will get nothing else that is due to you.*

A stark warning. A chilling one.

Leaving Janyn in a restless sleep, I began to search.

Nothing! Absolutely nothing!

Signora Damiata had done a thorough job of it while her brother
lay dying and I preoccupied with his dire sufferings or fallen into a
torpor of utter bone-weariness. His room of business—the whole
house—was empty of all items of value. There were no bags of gold in
Janyn's coffers. There were no scrolls; the ledgers and tally sticks had
gone. She had swept through the house, removing everything that
might become an attraction for looters. Or for me. Everything from my
own chamber had been taken. Even my new mantle—especially that—
the only thing of value I owned and that the Signora would covet.

I had nothing.

Above me in his bedchamber, Janyn shrieked in an extremity of
agony and I returned to his side. I would do for him what I could, ruling my mind and my body to bathe and tend this man who was now
little more than a rotting corpse.

In the end it all happened so fast. I expect it was Janyn's wine that
saved me, but the decoction of green sage from the scrubby patch in
Signora Damiata's yard, used to dry and heal the foul ulcers and boils,
did nothing for him. Before the end of the second day he breathed no
more. How could a man switch from rude health to rigid mortality
within the time it took to pluck and boil a chicken? He never knew I
was there with him. Did I pray for him? Only if prayer was lancing the

boils to free the foul-smelling pus. Now the house was truly silent around me, holding its breath, as I placed the linen gently over his face, catching a document that fell from its folds at the foot of the bed. And then I sat on the stool by Janyn's body, not daring to move for fear that death would notice me too.

It was the clatter of a rook falling down the chimney that brought me back to my senses. Death obviously had no need of my soul, so I opened the manuscript that I still held. It was a document of ownership in Janyn's name of a manor in West Peckham, somewhere in Kent. I read it twice, a tiny seed of a plan beginning to unfurl in my mind. Now, here was a possibility. I did not know how to achieve what I envisaged, but of course I knew someone who would.

Where to find him? I walked slowly down the stairs, halting halfway when I saw a figure below me.

"Is he dead?" Signora Damiata was waiting for me in the narrow hall.

"Yes."

She made the sign of the cross on her bosom, a cursory acknowledgment, then flung back the outer door and gestured for me to leave. "I've arranged for his body to be collected. I'll return when the pestilence has gone."

"What about me?"

"I'm sure you'll find some means of employment," she said, barely acknowledging me. "Plague does not quench men's appetites."

"And my dower?"

"What dower?"

"You can't do this!" I announced. "You can't leave me homeless and without money."

But she could. "Out!"

I was pushed through the doorway onto the street. With a flourish and a rattle of the key, Signora Damiata locked the door and strode off, stepping through the waste and puddles.

It was a lesson to me in brutal coldheartedness when dealing with matters of coin and survival. And there I was, sixteen years old to my reckoning, widowed after little more than a year of marriage, cast adrift, standing alone outside the house, and homeless. It felt as if my feet were chained to the floor. Where would I go? Who would give me shelter? Reality was a bitter draft. London seethed around me but offered me no refuge.

"Mistress Perrers . . . !"

"Greseley!"

For there he was—I hadn't had to find him after all—emerging from a rank alley to slouch beside me. Never had I been so relieved to see anyone, but not without a shade of rancor. He might have lost a master too, but he would never be short of employment or a bed.

"What did the old besom give you?" he asked without preamble.

"Nothing," I retorted. "The old besom has stripped the house." And then I smiled, waving the document in front of his eyes. "Except for this. She overlooked it. It's a manor."

Those eyes gleamed. "Is it, now? And what do you intend to do with it?"

"I intend *you* to arrange that it becomes *mine*, Master Greseley. Enfeoffment for use, I think you called it." I could be a fast learner, and I had seen my chance. "Can you do that?"

He ran his finger down his nose. "Easy for those who know how. I can—if it suits me—have it made over to you as the widow of Master Perrers, and now *femme sole*."

A woman alone. With property. A not unpleasing thought that made my smile widen.

"And will it suit you, Master Greseley?" I slid a persuasive glance at the clerk. "Will you do it for me?"

His face flushed under my gaze as he considered.

I softened my voice. "I cannot do this on my own, Master Greseley. But you have the knowledge. . . ."

He grinned, a quick slash of thin lips and discolored teeth. "Why not? We have, I believe, the basis of a partnership here, Mistress Perrers. I'll work for you, and you'll put business my way—when you can. I'll enfeoff the manor to the use of a local knight—and myself."

So that was it. Master Greseley was not entirely altruistic, but he was willing with a little female enticement. How easily men could be seduced with a smile and outrageous flattery offered in sweet tones. He extended his hand. I looked at it: not overclean but with long, surprisingly elegant fingers that could work magic with figures far more ably than I, and I knew his mind to be just as clever. There on the doorstep of my erstwhile home, I handed over the document and we shook hands as I had seen Janyn do when confirming some deal with a customer.

"You'll not cheat me, will you?" I made my voice stern.

"Certainly not!" His outrage was amusing. And then his brows twitched together suspiciously. "Where will you go?"

"There's only one place." I had already made my decision. There really was no other to be made. It would be a roof over my head and food in my belly, and far preferable to life on the streets or docks as a common whore. Should I have turned up on the doorstep of my property in Gracechurch Street and demanded entry? Today I would have done just that—but then I was too inexperienced, too ill-prepared to fight for my legal claim. Besides, I looked no better than a kitchen wench. "Back to St. Mary's," I said. "They'll take me in. I'll stay there and wait for better times. Something will turn up."

Greseley nodded. "Not a bad idea, all in all. But you'll need this. Here . . ." He rummaged in the purse at his belt and brought out two gold coins. "I'll return these to you. They should persuade the Abbess to open the doors to you for a little time, at least. Remember, though: You now owe me. I want it back."

"Where do I find you?" I shrieked, coarse as a fishwife, as he put distance between us, the proof of ownership of the manor at West Peckham stowed in his tunic.

"Try the Tabard. At Southwark."

That was as much as I got.

So I went back to the convent, where I had vowed I would never return, wheedling a ride in a wagon empty of all but the rank whiff of fish. I might own a manor and a house in London—I had left both precious documents in Greseley's care—but I was in debt to the tune of two gold nobles to my partner in business. And though those coins opened the doors of the Abbey to me, they bought me no luxury. It was made clear to me that I must earn my keep, and so I found myself joining the ranks of the conversa: a lay sister toiling for the benefit of the Brides of Christ. Perhaps it was the stink of salt cod clinging to my skirts that worked against me.

Why did I accept my diminished status?

Because the sanctuary the convent offered me was a temporary measure. I knew it deep within me. I had supped in the outside world and found it to my taste. In those days of silent labor, a determination was born in me. I would never become a nun. I would never wed again at anyone's dictates. At some point in the future, in Greseley's clever hands, my land would bring me enough coin to allow me to live as a *femme sole* in my own house with my own bed and good clothing and servants at my beck and call.

I liked the image. It spurred me on as I scrubbed the nuns' habits and beat the stains from their wimples to restore them to pristine whiteness. I would prove Countess Joan wrong. I would make something of my life beyond the governance of others, neither nun nor wife nor whore. I would amount to something in my own right. But for now I was safe in the familiar surroundings of the Abbey, accepting the unchanging routine of work and prayer.

"I'll stay there and wait for better times," I had said to Greseley.

And I would. But not, I prayed as my arms throbbed from wielding the heavy hoe amongst the Abbey cabbages, for too long.

I regretted the loss of my warm mantle.

Chapter Three

"**S**he's here. She's come." The whispers rustled like a brisk wind through a field of oats.

It was Vespers. We entered the Abbey church, the hush of habits and soft shoes a quiet sound against the paving, and we knelt, ranks of black veils and white wimples, I in a coarse fustian overkirtle and hood with the rest of the conversa. Ordinarily the mind of every sister, choir or lay, centered on the need for God's grace in a world of transgression. But not tonight. The sin of self-indulgence was rife, bright as the candle flames. Excitement was tangible, shivering in the air. For in the bishop's own chair, placed to one side of the High Altar, sat the Queen of England.

From my lowly place in the choir stalls I could see nothing of Her Majesty; nor could I even hazard a guess as to why she would so honor us. The service proceeded as if that carved chair were unoccupied, and once the final blessing was given, the nuns and conversa stood as one, with heads bowed and hands folded discreetly within their sleeves. Mother Sybil genuflected before the altar, and Her Majesty, still outside my vision, moved slowly through our midst toward the transept.

Slowly. Very slowly.

Which allowed me my first sight of true royalty.

Even today I recall my astonishment. Where was Countess Joan's

show of ostentatious wealth and power? There was no such magnificence here. I had envisaged a noble bearing, a gown in rich colors,
sumptuous materials stitched with embroidery, with train and furred
oversleeves. A crown, a gold chain, gold and silver rings heavy with
jewels. A presence of authority and elegance, of royal beauty. Joan's
arrival had been announced to us by courier and trumpet blast. I
looked at the Queen of England, and looked again.

She was well-nigh invisible in her anonymity.

Philippa of Hainault.

The years had not treated this woman with gentleness. All trace of
youth, any beauty she might have had as that young bride who had
come to England from the Low Countries to wed our vigorous King
Edward more than thirty years ago now, were lost to her. And where
was the expression of regal power? Her gown might be of excellent
quality, but it lacked glamour, the colors of the silk damask more
muted than glowing, in browns and ochers and russet. Nor was the cut
of the cloth in the fashionably sleek, close-fitting form, but wide, ample
enough to hide the lady's stout figure and broad hips. She was not elegant. She was not tall. She did not overawe. She wore no jewels. As for
her hair, it was completely obscured, every wisp and curl, by a severe
wimple and veil. Queen Philippa was neither a handsome woman nor
a leader of fashion.

How disappointing!

My first thought was of Countess Joan, who would eclipse this
dowdy little woman after wedding her royal prince. The frivolous royal
Court would circle 'round the vivacious new Princess rather than this
fading, unprepossessing Queen. Was that not the order of things? Who
could admire this aging, shuffling woman?

The Queen halted. There was the faintest gasp for breath. She must
be even older than I had thought. I looked again—longer than a
glance—and instantly chided myself for my lack of compassion. There
was a reason for the excruciatingly slow progress. The Queen was ill.
She was in pain. With a hand resting heavily on the arm of her attendant, she continued to make her small, uneven steps because each one
pained her beyond endurance. It seemed to me that she could barely
move her head, her neck and shoulders were so rigid with a spasm of

the muscles. The hand that clutched the arm of her woman was swollen, the flesh as tight and shiny as the skin of a drum. No wonder she wore no rings. How would she push them beyond her swollen knuckles without unbearable discomfort?

We curtsied as Her Majesty passed. She inclined her head in unsmiling recognition, pausing almost as she drew level with me to take in another breath. I saw the substantial bosom of her gown rise sharply on the inhalation, her nostrils narrow, and a crease deepen between her brows. Then the royal feet moved on—only to stumble on the uneven paving so that she fell. Without her grip on the arm of the young woman at her side, it would have been a disaster. As it was, she sank to her knees with a cry of agonized distress. Horrified by the quality of her suffering, I gave up pretending not to look.

"Help me," she murmured, to no one in particular, eyes closed tight in agony, her free hand outstretched to snatch at some invisible aid. "Dear God, help me!" And Queen Philippa dropped her rosary beads. They slid from her fingers to fall with a little clatter of pearls and carved bone on the stones before her.

"Help me to my feet. . . ."

And because it seemed the obvious thing to do, the only thing to do, I stretched out my hand and took hers in mine. The Queen's hand bore down, and as it did I froze, my mind skittering to the past. The rescue of Joan's monkey, a selfishly calculated action, was one thing. But to take the hand of the Queen of England on sheer impulse? I would surely be punished for my presumption. I fell to my knees beside her as she gripped me as hard as she could. There was not much force in it, but she groaned as the skin covering her swollen flesh tightened with the effort.

"Blessed Virgin!" she murmured. "The pain is too much!"

The tension around us, the shocked stillness, held for a moment. Then all was movement and sound: the lady-in-waiting lifting Her Majesty to her feet in a flutter of anxiety, the Queen's feverish clasp of my hand broken, the distress of her labored breathing deepening. Looking up from where I was still on my knees, I discovered Queen Philippa in the midst of all the fuss regarding me. Once, those eyes might have sparkled with happiness, but now their rich brown hue was strained with years of suffering. I could not bear to see it, and lowered my gaze to where the rosary still lay on the floor. She was quite unable to stoop to recover the beads for herself, even if a woman of such rank would deem to pick up her own belongings.

So I did it.

I lifted the rosary and held it out, startled at my temerity even without the sharp warning murmur of Mother Abbess, who was approaching, her habit billowing with the speed of her passage like a cloak in a gale, intent on snatching the rosary from me.

"Thank you. I am very clumsy today, and you are very kind."

Incredibly, the Queen's words were for me. I felt the touch of her fingers on my hand. For a brief moment the devastation in her face was overlaid by a softness of gratitude.

"Accept my apologies, Majesty." Mother Abbess directed toward me a look that boded ill for me in the Chapter House the following day. "She should not have pushed herself forward in this manner. She has no humility."

"But she has come to my aid, like the Good Samaritan to the traveler in distress," the Queen observed. "The Holy Virgin would honor such help to an old lady. What is your name, my child?"

Before I could reply, she cried out, more sharply than before, one hand spread across the damask folds over her abdomen.

"I need to sit down. My room, Isabella—take me to my room."

And her attendant, with a fierce frown and a firm grip, lifted her to her feet.

"I am so sorry, Isabella. . . ." The Queen's voice caught on a sob.

"You're tired, *Maman*. Did I not say this was too much for you? You should listen to me! And now you need to rest."

"I am aware, Isabella. But some things needed to be done, and I could not wait."

For the first time I did more than give passing cognizance to the Queen's companion. So this was her daughter, the Princess Isabella, whose arm had been gripped so tightly: a tall, fair young woman with a sprightly demeanor and a barely disguised expression of displeasure. How could I have ever mistaken her for a mere attendant? The Queen might be clothed in muted colors, but the Princess proclaimed her position in every embroidered thread and jewel, from her gold crisp-inettes to her gilded shoes.

"Some things could be left until you are recovered," Princess Isabella remarked crisply. I watched with pity as the little group made their way along the nave. At the Abbey door the Princess looked back, briefly, over her shoulder. Her gaze landed on me. "Don't just stand there. Bring the rosary, girl."

"Something will turn up!" I had said to Greseley. I did not need telling twice.

In spite of her daughter's determination, the Queen refused to be put to bed.

"I'll be in my bed long enough, and then my coffin, when death takes hold of me!"

I stood inside the door of the Abbess's parlor as the Queen was made comfortable in a high-backed chair with sturdy arms that would give her body some support. I could have put the rosary down on the traveling coffer beside the door and left, invisible to all as Isabella issued orders for a cup of heated wine and a fur mantle to warm the Queen's trembling limbs. *Stay!* my instincts urged. So I stayed. If I stayed, perhaps the Queen would speak to me again. The kindness in her voice had stirred my heart, and now as I saw the woman behind the face of royalty, my heart hurt for her. My first impressions were all confirmed. She was ill, and her suffering came not only from physical pain but also from grief. She was worn with it, and she had seen the truth in it: Black-cloaked death seemed to hover behind her shoulder. It did not take a dabbler in magic signs to see it. Never had I thought to feel sorrow for a Queen, but on that evening I did.

"And don't tell the King!" she ordered, voice harsh with exhaustion.

"Why not?" Isabella took her mother's hand and pressed the wine cup into it.

"Don't tell him, Isabella. I forbid it! I do not wish him to be worried over it!"

Her voice might be a mere thread, but how strong was her will. My admiration and compassion for her were profound. Did the King still love her? Had he ever loved her? Perhaps it was not expected between those of royal blood whose marriage had been contracted for political alliance. Was she ever the woman he had wanted as his consort, a mirror to reflect his magnificence? I could not imagine it. What must it be like to feel old and unwanted? And yet the Queen would protect her husband from concern over her pain.

As if she sensed the direction of my thoughts, the Queen pushed aside Isabella's hand with the cup and straightened herself in the chair. And there it was after all. There was regality. There was authority. In spite of the pain, she could give her attention to me and smile. Her face warmed, the harsh lines smoothing, until she became almost comely. Had I thought her broad, almost coarse features lacking charm and beauty? I was wrong.

She stretched out her hand with difficulty. "You have brought my rosary."

"Yes, Majesty."

"I told her to." Isabella poured a second cup of wine and drank it herself. "By God, this is poor stuff . . . ! We were too busy with you to worry about a string of beads, if you recall, trying to prevent you from falling on the floor before a parcel of ignorant nuns. . . ."

"Nevertheless, it was well-done." The Queen beckoned and I came to kneel before her. "A conversa, I see. Tell me your name."

"Alice."

"You have no desire to become a nun?" Putting a hand beneath my chin, she lifted it and studied my face. "You have no calling?"

No one had ever asked me that before, or even addressed me in so gentle a manner. There was a world of understanding in her eyes. Unexpectedly, unsettlingly, tears stung beneath my eyelids.

"No, Majesty." Since she seemed interested, I told her. "Once, I was a novice. And then a servant—who became a wife. Now I am a widow. And returned here as a lay sister."

"And is that your ambition? To remain here?"

Well, I would not lie. "No, Majesty. I will not stay longer than I must."

"So you have plans. . . . How old are you?"

"Almost seventeen years, I think. I am not a child, Majesty," I felt compelled to add.

"You are to me!" Her smile deepened momentarily. "Do you know how old I am?"

It seemed entirely presumptuous of me to even reply. "No, Majesty."

"Forty-eight years. I expect that seems ancient to you." Well, it did. It seemed to me a vast age, and suffering had added a dozen more years to the Queen's face. "I was younger than you when I came to England as a bride. It seems no time to me. Life flies past. . . ."

"Take another drink, *Maman*." Isabella replaced the cup in the Queen's hand, folding the swollen fingers gently around it. "I think you should rest."

I expected to be dismissed, but the Queen was not to be bullied.

"Soon, Isabella. Soon. But you, Alice . . . Have you no family?"

"No, Majesty."

"And your father?"

"I don't know. A laborer in the town. A tiler, I think."

"I understand." And I felt that she did, despite the distance between us in years and rank. "How sad. You remind me of my own daughters."

Isabella sighed heavily—"*Maman . . . !*"—whilst I shook my head. How could I remind anyone of a Princess of the Blood?

"Why should I not speak of them?" the Queen replied sharply. "If I don't speak of them, they will be forgotten. We exist on this earth only as long as the memories of us are shared. My two beautiful daughters. Mary and Margaret. Who will remember them when I am dead? You are of a similar age," she explained, as if I had spoken my doubt. "Such beautiful girls, full of promise. Both dead last September. Plague has a cruel bite."

Thus her grief.

"I miss them. That is why we are here, you see. To pray for them. I believe it is God's will that I make an endowment in their names. We buried them at Abingdon together, didn't we, Isabella? A sad day. It's too far for me to travel there now. All my girls gone . . ." Tears welled in her eyes.

"You have one daughter still at home, *Maman*!" Isabella handed her mother a square of linen.

"Yes! A daughter I wish were married and gone!" the Queen responded with a remarkable surge of spirit.

Isabella gave what I might have considered a grin, if she had not been a royal princess. "And I might be, if you provided me with the right suitor."

"We gave you the right suitor! More than ten years ago . . ."

"Who would have driven me to madness within a month!"

This weighty exchange that flowed above my head from mother to daughter intrigued me with its depth of affectionate tolerance. I imagined it to be a much-aired conversation. I was invisible between them.

"You should wed for suitability and power, Isabella, not for some ephemeral emotion such as love."

"You found love, *Maman*."

"My marriage to your father was arranged whether I found love or not. It was simply an added blessing that we discovered such pleasure together. You'll be an old unmarried woman, Isabella, with nothing but lapdogs, stitchery, and prayer to sustain you; you mark my words. But of course you don't!" The Queen turned her attention back to me. "You are young to be a widow. Would you seek to wed again?"

"No, Majesty!"

"Is it not what every young woman would seek?"

"They say I am too ugly to attract a man." For certain, Janyn had been guided by practical self-interest. "No man would look at what I could offer."

"What can you offer?"

I considered the sum of my talents. "I can read and write and figure, Majesty." Since someone actually showed an interest, there was no stopping me. "I can read French and Latin. I can write—and more than my name. I can keep accounts." Ingenuously, I was carried away with my achievements.

"So much . . ." I had made her smile again. And how did you learn to keep accounts?"

"My husband, Janyn Perrers. A moneylender. He taught me."

"And did you enjoy it? So tedious a task?"

"Yes. I understand what I saw."

"You have a keen mind, Alice of the Accounts," was all she said.

Perhaps I amused her, and I wished I had not boasted of my hard-won skills. She took hold of one of my hands, running her fingers over the evidence of hard digging in the heavy soil. My nails were cracked, the skin broken, and the aroma of onions was keen. "Blisters and blemishes. You look as if you have been digging."

"I have, Your Majesty. It is the time for sowing crops to feed us through next winter."

"I suppose it is. Do you like that work too?"

I shook my head.

"Nor would I."

And I laughed at the absurdity of such an admission from the Queen of England. The sound of my own laughter momentarily shocked me. I could not recall when I had last smiled or laughed aloud. I did not think I had much to smile about.

"You have a pretty laugh. And you should smile more. It brings a lightness to your face. If you could choose your future path, Alice, what would it be?"

I replied without hesitation, thinking of Greseley, of the hopes that kept me from despair in the dark hours of the night. "I would have my own house. I would buy land and property. I would be dependent on no one. . . ."

"An unlikely ambition!" Isabella's remark interrupted us, redolent of ridicule.

"But a commendable one for all that." The Queen's voice trembled. Isabella was instantly beside her. "Yes. I will rest now. Today is not a good day." She allowed her daughter to help her to her feet and moved slowly toward the bedchamber. Then she stopped and, despite the discomfort, looked back to me.

"Alice . . . keep the rosary. It was a gift to me from the King when I gave birth to Edward, our first son." She must have read astonishment on my face. "It is not very valuable. He had little money to spend on fripperies in those days. I would like you to keep it as a memento of the day when you rescued the Queen from falling on her face in public."

The rosary. I still gripped it in one hand, the gold enameled beads of the Aves clutched so tight that they left impressions in my palm. The pearls that marked the paternosters and glorias were warm and so smooth. The Queen would give this to me? A gift from her husband? I coveted it—who would not? I wanted it for my own.

"No . . ." I said. I could not. I was not courteous, but I knew what would happen if I kept the gift. "We are not allowed possessions. We take a vow of poverty." I tried to explain my refusal, knowing how crude it must seem.

"Not even a gift from a grateful Queen?"

"It would not be thought suitable. . . ."

". . . and you would not be allowed to keep it."

"No, Majesty."

"No. I was thoughtless to offer it. . . ." The tormenting pain gripped her again and I was forgotten. "By the Virgin, I am tired beyond endurance today—take me to my bed, Isabella."

Isabella maneuvered the Queen through the doorway into the bedchamber, and I was left alone. Before I could change my mind, I placed the rosary on the prie-dieu and backed out of the room until I was standing outside the door. Quietly I closed it, leaning against it. I had refused a gift from a Queen. But what would be the good in my accepting what I would not be allowed to keep? I had learned from hard experience. If I kept it, the rosary would fall into the hands of Mother Abbess. In my mind's eye, I could see it attached to her silver-decorated girdle, as she carried Countess Joan's Book of Hours into the church when she sang the offices. As I could imagine my mantle gracing the shoulders of Signora Damiata.

If ever I accepted anything of value in my life, I must be certain it remained mine.

Queen Philippa and her sharp-tongued daughter did not stay beyond the one night. As soon as the service of Prime was sung the next morning, they made ready to depart. The Queen was helped into her well-cushioned traveling litter by Sister Margery, who had made up a draft of tender ash leaves distilled in wine to lessen the agony of a bone-shaking journey. I knew what was in it. Had I not helped to make the infusion?

"Her Majesty suffers from dropsy," Sister Margery had pronounced with certainty. "I have seen it before. It is a terrible affliction. She will feel the effect of every rut and stumble."

Sister Margery instructed Lady Isabella: Too much of the draft would cripple the digestion; too little and the pain would remain intense. And here was a little pot of mutton fat pounded with vervain root. Smoothed on the swollen flesh of hands and feet, it would bring relief. I had done the work but it was not I who held the flask and offered the little pot. It was not I who received the Queen's thanks. I was not even there. I heard the departure from the cellar where I was engaged in counting hams and barrels of ale.

Take me with you. Let me serve you.

A silent plea that the Queen did not hear.

Why would she remember me? Because it was an occasion of moment in *my* life had no bearing on what a queen might remember. She would have forgotten about me within the quarter hour of my returning the rosary. But I did not forget Queen Philippa. She had the loving kindness in her homely face of the mother that I had never known.

I wondered what Greseley was doing. Whether I would ever see him again. Whether he was taking care of the houses in Gracechurch Street and the little manor in West Peckham. Surely he could raise enough money from them for my own needs.

I prayed even more fervently over the hams than I had over the cabbages that it would be *soon*, before my hopes died.

The early blossom on the gnarled trees in the orchard was over, setting into fruit the plums and damsons that we would preserve against the long winter months. I was engaged in collecting dead branches for firewood to heat the old bones in the infirmary, and scooping up the June drop of fruit that would attract wasps. An unpleasant task, all in all.

Sister Matilda stood at the gate beckoning me, her black sleeves flapping like the wings of the blackbirds that competed with me for the fallen fruit.

"Hurry, girl. Leave that."

My mind scrabbled through any recent sin, of omission or commission. Even as a lay sister who was not required to observe every service,

I was still bound by the tenets of Saint Benedict. It was too early in the day to have broken many of them; my silence in the orchard was complete, since I was alone. I was conscious of my disheveled skirts where I had knelt beneath the low branches, and of the mud on my shoes. Was that it? I made a desultory attempt to beat away the soil and grass.

"No time for that . . ." Sister Matilda took hold of my sleeve and pulled me along.

Where? Clearly not to the Chapter House. Nor the Abbey church. Instead we turned into the roofed passage between cloister and refectory that led through to the enclosed courtyard before the Abbess's lodgings, which was so full of people and horses there was barely room for us. Mother Abbess, heavy with satisfaction, stood on the steps out of the way of the melee caused by a small party of travelers: a tall, well-dressed man, perhaps a courier, judging from his riding gear of fine wool and leather; an elderly thickset groom who held the reins of a fine gelding; and a small but well-armed escort, sword and bow very evident.

As Sister Matilda and I flattened ourselves against the wall out of the way of teeth and hooves, I had the impression that a conversation between the Abbess and the courier had just come to a satisfactory end, and a small coffer was handed into Mother Sybil's keeping. But why was I here? This was nothing to do with me. Then the courier turned a penetrating gaze toward me.

"You are Alice?"

"Yes, sir."

"You are to go with me, mistress." He looked me up and down and, from the narrowing of his eyes, found me wanting. "You will need a cloak." And to the Abbess: "Provide one for her, if you please."

I looked to Mother Sybil for instruction. She lifted a shoulder, as if denying any complicity in what had been arranged. Had my labors been bought again? Holy Virgin! Not another marriage! The man continued to address me, impervious and uninformative.

"Can you ride, mistress?"

"No, sir."

He motioned to the groom. "She'll ride pillion behind you, Rob. She's no weight to speak of."

Within minutes I was bundled into a coarsely woven cloak and hoisted onto the broad rump of the groom's mare, as if I were the cordon of firewood I would now never collect from the orchard.

"Hold tight, mistress," the man called Rob growled.

I clutched the sides of his leather jerkin as the animal stamped and sidled. The ground seemed far away and my balance was awry. At a signal from the man who had thus so smoothly rearranged my future, the escort fell in and we rode through the streets of the town and into the open country without a further word being said on either side.

Obviously my escort preferred the silence, and hoped it would continue. But what woman would keep a still tongue when her inquisitiveness ran rampant?

"Sir?" I addressed the back of the man who was now riding a little way ahead of me. When there was no reply, I raised my voice. "Sir? Where are we going?" One day, I vowed, I would determine the direction of my travels.

He did not turn his head. He might have addressed me as "mistress," but it seemed I was not worthy of any further respect. "To Havering-atte-Bower."

It meant nothing to me. "Why?"

"The Queen has sent for you."

Which meant even less. "Is Havering-atte-Bower, then, a royal palace?"

"Yes."

"Why? Why would the Queen summon me?"

The man slowed his horse and gestured the groom to pull alongside. On a level, he reined in his mount, allowing me to read his unspoken thoughts as clear as figures in a ledger. His mouth curved downward, as if it were all beyond his comprehension, and it took little imagination on my part to understand why. My kirtle and overgown bore the sticky remnants of the fallen fruit in St. Mary's orchard, my hair was bound up in a length of coarse cloth, and my borrowed cloak was far beyond respectability.

He kicked his mount into a walk, and we plodded on side by side as he considered what he thought of me and what he would deign to tell me.

"Why would the Queen send for me?" I asked again. Why were men so uncommunicative?

"I have no idea. Her Majesty will doubtless tell you."

He shortened his reins as if to push on with more speed, our conversation brought to a premature end. I wanted more.

"Who are you, sir?"

He gave no reply, through choice, I decided, rather than because he had not heard me, so I took the time to appraise him. Nothing out of the way. He was neither young nor old, with regular features, and a little austere. He was certainly used to command, but I thought he was not a soldier. Nor was he the courier I had first thought him. He had too much authority for that. His eyes were a mix of green and brown, sharp and bright, like those of a squirrel. I thought him rather pompous for a man who could not be exactly described as old. So we would ride to Havering-atte-Bower in total silence, would we? I thought not. I held tight to Rob's tunic and leaned toward my reluctant companion.

"I have much to learn, sir," I began. "How far to Havering-atte-Bower?"

"About two hours. Three if you don't get a move on."

I ignored the jibe. "Time enough, then. You could help me. You could tell me some of the things I don't know."

"Such as?" He addressed me as if I were the witless minion I doubtless appeared to be.

"You could tell me how to behave when I get to Havering-atte-Bower," I suggested solemnly, at the same time widening my eyes in innocent inquiry. And I saw him waver. "And how do I address you, sir?"

"I am William de Wykeham. And you, I suspect, are no wiser."

I smiled deliberately. Winsomely. How best to seduce information from a man than to get him to talk of what was important to him? I had learned that from both Janyn and Greseley. Talk about money and rates of interest and they would eat out of your hand. "I am no wiser yet," I replied. "But I will be if you will be my informant. What do I call you? What do you do?"

"Wykeham will do. I serve His Majesty. And occasionally Her Majesty, Queen Philippa." And I saw the pride in him. "I am destined for the church—and to build palaces."

"Oh." It seemed a laudable occupation, if not very exciting. "Have you built many?"

And that was it. The door opened wide. Wykeham proceeded for the rest of the journey to tell me of his ambitions and achievements. Turrets and arches, buttresses and pillars. Curtain walls and superior heating methods. Holy Virgin! He was as dull as a meatless meal in Lent, as incapable of luring a nun from her vows as Janyn Perrers or Greseley. Perhaps all men in essence were as dry as dust. What I wanted to hear of was the minutiae of life in a royal palace, the food, the fashions, the important personages, and all I got was a description of the new tower at Windsor. Still, I made no effort to deter him. Were all men so easy to encourage into conversation? Far easier than women, I thought. A smile, a question, an appeal to their achievements, their pride, was all it took. I learned very little about life at Havering, but much about castle building. And then, the two hours passing rapidly enough, we were approaching an impressive array of towers, half-hidden in the trees.

"Your journey is at an end, Mistress Alice. And I had forgot. . . ." Transferring his reins into one hand, Wykeham fished into his saddle-bag. "Her Majesty sent you this. She thought you might like it—to give you God's comfort on the journey." He dropped the rosary into my hand. "Not that I think you need it. You can talk more than any woman I know. . . ."

I was instantly torn between amazement at the gift of the rosary and the unfairness of the accusation; the unfairness won.

"You've done more talking than I have!"

"Nonsense!"

"Stop fussing, woman!" Rob gave a rough growl. "You're as fret as a flea on a warm dog!"

I laughed. "I ache!"

"Your arse'll recover soon enough. My sides are stripped raw with your clutchings!"

Even Wykeham laughed. "And I expect you're thirsty." A flask was found in his saddlebag and he handed it over. The wine, too warm for pleasure but of a quality I had never drunk before, even better than Janyn's, eased my suddenly dry throat. I was at the end of my journey, and what awaited me remained a mystery.

"Why would she send me something so precious?" I held the rosary up so that the sun caught the beads, turning them into a rainbow of iridescence.

My companion surveyed me, from my cloth-bound hair to my mud-smeared hem, as if it were far beyond his comprehension too. "I really have no idea."

Nor did I.

Chapter Four

Havering-atte-Bower. I knew nothing of royal palaces in those days when I arrived in Wykeham's dusty wake. Nor was the grandeur of the place my first priority. Every muscle in my body groaned at its ill usage. We could not come to a halt fast enough for me; all I wanted was to slide down from that lumbering creature and set my feet on solid ground. But once we were in the courtyard at Havering, I simply sat and stared.

"Are you going to dismount today, mistress?" Wykeham's tone was lacking in compassion. "What's wrong with you?" He was already dismounted and halfway up the steps to the huge iron-studded door.

"I've never seen . . ." He wasn't listening, so I closed my mouth.

I have never seen anything so magnificent.

The palace was strangely welcoming, owning a seductive charm that St. Mary's with its gray-stone austerity lacked. It seemed vast to me, though I was to learn that for a royal palace it was small and intimate. The stonework of the building glowed in the afternoon sunshine, a haphazard arrangement of rooms and apartments, the arches of a chapel to the right, the bulk of the original Great Hall to my left, then further outbuildings, sprawling in all directions from the courtyard. Roofs and walls jutted at strange angles as the whim had taken the builders over the years. And if that were not enough, the whole palace was hemmed about by pasture and lightly wooded stretches like a length of green velvet wrapped 'round a precious jewel.

It filled me with awe.

"It's beautiful!"

My voice must have carried. "It'll do, for now," Wykeham growled. "The King's grandfather built it—the first Edward. The Queen likes it—that's the main thing—it's her manor. It will be better when I've had my hands on it. I've a mind to put in new kitchens now that the King has his household here too." He fisted his hands on his hips. "For God's sake, woman. Get off that animal."

I sat where I was. The ground looked far away. "I need help."

"Then let Rob . . ."

I ignored the snort of amusement from the groom, who had made no attempt to aid me.

"I suppose, sir, I am too far below you to expect you to help me to dismount." I was all demure insouciance, except for the tilt of my chin.

"Yes. You are." But Wykeham's mouth twitched as he stomped back to my side. "And I suspect you are a baggage! Where did you learn that, enclosed in a nunnery?"

"I have been married," I informed him, hinting nothing of its brevity or its lack.

"Then that must account for it."

I did not think so. I think my wit—its immediacy—had always been there, hidden away until I had the freedom to be myself. With a hand to my arm, he helped me to slide from the animal's broad rump as adeptly as I could manage.

"Thank you, sir." I held on tight for a moment as my muscles quivered in protest.

"I am at your disposal. Tell me when you can stand without falling over!"

I loosed my grip with a pert smile for the irony.

Wykeham led the way up the shallow flight of steps, pushing open the door and stepping into the Great Hall. It was an echoing space, tables and trestles cleared away for the day except for the solid board on the dais at the far end. Cool after the heat of the sun, it was a pleasant place to be, the rafters above my head merging into deep shadows striped with soft bars of sunlight, like the coat of a tabby cat. Servants moved quietly, purposefully replacing the candles in the wall sconces. A burst of laughter came from behind the screens at the far end that closed off the entrance to the kitchens. The tapestries on the walls glowed with rich color, mirrored in the tiles beneath my feet. A maid-servant crossed the room, busy with a tray of cups and a flagon, with a brief curtsy in Wykeham's direction.

My eye followed her.

Was this, then, to be my destiny? To work in the kitchens of the royal palace? But why? Did the Queen not have enough servants? If she needed more, would her steward not find enough willing girls from the neighboring villages? I could not see why she would bring me all the way from the Abbey to be a serving wench. Perhaps she needed a tire-woman, one who could read and write, but, remembering Lady Marian, I could hardly claim the breeding for it. So why, in the name of the Blessed Virgin, was I here? Countess Joan had been cruelly quick to reject my offered services: The Queen would hardly stand in need of my meager talents.

"This way . . ." Wykeham was striding ahead. "Don't stand day-dreaming!"

Behind us in the doorway a commotion erupted, enough to make my nerves jump and skitter like rats in a trap. Both Wykeham and I, and everyone in the Hall, turned to look.

A man had entered to stand under the door arch. He was illumi-nated, silhouetted, by the low rays of the afternoon sun so that it was impossible to see his features, only his stature and bearing. Tall, was my first impression, with the build of a soldier, a man of action. Around his feet pushed and jostled a pack of hounds and alaunts. On his gaunt-leted wrist rode a hooded goshawk.

As the hawk shook its pinions, the man moved forward a step, into the power of a direct beam, so that he gleamed with a corona of light around his head and shoulders like one of the saints in the glazed win-dows of the Abbey. Crowned with gold. I simply stared.

Then, as he took another step, the moment passed. He was en-closed in soft shadow, an ordinary man again. And I was distracted when the hounds bounded forward, circling the Hall, sniffing at my skirts. I had no knowledge of such boisterous animals and automatically stepped back, wary of sharp teeth and formidable bodies. Oblivious to my discomfort, Wykeham bowed whilst I was engaged in pushing aside an inquisitive alaunt.

Wykeham cleared his throat in warning.

"What is it?" I asked.

In reply he took hold of the ancient cloak that still enveloped me from chin to toe and twitched it off, letting it fall to the floor. I stiffened at this presumptuous action and took a breath to remonstrate when a voice of command, a strikingly beautiful one, cut across the width of the Hall.

"Wykeham, by God! Where've you been? Why are you always impossible to find, man?"

It was a clear-timbred voice, filling the space from walls to rafters. And striding toward us was the owner. The man with the raptor.

Wykeham bowed again, with what could have been construed as a scowl in my direction, so I accepted the wisdom of curtsying. The newcomer looked to me like a huntsman who had strayed into the Hall after a day's exercise to find a cup of ale or a heel of bread. He covered the ground with long loping strides, as lithe as the hound at his side.

And then he was standing within a few feet of me.

"Sire!" Wykeham bowed once more.

The King!

I sank to the floor, holding my skirts, my flushed face hidden. How naive I was. But how was I to know? Why did he not dress like a king? Then I looked up and saw him not a score of feet distant, and knew that he did not need clothing and jewels to proclaim his superiority. What a miraculous, godlike figure he was. A man of some age and experience, but he wore the years lightly. He was handsome without doubt, with a broad brow and a fine blade of a nose complemented by luxurious flaxen hair that shone as bright as silver. Here was no dry-as-dust dullard. The King shone like a diamond amongst worthless dross.

"It's the water supply!" the King announced.

"Yes, Sire. I have it in hand," Wykeham replied calmly.

"The Queen needs heated water. . . ."

The King's complexion might once have been fair, but his skin was tanned and seamed from an outdoor life in sun and cold. What a re-markable face he was blessed with, with blue eyes as keen as those of the raptor on his fist, whose hood he was removing. And what a fluidity and grace there was about his movements, as he unclipped his cloak, one-handed, swung it from his shoulder, and threw it to a page who had followed him across the Hall. How had I not known that this was King Edward? At his belt was a knife in a jeweled scabbard, in his hat a ruby brooch pinning a peacock feather into jaunty place. Even with-out the glitter of gems, I should have known. He had a presence, the habit of command, of demanding unquestioning obedience.

So this was Queen Philippa's magnificent husband. I was dazzled.

I stood, my heart beating fast, aware of nothing but my own unfor-tunate apparel, the heap of the disreputable mantle at my feet. But the King was not looking at me. Was I not more poorly clad than any of the servants I had seen in the palace? He would think—if he thought at all—that I was a beggar come to receive alms from the palace kitch-ens. Even the raptor eyed me as if I might be vermin worth eating.

The King swept his arm out in a grand gesture. "Out! All of you!" The dogs obediently vanished through the door in a rush of excite-ment. "Will—I've been looking at the site for the bathhouse you proposed. . . ." He was close enough to clip Wykeham in an affection-ate manner on his shoulder. "Where've you been?"

I might as well not have been there. I was of less importance than the cold-blooded killer whose feathers he was smoothing with casual affection.

"I've been to St. Mary's at Barking, Sire." Wykeham smiled.

"Barking? Why in God's name?"

"Business for the Queen, Sire. A new chantry."

The King nodded. "Yes, yes. I'd forgotten. It gives her comfort, and—before God!—precious little does." At last he cast a cursory eye over me. "Who's this? Someone I employ?" Removing the beaver hat with its brooch and feather, he inclined his head in grave acknowledg-ment, even though he thought I was a serving wench. His gaze traveled over my face in a cursory manner. I made another belated curtsy. The King tilted his chin at Wykeham, having made some judgment on me. "St. Mary's, you said. Have you helped one of the sisters to escape, Will?"

Wykeham smiled dryly. "The Queen sent for her."

Those sharp blue eyes returned. "One of her waifs and strays, perhaps. To be rescued for her own good. What's your name, girl?"

"Alice, Sire."

"Glad to escape?"

"Yes, Sire." It was heartfelt, and must have sounded it.

And Edward laughed, a sound of great joy that made me smile too. "So would I be. Serving God's all very well, but not every hour of every day. Do you have talents?" He frowned at me as if he could not imagine it. "Play a lute?" I shook my head. "Sing? My wife likes music."

"No, Sire."

"Well, I suppose she has her reasons." He was already losing interest, turning away. "And if it makes her happy . . . Come here!"

I started, thinking that he meant me, but he clicked his fingers at one of the rangy alaunts that had slunk back into the Hall and was following some scent along the edge of a tapestry. It obeyed to fawn and rub against him as he twisted his fingers into its collar. "Tell Her Majesty, Will— No, on second thought, you come with me. You've completed your task for the Queen. I've demands on your time for my new bathhouse." He raised his voice. "Joscelyn! Joscelyn!"

A man approached from where he had been waiting discreetly beside the screen.

"Yes, Sire."

"Take this girl to the Queen. She has sent for her. Now, Will . . ." They were already knee-deep in planning. "I think there's the perfect site. . . . Let me get rid of these dogs and birds. . . ." Whistling softly to the raptor on his wrist, the King headed to the door. Wykeham followed. They left me without a second look. Both of them. Why would they not?

Sir Joscelyn, who I was to learn was the royal steward, beckoned me to follow him, but I hesitated and looked back over my shoulder. Wykeham was nodding, my last view of him gesturing with his hands as if describing the size and extent of the building he envisaged. They laughed together, the King's strong voice overlaying Wykeham's softer responses. And then he was gone, as if my last friend on earth had deserted me. My only friend. And of course he wasn't, but who else did

I know here? I would not forget his brusque kindness. As for the King, I had expected a crown or at least a chain of office. Not a pack of dogs and a hawk. But there was no denying the sovereignty that sat as lightly on his shoulders as a summer mantle.

"Come on, girl. I haven't got all day."

I sighed and followed the steward to discover what would become of me as one of the Queen's habitual waifs and strays. I stuffed the rosary that I still clutched into the bosom of my overgown and followed as I was bidden.

The Queen's apartments were silent. Finding no one in any of the antechambers to whom he could hand me over, Sir Joscelyn rapped on a door, was bidden to enter, and did so, drawing me with him. I found myself on the threshold of a large sun-filled room so full of color and activity and soft chatter, of feminine glamour, that it took my breath, more than even the grandeur of the Great Hall. The sheer vibrancy of it. Here was every hue and tint I could imagine, overlapping, entirely pleasing to the eye, creating butterflies of the women who filled the room. I stared. It was ill-mannered, certainly, but I couldn't stop from staring at so beguiling a scene. There they were, chattering like bright finches as they stitched, books and board games at hand for those who wished, not an enshrouding wimple or brow-hugging veil amongst them. Here was a whole world of which I had no knowledge, to enchant ear and eye. The ladies talked and laughed. Someone was singing to the clear notes of a lute. There was no silence here.

I could not see the Queen in their midst.

The steward cast an eye and discovered the face he sought.

"My lady." His bow was perfection. Learning fast, I curtsied. "I would speak with Her Majesty."

Princess Isabella looked up from the lute she was playing, but her fingers continued to strum idly over the strings. Now I knew the source of her beautiful fairness: She was her father's daughter in height and coloring.

"Her Majesty is indisposed, Joscelyn. Can it wait?"

"I was commanded to bring this person to Her Majesty." He nudged me forward with haughty condescension. I curtsied again.

"Why?" Her gaze remained on the lute strings. She was not the King's daughter in kindness.

"Wykeham brought her, my lady."

The Princess's eyes lifted to take in my person. "Who are you?"

"Alice, my lady." There was no welcome here, not even a memory of who I was. "From St. Mary's Abbey at Barking, my lady."

A line dug between Isabella's brows, then smoothed. "I remember. The girl with the rosary—the one who worked in the kitchens or some such . . ."

"Yes, my lady."

"Her Majesty sent for you?"

Her fingers strummed over the lute strings again and her foot tapped impatiently. "I suppose I must do something with you." The glint in her eye, I decided, was not friendly.

One of the ladies approached to put her hand on the Princess's shoulder with the confidence of long acquaintance. "Play for us, Isabella. We have a new song."

"With pleasure. Take the girl to the kitchens, Joscelyn. Give her a bed and some food. Then put her to work. I expect that's what Her Majesty intended."

"Yes, my lady."

Isabella had already given her attention to the ladies and their new song. The steward bowed himself out and took me with him, the door closing on that magical scene in the solar. I had not managed to step beyond the threshold, and I was shaken by a sudden desire to do so, to be part of the life that went on behind that closed door. I would like that colorful and intimate world for myself.

Sir Joscelyn strode off without a word, expecting me to follow, and I did. I should be grateful that I was being given food and a place to sleep. I *would* be grateful. Would life as a kitchen wench at Havering-atte-Bower be better or worse than as a conversa in the Abbey at Barking? Would it be better than life as a drudge in the Perrers household? I was about to find out, thanks to the effortless malice of Princess Isabella, for I knew, beyond doubt, that the Queen had not brought me all the way from Barking to pluck chickens in her kitchen. It was all Isabella's fault. I knew an enemy when I saw one.

"This girl, Master Humphrey . . ." The steward's expression away from the solar spoke his contempt for such as I. "Another of Her Majesty's gutter sweepings to live off our charity."

A grunt was all the reply he got. Master Humphrey was wielding a cleaver on the carcass of a pig, splitting it down the backbone with practiced skill.

"The Lady said to bring her to you."

The cook stopped, midchop, and looked up under grizzled brows. "And what, may I ask, do I do with her?"

"Feed her. Give her a bed. Clothe her and put her to work."

"Ha! Look around you, Jos! What do you see?"

I looked, although the instruction was not for me. The kitchen was awash with activity: On all sides scullions, spit boys, pot boys, bottle washers applied themselves with a racket as if all hell had broken loose. The heat was overpowering from the ovens and open fires. I could already feel sweat beginning to trickle down my spine and dampen my hair beneath my hood.

"What?" Sir Joscelyn growled. I thought he did not approve of the liberty taken with his name.

"I don't employ girls, Jos! See? They're not strong enough. Good enough for the dairy and serving the dishes. But. Not. Here." The cook emphasized each word with a down sweep of his ax.

"Well, you do now. Princess Isabella's orders. Kitchens, she said!"

Another grunt. "And what the Lady wants . . . !"

"Exactly!"

Sir Joscelyn duly abandoned me in the middle of the teeming life of Havering's kitchens. I recognized the activities—the cleaning, the scouring, the chopping and stirring—but my experience was a pale shadow to this. The noise was ear-shattering. Exhilarating. Shouts and laughter, hoots of ridicule, bellowed orders, followed inevitably by oaths and complaints. There seemed to be little respect from the kitchen lads, but the cook's orders were carried out with a promptness that suggested a heavy hand if they transgressed his line of what was acceptable. And the food. So much of it . . . My belly rumbled at the sight. As for the scents of roasting meat, of succulent joints . . .

"Don't stand there like a bolt of cloth."

The cook, throwing down his ax with a clatter, gave me no more than a passing look, but the scullions did, with insolent grins and crude gestures. I might not have much experience of such signs with tongues and fingers—except occasionally in the market between a whore and a dissatisfied customer—but it did not take much imagination. They made my cheeks glow with a heat that was not from the fire.

"Sit there." Master Humphrey pressed down on my shoulder with a giant hand, and so I sat at the center board, sharing it with the pig. A bowl of thick stew was dumped unceremoniously in front of me, a spoon pushed into my hand, and a piece of stale wastel bread thrown down on the table within reach.

"Eat, then—and fast. There's work to be done."

I ate, without stopping. The sin of gluttony was swept aside. I drank a cup of ale handed to me. I had not realized how hungry I was.

"Put this on."

As he carried a tray of round loaves to thrust into one of the two ovens, Master Humphrey held out a large apron of stained linen. It was intended for someone much larger than I. I hitched it 'round my waist, or I would have tripped on it, and was knotting the strings when the cook returned.

"Now! Let me look at you!" I stood before him. "What did you say your name was?"

"Alice."

"Alice! Well, then, Alice, no need to keep your eyes on your feet here or you'll fall on your arse." His expression was jaundiced. "You're not very big."

"She's big enough. For what I've in mind!" said one of the scullions, a large lad with tow hair. A guffaw of crude laughter followed.

"Shut it, Sim. And keep your hands to yourself or . . ." Master Humphrey seized and wielded his meat cleaver with quick chopping movements. "Pay them no heed, girl." He took my hands in his, turned them over. "Hmm. What can you do?"

I did not think it mattered what I said, given the continuing obscenities from the two lads struggling to manhandle a side of venison onto a spit. I had already been judged. I would be given the lowliest of tasks. I would be a butt of jokes and innuendo.

"Come on, girl! I've never yet met a woman with nothing to say for herself."

So I would. I would state my case. I would not hide. So far, I had been moved about like the bolt of cloth he had called me, but if this was to be my future, I would not sink into invisibility. With Signora Damiata I had controlled my manner, because to do otherwise would have called down retribution. Here I knew instinctively that I must stand up for myself as I had never done before.

"I can do that, Master Humphrey. And that." I pointed at the washing and scouring going on in a tub of water. "I can do that." A small lad was piling logs on the fire.

"So could an imbecile." The cook aimed a kick at the lad at the fire, who grinned back. "No skills, then."

"I can make bread. I can kill those." Chickens clucked unsuspectingly in an osier basket by the hearth. "I can do that." I pointed to an older man who was gutting a fish, scooping the innards into a basin with the flat of his hand. "I can make a tincture to cure a cough. And I can make a . . ."

"My, my. What an addition to my kitchen." Master Humphrey gripped his belt and made a mocking little bow. He did not believe half of what I said.

"I can keep an inventory of your foodstuffs." I was not going to shut up unless he ordered me to. "I can tally your books and accounts."

"A miracle, by the Holy Virgin." The mockery went up by a notch. "What is such a gifted mistress of all crafts doing in my kitchen?" The laughter at my expense expanded too. "Let's start with this for now."

I was put to work raking the hot ashes from the ovens and scouring the fat-encrusted baking trays. No different from the Abbey or the Perrers household at all.

But it was different, and I relished it. Here was life at its coarsest and most vivid, not a mean existence ruled by silence and obedience with every breath I took. This was no living death. Not that I enjoyed the work—it was hard and relentless and punishing under the eyes of Master Humphrey and Sir Joscelyn—but here was no dour disapproval or use of a switch if I sullied Saint Benedict rule, or caught Damiata's caustic eye. Everyone had something to say about every event or rumor that touched on Master Humphrey's kitchen. I swear he could discuss the state of the realm as well as any great lord, while slitting the gizzard of a peacock. It was a different world. I was now the owner of a straw pallet in a cramped attic room with two of the maids who strained the milk and made the huge rounds of cheese in the dairy. I was given a blanket, a new shift and kirtle—new to me, at any event—a length of cloth to wrap 'round my hair, and a pair of rough shoes.

Better than a lay sister at St. Mary's? By the Virgin it was!

I listened as I toiled. The scullions gossiped from morn till night, covering the whole range of the royal family, and I lapped it up. Countess Joan, who had married her prince, was little better than a whore. The Queen was ill, the King protective. The King was well past the days of his much-lauded victory on the battlefield of Crécy against the bloody French, but still he was a man to be admired. Whilst Isabella! A madam, refusing every sensible marriage put to her! The King should have taken a whip to her sides! Gascony and Aquitaine, our possessions across the channel, were in revolt. Ireland was simmering like a pot of soup. Now, the buildings of the man Wykeham. At Westminster, water directed to the kitchens ran direct from a spigot into a bowl! May it come to Havering soon, pray God.

Meanwhile I was sent to haul water from the well twenty times a day. Master Humphrey had no need for me to read or tally. I swept and scoured and chopped, burned my hands, singed my hair, and emptied chamber pots. I lifted and carried and swept up. And I worked even harder to keep the lascivious scullions and pot boys at a distance. I learned fast. By God, I did!

Sim was the biggest lout of them all, with his fair hair and leering smile.

I did not need any warning. I had seen Sim's version of romantic seduction when he trapped one of the serving wenches against the door of the wood store. It had not been enjoyment on her face as he had grunted and labored, his hose around his ankles. I did not want his greasy hands, or any other part of his body, on me. The stamp of a foot on an unprotected instep, a sharp elbow to a gut kept the human vermin at bay for the most part. Unfortunately it was easy for Sim and his slimy crowd to stalk me in the pantry or the cellar. His arm clipped my waist once, and did so a dozen times within the first week.

"How about a kiss, Alice?" he wheedled, his foul breath hot against my neck.

I punched his chest with my fist, and not lightly. "You'll get no kiss from me!"

"Who else will kiss you?" he demanded, followed by the usual chorus of appreciation from the crude, grinning mouths.

"Not you!"

"You're an ugly bitch, but you're better than a beef carcass."

"You're not, slimy Sim. I'd sooner kiss a carp from the pond. Now, back off—and take your gargoyles with you." I had discovered a talent for wordplay and a sharp tongue, and used them indiscriminately, along with my elbows. Self-preservation was a wonderful spur.

"You'll not get better than me." He ground his groin, fierce with arousal, against my hip.

I gave up on the banter. My knee slamming against his privates loosened his hold well enough. "Keep your hands to yourself! Or I'll take Master Humphrey's boning knife to your balls! We'll roast them for supper with garlic and rosemary!"

I was not unhappy. But I was sorry not to be pretty. And my talents were not used. How much skill did it take to empty the chamber pots onto the midden?

Then all was danger, without warning. Two weeks of the whirlwind of kitchen life at Havering had lulled me into carelessness. And on that day I had been taken up with the noxious task of scrubbing down the chopping block where the joints of meat were dismembered.

"And when you've done that, fetch a basket of scallions from the storeroom—and see if you can find some sage in the garden. Can you recognize it?" Master Humphrey shouted after me, still leaning toward the scathing.

"Yes, Master Humphrey." *Any fool can recognize sage.* I wrung out the cloth, relieved to escape the heat and the sickening stench of fresh blood.

"And bring some chives while you're at it, girl!"

I was barely out of the door when my wrist was seized in a hard grip and I was almost jolted off my feet.

"What . . . ?"

And into the loathsome arms of Sim.

"Well, if it isn't Mistress Alice with her good opinion of herself!"

I raised my hand to cuff his ear but he ducked and held on. This was just Sim trying to make trouble, since I had deterred him from lifting my skirts with the point of a knife, and the red punctures still stood proud on his hand.

"Get off me, you oaf!"

Sim thrust me back against the wall and I felt the familiar routine of his knee pushing between my legs.

"I'd have you gelded if I had my way!" I bit his hand.

Sim was far stronger than I. He laughed and wrenched the neck of my tunic. I felt the shoulder of my shift tear, and then Queen Philippa's rosary, the precious gift that I had worn out of sight around my neck, slithered under my shift to the floor. I squirmed, escaped, and pounced. But not fast enough. Sim snatched it up.

"Well, well!" He held it up above my head.

"Give it back!"

"Let me fuck you and I will."

"Not in this lifetime . . ." My whole concentration was on my beads.

So was Sim's. He eyed the lovely strand where it swung in the light, and I saw knowledge creep into his eyes. "Now, this is worth a pretty penny, if I don't mistake. . . ."

He would keep it for himself. But perhaps the value was too great even for Sim to risk. . . . I snatched at it but he was running, dragging me with him. At that moment as I almost tripped and fell, I knew. He would make trouble for me. Here was danger.

"What's this?" Master Humphrey looked up at the rumpus.

"We've a thief here, Master Humphrey!" Sim's eyes gleamed with malice.

"I know you are, my lad. Didn't I see you pick up a hunk of cheese and stuff it into your big gob not an hour ago?"

"This's more serious than cheese, Master Humphrey." Sim's grin at me was an essay in slyness.

In an instant we were surrounded. "Robber! Pick-purse! Thief!" came a chorus from idle scullions and mischief-making pot boys.

"I'm no thief!" I kicked Sim on the shin. "Let go of me!"

"Bugger it, wench!" His hold tightened. "Told you she wasn't to be trusted." He addressed the room at large. "Too high an opinion of herself by half! She's a thief!" And he raised one hand above his head, Philippa's gift gripped between his filthy fingers. The rosary glittered, its value evident to all. Rage shook me. How dared he! How dared he take what was mine!

"Thief!"

"I am not!"

"Where did you get it?"

"She came from a convent." One voice was raised on my behalf.

"I wager she owned nothing as fine as this, even in a convent."

"Fetch Sir Joscelyn!" ordered Master Humphrey. "I'm too busy to deal with this."

And then it all happened very quickly. Sir Joscelyn gave his judgment: "This belongs to Her Majesty." No one questioned his decision. All eyes were turned on me, wide with disgust. "The Queen is ill, and you would steal from her!"

"She gave it to me." I knew I was already pronounced guilty, but my instinct was to fight against the inevitable.

"You stole it!"

"I did not!"

I tried to keep my denial even, my response calm, but I was not at all calm. Fear paralyzed my mind. Much could be forgiven, but not this: For the first time I learned the depth of respect for the Queen, even in this lowly part of the palace. I looked at the faces and saw condemnation, disgust. Sim and his cohorts were enjoying every minute of it.

"Where's the Marshal?" Sir Joscelyn demanded.

"In the chapel," one of the scullions piped up.

With the rosary in one hand and me gripped hard in the other, Sir

Joscelyn dragged me along and into the royal chapel to the chancel, where two laborers were lifting a wood-and-metal device of cogs and wheels from a handcart. There, keeping a close eye on the operation, was Lord Herbert, the Marshal whose word was law. And beside him stood the King himself. It could not be worse. Despair was a physical pain in my chest.

"Your Majesty. Lord Herbert . . ."

"Not now, Sir Joscelyn." The King and Marshal were preoccupied. All eyes were on the careful lifting of the contraption. We stood in silence as it was positioned piece by piece on the floor. "Good. Now . . ."

Edward turned to our importunate little group. So I was to be accused before the King himself. I shivered as the evidence was produced, examined, and the ownership confirmed. I shivered even more as I was tried, condemned, and sentenced by Lord Herbert to be shut in a cellar in the short term, all without a word from me. As for the King, he could barely snatch his damned concentration from the inanimate monstrosity spread around his feet, whilst I suffered for a crime that had never happened. I was nothing but a troublesome tick that could be squashed with a fingernail to enable him to return to his paltry toy. Within the time it took to snap his fingers, he would pass me over to the Marshal. It must not be! I would get his attention and keep it. And the flare of ambition and fiery resentment that I had felt under the lick of Countess Joan's tongue once more flickered over my skin.

I am worth more than this. I deserve more than this.

I wanted more than the half life in the kitchens of Havering. I would *make* the King notice me.

"Sire!" I discovered in myself a bold confidence. "I am the woman the Queen sent for. And this lout, this son of Satan, who's fit only to be booted out of this palace onto the midden, calls me a thief!"

"Does he, now!" The King's interest was caught—but only mildly so.

I renewed my attack. "His words are as filthy as the garderobe. I appeal to you, Majesty, for justice! No one will listen to me. Is it because I am a woman? I appeal to you, Sire."

The royal eyes widened considerably. "The King will always give justice."

"Not in your kitchens, Sire. Justice is more like a clip 'round the ear or a grope in a dark corner from this turd!" I had absorbed a wealth of vocabulary during my sojourn. I had his attention now, right enough.

"Then I must remedy your criticisms of my kitchens." The sardonic reply held out little hope. "Did you steal this?"

"No!" Fear of close, dark places, of being shut in the cellar, made me undaunted. "It is rightfully come by. Wykeham knows I did not steal it. He'll tell you. . . ."

Little good it did me. "He might," the King observed. "Unfortunately he's not here but gone to Windsor. . . ."

"Her Majesty knows I did not!" It was my last hope—but no hope at all.

"We'll not trouble Her Majesty." The King's face was suddenly darkly contemptuous. "You'll not disturb the Queen with this. Lord Herbert . . ." The dark cellar loomed.

"No!" I gasped.

"What is it that you will not trouble me with, Edward?"

And with that one question the tiniest speck of hope began to grow in me.

A gentle voice, soft on the ear. The focus in the chapel changed in the blink of an eye, and I became an instant irrelevance. Sir Joscelyn and Lord Herbert bowed. The King strode forward, so close to me that his tunic brushed against me, to take the Queen's hand and draw her toward one of the choir stalls. His face changed, the lines of irritation with me smoothing, his lips softening. There was a caring, a tenderness, as if they were alone in an intimate room. The Queen smiled up into his face, enclosing his hand in both of her own. Simple gestures but so strong, so affectionate. There was no doubting it. Taken up as I was with my own miseries, I could still see it and marvel at it. It was as if he had kissed her in public, which the King proceeded to do, a tender kiss on her cheek.

"Philippa. My love. Are you strong enough to be here? You should be resting."

"I have been resting for the past week. I wish to see the clock."

"You don't look strong."

"Don't fuss, Edward. I feel better."

She did not look it; rather, she was drawn and gray.

"Sit down, my dear." The King pushed her gently to the cushioned seat. "Does your shoulder pain you?"

"Yes. But it is not fatal." The Queen sat up straight, cradling her left elbow in her right palm, and surveyed what I realized were the makings of a clock. "It is very fine. When will you get it working?" Then she noticed the surprising number of people in the chapel. "What's happening here?"

The Marshal cleared his throat. "This girl, Majesty . . ." He glowered at me.

As the Queen looked at me, I saw the memory return, and with it recognition. Awkwardly she turned her whole body in her chair until she was facing me. "Alice?"

"Yes, Majesty." I curtsied as best I could, since my arm was still in the grip of Lord Herbert, as if I might make a bid for freedom.

"I sent Wykeham to fetch you." Philippa's forehead was furrowed with the effort of recall, as if it were a long time ago. "You must have arrived when I was ill."

"Yes, Majesty."

"What are you doing?"

"Working in your kitchens."

"Are you?" She appeared astonished, then gave a soft laugh. "Who sent you there?"

"The Princess Isabella." Sir Joscelyn was quick to apportion blame elsewhere. "She thought that was your intent."

"Did she? I doubt my daughter thought at all beyond her own desires. You should have known better, Sir Joscelyn."

An uncomfortable silence lengthened until Lord Herbert pronounced, "The girl is a thief, Your Majesty."

"Are you?" the Queen asked.

"No, Majesty!"

Edward held out the rosary. "I'm afraid she is. Is this yours, my love?"

"Yes. Or it was. You gave it to me."

"I did? The girl was wearing it."

"I expect she would. I gave it to her."

"I told them that, my lady," I appealed, "but they would not believe me."

"To a kitchen maid? Why would you do that?" The King spread his hands, disbelief still rampant.

The Queen sighed. "It's a long story. Let go of her, Lord Herbert. She'll not run away. Come here, Alice. Let me look at you."

I discovered that I had been holding my breath. When the Queen held out her hand, I fell to my knees before her in utter gratitude, returning her regard when her tired eyes moved slowly, speculatively, over my face, as if she were trying to anchor some deep wayward thought that was not altogether pleasing to her. Then she nodded and touched a fingertip to my cheek.

"Who would have thought so simple a thing as the gift of a rosary would cause so much trouble," she said, her smile wry. "And why should it take the whole of the royal household to solve the matter?" Pushing herself to her feet, she drew me with her, taking everything in hand with a matriarchal authority. "Thank you, Sir Joscelyn. Lord Herbert. I know you have my interests at heart. You are very assiduous, but I will deal with this. This girl is no thief, forsooth. Give me your arm, Alice. Let me put some things right."

I helped her from the chapel, conscious of her weight as we descended the stair, and of the King's muttered comment that, thank God, I was no longer his concern. As we walked slowly toward the royal apartments, a warm expectancy began to dance through my blood. Maidservant? Tire-woman? I still could not imagine why she would want *me*, given the wealth of skill and talent around her, but I knew there was something in her mind, just as I sensed that from this point, my life, with its humdrum drudgery and servitude, would never be quite the same again.

My immediate destiny was an empty bedchamber, unused, I assumed from the lack of furnishings and the dust that swirled as our skirts created a little eddy of air. And in that room: a copper-bound tub, buckets of steaming water, and the ministrations of two of the maids from the buttery. I was handed over.

With hot water and enthusiasm, buttressed by a remarkable degree of speculative interest, the maids got to work on me. If I was to be turned off, at least I would be clean. I had never bathed before, totally immersed in water. I remembered Countess Joan, naked and arrogant, confident in her beauty, whereas I slid beneath the water to wallow up to my chin, like a trout in a summer pool, before my companions could actually look at me.

"Go away!" I remonstrated. "I'm perfectly capable of scrubbing my own skin until it's red and raw!"

"Queen's orders!" they simpered. "No one disobeys the Queen!"

With no arguing against such a declaration, I set myself to make the best of it, for the maids were audacious, and personal enough to point out my deficiencies. Too thin. No curves, small breasts, lean hips. They gave no quarter, making me horribly conscious of the faults in my unclothed body, despite my sharp observation that life in a convent was not conversant with solid flesh. Rough hands, they pointed out. Neglected hair. As for my eyebrows . . . The litany went on. "Fair is fashionable," they informed me.

I sighed. "Don't rub so hard!"

They ignored me. I was soaped and rinsed, dried with soft linen, and in the end I simply closed my eyes and allowed them the right to talk and gossip and put me in the clothes provided for me. And such garments. The sensual glide of them on my skin forced me to open my eyes. They were like nothing I had ever seen, except in the coffers of Countess Joan. An undershift of fine linen that did not catch when I moved. An overgown, close-fitting to my hips, in the blue of the Virgin's cloak—a cotehardie, I was told, knowing no name for such fashionable niceties—with a sideless surcoat over all, was sumptuous to my eyes with gray fur bands and an enameled girdle. All made for someone else, of course, the fibers scuffed along hem and cuffs, but what did I care for that? They were a statement in feminine luxury I could never have dreamed of. And so shiny, so soft were the fabrics that slid through my fingers. Silk and damask and fine wool. For the first time in my life I was clothed in a *color*, glorious enough to assault my senses. I felt like a precious jewel polished to a glorious sparkle.

They exclaimed over my hair, of course.

"Too coarse. Too dark. Too short to braid. Too short for anything!"

"Better than when it was cropped for a novice nun!" I fired back.

They pushed it into the gilded mesh of a crispinette, covered the whole with a veil of some diaphanous material that floated quite beautifully, and added a plaited fillet to hold it firm, as if to hide all evidence of my past life. But no wimple. I vowed never to wear a wimple again.

"Put these on. . . ." I donned the fine stockings, the woven garters. Soft shoes were slid onto my feet.

I took stock, hardly daring to breathe in fear that the whole ensemble would fall off. The skirts were full and heavy against my legs, moving with a soft hush as I walked inexpertly across the room. The bodice was laced tight against my ribs, the neckline low across my unimpressive bosom. I did not feel like myself at all, but rather as if I were dressed for a mummer's play I had once seen on Twelfth Night at the Abbey.

Did maidservants to the Queen really wear such splendor?

I was in the process of kicking the skirts behind me experimentally, enjoying the sensation of elegance even if I did not quite achieve it, when the door opened to admit Isabella. The two maids curtsied to the floor. I followed suit, with not a bad show of handling the damask folds, but not before I had seen her thin-lipped distaste.

She walked 'round me, taking her time. Isabella, the agent of my kitchen humiliations.

"Not bad," she commented as I flushed. "Look for yourself." And she handed me the tiny looking glass that had been suspended from the chatelaine at her waist.

Oh, no! Remembering my last brush with vanity, I put my hands behind my back as if I were a child caught out in wrongdoing. "No! I will not!"

Her smile was deeply sardonic. "Why not?"

"I think I'll not like what I see," I said, refusing to allow my gaze to fall before hers.

"Well, that's true enough. There's only so much that can be done. Perhaps you're wise," Isabella murmured, but her sympathy was tainted with scorn. Peremptorily she gestured, and so, in a silence stretched taut, I was led along the corridors to the solar, where Philippa sat with her women.

"Well, you've washed her and dressed her, *Maman*. For what it's worth . . ."

"You are uncharitable, Isabella." The Queen's reply was unexpectedly sharp.

Isabella was not cowed. "What do we do with her now?"

"What I intended from the beginning, despite your meddling. She will be one of my damsels."

Isabella's brows climbed. I suspect mine did too. I was too shocked to consider how inappropriate my expression might be.

"You don't need *her*," Isabella cried in disbelief. "You have a dozen . . ."

"No?" A smile, a little sad to my mind, touched the Queen's face. "Maybe I do need her."

"Then choose a girl of birth. Before God, there are enough of them. . . ."

"I know what I need, Isabella." The Queen waved her daughter away and handed the rosary back to me.

"My lady . . ."

What could I find to say? My fingers closed around the costly beads. In the length of a heartbeat, in one firm command and one gesture of dismissal of her daughter's disapproval, the Queen had turned my life on its head.

"You'll regret it! And don't say I didn't warn you." So Isabella had the last word.

She did not care that I heard her.

Why? Why me? The one thought danced in my head when the ladies were gone about their customary affairs. A damsel—a lady-in-waiting to the Queen.

"Why me?" I asked aloud. "What have I to offer, Your Majesty?"

Philippa perused me as if searching for an answer, her features uncommonly stern.

"Your Majesty?"

"Forgive me. I was distracted. . . ." She closed her eyes. When she opened them there was a lingering vestige of sorrow, but her voice was kind enough. "One day I'll tell you. But for now—let's see what we can do with you."

So there it was. Decided on some chance whim, with some underlying purpose that the Queen kept to herself, I became a *domicella*. A lady-in-waiting. Not a *domina*, one of the highborn, but a *domicella*, the youngest, least skilled, and least important of the Queen's ladies. But I was a part of her household. I was an inhabitant of her solar.

I could not believe my good fortune. When sent on some trivial errand—I do not recall it now—through a deserted antechamber, I lifted my skirts above my ankles and danced a succession of haphazard steps to the lingering echoes of the lute from the solar. Not well, you understand, but more than I had ever achieved in my life. It astonished me what confidence a fine robe with fur edgings could bestow on a woman.

I think I smirked. What would clerk Greseley say if he could see me now? "Waste of good coin," I suspected. What remark would Wykeham find to make, other than his ambitions to construct a royal bathhouse and garderobe? I laughed aloud. And the King? King Edward would notice me only if I had cogs and wheels that moved and slid and clicked against one another.

I tried a pirouette, awkward in the shoes that were too loose 'round the heel. One day, I vowed, I would wear shoes that were made for me and fitted perfectly.

As for what the Queen might want of me in return—well, it could not be so very serious, could it?

They tripped over their trailing skirts, the Queen's damsels, to transform me into a lady worthy of my new position. I was a pet. A plaything. A creature to be cosseted and stroked, to relieve their boredom. It was not in my nature; nor was it a role I wished to play, but it was an exhilarating experience as they created the new Alice Perrers. And perhaps I was still very young, thrilled to be the center of their wayward attention. I was not above playing.

I absorbed it all: anointed and burnished, my hands smothered in perfumed lotions far headier than anything produced in Sister Margery's stillroom, my too-heavy brows plucked into what might pass for elegant arches—if the observer squinted. Clothes, and even jewels, were handed over with casual kindness. A ring, a brooch to pin to my mantle, a chain of gilt and gleaming stones to loop across my breast. Nothing of great value, but enough that I might exhibit myself in public as no less worthy of respect than the ladies from high-blooded families. I spread my fingers, now smooth with pared nails, to admire the ring with its amethyst stone. It was as if I were wearing a new skin, like a snake sloughing off the old in spring. And I was woman enough to enjoy it. I wore the rosary fastened to a girdle enhanced with silver finials as fine as Mother Sybil's.

"Better!" Isabella remarked after sour contemplation. "But I still don't know why the Queen wanted *you!*"

It remained beyond my comprehension too.

The Queen's damsels were feminine, pretty, beautiful. I was none of those. Their figures were flattered by the new fashion, with gowns close-fitting from breast to hip. The rich cloth hung on me like washing on a drying pole. They were artlessly gifted in music for the Queen's pleasure. Any attempt to teach me to sing was abandoned after the first tuneless warble. Nor did my fingers ever master the lute strings, much less the elegant gittern. They could stitch a girdle with flowers and birds. I had no patience with it. They conversed charmingly in French, with endless gossip, with shared knowledge of people of the Court. I knew no one other than Wykeham. His fixation with building arches was the subject of laughter.

For the damsels, flirtation was an art in itself. I never learned it. I was too forthright for that, too critical of those I met. Too self-aware to pretend what I did not feel. And if that was a sin, then I was guilty. I could not pretend an interest or an affection where I had none.

Had I nothing to offer? What I had, I used to make myself useful, or noticed, or even indispensable. I had achieved a place in the Queen's solar and I would not be cast off, as Princess Isabella cast off her old gowns. I worked hard.

I could play chess. The ordered rules of the little figures pleased me. I had no difficulty in remembering the measures of a knight against a bishop, the limitations of a queen against a castle. As for the foolish pastime of Fox and Geese, I found an unexpected fascination in maneuvering the pieces to make the geese corner the fox before that wily creature could kill the silly birds.

"I'll not play with you, Alice Perrers!" Isabella declared, abandoning the game. "Your geese are too crafty by half."

"Craftier than your fox, my lady." Isabella's fox was tightly penned into a corner by my little flock of birds. "Your fox is done for, my lady."

"So it is!" Isabella laughed, more out of surprise than amusement, but she resisted a cutting rejoinder.

I could make silly, harmless love charms and potions to please the damsels, gleaned from my memory of Sister Margery's manuscripts. A pinch of catnip, a handful of yarrow, a stem of vervain, all wrapped in a scrap of green silk and tied with a red cord. If they believed they were effective, I would not deny it, although Isabella swore I was more likely to add the deadly hemlock in any sachet I made for her. And I could read. I read to them endlessly, when they wanted to sigh over tales of courtly love between a handsome knight and the object of his desire.

Not bad. Not bad at all for a nameless girl from a convent, and an abandoned wife.

And Isabella was wrong. I would never use hemlock. I knew enough from Sister Margery's caustic warnings to be wary of such satanic works.

But what service could I offer Queen Philippa when the whole household was centered on fulfilling her wishes even before she expressed them? That was easy enough. I made drafts of white willow bark.

"You are a blessing to me, Alice." The pain had been intense that day, but now, propped against her pillows, the willow tincture making her drowsy, she sighed heavily with relief. "I am a burden to you."

"It is not a burden to me to give you ease, my lady."

I saw the lines beside her eyes begin to smooth out. She would sleep soon. The days of pain were increasing in number, and her strength to withstand them was ebbing, but tonight she would have some measure of peace.

"You are a good girl."

"I wasn't a good novice!" I responded smartly.

"Sit here. Tell me about those days when you were a bad novice." Her eyelids drooped, but she fought the strength of the drug.

So I did, because it pleased me to distract her. I told her of Mother Abbess and her penchant for red stockings. I told her of Sister Goda and her inappropriate love poetry, of the chickens that fell foul of the fox because of my carelessness and how I was punished. I did not speak of Countess Joan. I knew enough by now not to speak that name. Joan, the duplicitous daughter-in-law, far away in Aquitaine with her husband the Prince, was not a subject to give the Queen a restful night.

"It was good that I found you," she murmured.

"Yes, my lady." I smoothed a piercingly sweet unguent into the tight skin of her wrist and hand. "You have changed my life."

A little silence fell, but the Queen was not asleep. She was contemplating something beyond my sight that did not seem entirely to please her, gouging a deep path between her brows. Then she blinked and fixed me with an uncomfortable gaze. "Yes. I am sure it was good that you fell into my path."

I was certain it was not merely to smear her suffering flesh with ointments. A shiver of awareness assailed me in the overheated room, for her declamation suggested some deep uncertainty. Had I done something to lose her regard so soon? I forced my mind to rove over what I might have said or done to cast her into doubt. Nothing came to mind. So I asked.

"*Why* did you choose me, Majesty? *Why* did you send for me?"

When the Queen looked at me, her eyes were hooded. She closed her hand tightly around the jeweled cross on her breast, and her reply held none of her essential compassion. Indeed, her tone was curt and bleak, and she drew her hand from my ministrations as if she could not bear that I touch her.

"I chose you because I have a role for you, Alice. A difficult one, perhaps. And not too far distant . . . but not yet. Not quite yet . . ." She closed her eyes at last, as if she would shut me from her sight. "I'm weary now. Send for my priest, if you will. I'll pray with him before I sleep."

I left her, more perplexed than ever. Her words resurfaced as I lit my own candle and took myself to bed in the room I shared with two of the damsels. Sleep would not come.

I have a role for you to play. A difficult one, perhaps. And not too far distant . . .

Chapter Five

I t became my habit to keep a journal of sorts. Why? Did I need a reason? Only that I should not lose the skill I had learned with such painstaking effort. No one needed me to write in a palace where men of letters matched the number of huntsmen. Sometimes I wrote in French, sometimes in Latin as the mood took me. I begged pieces of parchment, pen, and ink from the palace clerks. They were not unwilling when I smiled, when I tilted my chin or slid a long-eyed glance. I was learning the ways of the Court, and the power of my own talents to attract.

And what did I write? A chronology of my days. What I wished to remember, I wrote for more than a year.

Did I ever consider that the damsels might discover what I wrote? Not for a moment. They mocked my scribbling. And what I scribbled was excruciatingly dull. Once, to satisfy their curiosity, I read aloud. . . .

" 'Today I joined the damsels in my first hunt. I had no enjoyment of it. The King celebrates his fiftieth year with a great tournament and jousting held at Smithfield. We all attend. I am learning to dance. . . .' "

"By the Virgin, Alice!" Isabella yawned behind her slender fingers. "If you have nothing better to write about, what in heaven's name is the value of doing it? Better to return to scouring the pots in the kitchens."

Dull? Infinitely. And quite deliberate, to ensure that no damsel was sufficiently interested to poke her sharp nose into what I might be doing. But what memories my writings evoked for me, rereading my trite comments when my life was in danger and turmoil. There on the pages, in stark letters, in the briefest of record, the pattern of my life unfolded in that fateful year, as clear as a flock of winter rooks digging in a snow-covered field. What a miraculous, terrifying, life-changing year it proved to be.

Today I joined the damsels in my first hunt. I had no enjoyment of it. . . . What a mastery of understatement that was. The gelding I was given was a mount from hell. I would never see the pleasure in being jolted and bounced for two hours, to come at the end to a baying pack of hounds and a bloody kill. Truth to tell, the kill happened without me, for I fell off with a shriek at the first breath-stopping gallop. Sitting on the ground, covered with leaf mold and twiggery, beating the damp earth from my skirts, I raged in misery. My crispinettes and hood had become detached. The hunt had disappeared into the distance. So had my despicable mount. It would be a long walk home.

"A damsel in distress, by God!"

I had not registered the beat of hooves on the soft ground under the trees. I looked up to see two horses bearing down on me at speed, one large and threatening, the other small and wiry.

"Mistress Alice!" The King reined in, his stallion dancing within feet of me. "Are you well down there?"

"No, I am not!" I was not as polite as I should have been.

"Who suggested you ride that brute that thundered past us?"

"The lady Isabella! That misbegotten bag of bones deposited me here. . . . I should never have come. I detest horses."

"So why did you?"

I wasn't altogether sure, except that it was expected of me. It was the one joy in life remaining to the Queen when she was in health. The King swung down, threw his reins to the lad on the pony, and approached on foot. I raised a hand to shield my eyes from the sun where it glimmered through the new leaves.

"Thomas—go and fetch the lady's ride," he ordered.

Thomas, the King's youngest son, abandoned the stallion and rode off like the wind. The King offered me his hand.

"I can get to my feet alone, Sire." I was ungracious, I knew, but my humiliation was strong.

"I've no doubt, lady. Humor me."

His eyes might be bright with amusement, but his order was peremptory and not to be disobeyed. I held out my hand, and with a firm tug I was pulled to my feet, whereupon the King began to dislodge the debris from my skirts with long strokes of the flat of his hand. Shame colored my cheeks.

"Indeed you should not, Sire!"

"I should indeed. You need to pin up your hair."

"I can't. There's not enough to pin up, and I need help to make it look respectable."

"Then let me."

"No, Sire!" To have the King pin up my hair? I would as soon ask Isabella to scrub my back.

He grunted, a sign of annoyance I recognized. "You must allow me, mistress, as a man of chivalry, to set your appearance to rights. . . ."

And tucking my ill-used crispinettes into his belt, he proceeded with astonishingly clever fingers to repin my simple hood to cover the disaster, as deft as if he were tying the jesses of his favorite goshawk. I stood still under his ministrations, a stone statue, barely breathing. Until the King stepped back and surveyed me.

"Passable. I've not lost my touch in all these years." He cocked an ear to listen, and nodded his head. "And now, lady, you'll have to get back on!"

He was laughing at me! "I don't wish to!"

"You will, unless you intend to walk home. . . ." Thomas had returned with my recalcitrant mount, and before I could make any more fuss, I was boosted back into the saddle. For a moment as he tightened my girths, the King looked up into my face, then abruptly stepped back.

"There you are, Mistress Alice. Hold tight!" A slap of the King's hand against the wide rump set me in motion. "Look after her, Thomas. The Queen will never forgive you if we allow her to fall into a blackberry thicket." A pause, and the words followed me. "And neither will I!"

And Thomas did. Only seven years old, and he had more skill at riding than I would ever have. But it was the King's deft hands I remembered, not Thomas's enthusiastic prattling.

The King celebrates his fiftieth year with a great tournament and jousting. . . . Magnificent! The King was superlative in his new armor. I could not find the words, burnished as he was by the sun, sword and armor striking fire as his arm rose and fell, the plumes on his helmet nodding imperiously. And yet I feared for him, my loins liquid and cold with fear. I could not look away, but when blood matted his sleeve, dripping from his fingers, I closed my eyes.

No need, of course. His energy always prodigious, he was touched with magic that day. Fighting in the melee with all the skill and dash and finesse of a hero of the old tales, he had the grace at the end to heap praise on those whom he defeated.

That day he was all hero to me.

Afterward, when the combatants gathered in the banter much loved by men, the Queen's ladies threw flowers to the knight of their choice. I had no one. Nor did I care, for there was only one to fill my vision, whether in the lists or in the vicious cut and thrust of personal combat. And I was audacious enough to fling a rosebud, when he approached the gallery in which we women sat with the Queen. He had removed his helm. He was so close to me, his face pale and drawn in the aftermath of his efforts, that I could detect the smear of blood on his cheek where he had wiped at the dust with his gauntlet. I was spellbound, so much so that the flower I so ineptly flung in his direction struck the cheek of the King's stallion; a soft blow, but the high-blooded destrier instantly reared in the manner of its kind.

"Sweet Jesu!" Startled, the King dropped his helm, tightening his reins as he fought to bring the animal back under control.

"Have you no sense?" Isabella snapped.

I thought better of replying, horrified at what I had achieved, steeling myself to withstand the King's reproof. Without a word he snapped his fingers to his page to pick up the helm and the now thoroughly trampled flower. I looked at him in fear.

"My thanks, lady."

He bowed his head solemnly to me as he tucked the crumpled petals into the gorget at his throat. My belly clenched; my face flamed to my hairline. Proud, haughty, confident, the King would treat me with respect when I had almost unhorsed him.

"Our kitchen maid cannot yet be relied upon to act decorously in public!" Isabella remarked, setting up a chorus of laughter.

But the King did not sneer. Urging his horse closer to the gilded canvas, the fire dying from his eyes as the energy of battle receded, he stretched out his hand, palm up.

"Mistress Alice, if you would honor me . . ."

And I placed mine there. The King kissed my fingers.

"The rose was a fine gesture, if a little wayward. My horse and I both thank you, Mistress Alice."

There was the rustle of appreciative laughter, no longer at my expense. I felt the heat of his kiss against my skin, hotter than the beat of blood in my cheeks.

I am learning to dance. "Holy Virgin!" I misstepped the insistent beat of the tabor and shawm for the twentieth time. How could I appreciate the ability to count coins under the stern tutorship of Janyn Perrers, yet not be able to count the steps in a simple processional dance? The King's hand tightened to give me balance as I lurched unforgivably. Should it not have been a graceful dance? The King was a better dancer than I. It would be hard to be worse.

"You are allowed to look at me, Mistress Alice," he announced when we came together again and snatched a conversation.

"If I do, I shall fall over my feet, Sire—or yours. I'll cripple you before the night is out."

"I'll lead you in the right steps, you know." I must have looked askance. "Do you not trust me, Alice?"

He had called me by my name, without formality. I looked up at him to find his eyes quizzical on my face, and I promptly missed the next simple movement.

"I dare not," I managed.

"You would refuse your King?" He was amused again.

"I would when it would be to his detriment."

"Then we must do our poor best, sweet Alice, and count the broken toes at the end of the evening."

Sweet Alice? Was he flirting with me? But no. That was not possible. I exasperated him more often than I entertained him. As was quickly proved, if I had had any doubts.

"By God, Mistress Alice. You did not lie," he stated ruefully as the procession wound to its end. "You should issue a warning to any man who invites you."

"No one will! Not every man is as brave as you, Sire."

"Then I'll remember not to risk it again," he said as he handed me back to sit at Philippa's side.

But he did. Even though I still fell over his feet.

The Queen did not forbid me to dance with the King, but she appeared to find little enjoyment in the occasion.

The Queen has given the King a lion. Ah, yes! The affair of the lion. Observing the damsels with scorn where they huddled, hiding their faces, retreating from its roars in mock fear, and keen to find a comforting arm from one of the King's gallant knights, I walked toward the huge cage, where I might inspect the beast at close quarters. I was not afraid. I would not pretend to be so. How could it harm me when it was imprisoned behind bars and locks? Its rough, tawny mane, its vast array of teeth fascinated me. I stepped closer as it settled on its haunches, tail twitching in impotent warning.

"You're not afraid, Mistress Alice?" Soft-footed, the King stood behind me.

"No, Sire. What need?" We had returned to formality, and I was not sorry. Was he not the King? "The girls are foolish, not really afraid. They just wish to . . ."

"They wish to attract attention?"

"Yes, Sire."

We looked across to where the fluttering damsels received assurance and flattery.

"And you do not, Mistress Alice? Does not some young knight take your extremely critical eye? Is there no one you admire?"

I thought about this, giving his question more consideration than perhaps was intended, appraising the wealth of strength and beauty and high blood around me.

"No, Sire." It was the truth.

"But you admire my lion."

"Oh, I do."

The lion watched us with impassive hatred. Were we not the cause of its imprisonment? I considered its state, and my own past experience. Both kept under duress, without freedom. Both existing on the whim of another. But I had escaped by miraculous means. There would be no miracle for this lion. This poor beast would remain in captivity until the day of its death.

"Does nothing fill you with terror? Other than horses, of course."

There! He had unnerved me again. "Yes," I replied. "But it's a fear *you'll* never know, Sire."

"Tell me, then."

Before I could collect my wits, I found myself explaining, because he was regarding me as if he really cared about my fears. "I am afraid of the future, Sire, where nothing is permanent; nothing is certain. Of a life without stability, without friends or family, without a home. Where I am nobody, without name or status. I don't want to be dependent on the pity or charity of others. I had enough of that from Sister Goda. And at the hands of my sister-in-law, Signora Damiata. It is a lonely existence and I fear it. I want to make something of myself, for myself. I don't want to die in penury."

Holy Mother! I looked fixedly at the lion, horrified. Had I really admitted to all that? To the King?

"It's a lot to ask," he replied simply. "For a young woman in your situation."

Countess Joan had observed as much, if with less courtesy. "Is it impossible?"

"No. That was not my meaning. But it's a hard road for a woman alone to travel."

"Must I then accept my fate, like this poor imprisoned beast?"

"Are we not all governed by fate, mistress?" I was aware that his attention was turned from the lion to me and, with just as much speculation, that the conversation had taken a very personal turn, and I sought for an innocuous reply.

"I don't intend ingratitude, Sire. I'm aware of how much I owe the Queen."

"I didn't know that you saw your future in so bleak a light."

"Why would you, Sire? You are the King. It is not necessary that you either know or care." For that was how I saw it.

"So you think I don't care? Am I so selfish?" He was clearly startled; his fine brows met over the bridge of his nose, and I wondered whether I had displeased him. "Or is it that you have a low opinion of all men?"

"I've no reason not to. My father, whoever he was, gave me no reason to think highly of them. Nor did my husband, who took me into a sham of a marriage to ward off his sister's nagging. I did not matter overmuch to either of them."

For a moment the King looked astounded as my bitterness overflowed, as I thought he might if one of his hounds dared to bite him on the calf.

"You don't hold back with the truth, do you, mistress? It seems I must make amends for my sex."

"You owe me nothing, Sire."

"Perhaps it is not a matter of owing, Alice. Perhaps it is more of what I find I wish to do."

The lion roared, lashing out with its claws against the metal, interrupting whatever the King, or I, might have said next. He led me away as attendants from his menagerie came to transport the beast, and I thanked God for the timely intervention. I had said quite enough to damn myself.

But the King was not finished with me quite yet. "You are not justified in your reading of my character, Mistress Alice," he said as we came to the door, a wry twist of his lips. "I know exactly what you fear. I lived through a period of my life when my future hung on a thread, when I did not know friend from enemy, and my authority as King was under attack. I know about rising every morning from my bed not knowing what fate would dish out for me that day—whether good or evil."

I must have shown my disbelief that a King should ever know such insecurity.

"And one day I will tell you."

He walked away, leaving me dumbfounded.

I have a gift. From Edward himself. I frowned at my gift, all spirit with a mane and tail of silk, as neat as an illustration from a Book of Hours, as she fussed and tossed her head in the stable yard.

"You don't like her?"

"I don't know why you should give her to me, Sire."

"Why should I not?"

"And why do you always ask me questions that I find difficult to answer?"

Edward laughed, not at all disturbed by my retort. "You always seem to find one!"

"She's never short of a pert comment, that's for sure." Isabella had arrived to stroke the pretty dappled creature. "When did you last give me a new horse, sir?"

"When you last asked me for one, as I recall. Two months ago."

"So you did. I must think of something else, since you're generous today."

"You have never had need to question my generosity to you, Isabella," the King replied dryly.

"True!" she declared, giving a final pat to the mare. "Get what you can, little Alice, since His Majesty is in the mood for giving! Here's your chance to make your fortune from the royal coffers." And she wandered off, restless as ever.

"My daughter is free with her opinions." He watched her go. "I apologize for her lack of grace."

It had been an unnerving little interlude, leaving the King with less of his good humor, but still I asked: "You have not told me why you have given me the mare, Sire."

"I have given you the mare because you need a mount to take care of you when my son cannot. She will treat you very well. If you will be so good as to accept her."

His reply was curt, giving me a taste of his latent power, his dislike of being thwarted or questioned, his very masculine pride. I would not be ungrateful and would accept with more elegance than Isabella had shown. I set myself to charm. King or not, he did not deserve to have his openhanded magnanimity to a servant thrown in his face.

"I am not ungracious, Sire. It is just that no one has ever given me a gift before. Except for the Queen. And once I was given a monkey." He began to smile. "It was a detestable creature."

Edward laughed. "What happened to it? Do you still have it?"

"Fortunately not. I fear its fate was sealed at St. Mary's. Repentance—or some dire punishment—as I know to my cost."

His laughter became a low growl. "Then if you are so short of gifts, I must do what I can to remedy it."

I considered this, conscious of how singular this must seem. "The King does not give gifts to girls of no family."

"This one does. He gives what he wishes, to whom he wishes. Or at least, he gives a palfrey to you, Mistress Alice."

"I can't, Sire. . . ." I was not lacking in good sense. It would be indiscreet. The mare was far too valuable.

"What a prickly creature you are! It is nothing, you know."

"Not to you . . ."

"I want you to enjoy her. Will you allow me to do that? If for no other reason than that you serve the Queen well."

How could I refuse? When the mare pushed against my shoulder with her soft nose, I fell in love with her—just a little—because she was beautiful and she was the King's gift.

The Queen is ill. She cannot move from her bed and begs me to read to her. When Edward visited, I stood to curtsy, already closing the book and putting it aside, expecting to be dismissed. Edward's time with his wife was precious, but he waved for me to read on and sat with us until I had finished the tale.

It was a dolorous one in which the Queen found particular enjoyment.

She wept for the tragedy of the ill-fated lovers Tristan and Isolde. The King stroked her hand, chiding her gently for her foolishness, telling her that his love for her was far greater than that of Tristan for his lady, and that he had no intention of doing anything so spineless as turning his face to the wall to die. Only a sword in the gut would bring him to his knees. And was his dear Philippa intending to cast herself over his body and die too without cause but a broken heart? Were they not—after so many years of marriage—made of sterner stuff than that? For shame!

It made the Queen laugh through her tears. "A foolish tale," she said, with a watery smile.

"But it was well read. With much feeling," Edward observed.

He touched my shoulder as he left us, the softest of pressures. There was no need for it—and yet he had chosen to do it. Did the Queen notice? I thought not, but she dismissed me brusquely, pleading a need for solitude. She covered her face with her hands.

Her voice stopped me as I reached the door.

"Forgive me, Alice. It is a grievous burden I have given myself, and sometimes it is beyond me to bear it well."

I did not understand her.

Edward has had his clock placed in a new tower. I stood and watched in awe. Edward's shout of laughter was powerful, a thing of joy, for at last his precious clock had come to the final steps of its installation, the tower to house it complete and the pieces of the mechanism assembled to the Italian's finicky satisfaction. Here was the day that it would be set into working order, and the Queen had expressed a desire to witness it. Had Edward not had it made for her, modeled on that belonging to the Abbot of St. Albans, with its miraculous shifting panels of sun and stars?

"I can't!" Philippa admitted. "I really can't!" when she could not push her swollen feet into soft shoes. "Go and watch for me, Alice. The King needs an audience."

"Thank God!" Isabella remarked.

"For what precisely?" Philippa was peevish. "I fail to see any need to thank Him this morning."

"Because you didn't ask me to go to look at the monstrosity."

"Well, I wouldn't. Alice will enjoy it. Alice can ask the King the right questions, and then tell us all about it. Can't you?"

"Yes, Majesty," I replied, not truly understanding why I had been singled out.

"But not in great detail," Isabella called after me as I left the room. "We're not all fixated with ropes and pulleys and . . . wheels!"

So I went alone. I was interested in ropes and pulleys and cogs with wooden teeth that locked as they revolved. I wanted to see what the Italian had achieved. Was that all I wanted?

Ah, no!

I wanted to watch and understand what fascinated Edward when he didn't have a sword in his hand or a celebration to organize. I had no excuse. I wanted to see what beguiled this complex man of action. So I watched the final preparations.

We were not alone. The King had his audience with or without my presence, the Italian and his assistant as well as a cluster of servants and a handful of men-at-arms to give the necessary strength. And there was Thomas, who could not be kept away from such a spectacle.

"We need to lift this into position, Sire." The Italian gestured, arms flung wide. "And then attach the weights and the ropes for the bell."

The ropes were apportioned to the men-at-arms, the instructions issued to hoist the weights for the winding mechanism. Thomas was given the task of watching for the moment when all was in place. I was waved ignominiously to one side.

"Pull!" the Italian bellowed. And they did. "Pull!"

With each repetition, the pieces of the clock rose into position.

"Almost there!" Thomas capered in excitement.

"Pull!" ordered the Italian.

They pulled, and with a creak and a snap one of the ropes broke. The weight to which it was attached, now without the tension, crashed down to the floor, sending up a shower of dust and stone chippings. And before I could react, the loose remnants of the rope flew in an arc, like a whiplash, snaking out across the stone paving, to strike my ankles with such force that my feet were taken out from under me.

I fell in an inelegant heap of skirts and frayed rope and dust.

"Signorina!" The Italian leaped to my side with horror.

"Alice!" The King was there too.

I sat up slowly, breathless from shock and surprise, my ankles sore, as the Italian proceeded to wipe dust from my face before discreetly arranging my disordered skirts.

"Signorina! *Mille pardons!*"

It all seemed to be happening at a distance. The cloud of dust settling, the soldiers lowering the still-unfixed pieces of the clock, now forgotten in the chaos. Thomas staring at me with a mixture of fright and ghoulish fascination.

My eyes settled on the King's anxious face. "Sire . . ." I said. I was not discreet.

"You are quite safe now." He enclosed my hands within his and lifted them to his lips.

And my senses returned.

"I am not hurt," I stated.

Ignoring this, Edward sent Thomas at a run: "Fetch my physician!"

"I am not hurt!" I repeated.

"I'll decide whether you are hurt or not," Edward snapped back, and then to his Master of Clocks, who still fussed and wrung his hands: "See to the mechanism. It's not your fault, man! I'll deal with Mistress Alice."

Never had I been so aware of his presence, the proud flare of nostrils that gave him a hawkish air even when he was not. Even when rank fear was imprinted in his face.

"Can you stand?" he asked abruptly.

"Yes."

Gently, he lifted me and stood me on my feet. To my surprise I staggered and was forced to clutch at his arm—no artifice on my part, but a momentary dizziness. Without a second thought Edward swept me up into his arms and carried me away from the dust and debris.

For the first time in my short existence I was enclosed in the arms of a man. All the feelings I had imagined but never experienced flooded through me. The heat of his body against mine, the steady beat of his heart. The fine grain of his skin beneath the weathering, the firmness of his hands holding me close. The pungency of sweat and dust and sudden panic when life came under threat. My throat was dry with an inexplicable need, my palms slick with it. Every inch of my skin seemed to be alive, shimmering in the bars of sunlight through the glazed and painted windows. I was alight, on fire, my heart thundering against the lacing of my gown. . . .

Until I was brought back to reality.

"Put me down, Sire!" I ordered, horrified. "You must not worry the Queen with this. She is ill today. Where are you taking me?"

He came to a sudden halt. "I don't know." He looked down at me, as jolted as I. How close his eyes were to mine, his breath warm against my temple. "In faith, Alice, you frightened me beyond reason. Are you in pain?"

"No!" I was too aware, far too aware. "Put me down. Why are you carrying me when I can walk very well on my own?"

"It seemed the right thing to do at the time." The lines that bracketed his mouth began to ease at last. "Allow me to be gallant, if you will, and carry you to safety."

I could hear the Italian tending lovingly to his mechanism, and the voices of the soldiers, the proximity of the servants. "Put me down, Sire. We shall be seen."

"Why would that matter?" His brows winged upward as if he had not considered it.

But I knew it would matter. I knew all the Court would know of this altercation within the hour. "Put me down!" I abandoned any good manners.

Edward turned abruptly into the chancel, marched along its length, and set me down in one of the choir stalls, allowing me some degree of privacy.

"Since you insist . . ."

And, kneeling beside me, he kissed me. Not a gracious salute to my fingers. Not a brotherly caress to my cheek as I imagined such a one to be. Not a chaste, husbandly peck on the lips such as Janyn Perrers would have employed if he had ever come so close to me. Edward gripped my arms, hauled me against him, and his mouth descended on mine in a firm possession that lasted as long as a heartbeat, and more.

He lifted his head and I looked at him, stunned. My blood hummed;

my thoughts scattered. "You should not have done that," I managed in a whisper. "That is not the right thing to do."

"Would you lecture the King on his behavior, Mistress Alice?"

He smiled ruefully before he kissed me again, just as forcefully. Just as recklessly. And when it was ended: "You should not have looked at me so trustingly," he said.

"So it was my fault?" My voice, I regret, was almost a squeak. "That you kissed your wife's damsel?"

For a moment, Philippa's presence hovered between us. We felt her with us. I saw the recognition in Edward's eyes, as I was sure it was in mine. And I saw regret there as his voice and features chilled.

"No, Alice. It was not your fault. It was all mine. You could have been injured and I should have been more careful with you." It was difficult to keep my breathing even, and when I shivered with a sudden onset of nerves, Edward stood. "You're cold." He shrugged out of a sleeveless overtunic he had worn in the church for warmth, and draped it around my shoulders. And when his hands rested there, heat surged through me so that my temples throbbed with it.

"Sire . . ." I warned as footsteps approached. Edward stepped back, struggling to be tolerant of his physician's meaningless questions and orders for me to rest to allow my humors to settle.

"I'll return you to the Queen," Edward said when the physician was finished and had gone about his affairs.

Yes, I thought. *That would be best.* To be away from this man who was all too compelling. And then on a thought I asked, "How is the clock after the accident, Sire? The Queen will want to know."

And he rounded on me with a blaze of anger. "To hell with the clock. I don't regret kissing you. I find you alluring, intoxicating. . . ." He glared at me as if it were indeed my fault. "Why is that?"

"A moment's fear, Sire. I doubt you will even remember this interlude tomorrow when the danger is over and the clock restored." Ah, but I would.

"This is not a sudden impulse. Do you feel nothing?" he demanded, the hawkishness very pronounced.

I dissembled. "I don't know."

"I think you do!"

"Would it matter whether I did or not? I am the Queen's damsel."

"As I very well know, God save me!" he exclaimed, his temper still simmering. "Tell me your thoughts on this debacle, Alice."

"Then I will. For it is a debacle. Yet I think you are the most amazing man I have ever met." For was that not true?

"Is that all? I want more from you." He was all authority, his hand strong on mine, his whole body as taut as a bowstring. "I want to see you again before tomorrow. I will arrange it. Come to me tonight, Alice."

No permission. No soft promises. A Plantagenet order. I had no misconceptions of what would await me. I think for the first time in my life I had nothing to say, not even in my head.

I told the Queen that the clock was experiencing difficulties but that the King had it all in hand.

Did I know what I was doing? Had I seen it developing, unfurling, from the very beginning? Did I see the pits and traps that were opening before my feet? Was I denying the truth even to myself?

Oh, I knew. I was never a fool. I saw what I had done. I saw when his attention was caught. I noted with the first scratch of my pen in my puerile writings when I had called him Edward rather than "the King," when he gave me the little mare, when I began to think of him as Edward, the man.

Did I enchant, entrap, weave him into my toils, as the malicious tongues were to accuse many years later? Was I complicit in this seduction?

Complicit, yes. But entrapment? I was never guilty of that. When did any woman entrap a Plantagenet? Edward had his own mind and pursued his own path.

Was I malicious?

Not that either. Never that. I was too loyal to the Queen. Guilt was not unknown to me, whatever slanders were aimed at me. Philippa had given me everything I had, and I was betraying her. Regret had teeth as sharp as those of the ill-fated monkey.

Ambitious, then?

Without a doubt. For here was a certain cure for the ills of obscure poverty. When a woman spends her young years with nothing of her own, why should she not seize the opportunity to remedy her lack, if that opportunity should fall into her lap?

Ah! But could I have stopped the whole train of events before I became the royal whore? Who's to say? With Edward I could be myself, not a silly damsel without a thought in my head but gossip and chatter. Edward listened to me as if my opinions mattered. I found his authority, his dominance, his sheer maleness intoxicating, as would any woman. When I saw his clever, handsome features, when his eyes turned to mine, it was as if I had just drunk a cup of finest Gascon wine. He was the King and I his subject. I was under his dominion as much as he was under mine.

Could I have prevented it? No, I could not. For at the eleventh hour it was taken out of my hands. *I* was not to be deus ex machina.

That night I waited, apprehension churning in my belly to the extent that nausea threatened to send me running to the garderobe. Taking a sip of ale, I sat on the side of my bed, feigning interest in the gossip of the two damsels as they plaited each other's hair for the night. I pretended to be unraveling a stubborn knot from a length of ribbon, except that I made it worse. Abandoning it, I took off my veil and folded it. Refolded it. Anything to keep my hands busy. I could not sit. I stood abruptly to prowl the room.

What division of loyalties was here in my mind, my heart. Commanded by the King, recipient of his kisses. Servant of the Queen, who honored me with her confidences. This was a betrayal. A terrible riding roughshod over the Queen's trust, stealing from her what was rightfully hers. It was impossible to argue around it.

I looked around the room, at the damsels quietly occupied. What to do now? Was it all a mistake? Had I misunderstood? There would be no royal summons after all, and my guilt could be laid aside.

A knock sounded on the door. I jumped like a stag, and my hands were not steady as I opened the door to a page in royal insignia.

"It is the Queen, mistress. She cannot sleep. She has sent for you. Will you come?"

"I will come," I replied quietly.

So this was how it was to be arranged. A royal stratagem. A clever, supremely realistic ploy to remove me from my room without rousing the least degree of suspicion. Would I be waylaid in some dark corridor, product of some careful planning, to be led to the King's apartments instead of the Queen's? I detested the thought of such secrecy, such underhanded deceit. I did not want this—but I was trapped in a web that might have been some of my own making.

While the page waited I wrapped a mantle around me and made to follow.

"I may not return before dawn," I told the other damsels, my hand on the latch, impressed that my voice was steady. "If the Queen is ill and restless, I'll sleep on a pallet in the antechamber."

They nodded, lost in their own concerns. It was so easy.

The King wants you in his bed.

I shivered.

I was not to be waylaid after all. Instead I was shown by the incurious page into the smallest of the antechambers, with a second door leading into the Queen's accommodations. It was a room I knew well, often used for intimate conversation, or to withdraw into if one felt the need for solitary contemplation. Had I not used it myself in the hour after the King made his intentions plain, after the affair of the clock? Built into one of the towers, it had circular walls, the cold stone covered with tapestries, all flamboyant with birds and animals of the forest. As I stood uncertainly in the center, deer stared out at me with carefully stitched eyes. Wherever I turned I seemed to be under observation. An owl fixed me unblinkingly with golden orbs; a hunting dog watched me. I turned my back on it to sit on one of the benches against the wall. I started at every sound, and strained in the silence when there was no sound.

What now? I could do nothing but wait. Whatever was to transpire within the next hour was not within my governance. What would I say? What would I do? The palms of my hands were clammy with sweat as my thoughts flew ahead. What if I displeased Edward? My knowledge of what passed between a man and a woman within the privacy of the bed curtains was so limited as to be laughable. My education with the nuns had not fitted me for the role of mistress, royal or otherwise. As for Janyn . . . I gripped the edge of the bench on either side of me until it hurt.

Holy Virgin, don't abandon me!

But how was I fit to call on the Queen of Heaven?

The door opened. I leaped to my feet.

In my anxiety I had not noticed that it was the door from the Queen's rooms, not the one from the corridor. I faced it, expecting another page to take me further along this treacherous journey.

Ah, no!

My blood froze. My feet became rooted to the spot. Fear was a stone in my belly.

The Queen stood there on the threshold.

She stepped slowly forward, as regal as if entering a state chamber, and closed the door behind her with the softest of clicks. She might be clad in a night shift beneath her loose robe, her hair might be plaited on her shoulder, but she was every inch a queen. Her face might be lined and pinched with long-suffered pain, but her innate dignity was superb. For a drawn-out moment we stood, alone in that little room except for the static gaze of hundreds of embroidered eyes, and regarded each other.

Philippa held herself stiffly, the elbow of her damaged arm supported by her opposite hand, yet still she had come here to see me, to remonstrate, to curse me for my presumption. It was as if she cried out to me in her agony.

And because I could not speak, I sank into a deep obeisance, hiding my face from her. Was I not stripping from her the duty and honor of her husband's body and name? Was I not about to create a scandal that would cloak her in humiliation? What I was about to do could destroy her. . . .

At that moment I knew in my heart: I could not do this thing.

"Alice . . ." My name was little more than a sigh on her lips.

"My lady . . . Forgive me. . . ."

"I knew you would be here."

She *knew.* Of course she knew. How would she not? Such an emotional tie as I had seen between them. Sometimes it seemed to me that Philippa knew Edward was present even before he entered the room. So she knew. She must know, through that same inner sense, that her husband, the one love of her life, intended to betray her.

I could not do this to her.

I fell to my knees before her. "Forgive me. Forgive me, my lady."

Without words she touched my hair and I looked up. Her face was wet with tears, so many that they dripped to leave dark spots on the damask of her robe. So much sorrow, it struck at my heart. I lifted my hands to cover my face so that I could not witness such depths of grief. There were tears in my own eyes.

"I would never harm you, Lady. . . ."

"I know."

"I'll go back to my room." I heard my words muffled by my hands. "I'll not do it. I promise I will not."

Bending awkwardly, the Queen gripped my forearm and with a grunt of pain urged me to my feet.

"I'll tell the King that . . ." I continued, shame a bloody sword in my flesh. Tell him what? The words dried on my lips.

"What will you tell him, Alice?"

"I don't know. I'll leave Court if I must. . . ." Anything to heal the wound of bitter betrayal. I turned my face away. I could not look at her.

"No, Alice."

I shook my head. "I don't deserve your forgiveness, but . . ."

The grasp of Philippa's fingers, which must have hurt her as much as it did me, silenced me. "No, Alice," I heard as she took a breath. "You will do as the King wishes. Do you understand?"

It made no sense. No sense at all.

"No . . . no!"

"You will go to the King. When the King's page comes, you will go with him." How accepting her voice was.

"I can't. I can't be so disloyal . . ." I protested.

"You are not disloyal. I *want* you to go to him."

Which confused me beyond reason. "No . . . !" I covered her hand with mine even though she was Queen, as if I could force her to acknowledge what she was saying. "You can't want that! Don't you see . . . ?" I could not put it into words.

The Queen raised her free hand to hold my chin so that I must look at her, and she at me. She gave an infinitesimal nod of her head, then released me and took a step away, creating a little space between us.

"Look at me, Alice. Look at *me!*" she insisted. "Not as the Queen but as a woman." She lifted her hands so that I had no choice but to see the ravages of the disease that was slowly but inexorably engulfing her. "I am almost fifty years old." She smiled with her lips. "I have worn my years less well than my lord. My body is wearing out. My fortitude might have been strong but the deaths of my children have robbed me of that too. I feel death treading on my hem, Alice."

"No," I urged. "I can make the pain less for you. . . ."

"I know you can. And you do. But sometimes it is so great. And I cannot bear to be touched. . . ."

The Queen sighed and I took her meaning. The swollen flesh, the stretched skin, the displaced shoulder. Some days it took the Queen all her willpower to walk from bedchamber to solar. "I know, my lady."

"Of course you do. Edward is virile, as much as he has always been. He has needs, as all men do. He needs a woman to warm his bed and pleasure his flesh. How can I do that? The weight of the bed linen is an agony to me. I have loved my lord. I have borne him twelve children and was honored to do so. I still love him more than life itself—but I cannot be a wife to him in the flesh. It hurts my heart, but I cannot."

"No . . ." There was nothing more to say.

"Once, I could barely wait until he came to me at night. My skin warmed. My loins melted. Now I fear what he might demand from me—not that he is ever cruel or thoughtless, you understand. He does not demand what I cannot bear. I don't want fear to stand between Edward and me—so I must make my own remedy."

How honest she was. How heartbreakingly transparent. I watched every stark emotion chase across her face and waited for her decision. And there it was.

"Do this, Alice. Do this for me. I thought I could stand back and allow it to happen without speaking to you. But I could not. You deserve to know what I have done. You are too intelligent to be treated as a cipher, your will to be disposed of at a whim in so personal a matter." She ran her tongue over dry lips as if she had to steel herself to continue. But she did. "I have told my lord to take a lover because such intimacy is beyond me."

Oh, Philippa! I could imagine what it had taken her to do this. How she had to deny her pride and her position as Edward's wife.

"I want him to have you, Alice. Why do you think I have placed you in his way?"

A new emotion began to surface in my mind. "So you planned this. . . ."

"Planned? Perhaps I have, although I do not like the word. It has been in my mind, let us say."

"Does the King know?" I was suddenly horrified that it had been arranged between them, with me as the pawn to be moved on the chessboard at will, and I felt the heat of resentment in my belly.

"No." Philippa's brief laughter was harsh. "He is a man who has always made his own decisions, and he will do so in this. Would any Plantagenet prince allow a woman to choose his lover? Never! We all dance to Edward's tune."

The crawling horror subsided a little. "But with all the beautiful women at Court . . ."

"My husband is well aware of the beauty around him. If he wanted a particular woman as his lover, he would take her. But you have a strange charm, Alice. I have prayed he would see it and respond to it."

"But it is betrayal! And is it not degrading to him? Even for us to be speaking in this manner?" I found my voice had dropped to almost a whisper, as if the vividly embroidered creatures might hear. "It is a dishonor to his manhood."

"No, my dear girl. Never think that. It would be too much of a burden for him to embrace chastity—he is a high-blooded man—yet he has done so in recent months for my sake." Her smile held a world of acceptance. "This is my gift to him—and yours to me. I lifted you up from nothing, Alice. Now you can repay me."

"My gift to you." I let the words filter through my mind.

"Yes. You speak of humiliation. But think! How could I bear it if he were to take a common whore in the heat of frustrated passion? Or a titled woman of my own Court? A man in the throes of passion does not always discriminate. And I could not bear the scandal. . . . The worst is always believed, and I haven't the strength to hold up my head against it. . . ."

Soft footsteps sounded in the distance, drawing nearer.

"Are you sure about this, my lady?" I asked. The moment had arrived. There would be no going back for either of us.

"More sure than I have ever been of anything." She leaned forward, clumsy but determined, to place a kiss between my brows. "I must go—I don't want us to be found here together. This is no plot, and Edward must not consider it as such. Give him what he wants, Alice, knowing it is with my blessing."

She turned to go, but I stopped her with my question.

"You once told me that you had a role for me to play. Is this it?"

"Yes." She looked back. "You will find that Edward is a magnificent lover." The grief was almost her undoing; I heard the sob in her throat. "I will make it as easy as I can for you."

For the length of a breath, but which seemed an age, we regarded each other: Philippa with a certainty born of desperation, I with astonishment at her courage and knowledge that it would not prove to be a simple role for her or for me. How could a loving wife accept her husband's whore as her own daily companion? It would be beyond my tolerance. Now I understood exactly what the Queen had meant by a grievous burden.

Then she was gone, and I was left in a quagmire of unbelief, my mind racing. The door to the corridor opened as the one to Philippa's rooms closed. I raised my chin and prepared to become the King's mistress with the blessing of his wife. All I had to do was follow the royal page. . . . Before God! This was a night for courage, and I suspected I had used all that was allotted to me.

There was Wykeham, regarding me as if I were a louse to be burned in the candle flame.

He stepped aside with the most dismissive of gestures. Not once did his eyes meet mine, not even fleetingly, but stared somewhere over my left shoulder. It was as if he could not look at me, for fear of acknowledging the terrible transgression that was about to be branded on my soul.

"You are to come with me, Mistress Perrers."

So Wykeham was to be Edward's minion on this sensitive mission. Yesterday he would have called me Alice. Yesterday he would have greeted me with a smile and asked after my health. Today he scorned me as the most despicable of creatures.

"This is a sin!" he growled in confirmation, if I had needed it, as I walked past him from the room.

"It is the King's will." The less I said, the better.

"You should not be part of it."

I was brief but defiant. "I am summoned."

"By your own contriving, no doubt. What you do must disgust any man possessing even an ounce of decency. The Queen has given you everything and this is how you repay her." Wykeham's mouth shut like a trap.

"I think we should go," I replied, and turned away so that I need not see his vile disgust of me glitter in his eye. What had passed between me and the Queen must remain locked away, and so I must be content to let this man I had called a friend think what he wished of me, even though he condemned me for a sin not of my committing.

He led me through the deserted corridors. Had everyone been sent away deliberately? Not one page, no clerks or body servants, not one of the royal household was about on that night that set my feet on a new and dangerous path. My escort was unnervingly silent, so that I could taste his disapproval in my mouth, feel the burn of it on my skin. For the length of a single breath I stumbled almost to a halt. What if I didn't comply? Was this how I wished to lose my virginity, as a creature in the clever royal scheming to benefit King and Queen? My mind was clouded with uncertainty, my heart encased in ice. So, what if I refused? What if I . . . ? But events had moved on too far and too fast, as I knew, and I was being carried along, a mindless leaf in a stream. Quickly I pattered after Wykeham, until he came to a halt so abruptly that I all but trod on his heel. Wheeling 'round, he forced me to retreat a step, but he seized my wrist in an unpriestly grip.

"You should not be here!" His eyes were furious, his lips stretched in anger.

"Will you deny me to your King?" I would say anything to stop the accusations. "Not even you could do that, Wykeham." I put a sneer into my voice. "You can build walls and arches, but you can't dictate to your King!" Anything to shut him up.

Instantly he released me, thrusting me away so that I staggered against the wall.

"Wykeham . . . !" I gasped.

His mind was closed against me. And what could I have said without betraying the Queen's carefully crafted deceit? With a brush of his knuckles against a door, Wykeham opened it, stood back, and gestured me to go through. I stepped into the room. The door closed at my back.

Chapter Six

*I*t was Edward's private chamber, redolent of masculine luxury. Wood paneling hung with tapestries, a fireplace with burning logs and a favorite hound curled there. A prie-dieu and a crucifix. A coffer, a standing table, a high-polished chair with carved arms and back—opulent, I decided as I took it all in at a glance, used as I now was to such magnificence. Here was everything a nobleman with a taste for prayer and erudition and comfort could wish for. Edward might have spent most of his life engaged in the hardship of campaigning in France, but at Havering, despite its insignificance compared to the royal dwellings at Westminster and Windsor, he enjoyed all that his consequence could bring him. And there were signs of recent habitation. A pole with a falcon that appeared to be asleep. A sumptuous damask and fur chamber robe in deep glowing red cast over the coffer. A flagon for wine and cups, and a platter of what remained of a meal. Books, one open, and a rosary cast on the bed; a bowl and ewer flanked by a candle stand, the fine quality of the candles casting a soft glow.

And a quite superlative bed.

My eye slid quickly away from its silk covers, its red and gold curtains. After the emotion of the past half hour, my control was compromised. I stood hesitantly with my back to the door, an animal at bay, so it seemed, as I waited for the predator to pounce. For surely the King of England was as much a predator as his hawk.

The hawk rustled its feathers and sank further into somnolence. The hound twitched and whined in the throes of some hunting dream.

And Edward walked toward me from where he had been sitting perusing the pages of a book, hand outstretched in greeting. How beautiful he was. How carelessly he wore that beauty, how unself-consciously, how unaware of the impression his fine-carved features and magnificent stature would make on the beholder. Would make on me.

"Alice." The stern lines of his face softened into the vestige of a smile. "You look as if you're considering that I might pounce and dismember you."

"I think I am," I replied.

Edward's laugh rumbled. "I'll not do that." His hand closed over mine. "You're freezing—or frozen with fear. Come to the fire. . . ." Pulling me gently forward, he placed me in his own chair, speaking all the time as if I were some flighty, unbroken filly in need of reassurance. Leaving me to look around, he poured two cups of ruby liquid. "Here. It's from Gascony. The best wine we have." He pushed the cup into my hand, hooked his toe around the leg of a stool, and sat at my feet, lifting his own cup to his lips.

"Drink, Alice." He nudged my forearm. I realized I had been staring at him, my thoughts paralyzed with uncertainty. I still could not look at the bed. For sure the King had not invited me here to have me copy the nation's accounts into a ledger.

Edward drank, his eyes never leaving my face. Under that intense gaze my nerves faltered, and I looked down at the chasing on the fine silver cup, inconsequentially following the outline of a superbly tined stag with my finger.

"Would it please you to be my mistress?" he asked, as if inquiring about my health.

"I don't know."

"That's honest, by God!"

"It has to be, Sire. I don't know how to answer you otherwise."

I took a careless gulp of wine and coughed. One of the logs collapsed with a sigh. The hawk shuffled on dry feet.

"You are a widow."

"Yes."

"Then you should not fear this." His hand gestured toward the bed.

I swallowed. "I am a virgin. My marriage was never consummated. He couldn't. . . ." I really had begun to tremble, now that the moment had come upon me. I glanced up to see that Edward was frowning at me. So that was not the answer he had wanted. He had wanted a mistress with some knowledge of what occurred between the sheets. All Philippa's planning would go for naught. "I can leave, Sire. If you don't want me here . . ."

"I'll tell you when I don't!" A flash of eye, a brush of temper that surprised me, and then it ebbed as fast as it had flared between us. His voice was very gentle. "Forgive me. This has to be a very private transaction between us."

"And you don't trust me to keep my own counsel?"

"That's not what I meant." His eyes were on mine, fierce and searching again, and I could not look away.

"I know what you meant. I know you don't want to hurt Her Majesty."

"You think it won't hurt her to know?" Surging to his feet, he was suddenly as far from me as he could get, at the other side of the room. Who was the animal at bay here? I watched him cautiously. "Sins of the flesh," he murmured. "They will return to haunt us."

"I am no gossip, Sire," I replied.

"How old are you?" he asked harshly.

"Seventeen years, my lord, perhaps eighteen."

"So many years between us, so much experience that I have and you do not. Do you know, Alice? I've never been unfaithful to her. Not in all the thirty years of marriage. No matter the rumors that I have taken lovers—from the day I wed her I have not broken my oath. But now . . ."

But now she has told you to take a lover!

How to keep all the secrets? Was I to be a deft juggler, keeping the separate items aloft in an orderly pattern, dropping none? Or a skilled weaver, melding all the colors into one seemly whole? Was I capable of such discretion? Such skill? Countess Joan's words slammed into my mind. *It is important for a woman to have the duplicity to make good use of whatever gifts she might have.* And there she was with her cruel smile. Until I banished her. There was no place for Fair Joan's cynicism in this maneuvering between Edward and myself. I waited, the nerves in my belly fluttering like finches in a cage.

"When I touch her she has to sink her teeth into her lips not to groan with the agony." Edward turned away from me to brace his hands against the edge of the coffer, head bent, shoulders rigid as he made his confession. "I love my wife. But I desire you, Alice. Is that very bad?"

"Wykeham would say so, my lord." I was still chafing at his reproof.

"What would *you* say?"

The only thing I could. "That you are my King and can demand my obedience, my lord."

His mouth twisted. "A simplistic answer to smooth over any complication." Silence fell. Heavy. Full of decision and indecision. And then: "If you are to share my bed, you must call me by my name."

"Edward." I tried it, as I had written it of late. I smiled. And the King must have heard the smile in my voice and he looked back at me over his shoulder.

"What is it?"

"It sounds strange."

"Strange . . . Do you know how few people call me by my name?"

"No, Sire."

"I could count them on the fingers of one hand. All the friends of my youth—dead within the last two years. Northampton—the bravest of my generals. Sir John Beauchamp, who carried my standard at Crécy. Lancaster—the most trusted of all my friends. The years are cruel, Alice. You're too young to see it yet. They rob us of our health and our friends and our hopes, and give nothing back." His sight was turned inward, his expression melancholy. Another log fell into ash, dislodging others, and as if the sound prompted him to what he was and what he must be, Edward slowly raised his head. His spine straightened visibly, and the lines of his face firmed as his lips compressed. "I am not allowed to grow old. I am King."

I stood, my own anxieties obliterated by compassion, not that I would ever have dared reveal it. Here was a proud warrior who had lived and fought for a lifetime, yet there was no comfort for him. Nor would he ask it—he would bear the burden of kingship to the grave, whatever the depth of loneliness it demanded from him. I walked slowly toward him, presenting him with my own cup, since his was forgotten on the coffer.

"You will not grow old. You will live forever. And I will call you Edward, if that is what you wish."

I touched his hand as he took the cup from me, marveling that I could so easily transgress the honor due to the King; all my fears seemed to have fallen away. I let my fingers rest lightly on his, as his eyes captured mine.

"I remember the softness of your mouth. When you smile, your face is illluminated as if a candle is lit behind your eyes," he said. "It lights you from within."

"You flatter me."

"Then we will flatter each other."

Edward kissed me. His lips were firm and warm against mine. An intimate kiss but with no heat of passion. He was not aroused. Perhaps it was the desire of courtly love he wanted to give me rather than the fulfillment of the flesh.

"God will damn me for this, but . . ."

He let his hands drop from my shoulders, for there was harsh conscience again. I thought that in his youth there would have been no hesitation in Edward taking what he wanted, but he was not at ease with either his conscience or with me. His authority, within the bedchamber or without, was supreme, but his memories had roused the specter of death and decay.

So what was my role here? It came to me that I wanted nothing more than to give him some level of contentment. To make him smile again. But how . . . how to distract him from these morbid thoughts that gave him no pleasure? What skill did I have to achieve that? The arts of seduction were unknown to me. What might he want most from me that I was capable of giving? What could I do? Well—I could argue and hold an opinion. . . .

My eyes were caught by the documents strewn across the table. Affairs of business and policy. I walked to stand before them.

"Tell me what you are doing here, Edward."

"Interested in royal policy, are you?" Intrigued, he had watched me go.

"Yes." I looked back at him, a deliberate challenge that he was free to accept or reject. "I am capable of far more than deciding the color of the gown I wear or how my hair should be dressed!"

"Are you, now?" Accepting the challenge, Edward directed me to sit on a stool and reached to select one of the documents, handing it to me. "Family affairs," he said, resting his weight against the table, interest in my precociousness replacing the melancholy. This was better!

"You are fortunate. I have no family," I said. "I know nothing of such."

"I have sons. Magnificent sons. And they bring me power." And there was the King again rather than the man, his finger on every pulse, his hand wound tight in the reins to keep ultimate control of the kingdom. "What do you see on that document?"

He tapped the one I held. The Latin was close-written in the crabbed script of a clerk, but I could read enough. "Ireland," I said.

"Good! This is Lionel. He's in Ireland. A difficult province, a tough job. Once, I'd have gone myself, but I've sent Lionel as King's Lieutenant. He'll have to tread a path between all the damned interests. God knows it's a morass of bad blood."

He took the document from me and gave me another. I felt like a novice again, under instruction, or a clerk under Janyn's scrutiny, but my fascination with the documents was keen. "And this?" he asked.

This one was more difficult, but the names were clear. "This is Aquitaine."

"Edward, my heir." The pride in his voice was unmistakable. "He'll rule Aquitaine well as long as he curbs his tendency to stamp on the interests of those he rules. Gascony's restive—he must learn to be patient at the same time as he learns to be king. He is a good commander, a man after my own heart. Now, this . . ."

He was enjoying himself. A man confident and assured as he spread out before me the heirs to his power who would carry the Plantagenet blood and name into history. I took the new document.

"This is John. John of Gaunt. The Duchy of Lancaster is now his.

And Edmund? I was planning on the Flanders heiress for him"—he frowned at a document with a heavy red seal that had cracked on its journeys—"but the French want her, and they have the ear of the new Pope. I'll have to look elsewhere for him. And then there's Thomas. . . ."

"Who's only seven, and hunting mad like his father."

"Yes."

The success of my simple ploy glowed in my heart. Edward was at ease.

"Isabella is the other problem." He took my cup again and drank as he considered her. "She'll marry as she sees fit. If I took a whip to her sides it would do no good."

"I think she will not be averse to any husband of your choice." I had seen the raging dissatisfaction in Isabella.

"She was more than averse once!"

"But now, with the years passing . . . she'll accept any man you choose for her—as long as he is young and good to look at and powerful!"

"I'll remember that. You see more than I in the domain of the solar. . . . My fear is that she'll make her own choice—and someone outrageously inappropriate."

"Then let her do it."

"But I need her to make an alliance for the good of England—not to choose some landless knight with a pretty face and formidable muscles to entice her into bed . . . !"

He stopped abruptly. I looked up from the vellum to his face, unsure what had silenced him. He was looking at me.

"What have you done?" he demanded.

"Nothing, my lord!"

"You are a cunning woman, Alice Perrers!"

And Edward cast the curling documents onto the table and laughed, enough to reverberate from the walls and wake the hound. With a smooth flex of muscle and sinew he pushed himself from the table, stooped with a hand below each of my elbows, and lifted me from the stool to place me firmly on my feet. He held me there before him.

"Did I bring you here to discuss matters of policy?" His eyes were now a clear blue, all shadows obliterated, full of humor. And desire. "Not only cunning, I think. You are a clever woman."

"Do you think so, Edward?" I tilted my chin, deliberately somber, exquisitively provocative.

"You've made an excellent attempt at distracting me."

"Yes," I admitted.

"And very successfully. I can only apologize for my ill humor."

"There is no need." And because I was so close, I touched the King's lips with the tips of my fingers. "I am pleased to give you pleasure."

It was a blatant invitation—and it was meant to be.

Edward needed no invitation. With grave courtesy he helped me remove my gown—how did a man of war deal so knowledgeably with female ties and laces?—allowing me to keep my shift for modesty's sake. His patience lulled all my virginal fears. Turning back the bedcovers, he helped me to sit against the pillows, then doused the candles except for one, standing far enough away to give me the benefit of shrouding shadows. Without any modesty on his own part, he stripped off hose and tunic, and stood beside the bed.

"I'll make this as good as I can, Alice."

"I am not afraid." Nor was I. Now that the moment had come I knew that Edward Plantagenet would not hurt me.

Curious, I allowed my gaze to travel over what I could see of his body in the single flickering flame. I expect the soft light flattered him. Half a century he had lived, but his flesh was still firm and smooth on flanks and chest; nor could the scars and abrasions from a lifetime of battle and tourneys detract from his splendid physique, despite there being more silver in his fair hair than he might wish for.

The evidence of his desire for me was formidable.

"Do you like what you see, Mistress Alice?" he asked.

I flushed brightly, realizing that I had been staring with open admiration.

"I like it very well," I replied as calmly as I could. "I can only pray that you will find me as pleasing to the eye and the senses."

"I'll let you know! For now, my pleasure in your company is obvious to us both."

So I lost my virginity to Edward Plantagenet, King of England. It was not an unpleasant experience, and my trembling was from neither fear nor pain. I followed his lead and was brave enough to return his caresses with my own. Sometimes I allowed my own needs, when I recognized them, to prompt a kiss or a caress. Sometimes I made him hold his breath.

He liked it.

And how did I feel? Edward made me feel desired. For the first time in all my seventeen years he made me feel valued, beautiful, even when I knew I was neither. I clung to him, drowning in his embrace.

"How did our lives cross, Alice?" he asked when passion had ebbed.

Your loving wife had something to do with it.

I shook my head.

"We keep this between us," he murmured, "and Wykeham, who's to be trusted."

"Yes."

Wykeham will damn me rather than you!

And so it was begun: this strange ménage a trois, with the Queen a silent partner who neither needed nor wanted to know more than she did, and Edward unaware of his wife's complicity. I would keep the secrets of both. And when his hands explored and his body possessed, we tacitly agreed to keep the Queen distant from the room and the bed. We did not speak of her. Enough time tomorrow to allow guilt to creep in. For now the fluid strength of his body, the slide of heated skin against heated skin, occupied all my thoughts.

At the end Edward fell asleep, the fingers of one hand interlaced with mine, but I lay awake, considering the responses of my body. What was love? Love, I suspected, was whatever Edward felt toward Philippa. Perhaps he loved me too in his way, unless it was merely lust. But did I love Edward? Perhaps I fell in love with him a little, if admiration and respect and loyalty amounted to love. My belly clenched with longing when he kissed me, when his hands stroked down my breast to the dip of my waist. I was overwhelmed by his glamour, that this was the King of England who wanted me enough to throw caution to the winds and own me.

Perhaps that was love after all.

Later—how many hours later, for time had no meaning—Wykeham escorted me back to the antechamber in the Queen's rooms. It was the same journey, in reverse, but even more spiked with his loathing of what had been done. He was beyond censure. He bowed and left me at the door, not even opening it for me, the bow an empty gesture that denied any courtesy.

I had forfeited all his approval. I suspect he thought I had forfeited my soul.

A page returned me to my room, where the damsels slept on in ignorance.

A new day and early sunshine filtered into the room as if it were an ordinary day. I washed my hands and face from the ewer of cold water, flinching from the chill. A day like any other day, and yet not so. I dressed hurriedly before my two companions were astir, with the ready excuse that the Queen might need me if she was still in pain, to give her the strength to attend Mass in her chapel.

What would I say to her? I knew only that I must see her, to learn what she might find to say to me in the cold light of day. Last night was a time of tension and high drama, when we had both allowed emotion to rule. Today might be a time for regret. The Queen might consider my dismissal a just punishment for what I had done, and, in truth, I could not blame her. I must know. I hurried to her rooms, only to be informed by her tire-woman that she had risen even earlier than I—was that a bad sign or good?—and was already at prayer. I slipped into the chapel. No priest was there, but the Queen knelt before the altar, clasping the altar rail to steady herself. I sank to my knees just within the entrance. I would wait. It seemed to me that the fair face of the statue of the Holy Virgin was particularly austere.

"Alice . . ."

The Queen's private devotions were complete. I stood, moving quickly toward the altar to help her to her feet.

"Well?" Her eyes were bright and aware. The pain was less this morning.

"It is done, Majesty."

"It was . . . satisfactory?"

"Yes."

How few words, so inconsequential in themselves, to encompass so momentous an act. Any deliberate eavesdropper would have abandoned us for meatier gossip.

"He will . . . he will send for you again?"

"Yes, my lady."

"Good. We will not speak of this again."

A strange relief trickled through my blood, that this three-stranded interweaving might not be impossible, if I had the skill to keep the secrets of both and remain true to each. Perhaps I could be loyal to both Philippa and Edward, betraying neither, harming neither. . . . But still the claws of treachery fastened in my flesh. I felt the rip of them as the Queen turned her gaze away from her husband's whore.

When the door opened, disturbing the air so that the candles wavered wildly, we both looked 'round, expecting a priest. And in a heartbeat the serene, ageless atmosphere of the chapel became heated with fury. It was written on her face, in every gesture. She barely waited to approach us before her voice rang out. For here was Isabella.

"God's Wounds! How could you . . . !"

She covered the distance with long strides, kicking aside her skirts. I thought her attack was for me, but Isabella swept past me as if I were detritus beneath her feet and pounced on her mother.

"Why are you here with her? Do you know what she's done? Wykeham will not talk—at least he's loyal and will keep his mouth shut about this family's affairs—but he was seen last night—with her! And do you know where he took her?" She all but spit the words, her beautiful face contorted. "She has betrayed you. Your little gutter sweepings, rescued from nonentity and squalor, spent last night in the King's rooms! In his bed, I presume! And here you are, all but holding her hands!"

"Isabella . . . !" the Queen remonstrated, to no avail.

"You didn't even know, did you? Don't touch her! She is a vile serpent!" And Isabella struck out at me, making contact with her hand against my shoulder with a forceful blow, so surprising me that I lost my balance and fell against the altar rail. "You will dismiss her. Do you hear me? And if you will not, I'll arrange it myself!"

"I hear you, Isabella." The Queen sighed.

"Look at her!" Isabella turned on me and snarled as I dragged myself upright. Prudently I stepped away as the Princess's fingers curled into claws. "You have dressed her and polished her until she's halfway presentable. And what has she done? Warmed your husband's bed. As for the King . . . ! Is no man honorable? After all you have given him—the respect, the children. I despise him! But I despise you more, little Alice from the gutter!"

"Isabella! You will be silent!" If I had thought Philippa's dignity a thing of amazement last night, today she was glorious in facing her furious daughter. "I know exactly . . ."

"She has cheated you! She has turned the gold of your generosity into dross! She should be flogged!" Isabella advanced on me once more.

"I have not cheated." I would not retreat again, even at the risk of Isabella's ire, but my fear was lively.

The Queen in timely manner grasped her daughter's sleeve. "Isabella!"

"You're not going to make excuses for her, are you?"

"No. I am going to make them for myself."

"I don't understand you."

"Then curb your passions, and listen. I know exactly what passed between my husband and Alice. Listen to me, my daughter. Forget your sense of ill usage and injustice. This is the reality." The Queen waited until Isabella had regained at least a semblance of calm. "What do you think? Am I capable of fulfilling my duty to your father?"

"Your duty . . . ?" Isabella looked as if she would rather not discuss it. "I don't see . . ."

"Yes, you do see it. Every day you see it. You are not a fool, Isabella. I am incapable of turning back the sheets on my bed for your father. That is the brutal truth."

"That's not . . ."

"If you were going to say something so foolish as 'that's not important,' you're no daughter of mine. It is always important. Your father is the man he ever was. Do I condemn him to a lifetime of abstinence because I cannot . . . cannot . . ." She brushed aside the words she could not speak. "Do you understand me, Isabella?"

"Yes!" Isabella's fair skin was flushed.

"And if I cannot give him what he needs . . ."

"You would procure a mistress for your own husband?" Isabella's disbelief was as strong as mine had been. That gentle, loving Philippa should give her blessing to her husband's lover. "Why not let him take a palace whore? There are enough of them willing to lift their skirts. . . ."

"No. Before God, Isabella! You try my patience. If it has to be, I would rather it be someone I know and trust. . . ."

How I detested this! In that moment I saw the truth. There was nothing new to learn of the Queen's motives here in this confrontation between Queen and Princess. Had she not bared her soul to me, in all its agony, the previous night? Yet hearing her state the words again made my blood chill. In spite of my loyalty to the Queen I was forced to acknowledge that I was being used. Snarled over like a bone between two royal curs. It was like the creation of an entirely new tapestry, stitched with clever fingers to reveal the whole before my eyes. Better for the King to sleep with an unimportant *domicella* than with a highborn titled lady who would use her position to sneer at the Queen's failure as she crowed over her success in bedding the King.

Degradation lapped over me, bitter as the leaves of hyssop. I might have sympathy with the Queen's motives, but the role that had been created for me was a wretched one. I was a creature, a pawn, to be moved around the chessboard at the whim of the player. And what a skilled player the Queen was. How long, before her eye fell on me, had she been plotting this deep scenario to preserve the Plantagenets from dangerous scandal?

"Could you not find a more acceptable bedmate than this?" Isabella continued to rage, stabbing her finger at me.

Nor, I realized, my blood now humming with my own brand of anger, did I appreciate this exchange of opinion that stormed over me as if I were invisible. I was not the same powerless woman that I had been yesterday.

You are the King's mistress. You are no longer invisible. Nor are you voiceless. You have his ear. He wants you to come to him again. You do not have to tolerate this. You have a power of your own. . . .

The words revolved and repeated like the cogs of Edward's precious clock.

"You will pretend you know nothing, Isabella. You will treat Alice with the respect she deserves for her obedience to me. Do you understand me?" The Queen was laying down her directives with the precision of an army commander.

"And you trust her?" Unimpressed, unmoved, Isabella flung a contempt that would have coated my skin in shame if my fury had not built mightily from a hum to a roar in my belly. "What else will she get from him? What gifts will she persuade my besotted father to give to her?"

How much more of this could I withstand? As hot as I was, the Queen was glacial.

"What do you mean?" she demanded.

"She'll not do it for nothing. What whore does? Jewels, money—a title even."

"And if she does gain material benefit? If Edward chooses to reward her with gifts . . ."

"You're wrong, *Maman*! You're making the gravest mistake of your life."

"Not so! It's the best decision I have ever made."

I could remain a silent onlooker no longer. "Stop!"

My voice sounded weak even to me. I might as well not have spoken.

"It is an obscenity. . . . That she should act as one of your simpering maids of the bedchamber and slither into your husband's bed at the same time." Isabella was beyond subtlety. "I'll not trim it with the words and gestures of romance. It's lust, and you should be ashamed to encourage it."

Enough! After my night with him, I could not bear that Edward be discussed in this manner. This time I raised my voice, caring nothing for the words I used in the presence of royal blood.

"Be silent!"

They looked at me, as startled as if the carved figure of the Virgin herself had come to life and spoken.

"I'll not be squabbled over like a piece of meat on a butcher's slab." There were things that must be said to Isabella. "Have you no respect for your father, the King? You denigrate him, defile him with crude words. Does he not have enough enemies across the sea to do that, without his own beloved daughter slandering him? His will is law in England, and you speak of him as if he were a toothless lion, an aging man who can be pushed and maneuvered at the will of others. Is he so weak that he needs his wife to arrange for a woman to warm his bed? I say he does not. I say his blood is high and his spirit great." I took a breath. I think I had never made so long a speech. "You do the King and yourself no honor. He is at the beck and call of no man. And I deny that he took a mistress at the behest of the Queen."

"Well . . . !" Isabella sought for words.

"I have not finished," I continued, my voice strengthening with conviction. "I will say what needs saying. You may consider me despicable, my lady, yet you will hear me. I am the King's mistress." How strange it sounded to say it aloud. I lifted my chin and held her gaze. "He chose me. He sent for me, and I will play the part with honor. I will be discreet as long as His Majesty wishes me to fulfill that role. I will not draw attention to what I do—that is in the King's gift. I will ask for nothing, take nothing but what the King gives me. If he wishes to reward me, then so be it. It is his decision. For myself, I will be loyal. I will not gossip or spread unseemly calumny. And I will continue to serve the Queen in every way I can. For as long as she wishes it."

Slowly Isabella's lips curved, an expression of sour acknowledgment. "Well, now. The whore has found its voice. I must curtsy to you." She did so, all mockery.

"You may mock me, my lady, but this is the King's wish—and the Queen's. From this day I am the King's lover."

Isabella's eyes flashed. "And if the Queen, with some judicious thought over her poor choice for a King's whore, objects to your new Court position? If *I* object . . ."

I lifted my shoulders in a perfect, elegant shrug. "I wish you no ill will, my lady, but I serve the King first and the Queen second. And I think *your* wishes are irrelevant."

"We'll see about that!" And Isabella marched from the chapel.

I was left to the mercy of the Queen. How could I have been so insolent, so careless of the difficulties of my new status? I waited for Philippa's judgment.

"Alice!" She laughed shakily. "Well, I was right in my choice. You are intrepid enough—more than enough if you will challenge my daughter. King's lover, indeed . . . What a magnificent defense you made for the King."

She did not despise me, or if she did, she hid it well. Tears glinted momentarily on her seamed cheeks until she wiped them away. "Have you courage enough to withstand the hostility of the Court?"

With shocking naïveté, I had not considered the answer to that question. "We will be discreet," I said with more confidence than I felt.

"I'm sure you will. But it cannot be kept secret forever. And Isabella will be your adversary. I'll keep her from doing too much damage, but she is willful. . . ."

"And Wykeham is no longer my friend." I sighed.

"Can you live with that?"

I thought about it, my anger ebbing as I stood at the foot of the Virgin, who would surely condemn us both for casting this marriage into adultery. What an impossible burden for me to shoulder. The King's love. The Queen's respect. And then the vilification from those who knew. The loss of Wykeham's regard. Did I have the courage? Whether I took little or much from Edward's generous hand, I would still be damned as the adulterous enemy. Not the King for his uncontrollable lust. Not Queen Philippa for her connivance worthy of a sinful daughter of Eve. Only I would be anathema.

I studied the serene painted face, but the Holy Mother gave me no guidance.

I had promised Isabella that I would take only what the King offered me. And so I would. But the possibilities were suddenly far beyond my imagining. Woven through this complex tapestry I saw the strand of my own future. It could be as strong as steel if I had the will and the boldness to make it so. It glinted gold in the weaving. I thought, if stitched with a clever hand, it could shine as bright as the sun at midday, or the stars in the Virgin's crown. On the other hand, Edward might fall out of desire for me within the week and take a different whore to his bed. I would once again be cast into the pool of insecurity.

I gave a little shrug. I must make sure that he did not. I was young, and not without resources, it seemed.

"What is it?" the Queen asked. "You were smiling."

"Was I? I did not know, my lady. But in answer to your question: It is yes," I said. "Yes, Your Majesty. I can live with it."

The Queen left me to offer up what prayers I might.

I came of age during that night and the day that followed. I stepped over the painful line from innocence to a hard-edged maturity. I was finished with being a young girl, the pet of the damsels, allowed to play and continue my youth. I played no more. And perhaps I regretted it.

I was the King's mistress: Philippa's damsel by day, Edward's lover by night. What a strange two-sided coin it was.

And every day I waited for the repercussions.

Wykeham might be furiously circumspect and stonily silent, but my anonymity must be compromised, even though whoever had initially informed Isabella had been effectively silenced.

For weeks it was as if I walked on the thinnest of thin ice, waiting with every step for it to give way beneath me to plunge me into a freezing torrent. I was summoned. I obeyed. Wykeham was always my escort. The Queen's health was always the excuse to take me from my room. But was our subterfuge not obvious? I could see the cracks radiating out from my feet every time I trod the same route in that first month.

And then the whispers began amongst the damsels. A slide of eye as I entered the solar. A comment that died away behind a flutter of fingers. It was nothing more than the faintest breath of scandal; the whispering remained barely audible, like the soft shiver of spring leaves in the forest canopy, as if it were known but agreed that it would not be spoken of. A strange conspiracy of silence: everyone knowing the truth of it, but no one prepared to unwrap the secret and lay my deceit open for all to see. No one challenged me to my face.

And why?

Not out of any respect for me. The silence was for Philippa. Such was the love she engendered that it was agreed she should not be told the despicable truth, that her youngest damsel lay naked in her husband's arms.

How unfair. How appallingly unjust! The situation hemmed me in and forced me to uphold the pretense that the Queen was as innocent and ignorant as she was believed to be. I was the guilty one. I had slithered my way into the King's bed like Eve's snake. For in all those weeks, I heard not one word of condemnation of Edward, as if it were acceptable that he, the King, would take a woman to his bed to replace his poor suffering wife. The King was beyond reproach.

Why Alice? they asked. I could read it in the slant of their glances. Why not choose someone better-born, more talented—someone beautiful—if lust itched at his loins? I was no longer their pampered pet, no longer clasped to their collective bosom.

"Are you made to suffer for this?" Edward demanded in his forth-right way. "Any man who maligns you will be dismissed."

How typical of a man. It was in the world of women, the cruelly gossiping henhouse of the solar, where I was held up for judgment.

"No one speaks ill of me," I replied.

I lied. I lied well. What point in telling him that the sharp dagger of ostracism was held to my breast all day, every day? It was not that he was uncaring, simply that no one dared whisper when the King was present.

At least my enemies took their lead from Isabella, whose demeanor toward me was rigidly polite, so icy that her stare could have frozen the Thames in August. So cold that it hurt.

It could not last. It was not in the nature of women, enclosed in the hothouse of solar politics, to tolerate a sin for long without a bite, a snap, a pinch. How publicly I was brought to book. In the manner of its doing, I would never forgive them for it. The occasion was a royal visit in November of 1363, when I had been Edward's lover for a little more than a month: a celebration of true splendor, when the rulers of France, Cyprus, and Scotland visited the English Court to be overawed by our magnificence. At a tournament at Smithfield, Edward would joust and lead one of the forays in the melee. At Edward's request, we were to attend with the Queen, clad in royal colors to support the symbolic victory of England over her enemies. We gathered in the audience chamber before making our procession to the ladies' gallery, a mass of silver and blue and sable fur, an eye-catching display of royal power as we damsels clustered around the Queen, who also shone in blue and silver with sapphires on her breast. A flutter of anticipation danced through the ranks.

Until the flutter of anticipation evolved into a rustle of shocked delight as I became the center of attention. As I knew I must.

The Queen's eye fell on me.

"Alice . . ."

I could have made my excuses and absented myself. I could have hidden, motivated by cowardice, by humiliation, for was that not the intent?

My enemy had misjudged me. I would not hide.

"Majesty." I curtsied. My skirts, as all could see, were not silver and blue and furred with sable.

"Why . . . ?" The Queen gestured toward my threadbare clothing, which I'd deliberately chosen. I wore the garments I had first arrived in and kept for no good reason, since I had had no intention of ever wearing them again. Worn and crude, stained and creased from their long sojourn in my coffer, now they clothed me from head to foot as a lowly servant in coarse russet. I stood out in the midst of this jeweled throng, a sparrow worming its scruffy way into a charm of goldfinches.

So! I had thrown down my gauntlet. Now I considered my reply most carefully. Did I state the blatant truth? The idea appealed to me as my temper roiled beneath the rough overgown of a conversa. Every one of the innocent-faced damsels would know it, so why not unroll it like a valuable bolt of velvet for all to gloat over? Or did I exert some subtle dissimulation? Subtle? How could I be subtle? How could I lie, when fury beat in my head like a blacksmith's hammer?

All I could see in my mind was the beautiful gown laid out for me on my bed, the most beautiful I had ever owned. The silk and damask was slashed and torn beyond repair, the fur edging ravaged. The veil was rent in half, the embroidered girdle cut in two. I had worked hard on it for so many weeks, but in the space of an hour someone had wielded a pair of shears with no skill and much vengeance. All my hard-worked stitching—when I had employed more patience than I had ever dreamed possible—entirely undone. Someone had delighted in taking out their hatred of me on Philippa's gift: The soft leather shoes with damask rosettes had entirely vanished. I could have wept when I saw the destruction, but those who shared my room would have enjoyed my grief far too much. For a moment I had stood and looked, swallowing the tears, moved not so much by this evidence of my isolation but by the disfigurement of so beautiful a thing. I heard a choked giggle that hardened my resolve. I carefully folded the ruined garment and veil and with fierce deliberation changed into the cheap fustian fit for a domestic drudge. If I could not wear the best, I would not compete with second-best. I made no attempt to hide what I had once been and what had been done to me.

Truth or dissembling? I looked 'round at the waiting faces, hearing the words in my mind.

One of your damsels disfigured my gown out of spite, Majesty.

Well, that would get me nowhere. I had no proof, only the evidence. I would merely look foolish.

"She cannot attend like that," Isabella observed when I had still not explained.

"No," the Queen agreed. "She cannot."

"I suppose there is a reason for the disobedience." I could hear the smile in Isabella's voice. Not that I thought she was the guilty one. Such a vendetta was beneath her, and she knew the Queen's wishes in this.

I raised my eyes to Philippa's face. "I am not willfully disobedient, Majesty."

Her face was serene, her eyes clear. "A misfortune, perhaps . . ."

She had thrown me a lifeline. "Yes, my lady. It was my own carelessness."

"And so great a carelessness that the gown is beyond wearing?"

"Yes, Majesty. The blame is mine."

I looked at no one but the Queen, praying that she would understand and allow me to retire without punishment.

"Carelessness is not one of your sins, Alice," she observed.

"Forgive me, my lady." I lowered my gaze to the silver-and-blue rosettes on the toes of her shoes.

"Alice . . ." I looked up to see the Queen nod briskly. "I understand.

Come with me. And you too, Isabella. We have time, I think. Half an hour ..."

I heard an exhalation around me. Disappointment, perhaps. But what a sense of exhilaration I felt. I had proved stronger than my enemies. I had shown that their hostility meant nothing to me. I would make no excuses; I would not retaliate; I would keep my own counsel. They would see that I had no fear of them. For the first time I learned the true power of self-control.

And that half hour demanded by the Queen?

A half hour was all that was needed to put in place a transformation. The Queen was soon disrobed of her blue and silver and furred gown. My own disreputable garments were stripped from me—I never saw them again—and Philippa's robes became mine. They were far too large, but with some robust lacing I kept them from falling off my shoulders.

Not a word was spoken other than instructions to breathe or lift or step out.

"Good!" The Queen, regal even in her shift, watched as her silver-edged veil and girdle were added to my ensemble. "Tell the King we will be ready in five minutes, Isabella." And when the Queen and I found ourselves alone together, she asked: "Will you tell me, Alice?"

"There is nothing to tell, my lady."

She did not press me but turned again to the matter at hand.

"Fetch the crimson and gold with the gold overrobe. And the gold veil and the ruby collar."

We returned to the audience chamber, where the atmosphere was thick with the waiting. There the Queen stood in our midst, glowing like a priceless ruby in the silver-and-blue setting of her damsels, whom she addressed with hard-eyed severity.

"We will honor the King today. It is my will. Alice is a loyal subject to both myself and His Majesty." She looked around at the suddenly bland faces. "I am displeased by the discourtesy to myself and those who serve me. I will not tolerate it."

Silence.

"Do you understand me?"

"Yes, Majesty." There was a hurried bending of the knee on all sides.

What an oblique little statement, saying little but acknowledging everything, and as clear as day to anyone with wit.

"Mistress Perrers will sit at my side at the tournament," the Queen continued with a flat stare. "Now, let us put in a belated appearance. It is always good for a woman to be a little late when a handsome man awaits her. Give me your arm, Mistress Perrers."

The tournament proved to be a superb exhibition of manly warfare, a triumphal celebration of my position at Edward's court. And what a contest he fought. If the visiting monarchs had any thoughts of the waning powers of England's King as he entered his fiftieth year, Edward dispelled them with his mastery of the art of combat.

I should have rejoiced, not least at my own victory, but the whole performance proved to be an edged sword for me. Jealousy is a terrible sin and a vicious companion: an animal that eats and claws and gives no quarter. Thus it attacked me throughout that glorious afternoon. I might be Edward's lover, but it was to Philippa that he looked, to Philippa that he gave the honors and the chivalric adoration. Not once did he single me out in my royal blue and silver, neither with look nor gesture. Edward accepted Philippa's scarf as his guerdon and wore it pinned to the sash over his body armor. He kissed Philippa's fingers and vowed to fight in her name. At the end, when he received the victor's prize and Philippa's loving salute, Edward spoke to her alone.

And I? I was woman enough to resent it. Why could he not speak to me? I was ashamed, bitterly remorseful of my envy, but unable to quell it. It assaulted me, as a grub burrows into the flesh of an apple, and I watched the tournament with a smile painted on my face, empty words on my lips, and anger in my heart that the King would take my body in private but not acknowledge me in public. I knew my thoughts were all awry, unfair to both Philippa and Edward, and to the role I had undertaken with my eyes open to the consequences, but still I raged inwardly.

I was simply one of the damsels to fetch and carry.

Until I was in Edward's bed that night.

"That was a good day's work." He stretched and sighed, pinning me effortlessly to the bed, his body slick and sated.

"Which part of it?" I responded primly, similarly replete, the monster of discontent temporarily laid to rest. I had not known that I could be prim, but I was discovering a multitude of skills to beguile a potent man. Edward had pleasured me with skill equal to that shown in the lists, and with far more subtlety.

"Mistress Alice, you have a mischievous tongue. There's life in the old dog yet." He turned his face into the curve of my breast, kissing the damp hollow where my heart still shivered with physical delight. "I can still fell a knight half my age with a lance and a good horse beneath me."

"And still reduce a woman to abject surrender . . ." I trailed a hand down his shoulder, pressing my palm against his ribs, feeling the answering solid beat.

"I thought I was the one to surrender."

"Perhaps you did. You deserved to be defeated by a woman after all your male pride today. Wykeham will surely lecture you on how sinful it is."

He rolled to hold my face between his hands so that I could not avoid his gaze, even if I had wished to. "My victory was for you too, Alice. Never doubt that."

"No, it was not." The green-eyed grub in the heart of the sweet apple was not quite dead. "You didn't think to ask for my guerdon, as I recall."

My tone was light but not altogether teasing, and he took me seriously, as he often did when I challenged him. "The thought was in my heart. This duplicity does not sit well with me."

I stifled a sigh and kissed him, allowing him the victory. Were we not both guilty of hypocrisy? "The Queen was the obvious choice as your lady, and you fought magnificently for her," I assured him. "You gave her great pleasure."

It was like executing a complicated dance step to which I was not accustomed, but, by God, my skills were improving. "The Queen dressed in red and gold to please you. To be the center of your vision and wish you victory."

"Rich colors always suited her." He smiled reflectively, and then his eyes focused, sparkling. "Now, you were perfect in silver and blue. And are even more perfect without any clothing at all . . ."

Edward's energies were prodigious.

As I was preparing to leave him, braving Wykeham's silent enmity, Edward cast a jeweled chain around my neck with careless generosity. He had worn it at the feast that had followed the tournament. I lifted the links in my hand as it lay on my breast, and stared at it.

"What's wrong?" Edward asked gruffly.

"You don't know?"

"No. I think it becomes you."

"I cannot accept this, Edward. I really can't!"

"Why not?"

"I thought you wished to be discreet." I took it off and placed it over his head so that it gleamed with far more power against the muscles of his own chest. "There's nothing discreet about it. The golden links would curb a horse, and the sapphires are the size of pigeon's eggs." He was not pleased, as I could see by the flare of his nostrils. I must have a care with his pride, but I must also safeguard my still-precarious position. A wise woman would not stir up more trouble than she needed. "Give me this instead," I said, and reached to where the Queen's scarf lay. And with it the brooch that had pinned the scarf to his sash.

"It is a small thing, Alice," he remonstrated, brows flattening ominously into a line. "Of no value."

"It is of great value," I purred persuasively, holding it on my palm. "You wore it in the thick of battle. I would like it for my own. And I can wear it without ostentation. See sense, Edward. How could I wear a chain like that without every finger at Court being pointed at me?"

Edward grunted his acquiescence. "Very well, madam. I'll be persuaded. But one day I'll give you what I choose."

"And one day I'll let you." And I knew that, at some distant point in the future, I would.

He pinned the simple jewel, a gold circle set with pinpoints of emeralds, to the linen of my shift, where it gleamed with a strange ostentation against the plain fabric. "This is not easy for you, is it?" It was not the first time he had asked the question. Nor was my reply any different.

"No. How would it be easy?"

"Am I selfish in demanding that you play this role?"

"Yes. But you are King. Are you not allowed to be selfish?"

He laughed, his humor restored, if a little wry.

I kept the brooch. Amongst the jewels that Philippa had given me it went unobserved. One day, as Edward had intimated, I would not be so discreet. One day I would not have need to be, but the obvious reason for this broke my heart. As long as the Queen lived, discretion must rule.

"Are you going to remain silent?" I demanded of Wykeham as he escorted me once more along the route I knew only too well. "You can't refuse to speak to me forever. When did you become so prudish?"

"When I perjured my soul in keeping the King's disgraceful secret," he responded without looking at me. "I'm leaving Havering to undertake some building at Windsor," he added through his teeth.

"I wager you'll find that more rewarding than associating with me."

"God's Wounds, I shall!"

"But I'll still be here when you return," I could not resist adding with a spark of naughty levity.

"I'll pray for a miracle that you are not!"

Wykeham went to Windsor to build a new tower. I missed him. I missed his severity and his honesty, but I no longer needed him as an escort, for I was given a room of my own, with freedom to make my own way to the royal accommodations. So my position was laid bare before the whole Court, yet the conspiracy of silence for Philippa's sake continued.

And when it did not?

"Whore!" hissed an ill-advised damsel when her moral indignation got the better of her good sense.

The result was a succinct audience with the Queen. Her possessions were packed, and she left Court within the day. I had enemies, but I had friends too, who were far more powerful. I still trod carefully, but with growing poise and confidence in every step. How would I not? Philippa's royal gown—all blue and silver and costly fur—was recut and restitched so that it fit me perfectly. I gloried in its possession.

Chapter Seven

Philippa was ill—a return of the old complaint that never entirely left her. I rubbed salve into the taut skin of Philippa's hands as gently as I could.

"You are sad, my lady," I observed. Not even lute music lifted her spirits.

"I feel the weight of every year of my life today."

She missed Edward. She missed his company and the unquestioning love in his face when he looked at her. With him she was once again the young girl—but without him she sank into gloom, and the hours dragged their feet. As if latching onto my thoughts she winced and pulled her hand away, suddenly petulant.

"Forgive me, my lady."

She shook her head. "I need to consider the arrangements. . . ."

"Arrangements, my lady?" She allowed me to scoop up more of the salve, leaves and petals of violets pounded into mutton fat, evil-smelling but good to relieve hot swellings.

"For my death."

My fingers hesitated before continuing their task. I had not realized the depth of her melancholy. "There is no need. . . ." I tried to soothe her.

"But there is. I need to prepare an effigy—for my tomb."

"You have many years, my lady."

"I do not. You know I don't." I looked up to find her dark eyes fixed on me, willing me to tell the truth. "You *know*! Don't lie to me, Alice," she whispered. "You of all people . . ."

And so I told her what I saw in her face, because I owed it to her. "I know, my lady. I'll not lie," I whispered back.

A slight smile touched her mouth. "I want my effigy to look like me, not some slim young girl—something I haven't been for too many years. If ever . . ."

"Then we shall arrange it," I said. "Tell me what you want me to do to help you."

Philippa released her hand from mine and placed it under my chin, lifting and turning my face to the oblique light from the window. She ran her thumb over the line of my jaw.

I remained perfectly still, the silk of my bodice barely stirring.

"Well?" she asked. Her hands dropped away as if she had been burned, and thus released, I met her gaze as fearlessly as I could. "There's a translucence about you, Alice. And a fullness in your face that I don't recall. . . ."

Still I said nothing. The Queen sighed, her eyes clouded with a mix of emotion. "I've carried twelve children, Alice. With some I've suffered. With some I've rejoiced. I know the signs. I'm right, am I not?"

"Yes, my lady."

"I suppose he does not know?"

"No. He does not."

Because I did not know how to tell him. It had been the one thought in my head since that morning, almost two months ago now, when my predicament forced me to my knees with an oath of despair when I vomited into the noxious depths of the garderobe, then staggered to slide down the wall when my knees trembled and gave way. The King, potent in all things, had got a child on me within three months of Edward's eye and Philippa's mind alighting on me.

I now saw my predicament reflected in Philippa's expression. Edward valued his image as the King who upheld all that was good and moral in England: a mirror for his people. Would he want a bastard foisted upon him by a hapless girl whom he had honored with his attentions? Before God, he would not. And Philippa? If I were the King's legal wife, I knew how I would react to his upstart mistress swelling before my eyes with the evidence of his bastard, forcing her mountainous belly on the attention of the Court. If I were Philippa, I would have the whore whipped from my sight. Conscious of how vulnerable I was, I saw my precarious future hanging in the balance as I sat back on my heels, the violet salve forgotten by both of us, and waited for the blow to fall.

Philippa considered me. When she spoke her voice was as hard as the pestle with which I had ground the tender violet petals. "Go and pack your belongings. I think it's time you left Court."

"Yes, Majesty."

Did she mean forever? Yet how could I blame her? How could she live with this terrible evidence of her husband's unfaithfulness burgeoning before her eyes? I swallowed against the rock of dismay that lodged itself in my throat.

"I'll arrange it."

"As you wish, my lady."

Disregarding the pain, the Queen pushed herself to her feet, her face a stone mask. "I wondered whether you might refuse to go."

And I bowed my head. "How can I? I am your damsel, my lady, and if you dismiss me, then I must go."

Her lips twisted. "I thought you would insist on begging Edward's tolerance. To remain here and give birth under the shocked gaze of the whole Court. When were you going to tell me?"

"When I had to."

"Did you think I would disapprove?"

"Yes." It was little more than a sigh.

Suddenly she stooped to seize my hand, her nails biting deep into my flesh. "Of course I do. I hate it. I despise what you have done! Do you think I wish to see you like this, knowing what you do with my husband? Sometimes I despise you too, Alice! Holy Virgin—I wish I had never set eyes on you. . . ." Her bosom swelled as she took a deep breath and forced a vestige of a smile to her lips. "And I despise even more that I cannot blame you—when it was all through my instigation." Releasing my hands, she turned her face away. "Get out. I don't want to look at you."

So I was dismissed from the Queen's presence.

"Will you tell the King, my lady?" I asked.

"I will tell him everything he needs to know."

I walked out of the Queen's chamber, my hand throbbing where her nails had scored me deep enough to draw blood.

The next morning, as dawn touched the sky, I left Havering. There was no one in the courtyard to bid me farewell or see me settled into the litter provided for me. Thus my departure was anonymous and unrecorded, much like my arrival. But then I had had Wykeham with me. Now Wykeham was at Windsor and Edward at Eltham, neither cognizant of the Queen's decision. The Queen would be on her knees in the chapel. There was no one. Isabella, if she had known, would have spat on my feet.

This was it. The end. Dismissed with a royal bastard child and nothing of my own other than the clothes in the saddlebags. The greater the distance I traveled, the bleaker my future became. All was so uncertain. And not least what Edward would say when he discovered my absence and the reason for it.

My thoughts drifted. Where were they taking me? Nothing had been said, and I had been too distraught at the speed and finality of it to ask. Was it to be the Abbey? The thought hit me like a pail of freezing water, drenching me from head to foot.

Not that! I won't go. Not again!

But where would I go instead? There was nowhere.

And even though I had always accepted that my good fortune was finite, on this journey I was forced to accept the truth of it. How terrifyingly reliant I was on this Plantagenet family, with all its pride and ruthlessness and complicated plotting. With the presence of this child under my heart, I meant nothing to them other than an embarrassment to be removed. I could do nothing but allow them to decide my future.

The hours passed, a knot of fear and anger building that I should have so little control over what would become of me and this child who suddenly became very precious to me. Greseley, I thought. I must write to him at the Tabard, demand that he release some moneys from my properties to pay for a permanent sanctuary for me. But as the second day of my journey drew to a close, the autumn sun golden, the shadows extending across the road, dappling the horses, my mind grasped what should have been obvious. I had traveled too far for my destination to be the Abbey, and when I had the wit to acknowledge the movement of the sun, I realized we were traveling west.

A shout came from my escort, and the hoofbeats of the horses slowed. Curious, I pulled back the curtains despite the evening chill, and thus caught my first glimpse of the place that was to be my home.

A manor house. A little stone-and-plaster house glowing in the final rays of the sun, the gates to the courtyard and stable block pushed back to allow my little entourage to enter. And there was my new household waiting for me on the threshold: a steward, a housekeeper, to one side two serving maids who bobbed curtsies, and emerging from the stables an ostler. That night the soft welcome of the manor of Ardington—one of Edward's own properties, as I was to learn—closed around me like the folds of a velvet cloak.

I was not content. Despite the comforts of my rural retreat, I had no serenity, neither of body nor soul. As my belly grew, my spirits declined in counterpoint. I was provided with a home and all my needs, even coin for my purse so that I would not feel without resources, but how long would that last? What would happen to me when the child was born?

In a strange way it was like an imprisonment. Although I had my freedom, I did not feel free to use it. Nothing disturbed my calm day-to-day existence. I did not travel or visit neighbors. There were books to occupy my mind, and out of boredom I sewed—how frustrated I must have been. I played my part in the running of the household, relieved that Mistress Lacey, the briskly efficient housekeeper, was tolerant of my sudden appearances in her kitchen and dairy. The world of the royal Court seemed to be as far away from me as the fabled land of Cathay. After less than a week in this haven, I accepted that I was not made for the unchanging tranquillity of rural life.

I did write—of course. To Greseley, urgency making me curt and demanding.

Master Greseley—I have need of immediate funds. What can you send me?

Only to receive an equally stark missive in reply.

I will send you a return at Michaelmas after harvest. Do not look for a vast sum. Trade is poor and your manor not yet thriving. My advice, Mistress Perrers, is to be prudent in your demands.

How infuriatingly cautious he was! So over all hung the terrible storm cloud of what I would do when the Queen's charity came to an end. When the King's lust died, or was lavished on another. Perhaps my successor already trod the corridors to Edward's arms. What value would I and my child be to him?

For in all that time, I received not one word from the King. No letter, no gift. Not even a visit from the priestly Wykeham to pray over my sinful head. Nothing. I thought I would find it hard to forgive Edward that.

I gave birth to my son with little difficulty, my young body resilient and tolerant of the pain. One moment I was sitting in the kitchen with Mistress Lacey, helping her to strip the sloes from their prickly stems for want of anything better to do, and the next my waters broke. Helped to my chamber by Mistress Lacey and visited by the local midwife, who declared me to be too much in a hurry, me and the child both, I held my child in my arms within the day.

What a stalwart child he was, with lungs like the blacksmith's bellows until I pressed his mouth against my breast, for I nursed him myself in those early days. I watched him feed with wonder. His hair was fair but I could see no likeness of Edward. His cheeks were round like crab apples, his nose showing nothing of an eagle's beak. Perhaps he would grow into the King's fine features. I prayed that the child, in all his innocence, would be more comely than I.

"You will become a knight and a famous soldier," I informed him, but he fell asleep, replete, his head heavy on my arm.

I loved him. He was mine. He was dependent on me, and I loved him.

But he was also the King's son. I knew what I must do, whatever the outcome.

Finding a long-disused pen, I wrote a letter. My pen hovered over the parchment. To Edward or Philippa? I would write to Philippa, one mother to another, even though it was supplicant to queen. My pen continued to hover, spiked with defiance.

Tell the King. Am I allowed to return to Court? What does the King think of his absent lover and her bastard?

None of those sentiments found their way to the parchment. I erred on the side of ridiculous brevity and discretion.

Majesty,
I am well and my child born. A son. I have called him John.
Your servant,
Alice

That was all I had to say. Then all I had to do was to sit and wait, discovering that patience was not in my nature at all. Holy Virgin, rescue me from this life of solitude and stagnation. In my blackest hours I imagined the Queen consigning my letter to the flames with a vicious pleasure. And who could blame her?

It was Edward who rescued me. And not before time. Edward was astride the familiar bay stallion beneath the arch, the sun gilding his face and bare head, and at his back was a body of gleaming horseflesh and soldiery with the flash of royal pennons and the glint of steel at hand and waist. How many months had it been since I had seen him? Six, I thought. Half a year of separation. And in that time, it seemed to my critical and not very friendly eye, he had grown older, a cobweb of fine lines etched beside mouth and eyes, a new austerity in his lean cheeks so that the eagle prow was keener.

Then he smiled when his eye lit on me where I stood in Mistress Lacey's garden, and I decided I was mistaken. Dismounting, Edward strode forward, covering the grass, as energetic as he ever was.

I did not curtsy. I did not smile.

"Alice! My dear girl. You look . . ." His words died and he gave a shout of laughter, so that a startled blackbird flew up from the branches above me. Despite my standing as stiff as a pikestaff with the child in my arms, his hands were on my shoulders, his lips on my cheeks and mouth. He did not see my anger.

"How do I look?" I demanded, when his kisses stopped. I knew how I looked. I kept no state here: clad in my oldest gown, my skirts tucked up, my sleeves rolled to my elbow, even my hair uncovered.

"Disgraceful!" he replied promptly. "Like a penniless country wench."

"I *am* a country wench."

"And this is your son." Releasing me, he lifted the child from my arms with remarkable aplomb.

"And yours too. I have called him John," I said, not thawing one inch.

"A good name. I couldn't think of better. A splendid name for so small and helpless a creature. He's no bigger than one of my alaunts' pups." He held him high, so that John's fussing became gurgles of joy. "He has the Plantagenet nose, I see."

"I can't see it."

"Then you must look more closely!" Edward lowered the infant, placing him gently back in his basket at my feet. He tilted his chin. He would have been a fool not to have picked up on my mood by now. "And what's biting you, Mistress Alice? You're as bad tempered as a squirrel in a trap."

"Nothing's biting me!" I would not allow his pleasure at seeing his son to win me over.

The King looked at me, obviously considering his next move with this ill-humored shrew. He brushed a tendril of hair from my forehead and a few crumbs of earth from my sleeve. And he grinned.

"Don't smile at me!"

"Why not?" But he became sober. "I know what burr's got under your saddle, mistress. You thought I should have come to see you before now. And that's the truth of it," he added when I opened my mouth to deny such childish petulance.

So I agreed. "Yes. How many months is it, Edward?"

"Too many. But listen. Look at me." He shook my sleeve to get my attention. "You have to accept—you are not always my first priority. I knew you were safe. I knew you were well cared for. I knew that you and your son were in health and lacked for nothing."

Still I would not accept. "Why did you not come?"

He pulled me to a bank of grass, where we sat. "Chiefly because the King of France is dead." Edward leaned forward, his forearms braced against his thighs, staring at the grass between his feet.

I knew something of this from my Court days: King John of France, defeated in battle and a prisoner in England until his ransom was paid by his penurious kingdom. A man of honor who waited out his days with good humor.

"He fell ill in March," Edward explained. "A month later he was dead. I returned his body to France. His son—King Charles the Fifth now—is reluctant to keep the truce of Brétigny between us. So that means war, God help us! I'm negotiating an alliance with King Pedro of Castile—I think we'll need him. No war yet, but the storm clouds are looming and I don't . . ." His words faded. Never had I seen him so lacking in assurance. Then he turned his head and looked up at me. "I am King, Alice. I can't put you before my duties. I must keep England safe. But I am here now, because I needed to see you and could put it off no longer."

My cold anger melted. Here was no apology but an explanation that I could understand. An explanation from a man who was King, who did not need to explain. And yet he had. I placed my hand on his arm.

"Will you stay?" I asked.

"I cannot."

"What is it this time?"

"What it always is. I have summoned Parliament. It is imperative that the Prince in Aquitaine receives enough finance to pursue his foreign policy. Imperative . . ." And I saw the line of worry dig deep again between Edward's brows. "I went out of my way to come here!"

"And I suppose that I, being less important than England, must forgive you."

I could feel him smile as he sat up and pressed his mouth against my hair. I had gone too far in my selfish displeasure, and I forgave him in my delight at seeing him again.

"Have you time for a cup of ale?" My question was gentle, and I touched his cheek.

"I have, and for a kiss from a woman who no longer stares at me as if I were a leper. And let me see my son again."

Barely an hour we spent together, seated in the garden amidst the herbs and bees. Then he was mounted, the royal escort drawn up in good array, but with one matter still uncertain for me. Was it deliberate policy that he had not spoken of it? I must know. . . .

"Do I return to Court, Sire? Does the Queen wish me to return as a *domicella*?"

"Can you doubt it?" His regard was quizzical. I did not think that he understood my concerns.

"Yes," I stated.

"She does, Alice. She has missed you."

Or was this Edward imposing his will on a reluctant Queen? "When?" I asked. "When will you send for me?'

Edward's eyes flashed, temper suddenly simmering close to the surface. "When I don't have the Commons baying at my heels about the rise in prices. It's like trying to legislate against the incoming tide. We're trying to determine what men of rank and no rank might or might not wear—fur or embroidery—or whether the commons should—" Impatience lay heavily on him, and frustration, as he bit off the words.

"What about John?" I asked with false sweetness. "What does your new law say that a bastard—even a royal one—is entitled to wear?" I knew my humor had an unpleasant edge, but what woman would not dislike being set aside for a discussion of sumptuary laws?

And the temper died, as I had intended. "By God, Alice! I miss you. I forget to laugh when you are not with me."

And I reached up to touch the lines beside his eyes, regretting their presence. "I miss making you laugh."

"Never doubt that I want you back at Court."

Then he was gone, leaving me with much to think about that was unsettling. Not so much my own circumstances, which were still far from certain in my eyes, but the events that were putting the King under so great a strain.

I returned to Court as circumspectly as I left. Who should be the first to cross my path, to grasp the chance to put me in my place, if for any reason I misread my strange status in the royal household, but Isabella, who was crossing the courtyard from chapel to hall—just as gloriously beautiful and as querulous as I recalled. And quite as extravagant: The gown on her back and the jewels at her throat would have ransomed King John himself back to France, if he were still alive. No change here. In my absence no one had managed to wed her and carry her off to nuptial bliss. I was sorry.

She changed direction like one of Edward's ships under full sail, and came to block my path as I climbed the steps.

"So you're back with us." Her lip curled.

I took a few more steps before I curtsied. I did it well. The steps gave me an advantage of height over her.

"We haven't missed you." She eyed me. "Your looks haven't improved—although your figure has, I expect."

Her smile was thin, her demeanor haughty. The ladies, a little knot of the Queen's damsels who accompanied her, did not try to hide their amusement at my expense. So this was to be the tone of my life if Isabella had her way, mocked and ridiculed and despised. But I had grown daring in my absence and by Edward's visit. I felt strong and would not be provoked. I stood my ground, waited. Sometimes there is strength in silence.

"Nothing to say, Mistress Perrers?" Isabella cooed. "That's unlike you! And where is the bastard? Does he look like my father? Or one of the scullions perhaps?"

A declaration of war. I was provoked, after all.

"Your brother is well cared for, my lady. In His Majesty's manor at Ardington."

I had left John behind. How difficult that was. But it was necessary, and Edward had established a nursery for him with his own servants, a nurse and governess. He would lack for nothing. I had kissed him and promised never to abandon him. Now I used my height advantage against the Princess, chin raised. "He is a true Plantagenet. His Majesty is much taken with him."

Isabella's nostrils flared. The damsels held their collective breath.

"Airs and graces, Mistress Perrers. How ambitious you are. What do you hope for? A title? A rich marriage on the back of my father's misplaced generosity?"

I replied without inflection. Oh, I was far surer of myself now. "I hope for nothing but respect and recognition for my services, my lady."

Anger lay bright on her, the jewels glinting at her sharp inhalation. Isabella opened her mouth to reply with a stream of invective, but we were disturbed, a group of courtiers entering the courtyard from the direction of the stable block. Loud and well satisfied after a vigorous hunt, the gentlemen bowed. I heard Isabella's little intake of breath, saw a stiffening in her spine as her attention was arrested, her expression softening. She smiled.

Duly interested, I observed the group to see who had been honored with the Princess's wayward admiration. Whoever it was, I doubted it would come to more than a passing flirtation. It would have to be a man of character to put a curb rein on Isabella. Had she not refused every suitor offered to her, a positive string of the highborn sons of Europe? I could see no response to her in this group of gentlemen, who were all more intent on the excitement of the kill. The courtiers moved off, the damsels following.

"Jesu! He's good to look at." She forgot who I was. Her eyes followed the departing figures.

"Who?"

"Him!"

At the door one of the knights looked back over his shoulder toward us, but then, with no more acknowledgment than a nod of his undoubtedly handsome head, followed the rest. He seemed to me to be very young.

"I don't know him."

"How should you?" Isabella's scowl was ferocious. She had remembered again. "You'd better go and remind the Queen of your existence. She has a new damsel since your departure. You may find you're not as indispensable as you'd like to think. Take care, Mistress Perrers!"

"I am always careful, my lady."

But her blow had struck home. My fears bloomed large again. At the royal whim, I and my son could be rendered destitute. I would never forget sitting in the parlor of the King's little manor at Ardington, wondering where I would be the next day, the next week. I was nothing, had nothing, without the goodwill of my lover and my lover's wife.

Isabella flounced off, while I caught up with the damsels to discover who had taken the Princess's fancy. Enguerrand de Coucy: one of the knights who had come to England in the retinue of the ill-fated King John of France during his captivity, and still here, unsure of his welcome if he returned to the land of his birth. Was he a suitable mate for Edward's daughter? I doubted it. But if she wed him and de Coucy succeeded in returning to France, taking his new wife with him . . .

I hoped Isabella achieved her heart's desire.

The Queen sat in her solar, her embroidery unstitched in her lap, as I sank to my knees before her, unable to look at her. A silence played out, ominous, full of presentiment.

"Alice."

"Yes, my lady." Nothing to read in that. Her embroidery slid to the floor. My fingers curled slowly into fists as I waited.

"You have returned."

"Yes, my lady." My knees quivered with the strain of kneeling, but I tensed my muscles to show no weakness.

"Where is the child?" Her voice was harsh, and I remembered how she had ordered me from her presence.

"At Ardington, my lady."

Then Philippa's hands were stretched to cup my cheeks. "Look at me! Oh, I have longed to see you, Alice!"

My eyes flew to her face, where tears tracked their silvered path.

"My lady . . ." It shocked me to see such overt grief.

"Forgive me," she whispered. "I was cruel. I know it—and it was not your fault, but I couldn't . . ." Her explanation dried. "You do understand, don't you?"

"Yes, my lady."

For of course I did. I kissed her distressingly swollen fingers, rescued the stitchery, and helped her to dry the tears, all as a good *domicella* should. She had aged in my absence, but still she could manage a watery smile that wrung my heart. And so I slid back into my place in Philippa's household as easily and smoothly as a trout into a cooking pot of boiling water. Philippa—kindly, suffering Philippa—kissed my cheek, asked after my son, gave me an embroidered robe for the babe, and presented me with a bolt of red silk for a new gown.

In private, Edward enfolded me in his arms and kissed me with Plantagenet fervor. "It has been a long time, Alice."

"But now I have returned to you."

"And you won't leave."

"Not unless you send me away."

"I'll not do that. I've been too long without you."

Too long. I had missed him more than I had thought possible. It was balm to my soul to be kissed and caressed and loved in Edward's bed.

Isabella left us. Isabella, headstrong and in love, flirted, flounced, cajoled de Coucy, and defied her father in equal measure. De Coucy looked unconvinced at his good fortune in becoming the apple of Isabella's eye, perhaps wishing he were elsewhere. To wed an English princess was one thing; to take on Isabella and her formidable father was quite another.

"He's too young, too unimportant," Edward said, refusing her first request.

"Why can't *you* do something useful!" Isabella snarled privately in my direction. "You have the use of much of my father's body! Surely you have his ear as well! Persuade him, for God's sake!"

It pleased me to refuse with profound grace, merely to ruffle her royal feathers. "I fear that I am unable to do that, my lady."

For the King, with or without my interference, would make his own decisions. And he did. Recognizing a lost cause, Edward clamped a tight hold on his true feelings about the match and gave de Coucy the title of Duke of Bedford, made him a knight of the Garter to tie him to English interests, and silently wished the Frenchman well of her. They were wed in the felicitous month of July at Windsor Castle, with all the pomp and splendor that Isabella could persuade her father to pay for. By November they had taken themselves off to France.

"I hope you are no longer here when I next visit," she said to me before she left. Marriage had not sweetened Isabella's tongue.

"I wouldn't wager Edward's magnificent wedding gift on it!" I could hide my insecurities with great finesse, or even coarse wagering, when I had to.

Isabella managed the ghost of a smile. "Neither would I. A lifetime's annuity and a king's ransom in jewels are not to be risked on a certainty. I might even miss your sharp tongue, Alice Perrers."

Well, well. Was this some manner of a compliment?

"I'll pray you don't breed any more bastards," the Princess added.

No. Her final sally was not friendly, but I might even miss her, I decided as the year slid toward its end. The Court lacked a vibrancy on her departure. For both Philippa and Edward, I gathered my resources to relight the flame.

The year of 1366: It would not be forgotten in a hurry. We had a bad winter, appallingly bad, to bring suffering and worry and grief to the Court as well as to the commons. A hard frost kept us shivering from September to April, curtailing most of Edward's attempts to set up a hunt, hurling him into an uncharacteristically somber mood. Philippa's joints ached beyond tolerance, so much so that she kept to her bed. The approach of her death kept her occupied more and more as the days passed. Isabella might have brought some light into her shadowed existence, but Isabella was embracing motherhood in France. Edward was little help to Philippa, wrapped in his own melancholy.

Through those difficult months I tried my best to woo Edward from his moody silences. Would he read? No. Would he have me read to him? No. Play chess or the foolishness of Nine Men's Morris? Would he take out the hawks on foot along the riverbank, even if it was too dangerous for the horses on the impacted ground? Would he don skates and take exercise on the Thames like the rest of the frustrated and icebound Court?

"Come and play." I smiled, hoping to engage him in some lighthearted companionship as the sun consented to put in an appearance. "You can leave these documents and give me some of your time."

"Go away, Alice," he growled. "I have too much on my trencher to be reading and skating!"

I knew when I was beaten. So I went. I learned to skate and laughed with delight. I was still young and enjoyed the exhilaration.

I lured Edward to his bed on the coldest days, but he was not to be roused. He might kiss me but his manhood refused to be enticed—his mind was far distant from me. I wrapped him in my arms and read to him from Geoffrey of Monmouth's fine book about the kings of England, selecting the tales of King Arthur—until he closed the book and refused to hear any more about heroes with magic swords. He took himself off to badger Wykeham for news of his latest building schemes. Even that interest was halfhearted.

I could not blame him and bore no grudges. Had I not learned my lesson, that I did not always come first with a man of such grave responsibilities? For the King had reason enough for the blackness that wrapped his soul like a shroud. My heart ached for him. For the Prince, his glorious son and heir, lord of Aquitaine, had persuaded Edward to finance a campaign to reinstate Pedro of Castile, who had been deposed by his subjects. A risky project in the depths of winter, as Edward was well and truly warned by Wykeham—invasion would be a grievous mistake—but, like the King of old, he grasped at the chance to be conqueror once more, forced a war budget through Parliament, raised an army, and handed authority over this invading force to another warlike son, John of Gaunt. He, together with the Prince invading from Aquitaine, would bring a solution to Castile's inheritance problems and glory to England.

"What do you think, Alice?" Edward asked as I sat at his feet before the fire in his chamber, although I think he did not care what I thought. He sipped gloomily from a cup of ale, and I sought for something to cheer him.

"I think you are the most powerful king in Christendom."

"Will England be victorious?"

"Of course."

"Will I still be seen as the man who holds the power in Europe in his fist?"

He raised his hand and clenched it, the tendons proud against the flesh. Age pressed particularly heavily on him that night. In the shadows the pale gold of his hair was entirely eclipsed by dull gray.

"Undoubtedly you will."

He smiled. "You are good for me, Alice."

I took the rigid fist, smoothed out the fingers between my own, and

kissed them, aware of my ignorance and deficiencies as king's counselor. What did I know of the state of England's authority over the sea?
Very little, but we were all to learn the truth over the coming weeks.

The King should have listened to Wykeham.

Our invading forces, beset by storms and gales and a shortage of
food, were reduced to a fifth of their original size, with no booty or
prisoners to compensate. Sitting in his chamber or pacing the halls of
Havering, Edward could do nothing to determine events except to rely
on his sons to uphold the English cause. Inactivity gnawed at him day
and night. Why did he not go himself, to lead as he once had done?
Because he too saw the waning of his powers. The future was with his
sons, and it hurt him, seeing the end of his glory. However hard I tried
through that winter, I could not heal the wounds for him.

As for English affairs in Ireland, they seemed likely to sink to their
death into the famous bog. Edward's son Lionel scrabbled at an impossible
settlement, reducing Edward to vicious oaths against his son's ineptitude.

Philippa despaired and wept.

And I? How did I fare? Did we, Edward and I, emerge from the
morass of black despair? Holy Virgin! It was balanced on a knife's
edge, and I could have lost everything, for we faced a crisis that was, I
admit, of my own deliberate making.

Frustrated with the cold rooms of Havering, in a fit of pique Edward departed to Eltham at the turn of the year, and at Philippa's in-
sistence we moved also, the whole Court, to be with Edward.

"You'll see," she fretted as her possessions were packed around her,
setting her teeth against the prospect of a painful journey in a litter,
however luxurious the cushions. "Eltham has more *space*. He feels
hemmed in here. And we must hear good news from Gascony soon.
We can't leave him to brood. It does him no good."

But, despite the new planned gardens and Edward's own pride in
the newly planted vineyard, Edward brooded in the spacious accommodations at Eltham as effectively as he had at Havering. He roared
through the halls and audience chambers, patient with no one except
Philippa, insisting on taking out the hounds, hard ground or no, snarl-
ing at the grooms when they were slow to deal with icy fingers and
frozen leather. He snarled at me too.

"Come with me," he snapped. "I want you with me!"

He kept me waiting, shivering in the cold outside the stables, while he listened to a report of a courier just ridden in. Only the week before he had given me a mantle of sables, wrapping my naked body in his gift in a moment of brittle good humor. I wore it now, but I might have been wearing the lightest of silk for all the good it did to keep me warm in the bitter wind.

"Let's go!" he ordered, his temper on as short a leash as the hounds. "What are you waiting for?"

"Her Majesty is not well, my lord. I should be with her." It was not quite an excuse. The journey to Eltham had stirred her joints to a new level of agony. Sleep for her was a distant memory without a draft of poppy.

"We'll be back before noon."

"Jesu! It's too cold for this," I murmured.

"Then don't come. I'll not force you." He swung up into the saddle. The courier's news had not pleased him.

For a moment I considered accepting his surly irritability and leaving him to his ill humor. Then perversely I joined the hunt. I regretted it, of course, returning with damp hems and frozen feet and mud-splattered skirts. My blood felt sluggish in my veins. Nor had the hunt been a success. We put up nothing for the hounds, everything of sense having gone to ground. We were frozen to the bone and Edward in no better mood.

He had spoken not one word to me—other than to "keep up, for God's sake"—when we galloped after a scent that proved to be as ephemeral as the King's good temper. Back at the palace, our steaming horses led away to the stables, I trailed after him as Edward stripped off gloves and hood and heavy cloak, thrusting them into my arms as he strode into the Great Hall as if I were his body servant. Without even a glance in my direction, he raised his hand, a royal summons, without courtesy.

Rebellion spiked my blood. Was this all I was to him, a servant to fetch and carry and obey unspoken orders? I halted, my arms full of muddy cloak. It was only when Edward had crossed the antechamber to the staircase leading up to the royal apartments that he realized my footsteps were not following him. He halted, spun 'round. Even at that distance I could see that his jaw was rigid.

"Alice . . . !"

I moved not one inch.

"What's wrong with you, girl?"

I considered what I should say. What would be wise? I thought briefly that it might be prudent to say nothing and simply follow. And promptly consigned wisdom to the fires of hell and remained exactly where I was.

"I'm cold. Don't just stand there." Edward was already mounting the stairs.

I abandoned prudence too.

"Is that all you can say?" I asked.

Edward froze, his eyes a steely glint. "I want you with me."

For a moment we were alone in the vast arching chamber. There was no one there to hear us. I raised my voice. I think I would have raised it if we had had an audience of hundreds.

"No!"

"I want a cup of wine."

And at the same echoing pitch I responded: "Which you are perfectly capable of pouring for yourself, Sire. Or you can summon one of your many pages or even a servant to do it for you. I will not."

Edward stared as if he could not believe what I had just said. Nor could I. I had been his mistress for three years, and never had I addressed him in this peremptory manner. But then, I had never had the need. I watched Edward's face, the range of emotion as he absorbed my words, their tone. Astonishment. Affronted arrogance. A strange despondency. And a fury that suffused his face with color. I trembled, and not from the damp skirts clinging to my legs.

Arrogance won. Edward's manner when he replied was as icy as my fingers. "Mistress Perrers! I want you with me!"

"No, Sire. You kept me waiting until my feet were well-nigh frozen to the cobbles. You did not care whether I hunted with you or not. You told me as much after dragging me from the Queen's side. I made my own decision to hunt, and I will make it again now. I will not go with you. I will wait on the Queen."

My blood was up and I held my breath. This was no childish temper. This was a deliberate ploy, and a dangerous one to rouse the sleeping Plantagenet lion. I saw anger flash bright in his face as my refusal struck home. It brought the King striding across the chamber until he towered over me. Holy Virgin! In that moment he was the King, not Edward. He grabbed my wrist, even as I still had my arms wrapped around his cloak, and held it tight, unaware of his strength.

"God's Blood, Alice!"

"God's Blood, Edward!" I mimicked.

The silence was heavy. Thick as blood. Threatening as a honed sword edge.

"You will obey me."

"Because you are the King?"

"Why else?"

My shivering increased but I held his gaze. "When did anyone ever deny you anything, Sire?"

"Never! Nor will you!" His fingers tightened still further, but I did not wince. "Do you question my authority?"

"Your *authority*?" I tilted my chin. My control was superb. "I don't question your *authority*, Sire, only your bloody arrogance." I bit down on a hiss of breath. "Do you intend to command my obedience through pain, Sire?"

"Pain . . . ?"

"Your royal fingers are digging into my flesh!"

He eased his grip but did not release me.

When I was seventeen and newly come to Court, I would have obeyed the King without question, wary of the repercussions. I did not feel of a mind to do so now. It was a gamble, and filled with jeopardy. He might dismiss me out of hand, order Philippa to dismiss me. But now I was the mother of his son. Now I had been his mistress for three years. Now I was a woman full-grown and I did not think he would dismiss me. I thought I had more power than that, and I thought I had earned the King's respect.

Well, we would see. I would gamble on that power and respect to wean Edward from his black mood.

"You would defy me, woman?" he roared. No respect here. I might just be wrong.

"Yes, when you are boorish and unreasonable, Sire. I've been away from the Queen's side all day. I am her damsel as well as your . . ." I allowed a little pause. "As well as your whore."

"By God, I order it! You'll come with me!" His hand fell away.

"By God, I won't!"

Even as rank astonishment ripped across Edward's features, I opened my arms to deposit his garments in a heap on the floor, at my feet and his. Then I let the sables slip from my shoulders to join them. And I stepped around him and climbed the stair, leaving him standing alone with the heap of costly fur and velvet cloth on the muddied tiles. A page entered at the far door. What Edward might have said if we had remained alone I had no idea. At the top of the staircase I looked back to see him, as unmoving as an oak, hands fisted on hips, looking after me, the garments still at his feet.

I waited until I was sure his attention was wholly mine. Then I made a magnificent curtsy. Again I pitched my voice so that he would surely hear.

"There are other palace whores who will be more than willing to keep you company, no matter how sour your humor, Sire. You can give her my sables. I make you free of them."

I did not wait to see if he would respond. Or if he picked up the garments.

I admitted to a terrible apprehension as I closed the door of my chamber behind me. I might have destroyed everything, and the terrible melancholy might still hold Edward imprisoned in its shackles.

I did not wait with an easy mind. The King made his displeasure felt. When he hunted I was not invited. When he visited the Queen, if I was present, he made a point of shunning me, gesturing without words for me to vacate the chamber. There was no question of my sharing his bed linen. I missed my sable mantle. The damsels gossiped, engrossed in our obvious estrangement. The Queen was anxious, but such was our relationship that we both kept our own counsel. Until the tension, colder indoors than out, became more than she could tolerate.

"Have you quarreled with the King, Alice?"

"No, my lady." It was not exactly a quarrel.

"Have you displeased him?"

"Yes, my lady." Definitely.

"He's very, very restless."

"Yes, my lady."

"Should you apologize, do you think?" Her broad brow creased in concern.

"No, my lady."

So the Queen abandoned any attempt at reconciliation, and I waited with increasing anxiety. He was the King, after all, and I was nobody. I had risked all and must pray that I had not staked my future ill-advisedly.

It took a sennight.

I was combing my hair in preparation to sleep alone when a soft knock sounded on the door. Wykeham, I thought. Carrying a message from the King to attend his pleasure. I opened the door, the refusal leaping to my lips.

"I will not. . . ." The words dried.

Edward. He had come himself. And over his arm lay the glossy pelts of my mantle.

"My lord!"

I curtsied low on the threshold, hiding my face. The King had come to my room. Was this to be the dismissal I had feared, the sables a final gift to mark my ignominious departure? If I looked at him, what would I see? I raised my eyes to his—better to know immediately—but Edward, master of negotiation, was giving nothing away. If it was dismissal, it would be done in cold blood, not in the heat of passion at my lack of respect.

"Well, will you let me come in?" His voice was rough. "I don't think the King should be expected more than once in his lifetime to conduct an intimate argument in a public space for all his subjects to see and hear."

I stood back, pushing the door wide, but still for all his impatience, he did not step across the threshold. Instead he held out the mantle.

"This is yours, Mistress Perrers."

I took it from him, tossing it over a coffer beside me as if I did not care.

"I was wrong, mistress. I treated you with unforgivable discourtesy."

He was excruciatingly formal. As long as I did not waver . . . I remained mute.

"I'm here to ask your forgiveness." It was still more of an order than a plea.

"It is easy for the King to be uncivil and demand to be forgiven," I said.

"I don't demand."

"No?" I folded my arms in an uncompromising manner.

"Mistress Perrers . . ." Now he stepped in and thrust the door closed at his back. "You will doubtless accuse me of overbearing pride, but I really don't want an audience for this!" And he sank elegantly to one knee. "I ask your compassion for my lack of chivalry. No true knight would have been as . . . boorish . . . as I was. Will you forgive me?"

I angled my chin, considering. He looked magnificent, like a knight from one of the illustrated books, kneeling in a blaze of blue and red and gold at the feet of his lady. He'd dressed deliberately, regally, to impress me. Here was the King of England kneeling at my feet. What was more, he possessed himself of my hand and kissed it.

"No subject has ever challenged me before."

"I know."

"Well? Will you keep your King in suspense?" His expression was not that of a lover. The lines of irritation sharpened. "I have missed you more than I should. You're only a slip of a girl! How could I miss you so much? And all you could do was scowl at me from the ranks of my wife's damned women, or behave as if I did not exist."

"Until you dismissed me from the room."

"Well—I should not have done that."

"No. And I am not a slip of a girl. I am the mother of your son."

"I know. Alice . . ." The formality was waning.

"Nor am I merely your whore. I give you more than the pleasures of the flesh. I thought you cared more for me than that, Sire."

"I do. God's Blood, Alice. Have mercy! I was in the wrong."

"We both agree on that."

He released my hand and, still kneeling, spread his arms wide. "I have learned this for you, as any foolish troubadour would to woo his lady. How's that for love . . ."

And he pressed his hands over his heart like a lovelorn troubadour and spoke the verse. The words were ridiculous, foolish, but there was no mockery in his voice or his face. The sentiment came from his heart, and with it a sadness, a poignancy for things past. Like youth that was gone forever.

Fortune used to smile on me:
I didn't have to try:
Good looks and charming manners
Were mine in full supply:
She crowned my head with laurels,
And set me up on high. . . .
But now my youth has faded;
I've seen the petals fall. . . .

He stopped. "To hell with verses! My looks are fading and my manners have been less than charming. I have no excuse for either, but I beg your understanding."

"A Plantagenet, begging?"

"There's a first time for everything!" The poignancy was gone. Back was the pride, the authority, even though he still knelt. I swallowed my sudden tears. I was indeed charmed. "Don't leave me in suspense, Mistress Perrers."

"I would not dare! I have made my decision, Sire." What mischief prompted me to keep him in suspense for one more moment? I touched his shoulder, with all the grace of the lady in receipt of her knight's love, to urge him to his feet.

"Well?"

"I forgive you. It is impossible to reject so fine a wooing."

"Thank God!"

He drew me into his arms, carefully, as if I were some precious object made of glass. Or as if I might still reject him. His lips were cool against mine until I melted against him, and then his embrace became a brand of fire. I had missed him too.

"It's in my mind to give you a gift . . . perhaps a jewel. . . . You have given me a son, a gift beyond price. I should show my gratitude. . . ." His chin rested on the crown of my head, my hair heavy on his shoulder.

"No . . . not a jewel."

"What, then?"

The thought had come immediately into my head. I knew what I wanted. "Give me land and a house, Sire." My insecurities never left me, and Greseley had trained me well.

"You want land?" His chin lifted and I heard the surprise in his voice.

"Yes. It is in your power to give it."

"You would be a woman of property. Then it's yours. For Mistress Alice, who shines a light into the dark corners of my soul."

It took my breath away. "Thank you, Sire."

"On one condition . . ."

I was suddenly wary. It never did to underestimate a Plantagenct.

"That you call me Edward again. I've missed that."

The rock beneath my heart, which had been there since the day I dropped my sables at his feet, melted away. "Thank you, Edward."

There was love and gratitude in the giving of the gift, and in my receiving it. I offered my lips, my hands, my body. All my loyalty. My absence had stirred Edward's passions, and he had no thought of celibacy. He made love to me on my less-than-sumptuous bed that could barely contain his long limbs, and wrapped me again in my sable mantle. I was no longer just his whore. We both knew it. My challenge had awakened the King to the truth of our relationship. Here was a permanence.

"I will never dismiss you," he murmured against my throat in the dying of passion and with touching insight. "You are my love. Until death separates us."

"And I will never willingly leave you," I replied. I meant every word of it. My respect and admiration for him had reached new heights.

He gave me the little manor of Ardington for my own.

I carried a second child for Edward. Another son, Nicholas. A happy event. I was free to travel now as I wished to the manor, where John grew and played and shouted in his games of knightly conquest. I had no fears that I would not be free to return to Court as it pleased me. My position might still be unacknowledged, but it possessed a strange viability of its own.

"And what will become of you?" I asked the mewling infant who resembled Edward far more strongly than did his brother, John. "What will be your path to wealth and power?" I thought of Wykeham, an excellent example for any boy.

"When you are older, I will introduce you to a man who I can sometimes claim as a good friend."

"What do I give you in recognition of this new gift?" Edward asked later, holding his son in his arms. "Don't tell me. . . ."

Nor did I have to.

He gave me the wardship of the lands of Robert de Tilliol and the gift of the marriage of his heir. It was extensive, four manors and a castle far to the north of England, with the promise of gold for my coffers.

As gifts from the King to a queen's damsel, these were out of the ordinary. They began to draw attention, but I could withstand the sidelong glances. I simply informed Greseley that his management on my behalf would take more of his valuable time.

I trust you will pay me well for my time, Mistress Perrers, he wrote back in habitual complaint.

I will pay you when I see the results, I replied, then added, *I will be astonished if you too do not benefit from these investments.*

To receive back very promptly: *As do you, Mistress Perrers. Your acquisitions are bringing you—and me—an excellent return.*

I smiled at his final response. What an exceptional man of business Greseley was.

Chapter Eight

A sense of unease touched my spine, like the light scratch of a lover's fingernail on delicate skin. I shivered, every sense alert. Then, since there was no repetition, I concentrated once more on the explosion of ill temper unfolding before me.

This was a high-powered, formal reception, deliberately staged: King and Queen seated in carved chairs on the dais in the largest of the audience chambers at Westminster. Before them swaggered a young man, just entering his third decade, boldly clad with all the éclat of indulged youth. Despite his shining arrogance he bowed deeply, his entourage following suit. And what an impressive escort it was, weapons as visible as the jewels and embellished tunics. Philippa beamed, but the King was not in a mood to admire.

"Why are you here?" he demanded.

"I can do no more in that godforsaken, bog-ridden province." The young man was not rebuffed by the King's displeasure. Undeniably handsome, he had a hardness, a carefully shuttered expression, and a shocking lack of reverence. "I wash my hands of Ireland and all to do with the bloody Irish."

"Wash your hands? You young fool! Did you think it would be an easy task? What in God's name have you been doing?" Edward strode down from the dais to strike the young courtier on the shoulder, a punch of a fist, not entirely a sign of affection. "Are you trying to destroy all my good work in that damned province by leaving as soon as you meet opposition? Before God, Lionel . . . !"

So this was Lionel, Edward's second son to survive the rigors of childhood. Handsome, stylish, ambitious, and King's Lieutenant of Ireland for the past handful of years, he possessed an abundance of charm, so smooth and slick as to be like a coating of goose grease on the chest of a sniveling child. Still, his unwarranted return had brought a flutter of excitement to stir the dark days of the Court. At least Lionel, newly made Earl of Clarence in Edward's birthday generosity, had brought a smile back to the Queen's face. For that I could look on him with more favor than I was at first inclined.

"That's unfair, Sire! I met opposition from the first day I set foot there!"

"I've a good mind to send you back as soon as you can saddle a fresh horse. . . ."

"No, Edward . . . No!" Philippa could not stand. It was a bad day for her. "He is our son!"

"And a thorn in my flesh! No son of mine would have abandoned his charge. We'll have the whole place up in arms before we can sneeze."

"I see no cause for the peasants to object. . . ." Lionel's voice had acquired an unpleasant whine.

"Of course they will object!" Edward continued to stand eye to eye with him. "Your job was to keep the peace, not stir the hornets' nest!"

"Oh, Lionel . . ." The Queen stretched out her hands.

The young man promptly evaded his father and fell to his knees before the Queen, where he bowed his head in unctuous regret. "Mother. Forgive me. . . ."

"My dearest Lionel."

"I can explain. . . ."

"I'm sure there were reasons. . . ."

"But will my father listen?" He angled a sly glance from his mother's face toward the King. As for the rest of us, we might not have existed in this complex throwing down of a family gauntlet.

Ah . . . !

The chill, that same strange sensation of awareness, brushed along my spine again. And again I shivered, an unpleasant prickle of cold on nape and arm. It fluttered over my skin, strong enough that it was almost a knowledge. Someone in this room was taking note of me, watching me. Someone had more than a passing interest in me. I looked around, over the men of Lionel's entourage, but nothing came to snatch at my interest. I could see no face turned toward me. All were intent on the standoff between king and errant son. And why should anyone single me out? Here I was simply one of the damsels, anonymous, faceless, to serve and support the Queen.

Yet the feeling remained. Someone had an eye for me.

"Your father will listen," Philippa urged, soothed. "But not now. Later. When we have celebrated your homecoming. Five years—it's five years since I saw you last." Her face was luminous with maternal delight.

Edward expressed as little delight as he had admiration, but he exhaled on a grunt. "I suppose the recriminations can wait. Your mother's glad to see you. You need some lessons in managing a difficult province—not everything can be solved with a show of force and sharp-toothed legislation. It needs . . ." He closed his teeth on what was about to become a lecture in high politics. "But we'll feast your return first."

He gave the signal for the audience to end. As I began to help the Queen to her feet, I felt that same scrutiny, as if it were stripping away my skin to peer into my soul. But only Wykeham was interested in my soul, and he was still constructing battlements at Windsor. Quickly I looked up, around, determined to catch the culprit who dared to stare at me—and there he was. One of Lionel's coterie, he pinned his gaze on me in a vulgar stare.

I refused to return the contact. I would not be intimidated. I allowed my gaze to rove innocently over the ranks as if I sought someone I knew. And all the time I was aware that his gleaming appraisal did not waver.

Who was he?

How dared he!

So be it. Without pretense, I returned his regard, stare for stare.

He was a bold man, for sure. He neither looked away nor smiled in apology. He was older than the Prince but by no more than ten years, to my assessment. He had a harsh face, but was not unattractive—if it were not for the saturnine lines drawn from nose to mouth. No, he was not a handsome man. Clean shaven, I noted, not the usual fashion of the day, and his dark hair closer cropped than the prevailing mode. His eyes were unremarkable in color, dark rather than light, but direct and with no embarrassment at being detected staring at one of the Queen's damsels. His jaw was disfigured by a faint scar that showed white against skin ruddy from recent campaigning. His clothes were of fine quality but functional, as was his sword, a good steel blade without decoration. As for the jewels of a courtier, alone of all the company he wore none, but I did not think that he lacked the means, rather the inclination. His mouth was set in an uncompromising line. I imagined he gave away no secrets—unless he wished to.

He was a soldier rather than a courtier, I decided. And no, I did not know him.

I lifted my brows, forcing him into a reaction, and he made a curt little inclination of his head. It pleased me to give no acknowledgment whatsoever; I turned my back on him to take the Queen's missal into safekeeping as she made her slow progress to her rooms, Lionel beside her. I followed, feeling that stare continuing to stab between my shoulder blades until we had left the room.

Well! I did not like Lionel overmuch. I liked even less this man in Lionel's company who had had the impudence to single me out. He had too many dark corners for my liking.

In regal style, the King ordered a celebration. Edward reveled in celebrations. It was his delight to glory in splendor in which he could play the central role. Was there ever a king to match him, one who could prance and flap with supreme confidence in the gilded costume of a gigantic bird, purely for the entertainment of his children? But not on this occasion. This was a feast with a scant nod in the direction of music and dancing but little else: barely enough of a spectacle to drain the contempt for Lionel's failures in Ireland from Edward's face. Ed-

ward handed a purse of coin to Andrew Claroncel, his favorite min-
strel, to end the singing barely before it had begun. All in all it promised
to be a long evening. I took my seat below the high table with a sharp
glance at the man who had been placed beside me on my right.

My companion for the feast was the insolent man from the audience
chamber. And I would have wagered my sables that it was no coinci-
dence he had the stool next to me. How had he achieved that? A bribe
passed smoothly into the palm of Edward's steward? His eyes that
raked my face—dark gray, I noted now at far too close quarters—were
as audacious as I had first thought.

"Mistress Perrers."

He stood until I had taken my seat, and it pleased me to make him
wait, shaking out my skirts and disposing them elegantly. And wait he did,
forcing me to admit that his manners were excellent. With a bland courtesy and a neat bow he finally sat, his actions brisk and controlled, but with
a surprising elegance. So he had not spent all his life in the saddle; he
had absorbed some of the skills of the courtier, even in Ireland.

"You know my name, sir." I met his open appraisal with studied
disinterest. "How is that?"

"You are not unknown at Court, mistress." His voice was smoother
than I had expected, and his reply interestingly enigmatic. I thought he
masked the full truth. "You are even spoken of in Ireland," he added.

So he hoped I would ask what was said of me. I would not. I picked
up my cup and drank from it.

"What I *don't* know," he pursued, imperturbable, "is what is your
family?"

And I remembered, the past suddenly stark and bleak in my mind.
The gossip of my infancy. The abandoned child. The bastard of a
whore and a common peasant. The purse of gold coins that might or
might not have ever existed. And I shrugged. None of it mattered now.
But I resented his stirring of the memories.

"I have no family," I remarked.

And I turned my back, leaning over to exchange views with an elderly knight who sat on my left. It was astonishing, the range of topics
I could find to discuss with this aging soldier, who looked askance at
me and showed more interest in his food. I sighed, weary of his mono-

syllabic responses. And was unwise enough to glance in my silent companion's direction. He was watching me with rare humor.

"Well?" I should not have responded, but I did.

"Have you finished at last?" he asked, showing his teeth in a smile that made me instantly wary. "I would not have believed your conversation could be so fatally dull, lady. Sir Ralph must have fallen asleep with the excitement of it. Even I could find it difficult to be enthusiastic about the length of time it takes the Court to transport itself from Havering to the Tower of London!"

"At least I had the good manners to talk to my neighbor, sir," I retaliated. "You have failed lamentably." He had not exchanged one word with the damsel on his other side.

How did I know? Well, I had listened, hadn't I?

"I thought you might wish to know my name," he remarked inconsequentially.

"Not particularly. But since we are trapped here together for the length of this meal . . . Who are you?" I could not resist after all. Oh, I knew who he was well enough—I had used my time effectively between audience and feast—but it would not hurt to dent his male pride. "Since you know *my* name, sir, it would be only common courtesy to tell me *yours*. And since you arranged to sit beside me . . ."

With a glint of appreciation in his eye, he waited until a page had refilled both our cups with a smooth Bordeaux. He sipped slowly before placing the cup at his elbow. He would make me wait too. I might have smiled, but did not, suspecting that this man would be quick to detect weaknesses in friend and enemy alike, and be even quicker to make use of them. So far I had no idea into which category I fell.

"I am William de Windsor, madam."

I gave an impertinent lift of my shoulder, a gesture I had watched Isabella employ with finesse.

He was unimpressed. "I have worked in Ireland, for the Earl of Clarence."

Which told me no more than I already knew. He was looking at me, still smiling, and to my discomfort I found that my blood flowed warmly into my face.

"Why were you staring at me?" I asked.

"I find you interesting."

"Interesting? You make me sound like a new battle plan!"

"I think we are very alike, madam."

"Are we? I don't see it, William de Windsor. You are far prettier than I."

That took him aback. He gave a bark of a laugh. "And you are more forthright than I had anticipated. An unusual trait in a woman. In my experience women usually dissemble."

"I do not." I imagined that his experience with women was as wide as the Thames at Tilbury. "Tell me why we are alike."

"Oh, I don't think I will. Not yet." He raised his cup in a little toast.

And I turned back to make another dull stab at conversation with Sir Ralph, as if Windsor's reply did not engage my interest. But it did. He knew it did. He waited until my knight buried himself in his platter of roast venison, and picked up the conversation as if there had been no hiatus.

"I've changed my mind, Mistress Perrers. You are a woman worthy of my confidence, so I'll tell you the manner of our similarity. We are both ambitious."

I stared at him.

"We are both self-interested."

Again I kept my counsel, watching him over the rim of my cup.

"We both come from nothing."

I would not respond. What was this man implying?

"Have you not one acerbic comment to make to my observations, Mistress Perrers?"

"Do we both come from nothing, sir?"

"In the order of things, yes, we do. My father was a minor knight who made no name for himself in his long life. Windsor of Greyrigg, a poor backwater in Westmoreland with nothing to recommend it but sheep and rain. I abandoned Greyrigg as fast as I could and became a soldier, as any ambitious lad would. Fame, fortune, wealth—that's what I wanted, and that's what I got. I fought at Poitiers and made a name for myself. In recent years I have attached my star to Lionel. He may not be perfect, but I consider him to be the most able of the royal brood." I found myself laughing at so flagrant a criticism, regardless of who might be listening, as Windsor's eyes shifted to where Lionel sat next to the Queen, entertaining her with wit and sparkle. Then he came back to me.

"We have both made our way in the world. You as a damsel to the Queen"—his remarkable lack of expression told me that he knew exactly the nature of my relationship with the King—"and I as one of Lionel's counselors."

"And this is of interest to me, Sir William, because . . . ?"

He frowned. "I'm not sure, if truth be told. But for some reason I feel our stars might rise together."

Now, that intrigued me, but I raised my brows in some species of mild interest.

"My skills are in fighting and hardheaded administration," he pursued without self-deprecation. "What are yours? How bright will your star shine?"

I flushed. The implication was obvious, his stare as sharp-pointed as Master Humphrey's boning knife, but I refused to be needled into indiscretion. "I think my star shines very brightly without your intervention, sir."

"Not as bright or as fast as mine, mistress. Military service allows an able and ambitious man to build up a goodly fortune."

"Through embezzlement, corruption, ransom money, and loot?" I had done more than a little investigating of my own.

He laughed, a cheerful note above the noise of the roisterers, causing a few eyes to turn in our direction. "You have been gossiping, Mistress Perrers."

"I have, Sir William."

"And you knew my name from the first."

"Of course."

"Well, I can't blame you for it. It's a wise man who knows who he deals with."

"And, undoubtedly, a wise woman." I leaned a little closer to murmur in his ear, "But I will not deal with you."

He took the time to carve through a collop of beef, offering me some choice cuts from the platter. I shook my head.

"What do you want, Mistress Perrers?"

"I don't take your meaning, sir."

"Well, I'm not speaking of the choice between the venison or the beef—the beef's excellent, by the by; you should try some. If you are a woman of good sense—and I think you are—you should consider where you will be in ten years. It's not a life position that you hold, is it? I'd say you could add up the years left to you at Court on the fingers of your two exceptionally capable hands. Life is finite, is it not?"

And because I understood him perfectly, and it was not the length of my life he was discussing, I followed his eye to where the King sat, leaning back in his chair, listening to Lionel make his excuses. Edward looked well and at ease, but the creep of age was relentless. As for Philippa, her life hung by a fraying thread. William de Windsor was right, damn him. I had no security of tenure here.

And had I not known it from the very beginning? The fear that was always present in me began to stir into life again, dull and nagging like the pain from a bad tooth.

"He'll not last forever, Mistress Perrers. What's for you then?"

My breath caught at this outrage, fear ousted by anger that this man should read my thoughts. "What is it to you?" I snapped. "You're remarkably well-informed in Ireland." A knot of resentment made my tone hostile.

He was oblivious to it. "It pays to be so if you wish to make your way in life."

"Some would say you've done quite well enough for a man of little consequence."

"Oh, no. They would be wrong. My foot is barely on the ladder. I'll climb higher yet."

Such arrogance! I was right in my first assessment: I did not like William de Windsor. I studied Edward, remembering his reaction to Lionel's mishandling of Ireland, recalling the disdain that flattened his fine features as he had cast an eye over Lionel's minions. It gave me pleasure to turn the blade in Windsor's gut.

"I think you're wrong, sir. The King does not like you."

"He may not like me but he needs me."

I choked on a sip of wine. Would nothing put him down? "To do what?"

"To handle Ireland. It's not a task for a squeamish man. The King trusts my decisions. He may not like them, but still he'll send me back to Ireland with even more power than I had under Lionel."

"You are so sure of yourself!" I mocked.

"Am I not," he replied, cheerfully unrepentant. "And uncommonly perceptive. Take heed of my advice, Mistress Alice! Look to your future!"

And after that unwarranted familiarity, for the rest of the meal he gave his attention to the damsel on his other side, presenting me with a view of his perfect silk-covered shoulders, leaving me to the mercy of Sir Ralph, who gobbled the meat and bread as if the meal were his last. I yawned with boredom, until the trestles were cleared. William de Windsor waited for me as I stood to leave the chamber.

"Will you take some more wise advice, Mistress Perrers?"

"I doubt it." I was ruffled, intrigued beyond good sense, and in no mood to be wooed by this wolf that did not even bother to adopt sheep's clothing.

"Who is your enemy? And don't say you have none."

"You, probably."

"I'm no enemy of yours, Mistress Perrers! Think of some others who would do you ill."

"And if I do?"

"Be aware. Be cleverer than your enemy. That's the best advice I can offer. And if you ever need help to keep that enemy at bay, I am your servant. Don't let your unaccountable animosity toward me sway you." He bowed and kissed my hand, even as I felt an urge to snatch it from him. "And no, you are not pretty. But before God, you are the most striking woman of my acquaintance. How old are you?"

Holy Virgin! "I am twenty-two years. And how old are you, sir?"

"Thirty-seven!" he replied promptly.

"And are you wed, sir?" I asked sweetly, on impulse, while his fingers enclosed mine, warm and firm.

"Why?" He cocked a brow.

"I wondered whether you had a son to inherit this great wealth you see yourself earning."

"No. I have not. I am not wed."

"Good. Or I would have to pity the poor lady you took to wife."
His grin was sharp and uncomfortably attractive.

I remembered nothing of what I ate at that meal. The minstrels might as well not have opened their mouths for all the notice I took.

My exchange with William de Windsor at Lionel's feast was, it appeared, damnably on display, and I wished it undone. Not because I said or did anything amiss. On the contrary, I had guarded my tongue in the presence of this knight I considered to be more than dangerous. But I found that my reactions to him were unstable. I had no wish to talk about him.

"What did that rogue Windsor have to say to you?" Eagle-eyed as ever for who said what to whom, Edward lost no time in interrogation, his growled demand taking precedence over any loverlike endearments when I sat in the middle of his bed. Perhaps there was more than a dash of jealousy in his unsubtle demand. The Plantagenet had an eye to his own.

"Nothing," I replied, hands folded neatly in my lap. "Nothing that was not to puff up his own self-aggrandizement. The man speaks of no one but himself." Not quite true, but close enough.

"Hmm." Edward's brow furrowed in familiar disquiet. He began to loose my hair from its neat braids, although I thought his mind was not on the pleasures of the flesh. Windsor had even infiltrated the royal bedchamber. Edward tugged persuasively against my hair. "What do you make of him?"

"I don't like him."

"Nor do I. Would he be honest in government, d'you think?"

"I doubt it."

Edward grunted a laugh. "Well, that's plain enough. Would he be loyal to me?"

"Yes, if it brought him money and power." Which was as honest as I could be.

"You seem to have read the man in some depth in so short a time." The frown was back, now turned on me.

"It wasn't difficult." I smiled disingenuously. "A more boastful man

I have yet to meet. He thinks you will make use of him—send him back to Ireland." The frown deepened, so I turned my head to plant a kiss on his hands where they were wound into my hair. "Will you use him?"

"I'm not sure. I think he's got a chancy kick in his gallop."

So did I, and perhaps not for the same reasons.

Wykeham, returned to Court on the occasion of the feast, was less than polite. Our steps fell into line after Mass the next morning. He had not officiated but stood toward the back of the small body of courtiers. I had noticed him when I had glanced over my shoulder to see whether Windsor was present. My lips curled in high-minded satisfaction as I noted that he was not. But Wykeham was there. And he had waited for me by design.

"I see Windsor has singled you out," he stated without preamble.

"It is good to see you again too, Wykeham," I remarked. "Perhaps you are even pleased to see me?" Wykeham had achieved a remarkable elevation: Bishop of Winchester and Lord High Chancellor of England—high indeed for a man whose main interest was the supreme angle of a buttress to prevent a castle wall from collapsing on hapless soldiery. For his impertinence, it pleased me to needle him a little. "Or are you now too important to take note of one such as I?"

"It's always an experience, mistress, to converse with you." Wykeham refused to acknowledge my pert jibe. "Why do you think Windsor is sniffing 'round your heels?"

"Is he?" I sighed. "I have no idea."

"I'll tell you why. To get the ear of the King."

"Then he won't succeed. I'm no friend of Windsor's. Do you consider me gullible, to be flattered and taken in by every ambitious office seeker?"

I stared at him, hoping for an apology. There was no apology from the King's new Chancellor.

"I consider that you lack experience when dealing with a man of his mettle," Wykeham announced, pausing between every word, the echoing thud of his steps providing counterpoint. "He's proud, ruthless, avaricious, ambitious, opportunistic, and quite without principle."

"You omitted talented." I smiled at his glower. "And who isn't guilty of any one of those entirely useful commodities at this Court, my lord?"

Wykeham scowled.

"Even you, sir. Pride and ambition seem to me to be fair game for a priest newly appointed Lord Chancellor."

With a curtsy and a swish of my skirts, I left him standing at the door to the Queen's chambers.

Philippa pursed her lips. "I'd not trust him. I wonder why Lionel finds him such good company."

"I have no idea, my lady," I replied.

"You did not find him entertaining at the feast?"

I took a steadying breath. Had our conversation gone unnoticed in *any* quarter?

"No. I can't say that I did, my lady."

Good company? Entertaining? He had been positively sinister, the manner in which he had poked at my anxieties, undermining my carefully constructed self-possession. Within twenty-four hours of our meeting, it was as clear as the bell on Edward's clock: No one liked or trusted William de Windsor.

The question I was driven to ask myself: Did I?

For William de Windsor had an unpleasant habit of stepping into my thoughts and trampling any attempt I made to dismiss him.

I was present, in attendance on the Queen, when Edward summoned Lionel, flanked by Windsor, to a council of war, to hammer out the thorny matter of Irish administration. Philippa rarely concerned herself with matters of business or politics these days, but her concern for Lionel, and her fear for her husband's temper, brought her to the council table. I was not displeased. How could I have found a reason for being there, to watch Windsor in action, if the Queen had not made it easy for me? I wanted to hear Windsor's excuses for his own involvement in the Irish problems. I wanted to see him squirm.

The King did not use his words with care or reticence.

"God's Bones, Clarence! I thought a son of mine would have more backbone."

"Do you have any idea what it is like?" Lionel challenged with what I considered to be an unfortunate degree of heat. "The native Irish are untamable. The English born in Ireland are loyal to the English throne only when it suits them. The only lot you can rely on are the English born in England, and they, to a man, are naught but a rascally band of brigands."

"So you hold the balance between them! Do you leave the province in turmoil and make a run for it, leaving them to wallow in their own blood?"

"I feared for my life." Lionel's pretty face was unattractively surly.

"I expect you to communicate with them, not ban them from your august presence! I expect you to get them to trust you! And don't make excuses for him," he snapped at Philippa, who had placed a hand on Edward's arm, as if it were possible to stem the tirade. "Your son is a coward. You're lily-livered, Lionel." As his ire grew, Edward became colder, the skin taut and white around his lips, his eyes pale with ice. "In my day . . ."

I slid my gaze to William de Windsor. His attention appeared to be focused on the carved wainscoting behind the King's right shoulder. How would leaves and tendrils deserve such concentration? Then his eyes moved to mine . . . but I could not read them. Anger or caprice or even a cool distancing—impossible to say, but an unexpected self-consciousness came to me. I looked away, down at my clasped hands.

"As for the army." The King brought his fist down hard onto the wood, causing the metal cups to ring and jump. "I hear there's rape and pillage committed by my forces in my name. I hear they're forced to loot to maintain themselves. What happened to the revenues I directed toward Ireland? What happened to the taxes? Whose pockets did they disappear into . . . ?" Without warning, Edward swung 'round in his chair to change his target. "I hear no good of *you*, Windsor."

And what would William de Windsor have to say about that? I was holding my breath. Did I want him to emerge victorious from this bout, or be buried under the justice of Edward's recriminations? I did not know.

Windsor was entirely undismayed, his harsh features an essay in composure. His voice held neither slick apology nor Lionel's aggression. I should not have been surprised.

"I admit the problems in the province," he replied. "I carry out orders, Sire, to the best of my ability. I was paid what was due to me. My lord of Clarence is King's Lieutenant; his is the authority. I am merely a loyal servant of the Crown."

It was a formidable statement of innocence.

"You're quick to slough off any blame, Windsor," Lionel snarled.

"I suppose you take no action on your own authority," Edward demanded of Windsor, waving his son to silence.

"No, Sire," Windsor responded, undisturbed, outwardly at least, by either the King's contempt or Lionel's fury. Against my better judgment, he won my acclaim.

"You think Ireland's a lost cause?"

Windsor thought for a long moment, as if it were a new idea, studying his hands that were placed flat, palms down, on the council table before him. If he said yes, he would displease the King; if no, then Lionel's excuses would be undermined by one of his own officers. Which way would he jump? Windsor raised his eyes and cast his dice.

"No, Sire. I do not."

He did not even look toward Lionel. He had known what he would say from the outset. He had his future entirely planned out, with or without Lionel. Had he not admitted to being ambitious, thoroughly self-interested? He might have omitted unscrupulous, but I recognized it.

"Ireland is dangerous, unpredictable," Windsor stated. "It's on the edge of rebellion. But I think it can be remedied. It just needs careful handling."

"And you could do it." The King made no effort to hide his distaste.

"Yes."

"At a cost, I suppose."

"As you say, Sire," Windsor concurred. "With enough power and wealth behind me, I'll whip Ireland into shape."

"I'll consider . . ." Edward fell into an abstraction. His fingers began to tap on the table's edge. His deliberation stretched out in an endless, uncomfortable silence, and his fingers stilled. His gaze, turned toward the window with its colored glazing, seemed to lose its focus. Those around the table began to stir in their seats. Still the King made no pronouncement. I became aware of the slide of unnerved glances from one man to another around the table as Edward sat motionless, lost in some inner thought.

"Edward!" Philippa demanded his attention. She placed a hand on his arm. And then apparently apropos of nothing, she added, "Edward! We must find Lionel a new wife."

The King blinked as if drawing back from the edge of some dark precipice.

"Yes, yes. So we must. I have it in mind." He was uncommonly brusque, although I knew that Lionel's remarriage after the death of his young wife three years ago now was a matter of policy. A new royal wife would mean the prospect of a new alliance. "But first this other matter . . ." Edward frowned, hesitated.

"Who will you send, Sire?" asked Wykeham, who had been an observer throughout of the clash of royal tempers, and the unsettling royal indecision at the end. "Who will go to Ireland?"

"I'll sleep on it." Edward stood; so did everyone else apart from the Queen. "I'll give it some thought, Windsor. Come to me tomorrow, Lionel, and your mother and I will consider the merits of a new bride. . . ."

The council was over with little to say for itself but a lot of bad blood and no outcome. In his youth, I thought that Edward would not have allowed it to be so. Over Philippa's shoulder as I helped her to her feet, William de Windsor's eyes met mine, with a victorious gleam. Glancing up, the Queen noticed.

She said nothing but grasped my hand as tightly as she was able.

After Mass the next morning I found Windsor leaning with studied negligence against the wall outside the Queen's apartments.

"Mistress Perrers. At last."

His bow was a study in elegance. Or was it no more than a charade? Undecided, I made little attempt at courtesy, with the merest bend of the knee. The Queen would have condemned me for my ill manners.

"Sir William. I did not see you at Mass."

"That, Mistress Perrers, was because I was not there. Where are you going?"

I inhaled sharply. "Why?"

"I thought I might escort you."

"To what purpose?"

"Such grace! I had thought better of you, a queen's damsel—and other things." Oh, he was a worthy adversary. "Allow me to accompany you, and you will discover my purpose."

"If you wish." I strode ahead of him on my errand for the Queen, but not for long. His energetic stride brought him abreast of me soon enough, closer than I liked. I made a show of tweaking the fall of my sleeve. "Perhaps if you attended Mass, sir, prayer and supplication would aid your future."

"Do you think? I doubt it."

"Confession, then? It is said to be good for the soul."

"I've found it overrated. Now, *you* could do much more for my future, Mistress Alice."

"I?" I honored him with a glance. "What could I possibly do?"

"Persuade the King to send me back to Ireland, of course."

Truly perplexed, I stopped and turned to look at him, taking in the uncompromising set of his mouth, the reckless gleam in his eye. "I don't understand why you would wish to return to the scene of your previous debacle."

"Debacle? No such thing. Have faith, Mistress Perrers—and tell the King I'm his man. The advantages of having a man of my knowledge there, on the ground, would be invaluable. Will you do it?"

I discovered I was in a mood to be uncooperative. Just to see what he would do.

"No."

"Why not?"

I knew more about this than I was saying. Should I tell him? Or let him find out for himself? No, I would drop the poison into his ear: It would please me to disturb the smooth exterior. "There would be no purpose in my taking up your petition with the King, Sir William." He was on guard in an instant. My smile was serene. "The King will appoint the Earl of Desmond as the new Governor."

"What?" Oh, he was shaken, his flirtatious manner cast aside. "What?"

"Desmond. The King will make him the new King's Lieutenant," I reiterated.

"Will he, by God!"

"A man of birth and high principle," I added.

"And a man with the intelligence of a gnat. So I've rid myself of Lionel to be saddled with Desmond!" All the warning I saw in the expressive face was a furious clamping of lips before Windsor strode off, leaving me standing.

I laughed at the success of my ruffling. "I see you did not seek me out for the pleasure of my company, Sir William," I called after him.

At which he promptly marched back, brow black but the formidable control once more in place. "Forgive me—although I think my behavior might have been unforgivable," he snapped.

"It was."

Windsor seized my hand and kissed my fingers, but his thoughts were elsewhere. "At least Desmond—unless he's changed dramatically in recent months—will stir himself to do as little as possible and leave the ordering of affairs to me. It could be worse. I could be saddled with some interfering old goat who couldn't recognize an insurrection if it fell on his foot. . . ."

He was striding off again before I could think of anything else to say.

Windsor was at the Mass next morning. He returned my regard with an atrocious parody of religious solemnity, just as his concentration on the raising of the host was unsurpassed. I was impressed with his apparent unquestioning reverence in God's presence.

Until the end. His grin was quite satanic.

And I was impressed for quite other reasons.

Edward surprised me. Without any advice from me, he ordered Windsor back to Ireland to aid the newly appointed Governor, the Earl of Desmond. Thus a little subtle balancing, I surmised, keeping all parties satisfied and putting an able man at Desmond's right hand. A politic move, forsooth. So Windsor was to go. I did not know whether to be relieved or disappointed that so troublesome an influence should be removed from my life. The decision had more than surprised me.

"I thought you did not like him," I remarked to Edward when he told me he was planning to send the thrice-damned but clever bastard back to Ireland, where he might, with luck, receive his just deserts, skewered to the heart by the sword of an Irish rebel.

"I don't. But he understands Ireland."

"And you don't fear he'll use your confidence in him to feather his own nest?"

"Of course he will. But he's not without talent."

"Will you send him soon?" I inquired.

"The sooner, the better. It's a conflagration in Dublin, waiting to happen."

So William de Windsor's visit to the Court would be a short one. Good riddance! I decided. But I would make the opportunity to see him before he departed. And why would I do that? Had I no sense?

I had no idea. And sense was definitely in short supply.

I did not know where to find him. Pleading a sore tooth to account for my absence from the solar, I tried all the possibilities, and some I knew to be impossible. Chapel—unlikely—stables, audience chambers, a group of hard-drinking knights in one of the antechambers—now, that I would have expected. There was no sign of him. Had he gone already? Had he left at the crack of dawn under royal orders to get back to the source of his ambitions as soon as possible?

My heart, inexplicably, plummeted.

You fool, I remonstrated. *He is nothing to you but a thorn beneath the skin. He could not even find the time to bid you farewell. He likes you as little as you like him.*

And yet I had found exhilaration in our cut and thrust that gave no quarter.

I returned to the stables, and was told that he had not gone. His rangy roan was still there, and his pack animals. So where was he? Some whore's chamber, perchance? But I did not think so. Where might he spend his last day at Court?

And I knew.

Within minutes I was standing outside the room, my ear pressed to the door. And beyond the door I could hear the rumble of voices. Difficult as it was to distinguish them, I elected to wait to find out, still wondering why seeing him meant so much to me. Before I had settled on an answer that did not increase my sense of self-delusion, the door opened and there was my quarry stepping into the corridor. He came from an interview with Edward's treasurer. Of course he would be discussing finance. . . .

"Mistress Perrers, as I live and breathe!" He bowed.

"Sir William." I curtsied.

"I leave tomorrow."

"I know."

"And you have come to find me to say farewell. How kind of you!"

"Wasn't it."

"You could make my final night here memorable. Unless you have other engagements." His hand was beneath my elbow, and he was leading me toward an unoccupied sunny window embrasure. I pulled my arm away, shocked at the instant physical response that tightened like a fist in my belly. My words were icy.

"Do you think I would slide into your bed, Sir William? Betray my King?"

"I don't know. Would you?"

"We are not all unprincipled."

"Oh, I think most of us can be, to one degree or another." It was an uncomfortable echo of what I had said to Wykeham. Windsor's stare was brazen. "Is he a good lover? Does he satisfy you?"

"You are impudent, sir. And I'll not betray the King."

No, I would not betray Edward with one such as William de Windsor, but he was a damnably attractive man for all his impudence. And he surprised me by a sudden change in direction that I was to discover was typical of him. A clever stratagem to unsettle the listener.

"No. I don't suppose you will. Will you do one thing for me, Mistress Perrers?"

"Since you obviously don't desire me in your bed, what would that be?"

"Keep me acquainted with Court opinion and any change in royal policy in Ireland."

So! His interest was political, not personal. A little piqued at his rapid rejection of my charms—how inconsistent can a woman be?—I asked, "What's it worth?"

"Do I have to pay you?"

I assayed a simper.

And William de Windsor kissed me. Not a kiss of passion or of affection, but a firm pressure of his lips at the corner of my mouth, like a promise of what might be.

And in instant response, without thought, I struck him with the flat of my hand against his cheek.

Windsor gave a shout of laughter. "Sweet Alice! Such lack of control!"

"Such lack of respect!" I was shocked equally by both his action and mine, and fought to claw back the control. My heart was beating faster; my blood was hot, and not from the heat of the sun through the glass. "I see you've learned your manners amongst the sluts of Dublin."

"I match my manners to my company, mistress."

As his gaze disrobed me down to my skin, my control flew out of the window. I reached out to strike him again, fast as a snake, but he caught my wrist and dragged it to his mouth, kissing the soft skin where my blood beat like a military drum.

"Tempestuous Alice! But seriously." He released me as fast as he had taken possession. "Keep me informed. And get what you can for yourself. Without the King or Queen to cushion the blows, your enemies will swoop in and swallow you up. Unless your goal is to return to the gutter, fill your coffers now."

"I'm not so mercenary."

"We're not discussing something so trivial as being mercenary, woman! It's self-preservation. If you don't look to yourself whilst the power is to hand, no one else will. And if you're thinking, 'Does this make me too hard, too avaricious?'—then consider this: Who will give you a moment's thought the day that Edward goes to his grave?"

I shook my head, horrified by the picture he had thrust so forcefully into my mind.

"Answer me, Alice."

For a moment I saw compassion in his face. I hated to see it, but I replied with the truth. "No one."

With Philippa and Edward dead, the Prince would wear the crown, and Fair Joan would be his consort. There would be no place for me in Joan's Court.

"Did you think to be damsel to Joan the Whore?" Windsor asked.

His crude words, startling me with their mirror image of my own thoughts, drove home my predicament. It was the last thing I could envisage. As long as she was in Aquitaine I need not fear her, but returned to England she would be no friend to me. I recalled her scorn, her disdain of all things lowborn, her contempt for me.

"Even provision for your sons will not be secure. Have you thought of *that*?"

My hot blood ran cold and sluggish, but I tried to ward it off. "I am not in any danger. Nor am I without resources."

"Two tuns of Gascon wine for service to the Queen? Edward is hardly generous!" His laughter was hard and humorless.

"I have property . . ." I insisted.

"Enough to allow you to live as you do now?" Windsor fired back.

"I have manors and town property. . . ." I clung on desperately to what I had hoped would keep poverty at bay.

"So your manors and town properties will keep the wolf from your door, will they, in the hard times? You've had a taste of life cushioned by royal wealth. Will you be willing to accept less? It's a long winter when you have nothing. I should know. But if you will not be open to my advice . . ."

"I never said that."

"No. You didn't. But give it some thought."

I studied the harsh lines of his face, the marks of his experience, not all of them pleasant.

"Why do you do this?" I asked. "Why do you bother yourself with my future? I am nothing to you."

With one hand he raised my chin, tilting my face to the light, and I allowed it, since I had asked the question. But what would I make of the answer?

"In all honesty, I don't know," he said softly, as if searching in his mind for a reason that did not wish to be discovered. "You're cross and perverse and not my sort of woman at all. But for some strange reason I would not wish to see you bereft. Now, why should that be?"

I chose not to answer that question. Were we both dissembling? My own emotions were inexplicably in turmoil. Almost in a panic I turned to go, but his hand sliding down my arm to my wrist stopped me. I looked back over my shoulder.

"Well?" I asked.

"We'll not meet again."

For which I am eternally grateful, sprang to my lips. I saw him brace himself, the smallest stiffening, against what I would say. His fingers around my arm tensed. His eyes darkened as if my reply mattered. So—perversely, as he had accused—I said nothing. And his rigid shoulders relaxed.

"Have you nothing to say?"

"Good-bye, Sir William."

"Well, at least it's apt." His mouth had a wry twist. "And will you write?"

"I'll consider it."

His hand slid farther until he closed it around my hand.

"This is too public . . ." I remonstrated.

"I care not. And neither do you. I admire you, Mistress Alice. I admire your strength and your loyalty to the King. I admire your single-mindedness and your refusal to be influenced by any man's advice—until you know what is right for you." I must have looked my amazement. Was that how he saw me? "I admire your confidence." He pressed his lips to the palm of my hand. "I admire your determination to be yourself."

Windsor looked at me through his lashes. "Do you admire me at all, Mistress Perrers?"

"No."

He laughed. "Which does not change to any degree what I feel for you. I admire your honesty even though I do not always believe what you say."

With a little tug on my hand he drew me closer and planted another kiss, this time full on my mouth. His mouth was firm and cool and entirely seductive. The kiss lasted for no time, but it had a warmth that stroked across my skin.

"Farewell, Alice."

A bow, a wave of his feathered hat, and he was on his way to Ireland.

Thank God!

I could not banish the man from my thoughts.

What did I feel for Windsor? I had as little understanding of that as he had for his feelings for me. I knew my feelings for Edward with the intimacy of long association. Admiration, of course. Respect coupled with an affection born of deep gratitude. Even—when I was in a mind to admit it—the eroticism of forbidden fruit.

But this man who had pushed his way into my consciousness? A far harsher emotion stabbed at me when I recalled the pressure of Windsor's mouth against mine, against my palm. I did not wish to put a name to this emotion, but he made my flesh shiver, and I was honest enough to admit that it was not distaste.

I wished he had not gone back to Ireland.

Do you admire me at all, Mistress Perrers?

Go away!

You could make my final night here memorable.

I was delighted that he had gone! I scratched at the spot on my palm as if I could erase the memory. There! I need think no more about him.

But I did. He left with me a memento of his deplorable regard and his unwarranted warnings of those who had no cause to love me. In the early morning after his departure, I opened my door to a palace servant, one of the many grooms, judging by his overpowering aroma of horse and straw. He bowed and handed over a leather leash attached to a very youthful wolfhound. Then he left before I could question him.

"Oh."

It—she—sat obediently and looked at me. I looked back. No letter or introduction came with this creature that eyed me like a juicy bone. First a palfrey, now a hound. Suddenly I, who had no affinity with animals, had acquired a surfeit of them.

"I should tell you," I informed the creature, "I have no love of dogs, however noble their breeding."

Unblinkingly, she continued to regard me.

"Why do I know that Windsor sent you to me? And what do I do with you?"

She panted enthusiastically, tongue lolling.

"Send you back to the stables? There's no place for you in a *lady's* rooms."

The wolfhound sighed.

"As you say! Since I am no lady, I suppose you will stay. Does Windsor think I need a guard dog? But to protect me from whom, I wonder?"

So he did think I might be in danger. I would consider that later.

"What do I call you?" I asked as I walked cautiously 'round the animal. She sank to her belly in a patch of warm sun and closed her eyes. "Windsor, perhaps?" I suggested with a touch of whimsy. They both shared a knowing expression and more than a hint of ruthless will, even when the creature was half-asleep. As soon as I stepped away, she lifted her head, following my movements with heavy-browed eyes.

"I suppose I had better keep you. And I cannot in all conscience call you Windsor. It had better be Braveheart instead."

When I sat, Braveheart rested her great head on her paws and slept, and I set my mind to pick apart Windsor's warnings—a far more valuable occupation, I chided, than recalling his kisses. I could not afford to brush aside Windsor's warnings as inconsequential.

It was time to contact the Tabard at Southwark again.

Greseley had continued to be busy in his and my interests, even to the extent of a little private moneylending. I did not bother overtly with the details of this, leaving my clerk to his own devious devices, discovering my involvement only when the documents of the pertinent court case were sent to me in absentia. One Richard de Kent, a London fishmonger, was sued by Greseley for the return of two hundred marks that I, through Greseley, had lent him. Far more important, my agent had used income from the Gracechurch property to buy for me a life interest in the manor of Radstone in Northamptonshire. And, of course, I had Ardington . . . and the ambition to buy more.

With a sum of money borrowed from the royal treasury—with Edward's permission, of course, and to be repaid at a later date—I wrote my orders to Greseley. The manor of Meonstoke was acquired for me. My future suddenly seemed far less insecure.

And what do you have to say about that, Sir William?

I thought he would find something suitably disparaging. If our paths were ever unfortunate enough to cross again.

Chapter Nine

The royal castle of Windsor, with its massive walls and towers, was a magical place. Mirrored rooms glittered with reflected light or, under Wykeham's flamboyant hand, allowed roses to riot from floor to ceiling in blue and green and vermilion. It was too garish for my taste but much admired, and with enough gold leaf to cover Edward's warship, the *Christopher*, from prow to stern. The summer lay softly on this sumptuous statement of royal power, but the Queen of England lay immobile on her bed. Even the smallest movement of head or hand racked her with pain. I could do nothing for her. The willow bark now had little effect against such corruption of the body. It had not soothed her for many months, and the frequency of the drafts she was taking was a nagging concern to me. But Philippa begged for the cup of bitter wine and sank gratefully into sleep when she could tolerate her waking hours no more. I sat with her as she moved between delirium and a keen awareness that demanded the truth and gave no room for lies. The damsels were not slow to leave me the duties of the sickroom.

I was not sorry. Did I not owe everything to this generous woman who had so much love in her heart, who had a spirit strong as a mighty oak, as soft as the feathers on a dove's breast? She had seen enough in me to lift me from obscurity to my strange life in the royal household.

I owed her *everything*. No, I was not sorry to sit with her as her life ebbed.

"Is Isabella here?" she asked.

"No, my lady. She is in France with her husband."

"Of course." Philippa's lips tried ineffectually to smile. "I'm astonished she hasn't washed her hands of him." She managed a breath of a laugh. Then: "Where is Lionel . . . ? Ah, no . . . I remember now. . . ." Tears sprang to her eyes, for her beloved Lionel was dead. In the wine-fueled aftermath of a glorious marriage in Italy to the Visconti heiress, Lionel had succumbed to some nameless fever. Philippa sighed. "I am so weary, Alice. . . ."

I bathed her face and lips, my mind gripped with fear.

"Read to me from my missal. The prayer to the Virgin . . ."

So I did, and it gave her comfort.

"Am I dying, Alice?" The assent stuck in my throat. "I see it in your face. Tell me this, if the first reply is too hard. Will it be long now?"

"No, Majesty. It will not be long."

"Bless you. You have always been honest. Is the King still in England?"

"Yes, my lady. He is in London—at the Tower."

"I need him." Her breath barely stirred the air. "Send for him. Tell him . . . tell him not to delay."

"I will, Your Majesty. Immediately."

"Will Edward blame me?" she wept. "For diverting him from his duties in France?"

"No, my lady." I wiped away the tears from her cheeks, a task that she was unable to do for herself. How could I not weep with her? "The King will never blame you. He loves you more than life. The King would never forgive you if you did not tell him how you suffered."

I thought about Edward's sense of duty. It was what I admired in him. When the French had marched into Ponthieu and threatened the security of Gascony itself, Edward had abandoned his policy of peaceful coexistence and begun to plan for a new war, reclaiming his relinquished title of King of France. Some might whisper that he was too old to plan such a sustained invasion—not like the old days—but what choice did a man of such pride have? The Prince, still laid low, remained too weak to lead an army, so therefore Edward must resume the mantle of command. He was King. All that he had achieved in his lifetime must not be thrown away. So in that very month, he had sent John of Gaunt to Calais. Edward and an army would follow. Even now he was at the Tower, organizing the invasion.

But now he would not. He would come to Philippa's side, whatever the cost. England's power in France would weigh lightly in the balance if the Queen was in need. I prayed he would be in time. The shade of death squatted in the shadows in the corner of the room, obscene in its presence, growing stronger as the days passed.

Edward arrived by royal barge that beat its way against the tide along the Thames, and I went down to the landing stage with others of the household to greet him. Perhaps to warn him a little. I had not seen him for six weeks, and the change in him was unmistakable.

Oh, I doubt it was noticeable to a subject who simply saw the outer glory of the King of England. Still fair and upright, still handsome with regal presence, he had a smile and a word for those who had rowed him from the Tower. His tunic flattered his broad shoulders. The golden lions stitched against the red were truly resplendent, and the sun gilded his hair as the barge was maneuvered into the river landing.

But I was aware of the change from the moment he stood up from his seat at the stern. Once, he would have stood for the whole journey, dignified but approachable, the leader of his people, to see and be seen. Now he sat. Furthermore—I saw it even if no one else did—he took his page's arm as he stepped from barge to land, not heavily but enough to give him stability. He stretched as if his limbs were stiff, and his first strides were uneven. The lines around eyes and mouth were more deeply engraved than when I had kissed him farewell. Oh, Edward! How grief and the passage of years can leave their mark. How the burden of duty can wear away the body's resilience. My first thought was to go to him, to kiss away the sorrow that darkened his eyes, but I kept my distance. This was no time for greetings from the King's lover. I had no place in this homecoming, and I knew nothing I could do would assuage Edward's suffering. For a moment I wished I had not come, but stayed at the Queen's side, where I had an acknowledged role. And I felt a cold foreboding for the coming days.

No Queen. No place. No position. No reason for Alice Perrers to remain at Court.

I pushed away the bleak thought as fast as it assaulted me. Nothing new here, merely the imminent inevitability of it. Now, in this moment, all that mattered was Edward's reunion with his stricken wife.

The steward bowed. I curtsied. Edward acknowledged the waiting group of courtiers. I actually took a step backward, but the King's eyes sought me out.

"Mistress Perrers."

"Your Majesty."

"Speak to me of my wife." His voice was low and harsh with unshed tears. "She is dying?"

"Yes, Sire."

"Does she know?"

"She is aware. She regretted asking you to come."

"I could not leave her. How could I? She is everything to me."

"Yes, Sire."

I swallowed hard. The heartrending affirmation could not have made my situation clearer. I stepped back again as the King turned to stride up the steps toward the castle, his vigor restored with the urgency to get to Philippa's side before it was too late. But he halted with his foot on the bottom step and looked back.

"Come with me. She will need you."

And although I shrank from the task, I obeyed.

So I was witness to their reunion. It hit me harder than I could have imagined, illuminating as it did the lack in my own life. The love shone between them, undiminished by death. Briefly the image of William de Windsor stole into my mind, whether I wished it or not—typical of the man himself. There was something between us, but nothing like this. I could not imagine love like this, beyond the physical, beyond the passage of time. Philippa raised her hand from the bed linen and placed it into the hand of the King, her lord and her love. Edward fell to his knees at her side.

"Dear Edward. You came." The words were slurred but I heard the pleasure in them.

"Did you ever doubt that I would?"

"No—Alice said you would come." She glanced momentarily to where I stood beside the door, but I had no importance for her. All her focus was on the man at her side. "What a marriage we have had. All these years."

"I would wed you again. Tomorrow. This very minute." Edward smoothed the thinning, matted hair back from her brow.

"And you have as much charm as ever." The gasp might have been a laugh.

"You are all I ever wanted."

The words struck me with such force that I stepped back against the tapestry—I could feel the stitching and the underlying stone solid against my back—to give them space. *You should not be here!* My conscience was implacable.

"When we are separated . . ." I heard the Queen whisper.

"No!"

"When we are separated," she repeated, "will you grant me three requests, my dear lord?"

Edward inhaled. "Lady. Whatever you ask, it will be done."

"Then—settle my debts. I can't bear that they be left unpaid."

"You always were extravagant."

The gentleness in Edward's reply caused my tears to overflow.

"I know. Will you do it? And then fulfill the gifts and bequests I've made."

"I will."

"And at the last—Edward, my love, will you lie beside me in Westminster Abbey when your time on earth is finished?"

"Yes. I will."

Edward bent his brow to her hand. They remained like that, the room still about them, and I left them to their solitude, closing the door quietly. They did not notice. They did not need me.

I walked unseeing through the antechambers, making my way to climb to the deserted wall walk. My thoughts were appallingly self-absorbed, but I could not redirect them. I wept for the two I had just left, but where would I lie when I was dead? Who would lie beside me, at his or my request? I was as alone and friendless as I had always been, except for this fast-fading woman and her broken husband. Who could I call friend in the royal household? No one. Who would even have a thought for me? William de Windsor might—but his was a self-interest as strong as mine. Wykeham would condemn me.

So I wept out of grief for Philippa and Edward and myself. And out of fear of a future I could no longer see.

Her last moments came on the fifteenth day of August, when Wykeham gave the Queen the last sacrament. We were with her, Edward and young Thomas of Woodstock, and all her damsels, who wept bitter tears, as did the household, from falconer to meanest scullion. Philippa had left her mark on the lives of everyone who served her. I prayed for her comfort and her soul, touching for the final time her foot beneath the sumptuous bedcover with its embroidered sprawl of Plantagenet lions. Near the end, she raised her hand to beckon me, and whispered, her words barely stirring the air between us.

"Promise me!" she begged.

"I promise."

Did she know what she had asked of me? Did she understand how heavy the burden would become? I think she did not, yet I would do it. I would continue to repay the debt I owed her.

The King held the Queen's hand as she drew her final breaths, and kissed her forehead.

"Edward. My love. What a family we made together . . ."

Edward bowed his head and wept unashamedly. I might own his affection, his respect, the demands of his body. Philippa owned his heart and always would, even to her grave. Edward had lost his lodestar. His rock. His clear place in the firmament.

So passed the Queen from this life. It was as if the great castle had been hollowed out, robbed of its entity. Windsor became a dark place. Edward walked the rooms and corridors like a ghost, all his vigor and Plantagenet spirit eclipsed by grief. He did what he must, what was necessary, but it was as if a husk of a man issued orders. And he did it alone. I, his mistress, had no role in these preparations for his wife's final resting place. His dear Philippa's embalmed body would be transported to the Tower by royal barge along the Thames, and from there in procession through the streets before reaching Westminster, so that all might witness and mourn her passing. She would be buried in the chapel of Edward the Confessor, as she had wished, in the tomb long prepared for her, with an effigy that showed her as she was, a plain woman with an abundance of love in her heart.

In a voice devoid of emotion, Edward acknowledged all the Queen's gifts: The Exchequer would pay me—and the other damsels—the sum of ten marks twice yearly at Easter and Michaelmas for services to the Queen. We were given a length of black cloth for mourning garments. I was not singled out in any way.

So it was finished.

What now?

You are the King's lover. That will not change.

But Edward did not want me in his bed. He never sent for me, not once in all those endless days when I could see his suffering. My heart reached out to him, but it was as if he were shrouded in an impenetrable mist from which he was unable or unwilling to break free. He did not want me, did not need me, and so I must wait to see my fate.

The damsels had a final task to complete, and I took my place amongst them. At the King's command, we packed away all the Queen's possessions. The hangings and covers of her magnificent bed were cut and stitched into vestments for the clergy of York Minster in memory of that exultant day when Edward and Philippa were wed there. It kept our hands busy if not our minds, and I could not join in the mindless twitterings of the young women, who would go home to their families unless another Court position opened up for them.

And then it was Christmas, a festivity that we did not celebrate. The dancing chambers remained silent. In concern for the King, John of Gaunt returned from Calais to spend the doleful season with his father, shut away at the hunting lodge at Kings Langley, but Edward did not hunt. Chancellor Wykeham, who traveled frequently on royal business between Windsor and Kings Langley, wore a troubled expression. I did not see Edward again until I accompanied Philippa's embalmed body to the Tower in the first days of the New Year. When Edward stood beside Philippa's coffin as it was placed in the tomb, there seemed to be as little life in his still, silent figure as there was in the body they finally laid to rest. His face was gray and worn, head bowed, fingers flexing convulsively on the hilt of his sword. Age had placed its hand on him with cruel precision.

As the solemn words came to an end, I watched Wykeham at the King's side make the sign of the cross. His eyes moved slowly from Edward's ashen face to mine, then dropped when he saw me watching him, as if it had been a mere chance meeting of our eyes.

I did not think it was.

At Edward's orders the solemnities were to last for six days. I thought, in despair, that for Edward they would never end. He returned to the Tower and shut himself away from everyone.

What was I to Edward in these dark days? That was simple enough to describe. I was nothing. I did not exist. I saw him only once, and that a chance passing in an antechamber.

Edward walked through with Wykeham, the same easy stride, but there the similarity ended. There was no appreciation of his surroundings, no ready word for those who came within his recognition. I think he recognized no one.

I curtsied.

Without even a glance, Edward continued to stride ahead with some grim intent.

"Mistress Perrers is here, Sire," Wykeham murmured to the King, surprising me. He actually touched the King's arm to claim his attention.

The King stopped, bowed. "Mistress Perrers."

His eyes slid over my face but they did not linger, did not hold my gaze. His bow had been perfunctory, such as he might make to the lowliest of his servants who performed some menial task for him.

"Sire!" I smiled, struggling to mask my concern. "I trust you are well."

There was no answering smile. Was this the man whose ready laughter had echoed from the roof in the Great Hall at Havering? Somber black had replaced the crimson and gold of his tunic. Giving no reply, he proceeded toward the door, presenting me with a good solid view of his back. The lover who had stripped the gown from my body and wrapped me in furs was far removed from this man who passed me by without a second thought. I rose to my full height, watching him in astonishment and despair. Wykeham shrugged helplessly and followed. I was left standing alone.

It seemed that Philippa was not the only one to be interred in Edward the Confessor's chapel. It was as if a hand had been slapped down to still the vibrating strings of a lute.

"Where's the King? It is imperative that I see him."

"The King is in his private chamber. He will not see you." If I heard such conversations once in those weeks after Philippa was laid to rest, I heard them a dozen times, and the answer, delivered in the bleakest of tones by William Latimer, steward to the royal household, was always the same, whether the petitioner was noble or commoner.

"His Majesty will see no one."

A light had been extinguished in Edward's heart. Abandoning London, he shut himself away in his rooms at Havering, where Philippa had loved to stay, letting matters of government slide. The problems in France, where the Prince was increasingly under attack and still not restored to health, might not have existed for all the interest he took. The country shivered under ice and snow as the rooms of the palace echoed in a weird desolation. The Court whispered, uncertain, in a grip of gloom. A country without its head, without its King. Without leadership.

The whispers intensified. The King was as good as dead.

Philippa's ladies had dispersed to their families or to other noble households where their skills were in demand as confidante or companion. Not I. The pattern of my life hung on the decision of this king who shut himself away in his chamber. I had never felt so alone, not even when standing in the street, a new widow. At least Greseley came to find me then. No one saw my need at Havering.

I wrote to William de Windsor, perversely, since I had hedged on the promise to do so, informing him of the lack of policy toward Ireland and the reason for it, and perhaps to tell someone of my own insecurity.

The King gives no direction to government. I doubt he thinks of Ireland at all. You are your own man, free to administer affairs as you wish. I think you may expect no more information from me. I fear my days at Court are numbered.

And then, on a whim—perhaps an ill-considered one:

I miss your forthright conversation, Sir William. Sometimes I wish you were recalled again to London to answer for your sins. I think I might give you a hearing. At the risk of sounding weak and destroying your expressed admiration of me, I have no one to talk to here.

Such was my isolation. I sent the letter but had no knowledge of its arrival.

We were a Court in waiting for Edward to emerge from his mourning and take up his sword once more. Did not King Arthur sleep, to return to England in her hour of need? Surely Edward would do the same. He did not.

I tried to reach him, of course, only to find a guard on his door. I was not even announced. The King did not wish to see me. I wrote to Edward, persuading Latimer to ensure my plea was delivered.

Don't shut me out, my lord. Let me talk to you. Let me give you solace. We both suffer from the loss of your dear wife. We can mourn together.
Remember what we have been to each other.
Allow me to return to your side.

My pen hovered over the page as I considered whether to tell him of the child that grew in my belly. I did not. Latimer took the note but there was no reply.

"Did he read it?" I asked.

"I don't think he did." Latimer's face was stark with furrows of concern. "It is impossible to reach him."

Almost I admitted defeat. Short of running the guard through with his own sword and battering down the door, I could achieve nothing.

But it broke my heart to leave Edward in this trough of despondency. Who would talk to him? Who would read or play chess with him? Who would entice him out of the black pit that he had fallen into? "Get him to see me!" I ordered, even though I had no authority of my own to order anything. I almost laughed at the expression on Latimer's face. He was unsure whether I was an abomination in the sight of God and man or a heavenly courier sent to release the King from his travails. I closed my hand on his forearm, gripping hard. "Tell the King I carry his child, if you have to. And if you can't, get Wykeham to do it. But do whatever it takes to get me into the King's presence!"

Latimer eyed me.

"Do it, Latimer."

Do it! For all our sakes!

Well, my vehemence had some effect. We were walking, Wykeham and I, Braveheart pattering after us, through the antechambers into the old section of the palace that was now rarely used. At last the Chancellor had come to my room to summon me. Except that this was not the way to the royal apartments.

"Where are we going?"

He did not reply, striding so rapidly, robes billowing, that I could barely keep up. His expression was stormy, his features tight with displeasure.

"Is it Edward?" I asked. "Has he asked for me?"

"No."

Hope died. "Then where . . . ?"

"Just shut up and wait, woman. . . ."

He marched on in a surly mood, with me beside him. In truth I was intrigued. This part of the palace was empty and silent, the walls stripped of their tapestries, the floors unswept. I noticed with interest that others had walked this way before us, and recently, their boot prints and scuff marks plain in the dust. The prints stopped at a door that Wykeham pushed open, and I was directed with a brusque nod into a chamber I did not know, my wolfhound shut out to whine and scratch in the antechamber. Much like many others, it was a small room built into the curve of a wall, bright with bars of sunshine angling through the narrow window slits. A fireplace was built into the wall, but there was no fire, and the room was as cold as an unused room could be. A standing table occupied most of the space, with stools set around it, but they were unoccupied. The men in occupation stood in a little group by one of the windows. The room seemed crowded with a heavy presence. It looked, I thought, like a war council.

I glanced across to Wykeham for an explanation, and did not get it.

"Mistress Perrers. Allow me to introduce you."

His tone was clipped, hard with distaste—but with me or the body of men, or with the whole situation, I could not tell. Nor did I need the introductions. Had I not lived cheek by jowl with them in the various palaces since the day I had come into Philippa's employ?

I curtsied, my mind working furiously as Wykeham made the introductions. First was William Latimer, Edward's steward. Then John Neville, lord of Raby. A surprise: Richard Lyons—not a courtier, but a man of finance, a merchant and master of the royal mint. The others: Nicholas Carew, Richard le Scrope, Robert Thorp. All, I realized in that first greeting, united by one common factor: ambition. Their eyes were avid with it, young men who hoped to further their careers in service to the Crown. I did not know whether they were men of talent, but I thought that perhaps they were. As Wykeham closed the door behind me, I saw them more as a feral pack of wolves, ready to pounce on any opportunity to step up the ladder to high office and destroy any fool who dared to stand in their way. But how did I fit into their schemes . . . ?

And then there was one more. A royal son, no less. John of Gaunt. They bowed.

"Please sit," Wykeham invited.

I did. So did the conspirators—for surely that was what they were—except for Gaunt, who stood against the wall, arms folded.

"Why am I here?" I asked. I saw no point in adopting innocence or good manners. This meeting was not for public consumption, and I doubted that most of these fine gentlemen, except for Wykeham and perhaps Latimer, would give me the time of day in normal circumstances.

They exchanged glances. Who, I wondered, would be the spokesman?

It was Latimer. "Can we trust you?"

Well, that was forthright enough. I replied in kind. "Unless you are plotting rebellion, or the King's death, then I expect you can." There they all sat, faces shuttered. Wary. "Perhaps you are? Is this a plot?"

"Not quite." The twist of Latimer's lips in acknowledgment was bleak. "The King has . . ." He hitched a shoulder under the rich damask bearing Edward's heraldic device as he searched for a word. ". . . withdrawn."

"Withdrawn? A milksop judgment, by God!" I responded. "He has incarcerated himself in his rooms and refuses to come out!"

Latimer cleared his throat. "We must bring him back."

I looked 'round at the gloomy expressions. "And you cannot?"

I knew they couldn't. I caught the eye of Gaunt, who had paid a visit to his father less than a week ago, leaving again within an hour with a furious face and spurs used viciously against his horse's flanks. Now I thought he might reply, but the royal Prince deliberately turned his head to look out of the window, leaving it to Latimer to commit them to whatever devious policy had brought them—and me—here.

"The King sinks further into melancholy. His physicians despair," Latimer said, and looked at Wykeham, who nodded. "We want you to speak to him."

"He will not see me. I have tried." They must know of my failure.

"We can arrange that you do."

"And what do you want me to say to him?" I played the innocent, enjoying Latimer's discomfort.

"We want you to . . . to give him solace . . . to encourage him to . . ."

"Say it, Latimer!" Wykeham growled.

Latimer huffed out a breath. "We want you to give him physical comfort."

"In effect, you want me to play the whore."

"Yes." Suddenly Gaunt was there, stepping up to the table, dominating it. He was a vitally handsome man, with his father's height and fine features, but none of his ease of manner, a man notorious for enjoying the value of women in his own life. He waved Latimer aside and spoke bluntly. "The King is not incapable. He still has the ability to fuck a woman and reap the pleasure of it. It might bring him back to his senses."

I was shocked to hear the proposal stated so coarsely, and I was not inclined to be compliant when every one of them would have condemned me for daring to take that role.

"Then if that's what's needed, pay a palace whore," I replied with a tight smile.

"Unsatisfactory." Gaunt brushed the idea away like an annoying fly, with an openhanded swipe. "I hope for a more subtle solution."

"And you think I can be subtle."

"I think you have a whole range of talents, discretion being one of them. And you were well liked by the Queen. You could be the answer to our prayers."

I laughed, surprising them. What a turnabout from these men who viewed me as some form of pond life, dwelling in the filth of unspeakable sin. I had taken Philippa's place in Edward's bed; did they now want me to play the role of the loving, maternal Philippa too?

"He needs a confidante as much as he needs a whore." Gaunt confirmed it.

"A concubine, then."

He bowed. "Exactly."

"A wife but not a wife."

"In so many words . . ."

"Openly acknowledged by the Court?"

"If we must."

I looked 'round at them. Not one of them approved. Not one of them wanted this.

"Why me, my lords?" I would make them admit it. I would make them say what had been unsaid through all the years since I had lifted my shift in Edward's bed.

"Because he has enjoyed your body often enough in the past," Gaunt snapped.

Of course they knew. All the Court had known, even if it was not spoken of except in murmurings over wine cups or in whispers between lovers, in their efforts to protect Philippa. Even when she was the instigator of the scandal. The sheer hypocrisy of it beat against the walls that hemmed us in, stirring into rampant life my determination to be cowed by no one.

"So I return to Edward as his lover," I remarked conversationally. "What then?"

"Make him return to government. Make him pick up the reins of authority again. We can't continue as we are now with the King shut away and the Prince taken to his bed in Gascony." Gaunt's fist thumped the board.

"I don't know that I can." Gaunt would get no bloodless victory over me.

Wykeham sighed. "You can. You're a clever woman, Alice."

I tilted my head and looked at him, noting his use of my name.

"And you're our last hope." Latimer flushed at what he had admitted.

I stood as if I might refuse. As if I might leave. How exhilarating was power, knowing that I held them all in the palm of my hand. I took a step. . . .

"Needs must when the devil's in control!" Gaunt snapped. "Enough! Here's the truth of it, Mistress Perrers. We are in mortal danger. The days of England's greatness appear to be draining away, and I smell rebellion in the air. We need my father at the helm. He's not young, but he's still capable of wearing the crown and ruling, if only we can . . ." He lifted his hands in near despair. "If only we can catch his interest and bring him back to life."

We. We were in collusion. We were a circle of plotters, taut with expectation, all driven, all concerned for the future, our own and England's, but their repugnace for this negotiation with me smeared the air like the miasma of pestilence. A quick anger shook me, and I turned my stare on Gaunt. By God! I would make them beg.

He turned away to drive his fist into the stone lintel at the window. It was Wykeham, generous Wykeham, who spoke the words.

"Will you do it?" he asked. "Will you rescue our King?"

Again, a beat of hesitation, as I luxuriated in making these men of power and breeding wait on my decision.

Then: "Yes. I will." And I saw the relief sweep through them, muscles relaxing, smiles appearing. The business was done—or so they thought. But it was not—not to any degree. "And what, my lords, did it take for you to trample over your damned morality and ask me, the King's whore, for help?"

To do him justice, it was Gaunt who replied. "It will be worth the price if we can restore the King to his powers." Walking 'round the table, he took and kissed my hand. "We are grateful."

"How can I refuse so gracious an admission," I murmured.

There was a concerted sigh. And in that exhalation I realized the truth of what had been done here. The power of these courtiers—excepting Gaunt—their future preferment, their wealth and place in government might rest on the King's pleasure, but now their ambitions were dependent on me. We all had everything to lose if the King were allowed to fade into obscurity. We were indeed in collusion. But I would not let them off the hook quite yet.

"What's in it for me?" I asked, distressingly frank.

"What do you want, lady?" Latimer asked, amusing me with the form of address. Much had changed in the last hour. I took a little time, pretending the ideas were new to me.

"Nothing much, my lords." I smiled at their palpable relief. "A servant. A bedchamber and a parlor with an outlook over the gardens. Clothing and jewels befitting my new position. An income, so that I am not penniless. Am I not worthy of all of that?" And then—what I desired most of all to expunge my memories of past humiliations. "I want recognition, my lords. I want acknowledgment that I am the King's Concubine. I refuse to live any longer under the shadow of embittered silence and rancorous rumor. There is no one to hurt now by stripping the covers from my relationship with the King."

Their gratitude was risible; they thought that I had made an easy bargain. What fools they were, as were most men. Did they not know that I would have gone to Edward freely? My compliance did not need to be bought. But a woman must seize her opportunities, as Windsor would have said.

"Furthermore," I added, "if I am to be involved in the running of the royal household, I need access to the royal Treasury for funds. . . ."

There was an exchange of glances, an uncomfortable lift of shoulders, but what choice had they? "It can be arranged." And Gaunt led me to the door, his hand light on mine. I knew little of him other than that Edward had a high regard for him, knew nothing of his ambitions. He was not the heir to the throne. What did he hope for from this agreement? He did not have the look of a man satisfied with life. A premonition touched my nape with chill fingers: that one day I would find out.

At the open door, I smiled and curtsied again.

"I will do it, my lords. I will be Edward's concubine, openly in the full knowledge of the Court. I will, if it is in my power, restore your King to life."

So much settled in a dusty room in the old palace. But was it? Now I must turn my mind and all my persuasive powers to the one obstacle to the success of our venture. It was in my mind that it might not be an easy task.

"Will he respond to me?" I asked Braveheart, retrieving her from her unhappy vigil outside the plotters' door.

She sneezed as she stood and stretched. She foresaw the future as unclearly as I.

Not wishing to let grass grow under my feet, for I could not afford to be squeamish about such matters, I wrote immediately to Greseley.

I anticipate having considerable funds at my disposal, sir. Buy or lease whatever you can for my future comfort.

Greseley acted with exemplary speed. Within the month I was the leaseholder of the Orby lands, with the control of the wardship and marriage of the young heir. Ten manors all told. I was becoming a woman of means.

I had been Edward's lover for six years, but in all that time I had never been the one to take the initiative. Edward had always sent for me. Yes,

I had challenged him on the day of the hunt, but never again. I knew how difficult a proud man could be, how his pride must be allowed to dominate. Edward demanded and I obeyed. A Plantagenet never asked for favors. I had never removed my garments without his invitation or without his participation. I was his minion, and I would not have had it any other way. A strong woman needs a willful man to match her. If not, respect flies out of the window or is crushed underfoot.

Now I stood outside Edward's apartments, my limbs trembling, and not with the cold air that shivered the tapestries. My belly lurched at what I must do. Tactics, I decided. It must be like planning a battle campaign, knowing when to attack and when to retreat. What, I wondered, would William de Windsor advise this time?

Attack the weakest element in the fortifications and give no quarter until the battle is won. In fact, never give quarter, or the opponent gains ground.

That was no help to me. I must simply use my instincts as a woman and pray that Edward would respond. *Holy Virgin, let him not turn me away!* I stepped over the threshold, closing the door softly behind me.

First an antechamber, empty and uncannily still. Then an audience chamber in a similar state of abandonment. Finally the Halidon Hill Chamber, a private room, where a man could take his ease with books and music. I knew the room well, with its magnificent tapestry of Edward's first great military victory, when, still a young man, he had demonstrated to the Scots who was master. On a low stool was a chess game, set up but unplayed. A fire burned low, gleaming on the polished wood of a coffer and a settle and a cupboard. A great chair was set beside the hearth, next to it a coffer set with a flagon and cup, a neglected dish of sweet pasties. Someone had left a candle bracket that was in danger of burning out.

And there was Edward. Every inch the King, bejeweled and clothed in costly fabrics, the mighty Plantagenet, Edward, the third of that name, who had made England a great power for all of forty years, stood as if carved from stone. He did not even turn his head.

I waited, neither speaking nor moving.

"Leave the food and go." Edward's voice was rough.

He stared out over the gardens and enclosing walls to the distant meadows and encroaching forest. Or perhaps he stared at nothing at all. He stood straight, legs braced, shoulders firm, head raised. There was nothing amiss with his health, I decided. My heart lifted a little. But the room, apart from the neglected chess game, was curiously impersonal. No books. No documents on the table. No habitual hawk on its roosting pole. Only the magnificent battle scene on the walls, its colors stark, even brutal in their vibrancy as the golden sun glinted on blade and armor sewn in silver thread. It seemed to me that the stitched battlefield dwarfed the King with its splendor. He could not have chosen more apt surroundings in which to sink into oblivion.

Edward did not turn to see whether his order had been obeyed. I did not think he cared.

I would have to make the first move after all.

"A cup of wine, Sire?"

My request dropped into the heavy silence. His body tensed. Slowly, very slowly, he turned, one hand resting on the stone ledge against which I now saw that he leaned. Perhaps he was more fragile than I had first thought.

Then, as the light fell fully on him, I saw what had previously been hidden.

Oh, Edward! What have you done to yourself? And as it hit home: *Did you love her so very much?*

What weight could my scribbled notes possibly have against this evidence of abject loss? Edward's face had thinned, the lines between nose and mouth deeply gouged, cheeks hollowed. His throat and neck showed a deterioration of flesh that he could not afford. Worse—far worse—was the dimness of his eye, the blue faded almost to gray, and the pale transparency of his skin. His mouth had not smiled, I thought, for weeks. The hand on the window frame was almost translucent. It looked incapable of wielding a sword.

First compassion. It flooded through me, almost to reduce me to tears. Then came fury as bright as the King's gold-crowned helm in the tapestry.

What was he doing to himself? How could the victor at Crécy wallow in miserable self-pity! Almost I spoke the words aloud, but then forced my anger to drain away. Ungoverned emotion would achieve nothing. The air around me was stuffed full of it, like goose feathers in a cushion. Smothering. All-enveloping. Edward had allowed it to gain the upper hand. But I knew: Emotion would not serve to accomplish my quest, but female cunning might. It might just save this man from himself and restore him to his uneasy realm. Perhaps in the end Fair Joan's conclusions on a woman's need for guile and duplicity were not incomprehensible.

So be it. I trod into his direct line of sight. "My lord."

"Alice." His eyes were unfocused; his voice, without its impressive power, grated from disuse.

I walked slowly forward, halting within an arm's length, interested in Edward's reaction. He seemed uncertain. And so he would be. I had dressed most conservatively, quiet and discreet as a nun. As a wife! I had laughed as I had donned the somber dark-hued gown and cotehardie more fitting to a housewife than a royal mistress. And so I played out my allotted role: I neither curtsied nor lowered my eyes in dutiful respect. I certainly did not kiss him in greeting, as I might have in the past.

"Yes, Sire," I stated in a cool manner, hands folded demurely at my waist. "As you see. It is Alice."

He frowned. "Who let you in?"

"Wykeham."

"I don't want to talk to you."

This was not good!

"As I am aware. You don't have to. I'll talk to you."

There was quick surprise in his eyes. Perhaps irritation. "I didn't send for you."

"No. I gave up waiting."

Edward's initial response was now overlaid by disquiet. Not quite disapproval, but not far off. Good! That was what I wanted. Would he order me to go?

"I would rather you weren't here. I would be alone." Not quite an order to leave, although I doubted he would see the difference. . . .

My reply was as flat as Wykeham's new paving in the great Court at Kings Langley. "Time for reflection is good, my lord. And I have reflected much." I put a hint of bite into the words. "Over the two months I have reflected—since you last spoke with me."

"Two months?"

"It is more than two months since you buried Philippa and shut yourself up here."

The vertical line dug between his brows. "I had not realized. . . ."

"Then you should. It's far too long for a king to shut himself away from his subjects."

I waited to see whether the Plantagenet temper would surface, and was disappointed when it didn't. My success was not a certain thing, even though I had thought long over this, as I unpacked my clothes in the new rooms that had been immediately set aside for me—Latimer was nothing if not an efficient steward. If Edward rejected me now, how should I force him to take note of me? Sexual allure? Not that. He was too solitary, too worn down with grief. Later, perhaps, but seduction was not yet the path forward. Stern admonitions—not that either. Plantagenets did not react well to stern admonitions from their subjects, even their lovers. Compassion? No—he would see that as pity.

I was here to draw Edward back from the brink of whatever hell he had made for himself, with cold logic. Had I a view to my place at Court? My own financial security? Of course I had. But my future and Edward's healing need not be entirely separate. I had no guilt as I poured the two cups of spiced wine—no longer warm but still palatable—and held one out. He took it automatically.

"I'm leaving Havering tomorrow. Drink with me to my safe journey." I did not smile. I was brisk.

"Leaving . . . ?"

"There's nothing to keep me here now."

"Where . . . ?"

"Ardington. I have a mind to see if it suits me to live there permanently."

Edward did not reply. So I would stir the pot a little more. I sat, even when he did not—such a breach of royal etiquette!—sipped the wine, inspected one of the cherry tarts on the plate, and bit into it. "This is delicious. Come, Edward." I made deliberate use of his name. "I can't eat all these myself."

He sat, but not close, regarding me as if I had transformed into a hunting cat that had just unsheathed it claws. "Why are you going?"

"I am no longer a royal damsel. I am not needed."

I let the silence play out, finishing the tart, licking my fingers, but in a businesslike manner. And then: "Have you thought about me at all through the past weeks, Edward?"

He shook his head.

"What have you been doing?"

"I have been thinking. . . ." His voice trailed off.

"I expect you've been thinking of all you've achieved," I observed. "All that you've done since the day you cast off your mother's authority and seized the ruling of England in your own hands. I imagine that took a lot of courage for a young man who'd barely reached maturity."

"I have thought of that. . . ."

"Philippa helped you, didn't she?"

For the first time, Edward smiled, a strained affair. "She was my strength."

"Tell me about it."

"I don't think I could have done it without her. My mother was a ruthless woman, and I was of an age to need a regent. . . ."

It was as if a wall had been breached, allowing the pent-up waters to escape. First a trickle, but fast becoming a flood. The old tale of the beautiful but vicious Queen Isabella, who would have ruled England with her notorious lover, Roger Mortimer, at her side, keeping the young Edward as close as a prisoner. Until Edward arranged a coup to bring Mortimer down, to strip his mother of her regency. He was all of eighteen years old, but the memories of that night in Nottingham when he took back his power were as vivid as if they had happened yesterday.

I nodded. "And Philippa helped you to stand firm, claim your birthright."

Edward's face was alight with it. "She was magnificent."

"She must have been very proud of you."

The light vanished. The rush of words dried up in a summer drought. Edward frowned, staring down into the cup, and I saw his jaw clench at some unpalatable truth. I knew what it was. I would say it.

"Philippa would not be proud of you now, Edward."

"No . . ."

"She would be horrified. She would berate you! Philippa would order you to look forward, not back."

At last his eyes lifted from whatever images he saw in his wine and slid to mine, and I saw true recognition there, and a flash of resistance. Good. Excellent.

"Have you come to berate me too?" he asked. "It is not your place."

"No. How should I? I am the lowest of your subjects and no longer have a claim on you or the Queen. I have come to say good-bye."

"I suppose you wish to be reunited with your sons."

"Yes. *Our* sons. Sons are very important. They are the only family I have. So, will you drink to my safe journey?"

He sipped the wine absentmindedly, his thoughts still far distant.

"Edward . . . !" How difficult this was. Was the only way to get his attention to empty my cup over the royal head?

"My son. My heir, the Prince. He is so ill. . . ." His words were spoken with difficulty as if he had to search for each one. "When I was his age I rode at the head of my army. What a sight we were. . . . But my son cannot ride. He is carried into battle in a litter. All I have achieved, destroyed . . ."

Panic fluttered, rapid wings beneath my heart. I was losing him again between the victorious past and the unpalatable present. I stood up, placed the cup on the coffer. I had to throw the dice with callous disregard, and risk the outcome.

"It seems I must leave without your good wishes after all." I walked to the door. My hand reached for the latch, and still there was no response. I would have to admit my failure. To Wykeham and Gaunt and the rest. I would have to leave my king, even though every sense urged me to stay. . . .

"Don't go."

It was quietly spoken, yet firmly. I exhaled slowly, but still I addressed my question to the smooth grain of the wood under my hand. "Give me one good reason why I should not."

"I want you to stay."

I held my breath.

"I need you, Alice."

I held still, eyes closed tight. I heard the brush of his tunic as he stood, the click of metal on wood as he placed the cup beside mine, his soft footsteps. I felt his body fill the space behind me, but he did not touch me.

"I was wrong, Alice. Don't go."

Against all my inner compassion, I kept my back to him.

"God's Blood! Look at me! I would rather not be addressing the back of that excessively unattractive hood you've chosen to wear!"

There it was. The command was back. But I would not succumb too quickly. I was not a fortress driven into surrender by a light threat and a call to parley.

"Two months—and you haven't once asked to see me. You feel lost without Philippa—I understand that"—I resented the quick flame of old jealousies—"but you must know how unloved and unwanted *I* have felt," I said. "I see no future for myself here if you don't need me." His hands were on my shoulders, turning me around so that I must face him. He was really looking at me, seeing me. At last!

And Edward tilted his chin. "Is that why you've clothed yourself as a drab? Like some penurious widow about to enclose herself into a convent and fill her life with prayers and good works? Perhaps I should send you off with some new gowns. How will you catch a man's eye otherwise?"

And there was the humor I had missed, a glint of it as the sun struck obliquely across his features.

"The only eye I wish to catch is yours!" I remarked with the slightest lift of my chin to match his, some would say with arrogance. I would not smile yet.

Edward bent his head and kissed me, my brow, then my lips, at first as if it were a difficult thing for him to do, to make this contact with a woman, like revisiting an old memory, uncertain of what he would discover on the half-forgotten journey. But then his mouth warmed against mine as his hands slid from my shoulders and closed around mine.

"Why is it that you make me feel renewed?" he asked.

I could feel the growing strength of his intellect as he sought my face for the answer. And as if he had found it, he raised my hands, still cupped in his, and pressed his lips to each palm, to the tip of each of my fingers, reacquainting himself with me after a long absence. Yet still we had a way to travel.

"How I have missed you, Alice. Why did I not realize it?"

"Because you closed yourself off to all but grief."

"Will you change your mind and stay here?"

"You too might change your mind. Tomorrow you might banish me!"

Temper flashed in Edward's face. "I order you to stay! Your King orders you! I need you to remain here."

The temper. The possession. The authority. They were all returned in good measure. I hid my smile but stood on my toes to kiss Edward's cheek.

He was already stripping the maligned hood from me so that my hair, unbraided beneath it, fell over my shoulders. He clenched his hand in it, into a fist.

"What lovely hair you have. Why do I feel that I have been outmaneuvered? You have never worn anything half so ugly as this." He dropped the hood to the floor.

"I have not needed to," I replied. "I had to do something to catch your attention."

And Edward laughed softly. At last he laughed. I led him over to the settle against the wall and pulled him down beside me. I would not let him go quite yet. I didn't trust his mood sufficiently. Reaching for the platter on the tray, I offered it.

"Eat one of these. You must be hungry."

"I suppose I must. If you eat them all, you'll lose your figure."

The final attack, the lethal thrust against which I prayed he would be helpless.

"I will anyway, my lord, with or without the sweetmeats." His stare was instant and knowing, on my face, my waistline. "I am carrying your child. Are you pleased?"

The King abandoned the sweet delicacy and turned his face into my hair. "I didn't know. You have to stay with me. I'll not have a child of mine raised without my knowledge. Stay, Alice. In God's name, stay."

I kept my incipient victory close as I unraveled another skein of my plotting. Edward must return to his people too. "Only if you'll take me hunting tomorrow. Please do," I invited, leaning against his shoulder. "I have no one to ride with who does not damn me as a daughter of Satan. Wykeham has taken to praying over me. And my mare needs exercise. She's eating her head off in the stables."

"You have been lonely." How clever he was at reading between my words. "I've neglected you, haven't I?"

He was mine. Color stained his cheeks; the years dropped away. Inwardly I rejoiced as I saw that the Plantagenet had returned. "Yes, you have," I said solemnly. "And now you must make recompense."

He stood and pulled me to my feet. "As I will. What is it my lady wishes?"

"Call a hunt, Edward. Let your Court see you. Let them know that the King is come again. Promise me." Still the slightest hesitation. "Promise me! Soon it will be too late—I will be too large to climb onto a horse!"

"I promise. Stay, Alice. I have missed you."

So I did. His kiss was long and deep with relief and an awakening of passion. "Come to bed, Alice. It's been a long time."

And so we returned to the vigor and heat of past days in the royal bed, where we could pretend that all was well. Edward took me with mutual satisfaction, confirming Gaunt's crude assessment of his male powers, and I could make the King forget the encroachment of age.

"You are a pearl of great price, my beloved Alice."

"And you are King of England. The country needs you."

"I shall rule." The self-regard was restored. "With you at my side."

Triumph surged through my blood as I gave my body to him once more. *I will look after him, Philippa,* I vowed. *I will care for him, nurture him, and love him.* And I kissed his mouth for my own pleasure, even as I acknowledged within my heart: Edward was no longer the man who had first taken me to his bed, the man who had first commanded me to his bed. But for now I had pushed back the shadows.

The hunt met in the courtyard, the denizens of the Court clad in velvet and furs. Horses stamped in the cold and sidestepped at the delay. The huntsmen swore as the hounds swarmed under everyone's feet. There was a sense of anticipation in the air that had been missing for a long time.

We waited. Would the King come?

We shuffled and puffed clouds of mist into the icy air. Squires brought 'round cups of spiced ale. We began to shiver at the delay.

Dark and saturnine in the middle was Gaunt, astride a glossy bay that resented the lack of action more than most. Beside him in the hands of a groom was the rangy gray that Edward loved. Deliberately Gaunt's eye found me in the crowd. No need for him to voice his concern, his blame at what he obviously saw as my failure. I returned his stare with a stony expression. I had done all I could.

Time passed.

Expressionless, Gaunt motioned to the groom to lead the gray stallion away. He drew on his gauntlets. "We'll go."

He raised his hand to draw the attention of the crowd, for the huntsman to blow the stirring note to move off. I sighed and admitted defeat, turning my mare's head toward the stables. I had no belly for the hunt without Edward.

"You'll wait for me, Gaunt."

He always was the master of surprise, of display and self-aggrandizement. The King strode down the steps and across the courtyard, taking the reins from the groom and swinging into the saddle with all the agility expected of him. By chance—or was it royal command!—a shaft of sunlight broke through to gild his leather and fur, sparking glints off the ruby that pinned the peacock feather to his cap and the jeweled chain on his breast. He smiled at the expectant crowd.

"An excellent morning. My thanks for waiting for your King—and my apologies. You need wait no longer." He was self-deprecating, with the same formidable charm that had won him more friends than enemies during his long reign. There were murmured greetings from all sides.

The huntsmen began to move from the courtyard, Edward riding beside his falconer, taking a hawk onto his wrist as if he had never been absent, except perhaps for the first moments of stiffness in his posture as he settled into the saddle. The air of melancholy had vanished with the donning of the handsome wolfskin cloak against the cold. As I hung back to take my habitual place at the rear with the women, I felt a warmth spread through my chest and my belly where the child lay. And I heard what I had prayed I might hear as Edward turned his head to address his son.

"After the hunt, come and see me. We must make plans—for our armies in France. It's more than time."

"Yes, Sire."

Gaunt, in his swaggering arrogance, which was as much a part of him as his raptor's face, gave me no recognition, but I could see the depth of his gratification as the brisk wind whipped color into his cheeks. Father and son exchanged a handclasp, reunited and set to enjoy the occasion. I tucked my skirts securely beneath my legs and nudged my mare forward to follow the rest. I too would enjoy the hunt. When the huntsman lifted his horn to blow the gone-away, I gathered up my reins.

The huntsman did not blow, his action arrested by Edward's hand on his arm.

"Mistress Perrers . . ."

All eyes fastened on the King, who had called the halt, and then shifted to discover me in the crowd. My hands closed sharply on the reins, causing my animal to jib. Never had the King addressed me so openly in public.

"Sire." I sounded breathless even to my own ears.

"Ride with me."

I hesitated, but only for a moment before I pushed my horse through the brightly clad melee to Edward's side.

"Sire . . ."

"You said you wanted to hunt. So you shall." He grasped my bridle to pull my mare closer, took my hand in his, then leaned over and kissed my temple. "You were right. It's good to hunt, and I have been remiss." His voice fell to an intimate whisper. "You will not be lonely today."

Around me there was a general intake of breath. To single me out in so obvious a fashion! The Court was astounded. Hot blood rushed to my face so that my cheeks flamed with it. To be kissed so wantonly in public . . . ! But was this not what I wanted, this acknowledgment in the face of lords and commons alike?

"Will you ride with me?" he prompted, forcing me to make a statement of our relationship. No one was to be allowed to fail to understand its meaning.

"I will, Sire."

As I fell in beside him, my hand still in his, the courtiers streaming out into the water meadow, the huntsman blowing the gone-away at last, I could do nothing but smile as brightly as the fitful sun that chose that moment to bathe us in gold. Edward had given me recognition in public. I was the acknowledged royal favorite.

I suppose my enemies multiplied that day. Did I care? I did not, for the flame of my ambition burned fiercely. It was a momentous day. The hounds ran to ground a particularly fine and royally tined buck. Edward's features sharpened and glowed with the exercise as his body relaxed into the familiar demands of the saddle. His laughter rang out, and the Court breathed a concerted sigh of renewed confidence. Even Gaunt looked content, despite my having replaced him at the King's side.

I rode beside Edward for the whole of the hunt. When the hounds picked up the scent and the riders spurred into a gallop, he restrained his mount to stay beside me, conscious of my state of health. He could not have made his choice plainer if he had ordered the Chester Herald to announce the news with a blast of his trumpet.

Alice Perrers was the King's Concubine.

I had to ponder this reversal of my fortunes, and did so in my room, where I stripped off my hunting finery and ordered my maid to fill the copper-bound tub with hot water. I sank into it with a sigh. I had not hunted for some weeks; my muscles complained, but not beyond what was tolerable. In the herb-scented water I inspected my belly that was rounded with the growing child: It would not be possible for me to hide it, and nor did I need to. For the first time I could display my increasing girth brazenly.

My name, in one form or another, had been on every pair of lips that day. Edward's very public showing of what all the Court knew, but pretended not to, had seen to that. No longer secret, no longer hidden, no longer a source of shame for the Queen, my position was exposed naked for all to speak of. It was Edward's gift to me, his recognition before the whole of the Court, with a generosity I could never have imagined. Made public and acknowledged by all, I was secure under the King's protection.

I repeated the epithets I had heard as the hunt pursued the hapless deer.

Alice the whore: not one I would choose.

La Perrers: better—but it had been said with a sneer.

Royal mistress, royal paramour: a ring of authority here, perhaps.

But this one I liked much better: King's Concubine. Official. Untouchable. Powerful. My sharing of the King's rooms and the King's bed was an undeniable fact; it lacked legal sanction, but the King's stated preference gave me status. No one, *no one*, would dare slight me, the King's chosen companion. Even Gaunt had managed to honor me with a deep obeisance as the hunt dismounted. I had never dreamed of such a gift, made in the face of the great and good, of which I was neither.

"Thank you, Edward," I whispered, my hands protective over my belly.

I let my head fall back on the rim of the tub and closed my eyes, enjoying my achievement.

Chapter Ten

Edward went into immediate conference with Gaunt. I knew nothing of the discussions, always the preserve of men, but I saw the results. The King was once more at the head of affairs, the reins firmly in his fist: Gaunt was ordered to Gascony with an army to give the beleaguered Prince some aggressive support against French incursions. Even more impressive, Edward ordered a second attack from Calais under a tough old campaigner, Sir Robert Knolles. If I had needed any evidence of Edward's recovery, it was this: a two-pronged attack from north and south that he had used in his early campaigns to good effect. At the same time a whirlwind of envoys was dispatched to the Low Countries, to Germany and Genoa, to enlist allies against the King of France.

Edward's nights were spent with me, where anxieties still gnawed at him.

"I should be leading the attack," he fretted. "Am I not strong enough?"

"Of course you are."

But the depredations of Philippa's death had dug deep. His strength was much restored, but however much I might not like to admit it, Edward's mind had lost its incisive edge. While he was playing chess, reading a book of favorite poetry, enjoying the music of a well-played lute and sweet singing, his concentration could vanish, his awareness of his surroundings drifting away like high clouds under the strength of a summer sun. Even his confidence waned. And as it faded, my fears for him grew. He would never lead his troops with the same superb flamboyance, if at all. And yet I gave thanks: The isolation was over and Edward was reunited with his Court. A victory at Gaunt's hands in France would in some measure restore Edward's confidence in his ability to make well-balanced decisions. I poured two cups of fine Bordeaux, a wine symbolic of Edward's possessions.

"To England's victory!" I raised mine, and drank.

"To England! And to you, my love." Edward kissed me with all the passion of a mighty king.

I celebrated too soon, of course. The news that trickled in over the coming months was not good. In the north King Charles of France had learned from past mistakes and refused to be drawn into battle against a major force. Knolles, increasingly vilified, lost impetus and authority, his troops becoming separated and easy meat for the French vultures to pick off. In the south we fared better. Limoges was sacked and burned, which put a stop to the French cause in that vicinity, but all we heard were tales of the Prince's being forced to return to Bordeaux, abandoning the attack, defeated not by the French but by his own pain-racked body.

Edward's convictions drained away.

"Gaunt is there," I soothed. "He will take control. There is no need to worry."

But increasingly Edward looked inward and was reluctant to talk to me. Nor did I realize the problem until I saw him waiting on the battlements for news that did not come, with young Thomas clamped to his side by a heavy hand on his shoulder, even though Thomas shuffled and twitched, clearly wishing to be in the stables or practicing his swordplay—anywhere but with his burden of a father.

"Then go!" Edward snapped, releasing the boy, and Thomas went with alacrity.

When I took the boy's place, tucking my hand within his arm, Edward smiled, but there was a loss in his face. It was not I he wanted, and although the remedy was clear to me, it was not a pleasant one. I thought I would not enjoy the outcome, but I was woman enough and confident enough in my new role to do it. For the sake of the King's health, I would risk the consequences.

I wrote a formal invitation on good-quality vellum, complete with wax and Edward's seal, and prepared to dispatch it with a courier in full regalia. It was wholly illegal for the King's Concubine to employ the royal seal—but why not? It could not help but have the desired effect. With a duplicity for which I made no excuse, I kept it from Edward. What point in raising his hopes if by some chance it never came to pass? Nor did I sign my name—it crossed my mind that I might just live to regret this missive. Indeed, I stood before the fire in my chamber, holding it between my fingertips as I considered consigning the document to the flames.

Could I not provide all the affection that Edward needed?

But news arrived. Devastating news that drove Edward to his knees in the chapel, his face ravaged with distress. The Prince's tiny son and heir, Edward of Angouleme, heir to England's crown, had died in Bordeaux. The Prince was too ill and distraught to carry on the campaign. He would return to England, leaving the campaigning in the increasingly ineffective hands of Gaunt.

Edward wept.

In the same hour I sent the letter. I could not afford to change my mind.

I wrote again to Windsor, with rigid formality.

I am restored to Edward's pleasure. And to his confidences. He has no interest in Ireland. The Gascony situation takes all his attention, which at best is wayward. You are still your own man in Ireland and I think there will be no interference from London.

I received a reply by return of the courier, in Windsor's trenchant style—he wrote as he spoke.

I received your two letters within days of each other; such is the difficulty of communication. I am relieved that you are restored.

For me or for him? I grimaced cynically.

Keep my name in Edward's mind. This is a hard road and I need all the help I can get.

The final paragraph surprised me.

I would give you one more piece of advice. You have experienced what it will be like for you without royal patronage. I did warn you when we last met. You rejected my advice. Now you know it for the truth. Your position as royal mistress can be undermined in the blink of an eye. Make the most of your opportunities while you can. I doubt the Prince and his ambitious wife will make a place for you at Court.

And then I was more than surprised.

I think of our meetings more frequently than I might wish. Yours was not a comfortable companionship, but I find that you dwell in my thoughts. It might surprise you to know that you are, on occasion, impossible to dislodge. You have claws of steel. So, accepting that, I admit that your wit and charm give me consolation in my isolation in this place. With some regret, I do not see myself returning to London within the foreseeable future. I think we would have dealt well together if events had fallen out differently.

Keep well, Alice. Keep safe. Your supreme position will make your enemies livelier than you might imagine. Take care that you do not put any weapons into their hands.

Accept this advice from one who knows.

I laughed softly, and then stared as I unwrapped the package that accompanied the reply, its content obvious even before I unrolled the soft leather: a slim-bladed knife that could be secreted in a sleeve or bodice. A lethal means of protection from the assassin. How ridiculous of him! Who would possibly wish me physical harm?

I found that I too regretted Windsor's absence from Court. I doubted he would be faithful to that final less-than-chaste kiss. But then, as King's Concubine, neither was I.

He had my protection in mind. A foolish dog and a slim blade.

Should I have been afraid? I was not. My mistake, perhaps.

The reply to my royal invitation took longer to arrive than Windsor's letter, but was far more impressive when it did. It came in person, arriving at Windsor with palanquins, outriders, and an impressive military escort with its pennons fluttering bravely. Eye catching and ostentatious, such an entourage could only have one owner. Yes, I conceded. I might just regret this. But it was the only answer to the problem that I could see.

Family!

Edward needed family around him. He wanted—as he had all his life—his children and the memories they brought him. He might be heroic on the battlefield, he might be a superb administrator, his physical presence might be matchless, but at home he needed the anchor of family. The absence of humor and affection played on his temper, his spirits. Philippa and the offspring she had borne him had been so vitally important to him after his own childhood of loneliness and isolation under the selfish hand of his mother. Creating his own family had been all-important to him, giving him all the stability and love he had never had.

But what now, now that his family had dwindled? Two sons in France, both heavily committed to war. Lionel dead in Italy. His daughters, except for one, all dead. Young Thomas too young and self-interested with the occupations of youth to give his father real companionship. Edward needed family around him.

Why can't you *give him what he needs?* I demanded crossly, but honesty made me admit: I could give him much, but not the sense of belonging that Edward needed. And the one remedy was, regrettably, Isabella, his much-loved daughter. Willful, capricious, a lover of ostentation and show. She was the remedy.

Now, below me, emerging from the swagged and cushioned palanquin was the unmistakable figure of Isabella, without her much-desired husband but with two little girls with the same fair hair and dawning beauty as their mother. I watched her arrival from the little chamber above the main door. Hardly had she set foot on the ground than she began to issue orders as if she had never been away.

I tapped my fingers against the window ledge as Isabella laid claim to Havering. Should I waylay her or let her settle in and meet Edward on her own terms? I mentally tossed the choices. If I went down now, there would only be a clash of words and personalities, with no one to cushion the resentment that would erupt like a flame to dry tinder. Ah! But if I let her see Edward, make her own rules, order her own accommodations, I would immediately put myself at a disadvantage. Isabella would take control before we sat down together for supper.

Well, now! I stilled my fingers, considering the appropriateness of my garments for the occasion that I foresaw. Since when had I retreated from a little unpleasantness? Was I not chatelaine of this palace since my very public elevation at the hunt? Who supervised the money and the housekeeping? God help me to harness my words and my temper—I needed her as my ally. So, having the niceties of Court ceremonial for the welcoming of important personages at my fingertips, I was standing on the dais in the Great Hall, clad in Court finery, Latimer and a servant at my side, when she eventually swept in.

"Are my rooms prepared?" she asked of no one in particular, imperious as ever, magnificent as ever, superbly gowned in an overrobe of silver and dulcet green that I instantly coveted. If I had not deliberately selected my newest gown, very much to Edward's taste, rapidly replacing the insignificant robe of leaf green that I had been wearing when I set eyes on Isabella's splendor, I would have paled into anonymity. Isabella retained her old habit of cutting one's confidence off at the knees. But I was now prepared to herald my new wealth and status in a startling figure-hugging robe of violet silk patterned in vermilion and blue. It was impossible to pale into insignificance in such a gown coupled with a cotehardie of gold damask. I was mistress here, and I signaled to the servant to lead Isabella's entourage and her two daughters to the accommodations I had had made ready for them.

Isabella remained. Her eye avoided me with careful nonchalance and fell on Latimer instead.

"Latimer! It's good to be back. Some wine, if you please."

"Of course, my lady." Latimer bowed to the Princess, and then to me, before exiting to obey the command. Isabella caught the action, as she must, and her brows rose into perfect arches as her gaze fixed on me, as I knew it would when she deemed it suitable. She had seen me the moment she had stepped across the threshold. How could she be blind to violet and vermilion?

"Well! Mistress Perrers!"

"My lady." I curtsied.

"I didn't expect you to be here still. And what role do you occupy now that you are no longer a damsel?" The disdain might have cut me to the quick if I were of a mind to let it. "Can I guess? Palace whore?"

I stayed unmoving on the dais. "Things have changed, my lady."

"They must have, if you are giving orders to Latimer." She produced a sudden frown. "Does my father know? I presume he does."

"Of course."

"So you have stepped into my mother's shoes."

"One might say. . . ."

She was uncomfortable, and I enjoyed it. Would she ask me outright? A servant entered with a tray of wine and offered it, kneeling before me. I motioned him to offer it to the Princess instead. What pleasure it gave me.

Her lovely face had acquired the consistency of granite. "You are controlling the household, it seems."

I inclined my head. "Someone must. It pleases the King that I do it."

Isabella deliberately ignored the wine. "I'll soon change that."

"Certainly, my lady. If you intend to take on the burden yourself . . ."

I knew that the Princess had no intention of taking on such a role. So did she.

"Where is the King?" she demanded.

"In the stables, I believe." Isabella turned on her heel. "Wait!" I had to speak now. "There's something you should know. . . ."

She halted. "And that is . . . ?"

"The King has not been robust."

"So?"

"Have a care in your choice of words to him."

"I don't need you to tell me."

I stepped down and faced her, our eyes much on a level. "But you do. You have not seen him in the weeks—months—since Her Majesty's death. I have."

She considered this, momentary indecision clear in her pursed lips, then spun around to accost Latimer, who had stepped quietly into the Great Hall again. "I understand the King has been ill, Latimer."

"Yes, my lady. But he is now much improved."

So she did not trust me to give her the truth even about her father.

I had some bridges to mend if I would make use of this Plantagenet princess. And seeing the ingrained hostility in the set of her spine, in her rigid shoulders, I thought I might have wagered wrongly in that damned invitation.

"Have you taken advantage of his kindness?" she demanded, jealousy thick in her voice. "I see you've been more than busy." Now that I was close, her eyes narrowed on my expanding waist. "Another bastard? Who'd have thought you'd have the wit to rise so high. But beware, Mistress Perrers; you'll rise no more."

I swallowed a smart retort. Isabella was an intelligent woman and I must appeal to that. I walked beside her, keeping step even when she quickened hers as if she would shake me off. Isabella had no idea how single-minded the Queen's erstwhile damsel could be.

"He can't be too ill," she announced. "He invited me here to participate in a celebration."

"I know."

"He said he was arranging a tournament."

"Yes."

"Would a man who was ailing commit himself to a tournament?"

"No."

"When is it to be held?"

"It isn't." That stopped her. Once again we faced each other like two cats posturing on a roof ridge. "There is no such arrangement," I stated.

"Who wrote the letter?"

"I did."

I heard the intake of breath, saw her nostrils narrow, and awaited the outburst, but it did not come. Rather her stare turned speculative. "To what purpose? You would invite me here?"

"You sound surprised."

"If you wanted to rule the roost, you would not bring me back to England. We both know my inclination is also to rule."

"That I know."

"So why?"

"The King's spirits are low. The Prince's state of health is uncertain, and his little son is dead. The King's in no mood for tournaments. Unless you persuade him, of course."

"I'll speak with him." She eyed me thoughtfully.

I smiled thinly. "I wish you well, my lady." And I did. Edward needed the distraction. "And I should tell you: The King does not know I sent for you."

I watched her go; the energy in her step was undoubtedly a flounce. She would not like what Latimer had to show her. I sighed and looked down to Braveheart, who pressed against my leg. God help me! Had I invited a vixen into the chicken run?

Isabella was in a conflagration of temper when I walked through the gardens to join the royal father and daughter and test the air between them.

"I have been turned out of my rooms!"

"Turned out?" Edward chuckled at the drama of it. "I expect you've been provided with something larger and far more fitting—you've brought the children, I presume."

"The rooms were mine—you had them built for me!"

"So I did. But they were empty. Why not make use of them? You rarely visit, and Alice finds them very comfortable."

Did I not say? Edward had moved me into the sumptuous royal apartments. When I had listed what I had wanted, I could not have envisaged what I got: the suite of palatial rooms constructed for a princess. And how I relished them.

A taut silence fell on us like a hoarfrost, sharp and cold, broken only by the strident cry of a magpie in the stand of trees. Isabella took a breath. I wondered what she would say, whether she could manage to be diplomatic. The line of her jaw had the tension of a bowstring. She stopped on the path with a swish of embroidered skirts, and turned foursquare to Edward.

"You would put your mistress in my room?"

No diplomacy here. Careful! I breathed. *Careful, Isabella! He may be aging, but his pride is as strong as it ever was.* In confirmation, Edward's hand closed tightly into a fist.

"I think you should ask pardon for that," he remarked mildly enough.

"Do we pretend she is not? That she was not, in all those years when my mother was alive?"

The ermine mantle of royalty slipped invisibly but impressively back onto Edward's shoulders. Even they braced as if to take the weight of it.

"I'll tolerate much, Isabella, but not that. You will not judge me or your mother. I have given Alice the authority to administer my household."

"I don't like it."

"You don't have to. You are a guest. If you do not like it, there is no compunction on you to remain." Isabella's lips parted, then clamped together. "Exactly! You are not without intelligence." Edward smiled, but the warning was still there. He knew exactly what he had achieved for me. "Now that the formalities are over, how long will you stay? We must see what we can do to entertain you."

Isabella's glance slid to mine. I left them planning. They were two of a kind when it came to outward display and spending money. So Isabella would stay for some weeks, but I was secure in Edward's favor. Daughter and mistress could work very well together when they had to, to ward off the dread melancholy.

Isabella had other ideas, of course. She whispered in my ear as we entered the Great Hall together for supper. "Don't expect to win my regard. You won't succeed. You're an upstart, Mistress Perrers."

True. I was, and always would be, but I had worked hard for my position. I decided to flex my claws a little.

"I don't need your regard, my lady." I remained solemn as she raised her brows. "His Majesty needs me in his life far more than he needs you."

"He'll listen to me. . . ."

"No, he will not. Ah . . ." Edward was there to lead me to the chair at his right hand. "Perhaps your daughter should take the preeminent position," I suggested smoothly. "For tonight, at least. As an honored guest . . ."

I showed my teeth in a smile. Isabella returned it but with a flash of eye as she sat. It was an excellent evening, with food and wine and music and entertainment. The King's spirits revived under his daughter's ready wit. She paced beside me as we left the chamber.

"Have a care, Mistress Perrers."

"I always do, my lady! I always do. As I have a care for the King."

She was furious, she would remain my enemy, but I knew she saw the truth in what I had said.

I left the field to Isabella through necessity, for I could barely see my toes over the swell of my belly. When the child kicked incessantly and I began to find life at Court wearying, I announced my intentions. Edward kissed my lips and my hands and packed me into one of his royal barges as if I were a precious piece of glass.

I had just acquired the house and manor of Pallenswick through Greseley's clever negotiation and my borrowed gold coin, courtesy of the royal Treasury. And Pallenswick was a gleaming gem of a property on the banks of the Thames, to which I had moved my sons and my whole household. My access to Edward and the Court was as easy as donning a pair of silk slippers.

"I'll come if I can," Edward assured me.

"I'll do just as well without you." I knew he would be engaged in the progress of the war, and would be barred from the birthing chamber, King or no. Isabella would keep his spirits in good order.

"I'll have Masses said for your safe delivery. Send me word."

"I will."

"I'll be content if you bear me a daughter."

"As long as she's less combative than Isabella!"

"Difficult not to be." Edward's laughter startled the ducks that quacked in the shallows. Then, as I settled myself against the pillows: "Don't go!"

The tightening of his hands around mine was a consolation, but I knew I must. In some matters I valued my independence. I wished to be under my own roof when I gave birth. And so I left Court. There was no secrecy now. My departure was marked with banners and pennons and a royal escort, such that all the world was aware that the King's Concubine would bear him another child. Isabella found other affairs to occupy her so that she would not have to pretend a degree of concern. Good practice, all in all.

My wolfhound traveled with me, nervous of the water. A more mis-named animal I had never met. I carried Windsor's dagger in my sleeve.

A basket of new-laid eggs rested on the table in the kitchen at Pallens-wick, where I was engaged in helping my housekeeper to clear out boxes of wizened fruit from the previous autumn. And tucked between the eggs was a letter. An unconventional delivery, forsooth. Intrigued, keeping an eye to Joanne, my new daughter, who slept in her crib be-side the hearth, I retrieved it and unfolded the single page. A brief note, no superscription, no signature, no seal. So someone wished to remain anonymous but had gone to a lot of trouble.

It is necessary for you to return to Westminster. Personal circum-stances must not be allowed to stand in your way. It is for your good and that of the King.

A clerk's hand. But from whom? I tapped the note lightly against the brown egg on the top of the pile. Not Edward. It was not his style, and why the need for secrecy? Wykeham? He would not stoop to un-signed missives. He would not need to, surely, as Edward's Chancellor. Edward's physician? If Edward were ill, a courier would have arrived with a horn blasting out its warning. Certainly not Isabella . . . None the wiser, I dropped the letter into the fire with a wry smile. Who would actually want me to return? I might be the acknowledged con-cubine, but most would happily clap me in a dungeon as far away from the King and Court as possible.

For the length of time it took me to walk from kitchen to parlor, the sleeping infant now in my arms, I considered taking no heed of it. But then—it was a warning. It was for the good of the King. I could not afford to ignore it—or could I? I did not appreciate an anonymous request that smacked of an order. I would think about it overnight.

I wished the anonymous writer a close association with the fires of hell.

I was, of course, up betimes, ordering my belongings packed and a barge made ready. I kissed my new daughter—fair and blue eyed like her father, named Joanne after Edward's beloved dead daughter who had been taken by the plague. I had balked at the name, it being uncomfortably reminiscent of the woman who had disparaged my low birth and consigned me to a life of drudgery, but on this occasion Edward's wishes took precedence. So I bade my daughter and sons farewell, admonished nurse and tutor with a multitude of unnecessary instructions, and set off for London within the hour. The writer of the note would make himself known soon enough.

I arrived to find that in my absence Edward had summoned a Parliament. It did not disturb me in any manner. With a new campaigning season approaching, a parliamentary session to give approval for taxation to raise the moneys to pay the English forces was an obvious step. It gave the palace at Westminster, where Edward was in residence, an air of turmoil. There was an unusual scurry and bustle, the stabling overcrowded, and accommodations for lords and bishops at a premium. The commons had to make what shrift they could. It would not affect me. Closing my door against the commotion without, I sighed with the pleasure of arrival. But not for long. I expect I scowled.

"You took your time!" John of Gaunt announced.

"What are you doing here?" I was not gracious. Why was I rarely gracious around John of Gaunt? And to find him here in my rooms, without my invitation. I think I always feared him. Gaunt was as ever impervious, sitting on the window ledge, his foot braced against the stone coping.

"I'm waiting for you, Mistress Perrers."

He'd had little to do with me since our initial agreement. Oh, his public recognition of me was superb. He might be forced to accept my importance to Edward, but still I thought he despised me. So what was he doing here? Unless . . . Suspicion began to flutter over my skin.

"I came as soon as I could," I said.

"I expected you yesterday."

I was right. He was plotting again. "So you sent the letter, my lord."

"That's not important. It brought you back. It should have been sooner."

I resented his tone—the peremptory demand, his overt criticism. My response was biting. "You didn't have the courage to sign it, did you, my lord?"

"Nothing to do with courage. More to do with discretion."

"So that no one knows you sent for the King's paramour? How unfortunate for you that you are driven to consort with such as me, having to admit that you actually have a need of me. Once was enough. But to have to ask again! How can you tolerate it, my lord?" How savage my taunts, but he had caught me on the raw.

Gaunt was on his feet, striding toward the door. I had pushed his arrogant pride too far.

"Wait!"

He halted abruptly, his face stony. "I don't have need of you. I was mistaken."

"Obviously you do." I removed my mantle and hood, giving myself time to struggle against the inclination to let him go and slam the door at his back. It must be serious for Gaunt to come to me; therefore it was for me to make the first gesture to this man whose conceit was vast. "Let us begin again, my lord." I stretched out my hand in a gesture of conciliation. "Tell me what the problem is and I will answer you."

Serious indeed! Gaunt needed no second invitation. "He refuses to do it. And he must. You are the only one he'll listen to. Regrettable, but a fact. You've got to persuade him."

Typical of the man to dive into the middle of the problem without explanation.

"I presume you mean the King. And I might persuade him if you are more specific. Come and sit with me, my lord, and tell me what's stirred this particular pot. Is it Parliament?"

"By God, it is!"

He sat and told me all in short, incisive sentences.

Parliament had begun the session in unfriendly mood. Their list of complaints would carpet the floor from Westminster to the Tower. All the money granted by the previous session—what had happened to it? Vanished without trace and with no achievement for it! England's proud name had been ground into the mud of Europe. Gascony was more or less lost. Where was the English Navy? Were there not rumors of French invasion plans? And now the King was daring to ask them for more finance. Well, they wouldn't provide it! It was throwing good money after bad.

I listened, honestly perplexed.

"I do not see how I can help in this matter," I observed at the end.

"They are looking for scapegoats," Gaunt snarled, as if I were wit-less not to see it. "They are unwilling to attack the King directly, but they are intent on drawing the blood of his ministers, accusing them of poor judgment. And unfortunately Parliament has discovered a weapon. What do all Edward's ministers have in common?"

I saw the direction of this. "They are all men of the Church."

"Exactly! Priests, to a man. What do they know about warfare? Noth-ing! Parliament wants them removed before they'll consider taxation."

It was now very clear, my role in Gaunt's plans. "And Edward will not do it."

"No. He is driven by loyalty. I can't move him. And if he won't comply . . . we would have a crisis at home to match the one in France."

"If I persuade Edward to dismiss his clerics, who will replace them?" I asked.

Gaunt smiled bleakly. "Here's my suggestion. . . ."

I listened to his planning. It was masterly. I could not find fault with it.

"Will you do it?"

I stared at him. "Will your new ministers not be unpopular?"

"Why should they be? They're not clerics."

"But they'll be seen as your men."

"They're men of talent!"

So they were. But for a moment I simply sat and considered the whole, making Gaunt wait just a little, because I was in a mood to do so. I could see no fault with his plan—and it would rescue the King's relationship with Parliament. It had much to recommend it.

"I will do it, my lord."

"I'm obliged!"

The agreement was accepted by the curtest of nods, and Gaunt strode from my rooms, leaving my previous good humor disturbed. Damn the man! Gaunt and I might be allies in this, but it would never be an easy al-liance. It crossed my mind that it might be like getting into bed with a viper.

Together Gaunt and I found Edward engaged in some heated conver-sation with Latimer. He greeted me with a smile, saluting my cheeks, but the welcome was notable for its brevity, even a touch of irritation.

"You should have told me you intended to return, Alice. I can give you only a few minutes, because . . ."

The burdens were hemming him in again. I saw the strain of holding his far-flung possessions together dragging at the muscles of his face. He looked beleaguered.

"We're here to talk about your ministers, Sire," Gaunt intervened gently.

"You know my feelings about that. . . ."

There was an irresolution about Edward that worried me. I touched his arm, drawing his eyes to my face.

"I have talked with your son, my lord. My advice is to do as he says."

"My ministers have served me well. . . ."

"But Parliament will not give them the benefit of the doubt. You need money from Parliament whether you like it or not, Edward. How can you fight without their support? Dismiss your clerics, my lord. Now is not the time to be indecisive."

I think I said no more and no less than Gaunt must have said already, but Edward listened to me.

"You think I should bow to Parliament's will?" His mouth acquired a bitter downturn.

"Yes, Edward. I do. I think it would be good politics."

So he did it.

And the men who came forward in the place of the unfortunate clerics proved to be the exact same coterie of men who had met with me in the circular room. All friends and associates of Gaunt, able men, ambitious men. Men who would serve Edward well and be loyal to Gaunt. Within the week the reorganization was complete. Carew became Lord Keeper of the Privy Seal. Scrope took on the burden of Treasurer. Thorp became the new Chancellor. William Latimer was honored with the position of royal Chamberlain, while Neville of Raby replaced him as Steward to the royal household. Thus a Court clique to close tightly around Edward and cushion him against the world that he found increasingly difficult to recognize.

I watched them bow before the King. Gaunt had it right: They were his men and would be bound to him, and since it was my influence that brought them to the forefront, they would be loyal to me also. Not one

of them would dare oppose me, giving me friends at Court who would
not neglect my interests.

So I took my first overt step into government circles.

"You must not worry, my lord." I raised one of Edward's hands to
my lips. "They will serve you well." The days when his palms were calloused from rein and sword were long gone. The strain in him, his lack
of vision for the future, were pitiable. He was like an aging stag, still
leader of the herd but with the weight of years beginning to dim the
fire in his eye. Soon the hounds would be baying to drink his blood.
Perhaps they already were.

"It is good that you are back," he said. "Have you brought the infant?"

"No. She is with her nurse. But I will. You will see her."

I accompanied him to the mews to inspect a new pair of merlins
just taken into training, relieved to see him enjoy the moment as he
handled the birds. Edward must not worry. But I would. I would do all
I could to keep the dangers at bay.

Gaunt, I presumed, was satisfied with the outcome. He made no
genuflection in my direction, but I felt the shackles that bound us together drawing tighter: We were undoubtedly in league, although
whether I had sold my soul to Gaunt or he had sold his to me was open
to debate. This was a marriage of convenience, and could be annulled
if either saw fit. We were too wary of each other to be easy bedfellows,
but for better or worse, in this political manipulation we were hand in
glove.

The result of our conspiracy was immediate and inspiring. Edward
addressed Parliament with all his old fire and won their approval, and
the money was forthcoming. England could go to war again, whilst I
smugly castigated the far-distant William de Windsor. *Look to your
enemies,* he had warned me. He had been wrong. I had friends at Court
now. Perhaps I should write to tell him. I consigned his dagger to a
coffer.

"I don't need you!" I informed an entirely unimpressed Braveheart,
who had curled up on the hem of my gown.

And if I needed confirmation of the rise of my bright star in the
heavens of Court politics, that was immediate too. When gifts were

exchanged between the royal Plantagenets, as was habitual at Easter, the sense of Gaunt's obligation to me must have struck him like a blow to the gut, for he was astonishingly and unexpectedly generous.

He proffered an object wrapped in silk.

I took it, unwrapped it.

Holy Virgin!

It was an exceptional object, a hanap such as I had never seen—a bejeweled drinking vessel, fashioned in silver and gleaming beryls, fit for a king.

Oh, I read Gaunt well. He had a need to keep my allegiance. My voice in his father's ear was worth every ounce of silver, every one of the jewels set in the hanap, a gift to buy my favors if ever there was one. And why was it so very necessary for this Plantagenet prince to have a royal mistress on his side? Because, as every man in the land knew, of the uneasy state of the succession. Because with the rumors flying out of Gascony of the Prince's health, no one would wager against the Prince dying before his father, and then the crown would pass to the Prince's son Richard—a child of four years. A state did not thrive with its ruler not yet out of his minority.

Did Gaunt see the crown of England falling into his own lap? Children's lives were vulnerable. Richard's elder brother was already dead in Gascony. Richard might not live.

But Gaunt was not as close to the succession as he might like to be, for would not Lionel's issue stand before him? Lionel, who had died so tragically in Italy, had produced a daughter by his first marriage. This child, Philippa, who was wed to Edmund Mortimer, the young Earl of March, was now mother to a daughter. If that young couple proved sufficiently fertile to produce a large family, a Mortimer son would take precedence over any offspring of Gaunt.

Not something to Gaunt's liking, I judged. There was no love lost between him and the Earl of March.

My thoughts wove back and forth as I inspected the splendid cup, as any tapestry maker would create a picture of the whole. It was all too far in the future for speculation, but without doubt Gaunt had much to play for in this complex picture created in my mind. For who would be a better king within the next decade? The child Richard? A Mortimer son as yet unborn? Or Gaunt in his full strength?

And just supposing the situation was solved and Richard lived? Still all would not be lost for Gaunt. A governor would be needed for the young Richard, and it was no secret who would be the obvious choice to educate and protect and direct the young King. Gaunt, of course. Gaunt would be in control. And he might still see the Crown as a not impossible prospect for his own son, young Henry Bolingbroke. And what better than to have as an ally the King's Concubine, who had the ear of the ailing King. Gaunt saw me as a useful arrow in his quiver in ensuring that the succession fell into the best hands, for nothing would persuade me that he did not have some scheme in mind. He was not a man to take second place, even to his brother, the dying heir, however deep his affection for him might be.

Was this treason on Gaunt's part? Of course it was.

I smiled, in no manner seduced by the quality of the gift, understanding the motives of the giver perfectly.

"Thank you, my lord." I curtsied. I would accept the gift, but my loyalty would remain true to Edward.

"It is my pleasure, Mistress Perrers."

Gaunt too smiled, sly as a fox.

I was not without regrets in all this realigning of alliances and royal ministers. Wykeham, the man who trod the line between friend and enemy, was the one victim in the political maneuvering whom Edward truly mourned, and so did I. I doubted a more honest Chancellor ever existed, but Wykeham was swept away in the anticlerical hysteria. It was impossible to save him.

Edward's departure from his minister was formal. Mine was not. He was packing his possessions, his beloved books and plans for even more buildings that would never now see the light of day. Standing at the open door, I watched him fold and place everything with meticulous neatness. William de Wykeham, Chancellor no longer. He was the closest to a friend, even if an unnervingly judgmental one, that I had. I did not call Windsor a friend. I was not sure what Windsor was to me.

He did not even turn his head. "If you've come to gloat, don't bother."

"I have not come to gloat." Wykeham continued wrapping a bundle of pens in a roll of cloth. "I have come to say farewell."

"You've said it. Now you can go."

He was hurt, and with every justification. I had stood at Edward's side and listened to the empty phrases of regret and well-wishing. It had been necessary, and Edward felt the hurt just as keenly as Wykeham, but the man deserved more. I walked 'round the room to force him to face me. He foiled me by picking up and rummaging in a saddlebag.

"Winchester will see more of you," I remarked, holding out a missal to him.

He snatched it from me. "I will apply my talents where they are appreciated."

"I'm sorry."

Now he looked at me. And I saw the pain of betrayal in his doleful eyes. "I never thought *you* would be the instrument of my dismissal. I thought you valued loyalty and friendship." He sneered. "You have so many friends, do you not? You can afford to be casual with them." I felt the blood stain my cheeks. "How wrong a man can be when he doesn't want to see the truth!"

"I don't think I was the instrument," I observed, keeping clear of sentiment. "Parliament wanted you gone. All of you."

"For crimes none of us committed. For lack of ability—and with what proof? We've more experience than the whole job lot of Parliament put together!" He shrugged, placing two more books into the bag. "I didn't hear you trying to persuade Edward to be loyal to old friends!"

"No, I did not."

"Nor did Gaunt." Wykeham glanced up under frowning brows as if to seek proof of what he suspected, and read the answer in my face. "Take care, Alice. You're swimming with big fish in a small pool here. Gaunt is a powerful man and might wish to become even more powerful. And when he does—when he doesn't need you any longer—he will be quick enough to rid himself of you."

"He doesn't threaten me," I replied. I thought about our last exchange, when I had returned to Court after Joanne's birth. "I think he would protect his father by whatever means. And to do that he needs me."

"*I* think he would feather his own nest."

"Who doesn't?"

"One day you will not be indispensable." A traveling inkstand followed the two books. "Stay away from him. He's not known for being scrupulous." When he looked up again his expression was smoothly bland, as if it were simply a piece of advice to a friend. But it was not. I knew it was not. It was a warning.

"I can't afford to antagonize Gaunt," I stated harshly.

"What? When you are the King's sight and hearing? His right hand?" Wykeham was mocking me now.

"For how long? You know my circumstances better than most. I need all the friends I can get, as you so aptly stated."

"Then you should turn your mind to making some, rather than antagonizing the whole Court."

"How can I, when what I am to the King lies at the root of all the hatred? To my mind I am stuck between a rock and a hard place. If I lose Edward, I lose everything. The Court will crow with delight. If I stay with Edward, I have a legion of enemies, because they resent my power. What do I do, most sage counselor?" He was not the only one who could stoop to mockery.

He thought about that. "I don't know."

"Well, that's honest enough." I growled moodily. "You could pray over me, I suppose." I wished I hadn't come.

"I will. . . ."

"Don't! I could not bear your pity!"

"You need someone's."

I flung away to the window, leaving him to his books, fighting against a ridiculous urge to weep.

"You could try the Prince when he returns," Wykeham said eventually, when he had allowed me time to recover. A man of cunning politics, Wykeham, in spite of being a man of God. I shook my head. There was no path for me to follow there. Joan would be no friend of mine. "He's expected home any day now."

"That's as may be." Adroitly I changed the direction of our exchange. "But what of you? At least you'll not be without comfort in your political exile. A dozen castles, palaces, and houses to your name at the last count. . . ."

His smile was wry. "But all belonging to my office. None of them mine. I too am vulnerable." The warmth was gone, and I was sorry.

"I'll see that you are rewarded," I found myself saying.

"Now, why would you do that?" How calm his voice, how trenchant his words. "Do I look as if I need your charity?"

"No! And I've no idea why I offered it! Since you are so unfriendly I should consign you to the devil."

"I'll not go. I'm aiming for a place with the angels."

"Then my advice is this—don't associate with me."

His smile, a merest breath, was a little sad. "You do yourself down, Alice."

"I merely follow the fashion."

"I've seen you with Edward. You are good to him, and for him."

"But only for my own ends." The scathing quality of my reply mirrored his and shook me by its virulence.

"I'll not argue the case, since you're determined to douse yourself in self-pity today. You clearly don't need me to point out your sins." He looked 'round the bleak, empty room. "Well, that's it."

I was sorry I had tried to provoke him. "When do you go?"

"Now." He bowed, quite formally. "God keep you, Mistress Perrers."

"He's more likely to keep you, my lord bishop." And when he laughed, I leaned forward and kissed his cheek. "Do you know?" I whispered, in a moment of gentle malice. "Sometimes I have thought that we could have been more than friends, if you were not a priest and I not a whore."

Wykeham's solemn face creased. "Sometimes," he whispered back, "I have thought so too. If you ever need me . . ."

He stopped at the door, and then went out, closing it quietly behind him so that I stood alone in the deserted room. Finding a forgotten quill on the floor, I picked it up and slid it into my sleeve. Bishop Wykeham was a friend worth having, and he was right to castigate my slide into self-pity. I had made my bed and for the most part enjoyed lying in it. It would be an unforgivable weakness if I were to whine about the repercussions.

I must be strong. For Edward, if not for myself and my children.

I watched Wykeham ride out, astonished at the sense of loss that was almost as painful as the guilt. He should not have had to forfeit his offices and his estates, and my guilt increased when Edward gifted one of Wykeham's estates to me: the pretty, desirable, extremely valuable manor of Wendover in Buckinghamshire, with its fertile fields and timber, its easy routes to London, and I was nudged into making reparation. Greseley had acquired for me the manor of Compton Murdak, and so I granted its use and income to Wykeham. I grimaced as I signed the document. Who said I had a heart of stone? But the grant was for a limited term only, and Compton Murdak would return to me. I was not too softhearted. It behooved me to have an eye to my own wealth, after all.

So Wykeham left, and I turned my mind to a meeting I really did not wish to have, but could not avoid.

I was late. When I arrived, father and son were in the midst of clasping hands in what was undoubtedly a joyful reunion. The Prince had returned to England. It would have been a moment for national and personal rejoicing, if it had not been so shattering for any onlooker.

Shattering? It was a truly horrifying spectacle.

I knew the Prince had needed to be carried into battle as if he were a man of twice his age, that his strength had waned so rapidly that he resembled in no manner the knight who had led his troops at Poitiers. We had all mourned the death of his firstborn son. But nothing could have prepared me for *this*. Whatever the disease that afflicted him, he was wasting away, his face a gaunt death's-head. Even from a distance I could see that Edward was as aghast as I.

"Thank God . . . !" Edward wrapped an arm around his son's shoulders.

"It's good to be home." The Prince stiffened, as if he could not bear to be touched.

"I have longed for this day."

Edward ushered his son to a seat. Isabella spoke softly, with something like despair freezing her features into what might pass as a smile. And there at Edward's side, her hand on Edward's arm as she smiled up into his face, was the Princess Joan.

The Fair Maid of Kent.

I had last seen Joan brushing the dust of Barking Abbey from her skirts. Now I took stock. The years had not been kind to her, her face full and round like a new-made cheese, flesh encroaching on her slight frame so that her once-fastidious features were now flaccid, coarsened, and the remnants of her earlier prettiness wholly overlaid by excess. Over all, gouged in the soft flesh next to mouth and eye were lines of grief and worry.

Edward was busy with the Prince. Isabella and Joan stood a little apart, two forceful women. As I walked toward them, Joan looked 'round, her expression such as she would direct at a servant tardy in bringing wine.

"Here is Alice," Isabella announced with a face and voice as bland as a dish of whey.

"Alice?" Joan's lips pursed.

"Alice Perrers. The King's whore." Isabella stated it without inflection.

"We had heard. . . . So it's true. . . ." Joan stilled as she saw me, really saw me, for the first time.

I curtsied, my expression, my bright smile, one of disingenuous welcome. "My lady. Welcome back to England."

Joan's brows snapped together. Memory returned, as it must. "The Abbey!"

"Yes, my lady. The Abbey."

"You two know each other?" Senses instantly on the alert, Isabella was jolted out of her blandness, like a cat spying an approaching mouse.

"Yes," I replied. "The Princess was kind enough to give me a monkey."

"How unfortunate that it did not poison your blood with its bite," snapped Joan.

"I have proved to be exceptionally resilient, lady," I assured her with gracious serenity. "You will be gratified to know that I found your advice most pertinent."

"Your name was not Perrers," Joan responded, as if it made a difference.

"No. I have been wed."

"Fascinating . . ." Isabella purred. "A reunion. How charming . . ."

Joan's gift for razor-edged comment returned with polished venom. "She was naught but a clumsy, nameless servant lent to me to fetch and carry." She turned on me with fire in her eye. "By what ill chance did you become . . . ?" She gestured to my clothes, my person.

"The King's lover? No ill chance, lady. I am mistress of my own destiny now."

"Fortunes change, dear Joan," Isabella interposed with sparkling devilment. "As you yourself should know. Alice is a remarkably powerful woman."

"It's not fitting," she spat. "And now I've returned. . . ."

"I doubt you'll change the King's mind." Isabella was enjoying this.

"The King will listen to me!" Joan was not.

I waited, sure of my ground. I would not antagonize—that would not be politic—but neither would I give way before such impertinence at the hands of this woman who expected to slide into the preeminent role as the next Queen of England. The preeminent role was mine.

Edward became aware of my presence.

"Alice . . ." His touch of greeting on my hand was unmistakably intimate.

"My lord. The Princess has been telling me how much she anticipates renewing my acquaintance. It is my greatest wish," I said, placing my hand softly over Edward's. "We will do all in our power to make Joan's return a happy one. I have ordered the apartments at Westminster to be made ready."

"Excellent!" said Edward.

"A family reunion, no less!" Isabella smiled.

Joan scowled at my use of her given name, then quickly hid it behind a tight curve of her mouth and an unmistakable barbed response. "I cannot express my gratitude!"

So the battle lines were drawn. Joan regarded me as less than a beetle to be squashed beneath the sole of her foot. She might justifiably have expected to order affairs in England to her liking, with the approval of a father-in-law who remembered her fondly as a child brought up in the royal nursery. And now, in the space of a half hour, she had learned that she had a rival. I was the one to order affairs at Court.

But a warning tripped its way down my spine. At some point in the future, which I would not contemplate, Joan would be the one to hold all the power.

"We should celebrate my son's return," Edward announced, oblivious to the antipathy amongst the women in his household.

"I will be gratified to arrange it, my lord," Joan responded, seizing the chance to make her mark.

"No, no. We won't ask that of you. I think we can give you time to recover from your long journey, my dear." Edward looked across the Princess to me. "What do you think, Alice? A tourney?"

It was not done deliberately. Edward had little guile in him these days, but the effect was like a bolt of lightning. Joan inhaled sharply, hands clenched in her damask skirts.

"I should take up my responsibilities immediately," she stated. "As your daughter by marriage, I should be hostess at a Court function."

"But Alice has the knowledge and the experience," Edward demurred. "She's the one to ask. What do you say?"

"A Court banquet," I replied. "To organize a tourney would take too long."

"Then a banquet it shall be." Edward was turning away, back to his son, content.

"I would organize a tourney!" Joan's demand sliced through the air.

"As you will. Talk to Alice about it!"

With true male insouciance, Edward cast aside the matter to return to the discussion of military tactics with the Prince, leaving me to fight a war in his wake, but unlike the days in the Abbey, I had the skills now to avoid and maneuver. And attack. And surprisingly, I had an ally.

"It is my right, and you will not usurp it," Joan declaimed. "Now that I am returned—"

"Of course," I interrupted pleasantly. "I'll tell the King you insisted. A tourney? You'll need to speak to the Steward, the Chamberlain, the Master of Ceremonies. The Master of Horse, of course. Chester Herald if you intend to invite foreign knights—which I'm sure the

King will insist on. . . . I'll send them to you. I'll send Latimer to discuss the ordering of food. The annual cleaning of the palace, which is now pending. . . . And where will you live? Do you intend to stay at Westminster? The accommodations are not very spacious. . . ."

The planes of her face tightened. "The Prince has not yet decided. . . ."

"Then do you wish to interview them in my rooms?"

"No."

I spread my hands. "What do you wish?"

"Let it go, Joan." Isabella chuckled. "Hold a banquet. It's much less hard work in the circumstances. And let Alice do it."

"I thought *you* would understand."

"I understand that Alice is a past master at arranging these affairs."

"Which I intend to change . . ."

"And I also understand that you are *jealous*, dear sister."

"Jealous?" Joan's voice climbed. "She has no right!"

"Sometimes, Joan, it is necessary to accept the inevitable."

"That this woman rules the King?"

"Yes. And you should have the wisdom to give her credit for what she does astonishingly well."

"I will not listen to you!" Joan stalked away to her husband's side.

"Then you are a fool," Isabella murmured after her, sotto voce.

"Whilst I," I added, astounded at this turn of events, "am entirely perplexed!

"What I don't understand," I murmured to Isabella when the Prince and his wife had departed for a temporary stay in the royal apartments at Westminster, and I was left to consider the burden I had just been handed, "is why you would throw in your lot with me rather than with the Princess. Why not plump for a tourney and let her get on with it? Would it not please you to put my nose out of joint?"

"She's naught but a block of lard!" Isabella announced.

"So?"

"I dislike her."

"You dislike me!"

"True—but if truth be told, perhaps not as much as I dislike her. I always have."

"Joan will one day be queen," I warned. "I have no long-term prospects."

"I know who holds the power now, and it's not Joan."

"I still don't understand why you would stand at my back when Joan tried to stab it."

Isabella frowned at me, clearly considering whether to take me into her confidence. "We'll need a cup of wine. Or two . . ." Her eyes gleamed.

We sat in the solar, two conspiratorial women.

"Not a good marriage!" Isabella pronounced, and proceeded to inform me of all the facts that fair Joan had failed to impart to me about her marital affairs in those far-distant days at the Abbey.

Delicious scandal!

Joan had made a clandestine marriage, no less, at the precocious age of twelve, with Thomas Holland, who promptly abandoned his child bride to go crusading. Meanwhile Joan was forced by her family into a second marriage with William Montague, son of the Earl of Salisbury. Holland returned and for a good number of years became steward of William and Joan's household.

"Can you imagine," Isabella gloated in unseemly mirth, "what a convivial household that must have been! Whose bed do you think she shared?"

Then Holland petitioned the Pope for the return of his wife, and got her back, for good or ill, after an annulment of the Montague union. Holland died in the year I first met Joan.

"But Montague was still alive," Isabella stated. "A living husband, even a dubiously annulled husband, did not make Joan good material for a royal bride. It smacks of a bigamous relationship to me! Many might consider so unorthodox a situation to be an impediment to the legitimacy of any child my brother got on Joan. Is their child Richard a bastard?" Isabella wrinkled her nose. "Hardly good news for the succession! The Virgin of Kent she was not! But my brother closed his ears and the marriage went ahead. Joan had him in her thrall." Her lip curled. "She's an ambitious woman."

I could not blame her for that. "Like me?" I asked wryly.

"Exactly. That's why she hates you."

But Joan had every right to be ambitious. Furthermore, she would see her ambition fulfilled, and I would find myself effectively banished.

"Did you see her?" Isabella continued, oblivious to my thoughts, not mincing her words. "Joan the Fat! She still preens and smirks as if she were beautiful. And that makes it all the more incomprehensible to her—that you should have such power with the King when you are *not* beautiful." Her stare was uncompromisingly critical. "Famously ugly, in fact."

I stifled a gasp at the outrageous statement. "My thanks for the compliment." But I think I had become resigned to it. It no longer hurt.

"It's true."

"The King does not think so," I observed.

"The King is blind!"

And I thanked God for it. What a rewarding exchange of information this had been. Princess Joan would be my enemy. But Isabella . . . Here was a strange twist in our troubled relationship, yet it would be an unwise woman who put too much weight on any new intimacy. I raised my brows, determined to prod and pry.

"Do I understand that you will be my friend, my lady?"

The reply was as sharp as I expected. "I wouldn't go as far as that!"

"I have never had a friend," I added, poised to see her response.

"I'm not surprised. Your ambitions are beyond what most people can stomach." She perused me, her eyes bright with anticipation. "But I'll say this: It will be interesting to watch the battle royal between the pair of you. I'm not sure that I wish to wager on the outcome. It wouldn't surprise me if the banquet never happened."

In that moment I found myself wishing for the one thing I had never had—a friend, a woman to whom I could speak my mind with confidence and trust. A confidante. What would it be like to say what was in my heart, to bare my soul and know that it would be treated with respect? How would it be to have a woman to turn to for understanding, even for judgment? For balanced advice? I had never known it.

Was this a melancholy?

Briskly, I took myself to task. How was it possible to miss what one had never had?

I arranged a banquet to mark the return of the Prince and Princess.

I was suitably extravagant in my outlay of coin to make the desired effect. The only whining voice raised in protest was drowned out by the din of the feasting courtiers.

"What did you wager on this banquet ever coming to fruition?" I asked Isabella.

"Not a silver penny! I thought the planning would shatter on the rock of Joan's disgust."

I smiled in pure joy. "You were wrong."

"So I was."

Joan was not finished with me. She had not even started. With a smooth exchange of seats as the feasting ended and the wine flowed, as the minstrels dived into their—to my ear—unmusical renderings, encouraging the Court to leap and caper with riotous levity, she leaned close, her eyes hard as jade.

"When I am Queen of England, I will destroy you for what you have done."

I returned the gaze, a little contemptuous. "And what have I done?"

"You have entranced him! You have taken the King's mind and twisted it! You have usurped a role that is not yours to take. Nor ever will be. You have schemed and manipulated until he sees nothing but your desires. You trick him at every step and turn."

I was startled by her unsubtle accusations, but not perturbed. I would use her own words against her.

"As I recall, my lady, you advised me that a clever woman should always be capable of dissimulation, and mocked me when I did not comprehend." I smiled as her face became suffused with color. "I have no need for guile or trickery. I show the King the respect he deserves. Which is more than you do, my lady. Do you think him so weak of mind that he cannot withstand the wiles of a woman?"

For a moment she stared, openmouthed. "How dare you!" She had not expected me to retaliate.

"I have brought nothing but pleasure and contentment to an aging man."

She was quick to regroup; I had to give her that. "Is that all? I see more, Mistress Perrers! You dip your fingers into the royal Treasury. Who paid for those garments you wear? You walk these corridors as if you were queen. I've seen you—you wheedle and connive until you squeeze all you can of land and estates and wardships from the King. When I am queen I'll strip you of all you've filched and send you packing back to that dire convent with only the clothes you stand up in. And not even those, I swear . . ." Her eye traveled over my new velvet sideless surcoat in royal crimson, the jeweled cauls that encased my hair. "Then who will remember Alice Perrers! And if I discover you have at any time stepped even an inch outside the law, I'll make sure there is a cell to confine you for the rest of your earthly existence. A pillory would not be too good for such as you! Even a noose . . . !"

I looked across to where the Prince sat beside his father, allowing her bitterness to pass for the most part unheeded. Her accusations were not new to me. They could be heard in every quarter of the palace, with or without evidence to prove them. I had learned to live with them.

"Look!" I interrupted her with a nod of my chin. And she did, the invective drying.

"Do you truly look? And acknowledge what your eyes show you? When will you become Queen of England?"

Two men. One old, one in what should be his prime. One fading slowly as the years took their toll, the other racing to his death. Unless there was a miracle, there was not one man in the country who would wager a purse of gold on the Prince outliving his father. Edward might be fifty-nine, the Prince a mere forty-one years in comparison, but I knew who would die first.

So did Joan.

And I saw the emotion that took a grip of her features so that any remnant of good looks was transmuted into ugliness. So she loved him. Despite everything, I felt a tightening around my heart and an unexpected lurch of compassion.

"It must be hard for you to be so impotent," I said.

But my compassion was wasted. Joan's eyes might be bleak with despair, but she thrust aside my observation with the flat of her hand slapped down on the table. "My lord will recover with rest and good nursing. And your days will be at an end. The Prince will live—you'll see. And my son after him. I will be Queen of England. Your present good fortune will be laid waste before your eyes." Her hands curled into fists on the table.

"I wish you and the Prince well, my lady."

I shrugged off Joan's answering stare that could have pierced a shield at fifty yards. Her plans for the Prince would never come to fruition, and Joan was wretchedly, hopelessly building a bulwark against the truth. I went to stand beside Edward, enjoying the brightness of his face as he conversed with his son.

Edward's restored vigor with the return of the Prince had its own consequences. I fell for a child at Easter. A girl, Jane, to join her sister in their little household at Pallenswick. She was not a pretty child, for she inherited my heavy brows and dark coloring, but I lavished love on her because of it, and Edward presented her with a silver bowl that I stored away with the other three. Edward had no imagination for birth gifts, but the recognition of this dark-browed daughter was magnificent.

Edward's return to good heart proved not to be transient. Despite the Prince's weakness and his inability to visit Court with any frequency, Edward began to turn his ear to what was happening outside the walls of Westminster, where we were settled for the term.

"Consider Parliament's grievances," I advised Edward.

And so he did, meeting with his council at Winchester, as in the old days. Graciously conciliatory, he listened to the endless petitions, promising redress but doing nothing to undermine his own prerogative. Regal authority sat well on him with his ermine robes. When he returned to me from the success of his meetings, his enthusiasm filled the rooms of Westminster with a blast of energy. "I will rebuild our defenses," he said. "And then we will go to war again. I will restore Gascony to English hands. Gaunt will help me. . . ."

"You will do all that is necessary," I assured him.

His smile was almost a youthful grin. "I feel the years falling from my shoulders."

We went hunting, the best sign of Edward's renewed spirits.

Gaunt acknowledged his father's initiative with a bow in my direction. "My thanks."

"It is my pleasure, my lord."

I needed no more. Edward was himself again.

Beware fickle fate! Never turn your back on her. If you do, she will sink her teeth into your unprotected heel. If there is to be any maxim applied to the conceit of my life, that will be the touchstone. My spirits, one minute soaring as high as Wykeham's new towers at Windsor, in the next collapsed as if the foundations had been fouled by a detail of zealous sappers. Edward sat in stunned silence, his knuckles white as his hands gripped and kneaded the arms of his great chair. I stood at his side, even going so far as to touch his shoulder to remind him of my presence. I don't think he felt it. His mind, his inner vision, was across the sea with this ultimate, irreconcilable loss. All my hopes, all Edward's optimism, were destroyed in one piece of news from a royal courier. The King aged before my eyes.

"This date will be engraved on my heart," he murmured, his voice broken with grief.

I would have saved Edward from knowledge of the devastation, but how could I? It was his ultimate responsibility. Unaware of the latent strength in his hands, seeing nothing but the bloody massacre that had been recounted, he gripped my fingers as if to draw the lifeblood from them. And there was nothing I could say to him to soften the agony.

The English fleet was lost. All of it. Completely and utterly destroyed when pounced on by a Castilian fleet, in opportunistic alliance with France, in the seas off La Rochelle. Our ships were swept by fire. Terrified horses stampeded, breaking apart the wooden vessels that contained them. The English commanders were captured.

It was a terrible scene of wanton death and carnage.

Edward gazed at the wall before him, seeing nothing but the destruction of his life's work in this, his first major military defeat in his long reign. He said not one word, even as he sat through the night staring into the flames of the fire he insisted on having lit in his room despite the heat of the summer. I sat with him. I feared for his reason through those long hours. The next morning, as light filtered into the room, he stood.

"Edward . . . you haven't slept. Let me . . ."

His words startled me.

"I'll have my revenge," he said, low and even. "I'll lead the greatest army England has ever seen into France. I'll fight to take back all I have lost. I'll not return home until it is done."

But it was a charade laid bare by the transparency of his skin pulled tight over spare cheekbones, by the trembling in his hands.

Should I have tried to dissuade him? Should Gaunt? We did not. There was about Edward a hardness that I recognized and knew I could not fight against. He might be aging, but he was a lion still and needed to prove to himself and to England that he was a king worthy of his crown and people's loyalty. I let him be.

The preparations were magnificent, the army vast as, flanked by Gaunt and even the Prince, who was roused by the crisis of the moment, the whole force embarked on the Thames with appropriate fuss and splendor. Pride filled my heart, for a short time sweeping away my doubts as I watched from the shore. Edward stood at the forefront in gilded armor and helm, his heraldic lions resplendent above him as the war banners whipped in the wind: a sight to stir the senses. I had already made my farewell. Now I must leave him to God's grace and pray for his success.

"I'll die on French soil before I allow them to take what is my inheritance!" he had sworn as he boarded his flagship, *Grace de Dieu*.

It frightened me for him to tempt fate in such a manner. *By the Virgin!* My fears were well-founded.

Three weeks later, the vessels had not stirred from port, contrary winds battering Sandwich and the brave plan into pieces. In Gascony, our beleaguered town of La Rochelle fell to the French. In utter despair, Edward called off the campaign. It was a sad, hopeless old man who returned to London to my waiting arms, and I could offer him no solace.

The humiliation broke Edward. His world fell apart around him. Philippa's death had wounded him sorely, but the failure in war broke him beyond repair. And during the following months with Edward sitting helpless in London? Not one major battle to claw back English advantage, but any number of minor skirmishes, each English-held castle and town coming under attack. Every English defense was obliterated. By the end of it, Edward's Gascon territory was even smaller than that bequeathed to him by his father.

All his life's work destroyed.

Despairing, Edward galloped into a truce signed at Bruges to cease hostilities. If England was humbled, Edward was trampled underfoot. He had lost everything, a thing that his mind found it difficult to comprehend. He tired quickly, losing the thread of conversations in the middle of a thought. Sometimes he fell into a silence from which he could not be roused. Sometimes he did not recognize me.

Chapter Eleven

*S*ir William de Windsor! Back in England! Back within my orbit!
He might have thought it a matter of pure chance that I was
crossing the vast space of the Great Hall at Westminster when
he arrived, but I could have put him right if I had chosen to do so. I
knew exactly when he dismounted from his mud-spattered mount, dispatched his horses, baggage, and escort to the stabling, exactly the
moment when his foot struck the first of the steps into the great entrance porch.

I stood in the shadows cast by a pillar to catch a glimpse of him, the
first for nigh on four years. I had been expecting him, for before the
debacle of the English fleet off La Rochelle, when Edward had turned
his mind to England's precarious hold on Gascony, he had also picked
up the rumors emanating from Ireland.

It was not good news. It never was. The usual trail of accusations of
inefficiency, bribery, corruption, and backstabbing in the highest circles. Which put Windsor directly in the firing line, for no one doubted
that the power was in Windsor's hands rather than in the hapless Desmond's. Windsor had no warning from me. Had I not promised to
apprise him of royal policy toward Ireland? The last time I had written
was to tell him that there *was* no policy. By the time I knew of Edward's
renewed interest, events had overtaken me. In an unusual burst of

anger, and a flash of the old independence, Edward had ordered Sir William to get himself to London on the next available ship and deliver an explanation in person.

When he would come, *whether* he would come, was a matter for conjecture. It was easy enough to claim the message lost en route. But I thought he would obey the summons. Windsor was not a man to hide from notoriety. And so I had been watching for his arrival, unsettled by the range of emotions that was stirred up in me. Some trepidation, some anticipation, a good deal of mistrust. And more than a pinch of pleasure.

And here he was. My first impression—more than an impression, more a certainty—was that Windsor was not in a good mood. I would not have expected otherwise, given the tone of the royal demand. Crossing the threshold, he looked as if he had been thrust into the hall by a blast from a raging storm. His clothes were wet and mud-spattered; a hint of stiffness in his muscles told of long days of travel. Driven, furiously engaged with the direction of his thoughts, as if the storm had entered his brain, he marched forward. I thought he would stride straight past me. Did he even see me?

I waited until he drew level, even two steps beyond, picking apart my own wayward reaction to this man as my heart beat a little more quickly, my mind bounding ahead to the prospect of his caustic observations. Unexpectedly my lips warmed. That final kiss had been compelling.

If I did not speak now, he would be gone. . . .

"Sir William . . ."

He lurched to a halt, wheeled 'round, eyes fierce as if he expected an enemy to leap from concealment. Then he gave a sharp, impatient exhalation of breath.

"Mistress Perrers."

He made a scratchy bow, irritable beyond words, to which I responded with an equally brief curtsy. Braveheart, older but no wiser, pushed hard against my legs to give herself courage.

"Is that all you have to say?" I asked sweetly.

His eyes narrowed. "What do you want me to say? I'm back. And not best pleased."

An understatement, I realized, seeing his expression clearly for the first time. His face was set hard, engraved with a faint cobweb of lines by eye and mouth that were new since I had last seen him. His tight-lipped mouth and flared nostrils spoke of temper. His whole body was, in fact, an essay in contained fury, with all the allure of a shard of flint. But my heart shifted at the proximity of his lean frame and sardonic features. When he snatched his hat from his head in a gesture of furious impatience, his hair clung, sleek as moleskin from rain and sweat, against his skull. The eyes that were dark and hostile on mine as he waited for me to speak were no darker than his dangerous and volatile mood. And still I felt that uncomfortable thrill of attraction, new to me, but frighteningly appealing.

I set myself to speak of immediate affairs. Indeed there would be no point in doing otherwise, since the man was too caught up in the moment to think beyond his grievances.

"I hope you've come prepared to answer for your actions in Ireland, Sir William."

"I might have hoped you'd have warned me, mistress," he snapped back.

"And I would." I tilted my chin a little. I did not appreciate his criticism. "It was too late. The King's summons would have reached you before any warning of mine. Besides, would it have made any difference?"

He shifted his shoulders irritably. "So he's angry."

"He's not pleased."

"I thought the King was fading . . ." he growled. "I had hoped the Prince might have spoken for me."

"The Prince is ill."

"I had heard. . . ." Windsor sighed, his thoughts momentarily diverted. "And God knows I'm sorry for it. Once, we were close enough, fighting side by side, campaigning together—twenty years ago now." His frown deepened as he stared down at his fist clenched on his ill-used cap. "We were both young and loved the soldiering life. He was the best commander I ever knew. And now . . ."

"Now those days are gone; the Prince is dying."

"Is he, now? It raises a question over the succession."

"It does. A question where more than one has an interest."

"The child is too young . . . five years?"

I sighed silently. Politics and policy. Court intrigue. This was not what I wanted to talk of when my heart was beating and my blood racing: that same strange reaction to this man whose principles were questionable, whose motives were driven primarily by personal ambition, and whose actions did not bear close scrutiny. I realized that a silence had fallen between us, and that for the first time Windsor was concentrating on me.

"You look well," he announced brusquely.

"I am."

"I see my wolfhound fulfills her role."

"Not to any degree." I dug my fingers into the rough hair at Braveheart's neck, causing her to whine in delight. "She needs my company to make her feel brave, and even then a mouse would frighten her. Your choice was not a good one, Sir William."

"And the blade?"

"I have had no occasion to use it, unless it be to cut my meat."

"For which it was not intended!" For the first time his eye glittered with more than ill humor. "Tell me that you keep it in your bodice."

"I'll tell you no such thing."

I waited for a provocative reply, but he surprised me.

"I hear you've made a reputation for avarice. Your hold on power has grown apace since I saw you last. I commend you."

It hurt a little. I did not expect that from him. "And I hear that you are much disliked by those whom you rule." I would give as good as I got.

"I also hear that you are making a name for yourself acquiring rights over property by fraud."

Acquiring property? He would know, of course. It was no secret—but fraud? Oh, he was in a vicious mood. I raised my chin.

"Fraud? That's unproven! My agent, Greseley, is a man of high principle!" My response was sharp, for I would defend my business dealings until my last breath. "If you refer to the fact that I have just acquired the manor of Compton Murdak with some difficulty, then that is so. Are you so interested? Then let me tell you. I sued John

Straunge for poaching in my new rabbit warren—did you hear of that too? He was as guilty as hell and deserved the fine. His wife wore a rabbit-skin hood." I smiled at the memory. "I sat with the judges in the case and pointed it out to them. They were not pleased at my interference, but they ruled in my favor. How could they not? If that is fraud, then I am guilty." I grew solemn. "I hear that *you* are guilty of exploitation and bribery."

It was like setting a match to dry timber.

"God help me! Of course I am. Which governor of Ireland has never been guilty of bribery?" His jaw visibly clenched. "When will he see me?"

His admission shocked me. "I don't know."

"Then I'd better find someone who does."

"There is no one." I had not done with him yet. "Who knows but the King himself?"

His stare became ferocious. "The longer Ireland is without a head, the sooner it will descend into revolt and bloodshed. All my work undone in the time it takes for Edward to decide that he has no one, other than me, to take on the task."

And without another word or even a gesture of respect, he spun on his heel, damp cloak billowing and shedding pieces of twig and leaf, and marched off. I watched him go. I was sorry, despite his foul mood. I trusted him as little as I trusted Gaunt, but there was a visceral connection between us. I might have wished there were not, but so it was. I waited until he reached the staircase at the end of the Hall. I raised my voice.

"Windsor."

He turned but did not reply. Even from a distance I could tell that his humor had not softened to any degree. There he stood in the shadow, the light from a flickering torch picking out the edge of his cloak, the glint of the metal at his side. A man of shadows, a man of unplumbed depths. It would be a brave woman who claimed to know him.

"I can find out for you," I suggested.

"Then do so. Why stand there wasting time?"

Once, four years ago, he had marched back to finish a conversation, apologizing for his rude manner. Now he stood and waited as if I might approach him. I did not. A neat little stalemate of our joint making.

"I do not answer to your beck and call, Sir William." My reply echoed in the vast space.

Windsor bowed low, the gesture dripping with malice. "Sweet Alice, sweeter than ever. Will you be there when Edward tears my morals to shreds and damns my actions to hell and back?"

"Wouldn't miss it for the world."

"And will you speak out for me?"

"I will not. But neither will I condemn you until I've heard the evidence."

"So you are not my enemy?"

"Did I ever say I was?"

A hard crack of a laugh was his only reply. At least I had made him laugh. He ran up the stairs, every action speaking of annoyance but with perhaps a lessening of the anger. Until at the head of the stair he halted and looked down to where I still stood below.

"Were you deliberately waiting for me?"

"Certainly not!"

The bow, the flourish of his cap, suggested that he did not believe me for a moment. I watched him disappear through the archway.

What now? I was not satisfied, not content to leave matters as they were. Never had I felt this need to be close to a man of the Court. Yes—through necessity, through courting their regard, through a need to win their support in a bid to protect Edward. But this? Windsor's friendship—his regard—would bring me no good. And yet still I wanted it.

I considered as the distant sound of his boot heels died away. I did trust him more than I trusted Gaunt. And then I pushed him aside, unable to make sense of my troubled thoughts. Time would tell. And I would be there when Edward dissected his morals and his character. And no, I would not condemn him until I had heard his excuses.

Windsor's presence continued to nibble at my consciousness. Nibble? Snap, rather. Like a kitchen cat pouncing on a well-fed and unwary rat.

Edward ordered Windsor to present himself one hour before noon on the following day, with no prompting from me. The King was lucid, furious.

It was, I thought, very much a repetition of his interview with Lionel, without the close redeeming relationship of father to son. In the end Edward had forgiven Lionel. Here there was no softness, accusation following on accusation. Edward was angry and seethingly forthright: There was no impediment to his memory or his powers of speech that day.

Windsor proved to be equally uninhibited beneath the gloss of respect.

As I had intended, I sat beside Edward, fascinated at the play of will between the two men, impressed by Edward's grasp of events, anxious that Windsor would not overstep the mark. Why was I anxious? Why should I care? I did not know. But I did.

Edward's litany of crimes against his governor of Ireland rolled on and on.

"Bloody mismanagement . . . inglorious culpability . . . disgraceful self-interest . . . appalling fiscal double-dealing."

Windsor withstood it all with a dour expression, feet planted, arms at his sides. I did not think his features had relaxed for one minute since his arrival the previous day.

Was he guilty? Despite his callous acceptance of my initial accusation, I had no idea. He argued his case with superb ease, not once hesitating. Yes, he had taxed heavily. Yes, he had used the law to support English power. Yes, he had empowered the Anglo-Irish at the expense of the native Irish—to do otherwise would have been political suicide. Was not the revenue needed to finance English troops to force the Irish rebels to keep their heads down? If that amounted to extortion and discreditable taxation, then he would accept it. In Ireland it was called achieving peace. And he would defy anyone to instigate peace in that godforsaken tribal, war-torn province by any other means than threats and bribery.

Edward was not impressed. "And the royal grant made for such purposes?"

"A grant I thank you for, Sire." At least Windsor tried to be conciliatory. "But that was spent long ago. I am now on my own and have to take what measures I can."

"I don't like your methods, and I don't like the rumble of dissatisfaction I hear."

"When is there not dissatisfaction, Sire?"

"You are very voluble in defense of your innocence."

How would he answer that? I waited, my heart thudding against my ribs.

His eyes never flinched from Edward's face. "I would never claim innocence, Sire. A good politician can't afford to be naive. Pragmatism is a far more valuable commodity, as you yourself will be aware. And who knows what's happening while my back is turned?"

"They don't want you back," Edward accused.

Windsor shook his head, in no manner discomfited. "Of course they don't. They want someone without experience, to mold and turn to their own will. I am not popular, but I hold to English policy as best I can with the tools I have. A weaker man would have the Irish lords singing his praises and licking the toes of his boots, all while they are sliding Irish gold into their own pockets."

"They want me to send the young Earl of March," Edward announced. "At least I know he's honest."

"I rest my case, Sire. Doubtless an able youth, but with neither experience nor years to his advantage . . ." Windsor left the thought hanging, his opinion clear.

"He is husband to my granddaughter!"

Edward was tiring. He might wish to champion the cause of young Edmund Mortimer, Earl of March, wed to his granddaughter Philippa, but I could see the tension beginning to build in him, wave upon wave, as weakness crept over his mind and body. It was time to end this before his inevitable humiliation, I decided. Time to end it for Windsor too. I leaned across with a hand on Edward's sleeve.

"How old is the young Earl, my lord?" I murmured.

"I think . . ." A frightening vagueness clouded his eyes.

"I doubt he has more than twenty-one years under his belt." I knew he hadn't.

"But he is my granddaughter's husband. . . ." Edward clung to the single fact of which he was certain in the terrible mist that engulfed his mind, his voice growing harsh, querulous.

"And one day he will serve you well with utmost loyalty," I agreed. "But it is an appallingly difficult province for so young a man."

Edward looked at me. "Do you think?"

"There may be much in what Sir William says. . . ."

"No!" he huffed, but with agonizing uncertainty.

I had planted the seed. I looked at Windsor, willing him to a mood of diplomacy, and for the first time in the audience he returned my gaze. Then he bowed to Edward.

"Do I return to Ireland, Sire? To continue your work to hold the province? Until the Earl of March is fit to assume the role?"

It was impeccably done.

"I'll consider your guilt first. Until then you'll stay here under my eye."

It was not an out-and-out refusal, but I doubted Windsor accepted it in that light. He bowed again and stalked out. I might as well not have been there.

"Come," I said to Edward, helping him from his chair. "You will rest. Then we will talk of it—and you will come to a wise decision—as you always do."

"Yes." He leaned heavily on my arm, almost beyond speech. "We will talk of it. . . ."

So Windsor, against his wishes, was restored to the complex round of Court life, where all was seen and gossiped about, and it was increasingly difficult to keep Edward's piteous decline from public gaze. For the first week I saw nothing of Windsor. Edward languished and Windsor kept his head down. No decision was made about the future of Ireland. How did Windsor spend his time? When last at Court he had sought me out. Now he did not. When Edward was strong enough to dine in public with a good semblance of normality, Windsor was not present. After some discreet questioning I discovered that he visited with the Prince at Kennington.

I wished him well of that visit. I thought there would be little satisfaction for him.

And then he was back, prowling the length and breadth of one of Edward's antechambers, a black scowl on his face, a number of scrolls tucked under his arm. At least the scowl lifted when he saw me emerge from the private apartments. He loped across as I closed the door at my back. He even managed to smile, though there was no lightness in him. His mood gave me an urge to shock him out of his self-engrossment— except that I could think of no way of doing it. Nor did I have the energy. Edward had been morose and demanding. If there had been other courtiers waiting in the antechamber, I might even have avoided Windsor's harsh, brooding figure. As it was . . .

"The King has not decided?" he demanded without greeting.

"No."

"Will he never make a decision?"

I sighed, a weary hopelessness settling on me. "In his own good time. But you know that. You must be patient, Sir William. Are you waiting for me?"

"Certainly not." He flashed a wolfish grin as he deliberately repeated my previous denial.

Tit for tat! I laughed softly, some of my weariness dispelled. "What are you doing to pass the time?" We were close enough that I tapped my fingers against the documents.

"Buying property."

"In Ireland?" I was surprised.

"In England. In Essex, primarily." I was even more surprised, since his family estates were far to the north.

"Why?"

"Against hard times. Like you. For when we can no longer depend on royal patronage."

He looked at me, as if weighing up a thought that had entered his head. Or perhaps it had been there for some time.

"What is it?" I asked, suspicious.

"I have a proposition, Mistress Perrers."

I felt a little tingle in my blood, a faint warmth that dispelled the smothering lethargy, the product of sleepless nights.

"A proposition?" I turned to go, feigning disinterest. "Now, what would that be? You've had little enough to say to me in the past sennight."

"I've been busy."

"And so? Now that you are no longer busy?"

Again, for a long moment he studied me, then gave a decisive nod. "Let us find a little corner where the hundreds of courtier ears in this place will not flap. It's like a beehive, a constant buzz of rumor and scandal."

He escorted me—not that I was unwilling, for had he not stirred my curiosity?—into a chamber used by the scribes and men of law, angling me between desks and stools into a corner where we could sit. There were no courtiers here. The young scribes continued to dip and scratch and scribble without interest in us. Idly I picked up a document from a box on the floor and pretended to be engrossed in it. A bill of sale of two dozen coneys. Presumably we'd eaten them in the last rabbit pottage.

Windsor came straight to the point. "I think we could make a killing."

We? I said nothing, fanning myself with the coney document.

He grinned. "You give nothing away, do you? A killing of a financial nature."

I tapped my foot against the base of the box.

"Would you care to throw in your lot with me on the purchase of some excellent little manors?"

A proposition indeed. My interest was snared like one of the unfortunate rabbits—that he would desire someone to join in partnership with him—and that he would look to me. Playing for time, I smoothed out the roll of parchment in my hands as if the coneys were of vast importance.

"And why would I do that?"

"Against the hard times," he repeated. "They'll be harder for you than for me." And he began to juggle with two lumps of red sealing wax that he'd swept up from a nearby desk, adding a third and then a fourth with amazing dexterity.

"Perhaps." My eye might be caught by the clever manipulation of the wax, but my mind was working furiously. Would they be harder for me? I expected he was right. It was always harder for a woman alone. I slid my eye from the wax to the sharp stare turned on me. "Why invite *me* to share in your project?"

"You have an interest in purchasing land." The wax, unheeded, fell to the floor with a soft clatter. "You have contacts. I expect you have access to funds. You have an able agent. . . . Need I say more?"

It was an impressive tally, for which I was justifiably proud. "What do *you* have?" I demanded.

"Hardheaded business acumen." He was not short of arrogance.

"Do I not have that also?"

"Amazingly, yes, but . . ."

"Don't say it! Amazingly for a woman!"

"Then I won't." His mouth twitched. "What do you think?"

I waved the forgotten document to and fro, giving it some thought. "Don't you trust me?"

"No."

He laughed. "So what's your answer? Is that no, too?"

"My answer is . . ." And because I did not know my own mind: "Why do I need you? I have acquired land perfectly adequately without you."

"Sometimes you need a man to push the negotiation forward."

"I have any number of men who are ready to work with me, for our joint benefit."

"Do you?" He looked surprised.

So I allowed myself to crow a little. "Did you not know? In the last handful of years I have purchased any number of manors through the offices of a little cabal of most trusted men. I use them as feoffees who—Master William Greseley in particular—undertake negotiations in my name. It is a perfect arrangement for a *femme sole.*"

"Where did you learn that?"

"A long time ago—a different life." I remembered standing outside Janyn Perrers's room, my bride gift clutched in my hand. I smiled a little. How far I had come. Then I dragged my mind back to the mercurial man who sat before me, leaning forward, the wax rescued from the floor and being tossed irritatingly from hand to hand. "If I do not help myself, who will?"

"Clever!" Windsor's eyes narrowed as he considered what I had achieved. "I admit your success. Then tell me, a mere curious man, how many manors have you actually snatched up?" I shook my head. I would not say, which he acknowledged readily enough. "I'll find out one day! I still say you need an astute man, who has a more personal view of your future."

"And you are he."

He bowed.

"Ah, but I think my little cabal of moneyed men have a very personal commitment to my success. If I fall under attack, so will they, so they will defend me to the death. I find them hardworking and unswervingly loyal. And so my answer is, Sir William—no. You might need me, but I do not need you."

"Then our conversation is at an end, Mistress Perrers."

Abruptly, he tossed the wax on the desk and left me to the company of the incurious clerks. I had surprised him with my refusal, and he did not like it.

For the whole of the next week he kept his damnable distance from me!

During that time I considered Windsor's offer. I had many hours. The King was full of lassitude, his mind sluggish. When awake, Edward felt an urge to confess his sins and so spent many hours on his knees in the chapel. Sometimes he stood alone on the castle walls, looking abstractedly out toward France. Since I was not in demand, my thoughts turned inward to the unexpected proposal.

There was much to recommend it in spite of my cavalier rejection. Was it not always easier for a man than for a woman to indulge in binding agreements with those with land to sell or lease? Yes, I used Greseley, but would it not be more advantageous to have an equal partner, a man with some status and authority whose interest was as strong as mine? A woman was considered an easy target. I might have the King's ear, but not everyone was willing to accept my jurisdiction.

Yes, I had won my case over that amazingly unattractive rabbit cloak, but my mind swerved to a more recent clash with the local population near my manor of Finningley, a valuable little property in Nottinghamshire. My manor no longer! For what had the local mob done? Only attacked and stolen my cattle. And not only that: My crops were destroyed, my men and servants imprisoned until they took oaths to

renege on their oath of fealty to me. Which they did, the words trip-
ping over their tongues in their desire to obey the vindictive rogues
with hard words and harder fists who had set upon them.

Now, if I were in partnership with Windsor . . . would it be to my
advantage? I imagined him more than capable in negotiation. But
would I wish to work with one such as William de Windsor? *Do you
trust me?* he had asked. *No!* I had replied. And yet I thought it would
be exhilarating to work in tandem with such a man. I imagined him
taking a select group of armed men to sway the decision of the local
population, and ensure that Finningley remained my property.

On the other hand . . .

Holy Virgin! He would make me take the initiative here! If I kept
my distance, he would find someone else to work in partnership in his
ventures.

So must I agree to work hand in glove with him? A bold woman
might be persuaded to accept a glove from Windsor. A smile touched
my mouth. I would do it. But I would take him by surprise, on my own
terms. I would put him at a disadvantage, and enjoy every minute of it.

I wrote two fast notes, much with the same purpose: one to Master
Greseley, one to Windsor. The response from both was prompt. I set
myself, with some careful arrangements, to luxuriate in the outcome.

I was always fond of the drama of a mummers' play.

The whole occasion had a delicious frisson about it. I chose late afternoon, for obvious reasons, when the light in the audience chamber
would have dimmed, and I had no torches lit. I took my place on Edward's throne, clad in dark skirts and veil, Greseley at my side. Only
when I was ready did I raise my hand for the attendant at the door to
admit Windsor, who was waiting in the antechamber. I heard his words.

"You will be seen now, my lord."

And I recalled my little note. It was not malicious, only playful. I
had hoped Windsor would appreciate it.

*His Majesty has made a decision relating to the governorship of Ire-
land. You will be informed in the Paneled Chamber at four hours after
noon.*

He was very prompt. He strode in. Halted. Bowed, a keen eye to protocol.

"You may approach," the attendant advised before closing the door behind him.

So we were alone, the three of us, as Windsor advanced. He had dressed with impeccable neatness in dark hose and close-fitting cote-hardie in black and green damask, cinched with a jeweled girdle on his hips. It was very fashionable—even to a parti-colored shoulder cape and gold-edged baldric, although he had abjured the extravagant long toes for good-quality leather boots. He was out to make a good impression; he would not lose this position through inattention to detail. He was, I recognized anew, a man who could play whatever role he set himself.

The thought shivered momentarily along my spine, but I sat perfectly still.

When did he realize it was not the King who occupied the royal throne?

When he was halfway down the length of the room. I saw the moment, the second look, the recognition. To his credit there was barely a hitch in his step. He continued until he stood just below the dais and bowed again with the same depth of respect, the feathers of his cap sweeping the floor. Straightening, he looked up at me. His eyes were somber in the shadowed light, but they gleamed when I motioned to Greseley to light the bracket behind me. And there we were, a dramatic little scene in a pool of golden illumination.

"Sir William. How good of you to come."

"Isn't it? I could not resist the invitation."

"And so promptly."

"I dare do no other. Queen Alice, is it?"

I would not smile! "I think that is treason, my lord."

"I'm sure it is. As is impersonating royalty."

"Impersonation? I wear no crown."

"Forgive me! Is that not the throne that you are occupying?"

"Where would you have me sit, sir? On the floor?"

"Many would. . . ."

"I make no claims to royal authority, Sir William."

"Impressive, mistress. You may not claim it, but . . ."

My whole body felt alive, my breath quick and shallow. This was exhilarating. And beneath the sharp cut and thrust, did we not understand each other very well? I stilled my tongue; I made him ask. And he did.

"You have news for me?"

"Yes."

"Well?"

"I will do it."

"Do what?" And I saw the fingers of his right hand spread slowly against his thigh. So it did matter to him, as I had thought.

"I will become your associate in buying land. This is my agent, Master Greseley." Greseley bowed. "He deals with many of my ventures and handles the finances."

Windsor's brows snapped together. "Why have you changed your mind?"

"Sometimes it is necessary to work through a second party. I have decided that I will work with you."

He made no reply while his regard was fixed on my face.

"It is also," I suggested smoothly, "a woman's privilege to change her mind." I rose to my feet, considered remaining above him, then stepped down from the dais, so that we were all on equal footing. "I trust your offer is still open? If not, then Master Greseley and I will continue to purchase land in the same efficient manner that we have always done. But if you are still of a mind, Sir William . . ."

"I am." Was his reply not quite as smooth as was his wont?

"What do you think, Master Greseley?"

"I see advantages, mistress," he replied in his undemonstrative way, as if nothing could surprise him.

"So it is done," Windsor observed.

"So it is," I agreed.

We clasped hands, the three of us.

"Are we business associates, then, Sir William?"

"So it seems. I rarely enjoy being wrong-stepped by anyone, much less by a woman. But on this occasion . . . I believe it will be a lucrative venture."

Not only did he clasp my hand but he kissed it.

*   *   *

My carefully staged little drama had taken him by surprise. To the advantage of both of us, of course. But my planning was nothing to what Windsor achieved next, to all but shake me out of my wits. What's more, it took no staging on his part, merely a diabolical cunning and an outrageous confidence.

I suppose he thought I deserved it. And perhaps I did.

Meanwhile, as my new associate planned his campaign against me, we celebrated our first joint step into property with a cup of wine. It was a fine Bordeaux, to toast the acquisition of the land, rents, and services of the equally fine manor of Northbrokes in Middlesex. Greseley was lugubrious but satisfied. I was full of delight at our smooth purchase. Windsor was not. Although he worked hard to keep his frustrations smothered beneath a brittle jubilation, as we lifted our cups in mutual appreciation, his mood was somber.

"Can you not get the King to make a decision on Ireland?" he asked when Greseley had left us.

"Edward is not capable of deciding what he will eat to break his fast. You must be patient."

"It is not in my nature."

As I knew. I would miss him when he was gone.

I made an error. Or perhaps it was not an error, because it was an outcome I desired, but it turned out to be a dangerous choice on my part. Where had my sense of clear judgment gone? Buried under my successful enterprise with William de Windsor, I expect, thrust aside by my delight in Edward's return to health. We were at Woodstock, where the hunting was good and Edward, rallying as he often did in new surroundings, was renewed in body and spirit. Or perhaps I was driven by my lamentable ambition to own a king's ransom in fine jewels. Now, that I cannot deny.

Why was I incapable of seeing the consequences of my request to Edward? I had stepped carefully all my life, and yet here I leaped into a morass that would ultimately drag me down. And what was it that caused the conflagration? Philippa's jewels. Some inherited, some gifts, some brought with her to England all those years ago. All magnificent.

"They're yours." Edward placed them on the bed in the room he had had constructed with such love for Philippa, and which I now occupied. With the jewels was a letter in his own hand.

> *... we give and concede to our beloved Alice Perrers, late damsel of the chamber of our most dear consort Philippa, now dead, that to her heirs and executors all the jewels, goods, and chattels that the said Queen left in the hands of Euphemia, wife to Sir Walter de Hasleworth, and the said Euphemia is to deliver them to the said Alice on the receipt of this command. . . .*

Philippa's jewels. What woman would not want them? They took my breath as I lifted a string of rubies, a collar set with sapphires, a heavy emerald ring, and allowed them to fall back to join their glittering brethren in the metal-bound coffer. Edward had given them to me.

But on whose initiative?

On mine, for my sins. I had asked for them. Since Philippa's death they had never seen the light of day, but languished in safekeeping with one of the senior ladies of Philippa's household. And so I had asked for them, and Edward, in his magnificent generosity, had arranged it. Legally and officially they were now mine. And with this simple acquisition of Philippa's jewelery, I helped to dig my own grave. Thoughtlessness on my part. Greed? I did not think so. They ought to be worn—and who better than the King's Concubine?

I wore the sapphire collar when the court met for supper.

It was, of course, immediately recognizable, and the whispers began to circulate, between the minced meatballs in jelly and Edward's favorite dish of salmon in rich cream sauce, damning me for my impertinence. Did I not see the eyes slide disbelievingly over the wealth that gleamed on my bosom? And the murmurs multiplied when next morning I pinned a ruby brooch to my mantle. Disgraceful avarice and greed, they said. The jewels were not mine to take. The King must be besotted or bewitched, one as bad as the other, to give his wife's jewels to his whore. If they were to be worn, was it not more fitting for them to be seen around the neck of Isabella or even Princess Joan? Certainly not adorning the neck of Alice Perrers. Had Edward lost his wits entirely?

I could answer my critics. Not that I ever did—why would I? Any reasoning of mine would be rejected out of hand. But of what use was it for such glorious jewels to be shut in a box in a dusty cellar in the home of Lady Euphemia? Far better for them to be worn and enjoyed. It was not as if I were wearing the royal regalia, was it? If Philippa had wished them to be worn by Isabella or Joan, she would have willed them. She did not. Did she will them to me? She did not do that either, but I did not think she would object to seeing them on my person. And I think, truth to tell, she would have seen the humor in it.

Did I have an eye to the future? Of course I did. As Edward's life-force failed, my preparations for an uncertain future quickened. Greseley might decry gemstones against the lasting value of land, but both were of equal value to me—and what woman could resist a collar of sapphires and pearls? Besides, I could not afford to be complacent. And Edward knew it too, although we did not speak of it beyond his solemn assertion: "At least they'll put cloth on your back, Alice, and bread in your mouth when I'm not here to provide them."

Oh, yes. I could make every excuse, but I never did. All I knew was that Edward loved to see me wearing them, and to me that, and my own pleasure, were reasons enough to flaunt them before the censorious Court.

"They become you as well as they became Philippa." The smile that almost refused to come to Edward's mouth these days, so weak were his muscles, was very gentle.

"I am not Philippa, my lord." I was equally gentle. Some days I was not sure that he could even distinguish between us. But on that day he did.

"I know that very well. You are Alice and you are my beloved."

In response to my wearing a particularly fine emerald ring that Philippa had much loved, and a gold-linked belt set with equally fine stones, Princess Joan's descent on Woodstock was immediate and vicious. Someone had ensured that the gossip had reached her. "They're Philippa's!" She launched into her invective before the door to my parlor was closed. "By what right do you dare to even touch them, much less wear them!"

On that occasion I was wearing rubies. Well, she would notice those that adorned my hood, as large as cherrystones, wouldn't she? They were difficult to overlook. At least we were private when Joan grabbed my wrist for her inspection. "I don't believe it!" She twisted my arm so that the light glittered on the ring and the bloodred clasp around my wrist. "Did you steal them?"

I raised my brows. I would not answer such an accusation.

"Did you?" Joan was always obtuse. "I know you did. It's the only way you would get your thieving hands on them! They're the Queen's. They're not yours to wear."

"Oh, I think they are." My gaze never wavered beneath hers, and at last gave her pause.

"God's Blood! He gave them to you!"

"Of course he did."

"What did you have to do to get them from him? No—don't tell me! I might vomit!"

Without doubt I should have been more circumspect in my reply. "Am I not worthy of them?" I asked, in retrospect not circumspect at all.

"By God, you are not."

"By God, I am."

She dropped her hold, retreating in obvious disgust, lips drawn back from her neat teeth. But I followed her. I was no minion to be put in my place. And I was weary of baseless accusations.

"If we are talking of worth and payment here, then consider this, my lady: How many nights have I sat beside the King when he is sleepless? How many nights have I talked or read to keep the nightmares at bay? How many days have I devoted to the melancholy that drags him down?" I pushed on to make her think beyond her prejudices, to make her acknowledge me and what I had achieved. "You know what it is like when a strong man suffers. He is demanding, and yet inconsolable in his weakness. It is not easy for a woman to stand buffer against the horrors that attack him. You know this from your own experience."

For a moment I saw her hesitate. She understood what I meant. But not for long.

"The Prince is my husband! It is my right and my duty to stand with him! You have no right!"

Holy Mother! Any prudence I might have melted under Joan's scorn. "And the King is my lover," I rejoined. "He gave me Philippa's jewels and I will value them. I will wear them and enjoy them."

"You wear them like a slut—shamelessly, blatantly—a Court harlot who has demanded jewels for her body."

But I did not think I was. These were not gifts given in a spirit of payment for services rendered; the jewels had been given out of love. Yet I was without redress. My reputation was made and I must live with it, but sometimes it was very hard to accept the consequences. Perhaps Joan's savage attack wounded me after all. And that was why I said the unforgivable.

"I had no need to demand, my lady. The King obviously considers gold and gems suitable payment for my superior skills in the bedchamber."

"Whore!" She stormed from the room.

Joan never forgave me, and I was to pay a high price for my heedlessness, higher than I could have dreamed possible, even though I made an attempt at conciliation, for Edward's sake. I was not entirely heartless, you understand. Unfortunately my good intentions made matters worse.

Edward decided to visit the Prince at Kennington; I accompanied him with serious intent. Edward, I decided, deserved some peace in his household. War between his mistress and his daughter-in-law—both of us no better than two screeching, scratching cats—should be avoided. Within minutes, King and Prince were deep in discussion of the state of the present truce with France, and I, my feet on a path toward what I suspected would be a lost cause, was shown by the steward into Joan's solar.

She sat at her embroidery, by her side on the floor her young son, turning the illuminated pages of a book. A charming boy with fair hair and round cheeks, Richard leaped to his feet and bowed with quaint grace.

I curtsied. "My lord. My lady." I would be courteous.

Joan remained seated with disdain in her eyes. "Mistress Perrers." Her voice was as flat as her stare.

"His Majesty has come to speak with the Prince." I was very formal. How to broach this? Head-on as if in the tilting yard was the only way. "How is the Prince?"

I had not needed to ask. I had seen it for myself. His loss of weight was pitiful. Eyes feverish, skin gray, hair dull and lank. The basin positioned beside his daybed was ominous in itself. Joan's features closed, tight with distress. Unable to hide her fears, she shook her head. I knew she would not lie, would not pretend. For once, her guard was down, with even the moisture of tears in her eyes. This was my one possibility, for Edward's sake, of draining the poison from her hatred of me.

Grief strong in the set of her mouth, the hard lines deep from nose to chin in her soft flesh, Joan forgot she spoke to me. One tear rolled down her cheek. Then another. "I don't know what to do for him!" It was a cry from the heart.

"I can help."

"You! What can you do?" Furiously, she dashed away the tears.

I could have retreated. I would have, if I had known where this would lead, yet faced with such grief, knowing the terror of helplessness for myself when Edward looked at me as if I did not exist, I could not. In my arms I had a little coffer, a delight of sandalwood with ivory corners and metal hinges, and an intricate little lock and key. It was a costly gift in its own right, but its contents were of far greater value to the Prince. I had brought the only offering I could think of that might be acceptable. For sure the Princess would take nothing else from me. I placed it on the chest that held a tangle of her embroidery silks.

"What is that?"

"A gift."

"I have coffers enough, and of greater value than that." She barely looked at it, setting a number of stitches, stabbing clumsily at the panel for a purse or an altar cloth.

I thought it unlikely, given its value—for it was a gift to me from Edward—but I let it go.

"It is the contents that are valuable," I explained gently. The nuns would have been proud of my humility. "A number of nostrums and potions. They will give the Prince ease. . . ."

"And do these nostrums and potions work?" She stopped stitching.

"They soothed the King in his grief after Philippa died. They helped Philippa too."

Joan cast aside her sewing. I saw her fingers twitch over the domed lid. Surely such a gift was impossible to resist. She lifted it to reveal the carefully folded packets of herbs, the glass vials of intense color.

"They are distilled from common plants," I explained. "I learned the skills at the Abbey. Here are the leaves of lady's-smock to restore a lost appetite and soothe digestion. A tincture of primrose to aid rest and a quiet mind. White willow bark when the pain is too great to bear. I have written the amounts." I indicated the sheet of parchment tucked under the lid. "Either you or the Prince's body servants can mix them with wine as indicated. I'm sure the Prince would enjoy the effects."

Joan looked at the coffer, the neat arrangement of packets and bottles. Her teeth bit hard into her lower lip.

"I can speak well for their effectiveness," I encouraged as she made no move. "There is also the pulp of dog rose hips—to stanch bleeding and the loss of bodily fluids."

We had all heard of the Prince's appalling symptoms, the constant flow of blood and semen that could not be halted.

Joan moved. It was as if I had thrust a bunch of stinging nettles into her unprotected hand. With a jerk of her arm she swept the box from coffer to floor. It fell with a crack, damaging the hinges, so that glass from the vials shattered and the liquid ran. A dusting of herbs covered the whole, swirling into patterns. Richard squeaked in horror, then was quick to investigate, poking his fingers into the debris until Joan took a handful of his tunic to pull him away to stand beside her.

"Don't touch that spawn of the devil!"

"Indeed it is not . . ." I remonstrated.

"Satan's brew! And you are his servant!"

Her words were a shock, running cold through my blood as we looked at the mess between us, Joan still seated, I rigid with what she had implied. Until Joan raised her eyes to mine, holding them as she clicked her fingers for one of her women to approach from the far end of the room.

"Get rid of this. Burn it. And the box. I don't want to find any trace of this on my floor." And when the woman gawped at the detritus: "Do it *now!*" she hissed, like the kiss of a steel blade against its adversary.

As the woman busied herself, the Princess stood, gripped my wrist, and leaned close, her mouth against my ear. "Did you think I would be such a fool?"

I was still stunned by her outrageous response to a gift that could have brought nothing but good. "I thought you might accept what I could do to give your husband ease," I remarked, watching the play of fury—and was that fear?—across her face.

"Ease! Distilled from common plants!" she spat. Her voice fell to a whisper that hissed in the corners of the room. "I hear you employ witchcraft to achieve your ends, Mistress Perrers. I think you have *maleficium* in mind. Not *compassion!*" Spittle sprang to her lips on the word.

But there was only one word that I heard out of the whole rant.

"Witchcraft!" I repeated, my voice equally low. It was not a word to shout to the rooftops. I had heard much said of me, but not that. A little breath of fear beat in my mind, but I managed a sneer coated in laughter. "And what do *they* say? Whoever *they* are. That I eat the flesh of children? That I keep a familiar and feed it from the blood of my own body?"

"They say you call up the devil's powers. That you have skills and knowledge that no God-fearing woman should have." I watched as Joan's fingers on her left hand circled into the sign against the evil eye. "How in God's name could you explain Edward's fascination with so ugly and ill-bred a woman as Alice Perrers?" Her jaw snapped shut on my name.

It was the slide of a knife between my ribs, but I ensured that my reply gave away nothing of her wounding, or of the fear that spread to fill the spaces around my heart. The cold along the length of my spine deepened, as intense as ice in January.

"It is inexplicable, I grant you," I remarked. Refusing to defend my birth or my looks, I dragged my wrist free of her grasp. "But my lord's love for me is no product of witchcraft. Nor was this gift." I slid my shoe over the sifting of dried heartsease flowers that still marked the floor. "But if my husband suffered as yours does, my lady, I would use the powers of the devil himself to give his body relief. I would leave no stone unturned between here and the depths of hell, if it would allow my husband a restful night and an end to pain."

"Get out."

"My lady." I curtsied.

"Get out. Or I will lay evidence before the authorities that you plied me with witches' condiments."

"Your evidence is worthless." For Edward's sake, I would not allow my temper to rule.

"Get out of my sight."

I did. I did not try again. Joan was too eaten up with hatred. I told Edward nothing of my interview. He did not deserve to know.

Witchcraft. Maleficium.

The vicious accusation continued to buzz in my brain, like a persistent bee in the depths of a foxglove flower. There was no evidence that Joan could use against me; of that I was certain, since there had never been any bewitchment, but it was too dangerous an accusation to be taken lightly.

Evidence could be fabricated, could it not?

Chapter Twelve

I had caught Windsor off guard in the audience chamber. *Holy Virgin!* If I had jolted him out of his habitual sangfroid, he all but stunned me. He swept the rushes from beneath my feet.

It did not start off well. We had moved on in our royal perambulations from Woodstock to Sheen, where a weighty delegation had arrived from France to begin negotiations for a permanent truce. I intervened. On instructions from me, Latimer sent the delegation away. I watched them go, aware of their furious dissatisfaction. They made no attempt to hide it.

"Dangerous, Mistress Perrers!"

The voice was at my elbow.

"And what does that mean?" I scowled indiscriminately at the departing delegation of angry, highborn Frenchmen and at Windsor.

"It won't be popular."

"What won't?"

"Dictating who will and who will not see the King."

"Do you think I don't know that?"

How could I not know? This was not the first time Latimer and I had intervened between king and petitioner. Did I need Windsor to tell me how much resentment there was? As for resentment . . . I glared at the man at my side. I resented his presence. I resented his opinion. In that moment I resented everything about William de Windsor.

"You're playing with fire," he stated. Such an obvious statement.

"I know that too."

"It will put a weapon into the hands of those who would be rid of you."

"Tell me something I don't know."

"So why do it?"

He could think ill of me if he wished. There he stood, regarding me with an element of deep suspicion that did nothing to improve my mood. I did not need this, not at this precise moment. I'd had enough hard words from the Princess to last a lifetime. But if Windsor would condemn me without a hearing, then so be it!

"I won't talk to you now! I don't have to answer for my actions to you!"

And then suddenly, overwhelmingly, I wished he would wrap his arms around me and allow me to lean against him. What I would not give for a moment of ease, to realize that I was not alone. I would like him to stroke my arm as if I were a soft-furred cat, fold my fingers close within his, and tell me that all would be well. . . .

Of course, all would not be well! Immediately I took a step back, away from him, shivering at my appalling show of weakness, determined that Windsor should never read the turmoil in my mind. I would not make excuses. I would not explain. I realized that he was staring at me intently, and so I hurried to follow Latimer and the angry delegation, to make my escape. I did not think I could keep my reactions under a firm hand for much longer. I swallowed when hot tears gathered in my throat.

Windsor stopped me by the simple method of stepping in front of me. "Come with me," he ordered curtly.

"No!"

Regardless, he took my wrist and pulled me out of the now-deserted audience chamber.

"And let go of me. Do you want every riffraff in the palace to be talking of us?" He released me, but I followed, knowing that if I did not comply, he would repeat the performance. "Where are we going?"

Since I got no reply, I marched sullenly at his side, still disturbed by the recent confrontation, the disbelieving stare of the French when

Latimer offered to begin the negotiations himself. Even more unsettled by Windsor's judgment of my motives. When I found myself hustled into a corridor leading to an outer door, I balked. Halted.

"No!"

"Why is a woman always difficult when a man has her best interests at heart?" he asked, returning to intimidate me with his height and breadth in the narrow passage.

"You have only your own interests at heart. I've never met anyone as self-interested as you," I fired back, all my thoughts awry. "In fact . . ."

"By God, woman . . . !" He pinned me against the wall, regardless of who might be traversing the corridor—fortunately no one—and he kissed me. It was not a kiss of mild affection. I wasn't sure what it was. When he lifted his head, I had no breath left to speak.

"Silence! At last!"

"Are you out of your mind . . . ? Will you release . . . !" Lord, how that kiss had stirred my blood. My heart bounded against my ribs like a ferret in a hunter's cage.

He kissed me again. All heat and power, appallingly seductive, and my will to resist was stripped away. When he released my mouth I simply stood, my senses compromised.

"Excellent! Now be a biddable girl for once in your life. . . ."

He had kissed me, as far as I could tell, with thorough enjoyment, but his face was stern, his thoughts preoccupied. And because I wanted to, I walked beside him, conscious of his nearness, the brush of his tunic against my arm at a turn in the stair. And then we were out in the open, climbing to the wall walk, under clouds that were low and brooding, much like my humor. There we came to stand, looking east, and I waited, limbs still shaking, wondering whether he would kiss me again. I hoped that he might, despised him for trapping me in this unexpected passion; I despised myself. I had no intention of cuckolding Edward, in private or under public gaze. The palace guards were far too obvious, far too watchful, and I retained some sense of honor even as my heart galloped like a panicked horse.

"Tell me what's troubling you," he invited when the silence between us grew heavy.

"Nothing. Since you think the worst of me . . ."

"It's the King, I presume."

"How should it be . . . ?"

"Alice . . . ! You can't deny it any longer. He's beyond sense. At this moment you need a friend, and I'm the nearest you'll get. So tell me the truth."

My determination to keep silent, to protect Edward at all costs, drained away. Yes, I needed a friend to help me shoulder the increasingly difficult burden. Wykeham was in Winchester. I would not put myself in Gaunt's hands. So that left Windsor. . . . But was he that friend? There he stood, dark and saturnine, the epitome of louche self-serving. And yet there was in his face, completely unexpected, a kindness. . . . Why not . . . ?

"Yes. It's Edward."

"You're guarding him."

"Yes. What would you have me do? Put him on show in London for his subjects to gawp at?" Still I was defensive.

"At least then you could not be accused of manipulating an old man for your own ends. Keeping it secret is dangerous, Alice."

"I won't do it! You are not helpful!"

"I'm trying to be realistic!"

Still I resisted, but in the end I told him everything. How Edward's bright spirit was once more in eclipse, his actions unpredictable. Who could persuade him that it was not good policy to order *every* bridge in Oxfordshire to be repaired or rebuilt, simply because he wished to go hawking from Woodstock? I could not. The King was incapable of committing England to any future policy. How long could Latimer and I, and the rest of the loyal ministers, pretend that Edward was fit to be King? Edward barely knew the day of the week. His physicians could do nothing to alleviate his loss of awareness.

"And so that's why I try to protect him as much as I can," I finished.

"Next week—tomorrow, even—his senses may return."

"How admirable you are."

"No. I'm not. But I care too much to allow him to come under attack from those who might question his right to rule."

"Some would say that you do it for your own ends. To bolster the King's power is to preserve that of Alice Perrers."

"Which is entirely true, of course." Sharp irony coated the air between us. "How could anyone think I had any concern for the King's well-being?" I turned away, furious that once again he voiced familiar calumny against me.

"I didn't say *I* believed it," he retorted. "I think I need to distract you a little."

"By kissing me?" Suddenly I was afraid of my weakness with this man, afraid of the burn of tears beneath my eyelids. I was far too emotional. "I hope you won't."

"No. Or not yet, at any rate. Later I might. . . ."

The preoccupation was back. Windsor had other thoughts on his mind. Womanlike, I resented his preoccupation and strolled away, angry with my twisted emotions, despairing at how easily I was maneuvered into opening my heart to this man, leaving him to lean on the stone coping and sweep an arm over the battlements to take in the view.

"I have a handful of estates in Essex," he remarked.

Neutral territory. I strolled back. "I know."

"I plan to have more."

"I know that too. Have you brought me all the way up here to tell me something of so little news?" My mood was horribly unpredictable.

"No. I want to ask you something. And from the scene I just witnessed, it's becoming imperative."

He leaned on the parapet, chin resting on his folded arms, and glowered at the scene below, where one of the palace cats took its morning slink amongst the rabbit holes on the riverbank. I waited in silence. Then he turned his head to look at me.

"Alice . . ."

"William . . . !"

He eyed me speculatively.

"Alice, will you marry me?"

Marry . . . ?

My mind scrabbled for understanding, for any sensible response, and found none. After all the emotion of the morning, I could not deal with this. I was forced to drag air into my lungs.

"Are you mocking me?"

"Now, there's an intelligent reply. I often propose marriage to a woman in the spirit of mockery. The country is littered with my proposals. Will you marry me?" he repeated.

Did he mean this? I could read nothing in the hard lines of his face.

"Marriage . . . ! But why?"

Immediately he straightened, then, shockingly, went down on one knee. For a moment of blazing memory, I recalled Edward in his strength and power wooing me after my outburst. But there was no similarity here at all. Edward had wooed me from the heart; this was a charade, a travesty of honor and chivalry. Surely it was.

"I love you," Windsor announced. "Why else would a man ask a woman to wed him?"

"You are a liar, Windsor."

"Ah . . . but how do you know?" Those bold eyes glinted in a sudden bright stroke of sunlight through the heavy cloud.

"I don't. Sense tells me. . . . Stand up! The sentries will see us and the whole world will know within the hour that you are making mischief!" When he rose to his full height, the light spread over his harsh features, gilding him in an enticing softness that I instantly rejected. Pouncing, he clasped my hand and pressed his lips against my fingers.

"It's not such a bad idea, you know. Wife and concubine—not an easy role to pursue at one and the same time, but I swear you have the talent for it. Will you?"

"No." I had no breath, no wit to say more. What an appalling morning this had been. Was he ridiculing me? If so, there was an edge of cruelty to it that I would never have expected.

"Listen to me. I'm quite serious." He leaned back against the parapet once more, looking up to where a pair of crows somersaulted on the thermals. His voice was clipped, his hand still firm around mine. He was deadly serious. "I foresee advantages. . . ."

"You would, of course!"

"For you, woman! For you! Just listen. When Edward dies, what happens to you? Alone, unprotected, you will become a perfect scapegoat for those who have loathed you since the first day you crawled into the King's bed." How sordid he made it sound. "From the first day that you stood at the King's side and blocked their way to power. They'll not accept that the King was too ill to hold the reins of government. They'll blame you. And they'll take utmost pleasure in throwing you to the dogs." His eyes slid from tumbling crows to me. "And I wager that none of this is new to you. You've seen the threat of the storm clouds building on your horizon, just as those birds know the power of the thermals to lift them. Look at them! Storm crows. Birds of ill omen."

Who'd have thought Windsor would be superstitious! "I have seen the storm clouds," I replied. "And I see the crows every morning without fear. I have made provision."

"I'm sure you have. Squirreling away wealth for your old age." How cynical, how practical. No superstition here! Did he think I had been robbing the royal coffers? "But what if they target your sources of income?"

"I have taken precautions."

"I know. I know how clever you are." I thought it was no compliment. "But that's another reason for you to watch your back. Men don't like it when a woman oversteps the line of what is acceptable for her sex. A man would get away with it. A woman . . . ? She will be damned as impertinent, presumptuous at best. Immoral at worst. A woman who fights for herself, who is bold and outspoken and fearless, and is amazingly successful at what she sets her hand to, is instantly vilified, whereas a man is praised for his perspicacity. You've made yourself notorious."

"As have you . . ." I retaliated, horrified by his brutal brushstrokes of me and my character.

"That's not relevant," Windsor fired back. "Just as your innocence or guilt is irrelevant. They'll be snapping at your heels as soon as the King is laid out in the chapel. Now, if you wed me, I would stand protector for you and your property, through the courts if need be."

Ah! Of course! Not kindness at all! "And what would you get out of marriage?"

"Someone to watch over my interests in England when I'm in Ireland."

I frowned. "That's not an answer a woman wants to hear. It's a marriage, not a business deal." I pulled my hand free and turned my back on him. "Are you still so sure you'll be allowed to go back?"

"Yes. As I said—who else is there?"

"Then pay an agent to look after your properties for you. It's cheaper than marriage. With far fewer problems," I added dryly. "I'll get Greseley to recommend someone."

"I want someone who will do it for better motives than a paid clerk. I want you!"

I want you! I shook my head to jangle my thoughts into order. "No."

"Why *not*? Give me one good reason!"

I fell back on the practical, because I dared not contemplate my initial reaction. "I can't. Edward . . ."

"Edward would not need to know."

"What? We would keep it secret?" My shock doubled.

"Why not? Would it be so very difficult? If we did take so momentous a step, it would undoubtedly be better if the Court didn't know of it."

I followed his line of sight, the crows twisting and falling in unison, a mating dance, and, brusquely, asked the primary question in my mind: "Why would you consider—why would any man consider— making such a proposal to the King's mistress?" I swallowed against the constriction in my throat and made my question plainer. "Why would you wish to share your bed with the King's whore?"

"I've thought of that. I've decided it doesn't matter." When I looked at him in amazement, he returned my gaze with frank assessment. "What are you to him, Alice? What are you to him *now*?"

"I . . ." The question took me unawares, and I sought for a reply that would not betray Edward. I would never speak of what passed between myself and the King.

"What are you to him?" Windsor repeated. I must have looked momentarily lost, so he made it easy for me. Who would have thought that he would do that? "Friend?" he asked.

"Yes."

"Counselor?"

"Yes. When he asks—and sometimes when he does not." I smiled sadly. "Edward likes to talk. Or he did. . . ."

He cocked his head. "Confidante?"

"Yes . . . always . . ." I set my teeth. I knew what was coming.

"Lover?"

My reply stuck in my gullet.

"Be honest with me, Alice. For God's sake! I'll not spread it through the palace!"

Should I give him the answer he wanted? The one that was the truth? Blessed Jesu! I found my nails digging deep into my palms.

And, seeing, he took my hand, smoothing out my fingers, asking gently, "Are you still lovers?"

"No!" I cried out, with infinite sadness at this ultimate decline in so great a man. "No longer . . ."

"As I thought . . ."

"He cannot. . . ." I felt the need to explain, to defend the King when he could not defend himself. I could not bear that he be sneered at for losing that essential masculine power that made him the crowned stag, the vigorous stallion. Edward would hate it, shrink from it. But I did not need to explain. Windsor showed no scorn.

"The sad depredation of old age," he remarked matter-of-factly. "It strikes us all down eventually. How long since?"

"Two years or more now," I admitted.

"And yet you stay with him."

"Yes."

"For the power it brings you?" His eyes bored into my soul.

"I can't deny it, can I?" I demanded bitterly.

"I think you are better than that."

He reminded me of Wykeham. It should have been a comfort to have two men who believed that I had even an inch of a better nature, but it was not. When the whole world railed against me, sometimes it was difficult not to believe the defamation. Perhaps I did not deserve happiness. Not when the length and breadth of my sins were tallied up.

"He needs me," I stated, consigning self-pity to the devil. "I cannot leave him." To my relief, Windsor made no comment, letting the moment draw out between us. "He loves me, you see," I continued. "Even though he cannot play the man any longer, he loves me. Does he not deserve my loyal service to the end?"

Windsor turned back to the wall, resting his chin on his hands again. "Think of it like this. If you are not intimate, would it matter if you were wed to me? It would not be a physical betrayal, would it?"

"But the King would see it as a betrayal—and rightly so."

"I can't agree. How often does he not know you when you walk into his chamber?" He must have felt my resistance. "Be honest again. You've nothing to lose. I'm no gossip."

No, he was not. "Too often . . ." I sighed.

"Here's the thing," he drove on, the timbre of his voice deepening. "You are vulnerable. And when the King's dead you will be on your own."

"And if I wed you, you will stand for me."

"I will."

"And in return I will administer your property."

"Yes."

"Still a business arrangement, all in all."

"If you wish to call it that."

"It's what it seems to me." Dismay, like a reaction to the cool breeze after a hot day, shivered over my skin.

His glance was a direct challenge. "Wed me, Alice. Do you have the courage?"

"I don't think I lack for courage."

"Then accept!"

I let the idea tumble through my mind as the crows dived and rose once again on the air, a pair enjoying the freedom of their kind. I did not think that I had any freedom.

Windsor sighed. "Alice . . ."

"No. I won't. I can't."

He did not press me but abandoned me alone to ponder the joy of the two crows flirting above me. I was left trying to deny the effect of his mouth against mine, to deny what I wished for rather than what I was in duty bound to do.

Windsor's proposal made an uncomfortable bedfellow, and I did not sleep that night.

Marriage. A business agreement was one thing—but marriage? To a man whom I found inordinately attractive. It had an appeal, until integrity demanded that I consider my loyalty to the King. Did he not deserve my fealty, my steadfastness?

Edward smiled serenely, uncomprehendingly, as I wished him good night, kissing his cheek. I might have been the servant who brought him wine at the end of the day to help him to sleep. I had not shared Edward's bed for physical gratification since he returned from the desperate attempt to invade France. His failure had rendered him impotent, his physical desires vanished entirely, his passionate need for my body transfigured into mild affection when he recognized me. Just as we all knew that Edward would never again lead an army into France, I knew that he would get no more children on me. He might need me to share his bed, but for comfort only: He made no more demands on my body. The years had their cruel sway.

But marriage to Windsor?

When the tenure of my royal position ended, I would have the wealth I needed to bolster the rest of my life and ensure security for my daughters. What more did I need?

You need a man to stand protector.

Did I? No. I had married once and found no joy in it. I would not do so again. I did not even know if I *liked* William de Windsor. His touch might set fires ablaze in my blood, but that was mere lust. No, he was not for me. If I wed, it would be to some mild, biddable soul who could be managed by a strong-willed woman. I would be no one's chattel. No, I stated again, firmly in my mind as I considered that undesirable state, marriage was not for me. And it would be a brave woman who agreed to take on William de Windsor.

Are you not a brave woman?

I buried my face in my pillow. He said he loved me but I did not believe him. His proposal had smacked of a transaction to buy property. I should know, should I not?

Not one soft word had he spoken.

I abandoned sleep, taking up a quill to record my most recently purchased manor of Gunnersby, a property on the Thames that would prove far more trustworthy than William de Windsor.

"Good morning, Sir William." I stood in the little group of shivering courtiers with Edward, who had expressed a wish to fly the falcons. We were on foot, ambling along the riverbank at a speed that would suit the King, who seemed not to feel the cold. "I did not expect to see you so early in the day. Or are you hoping to win royal favor?"

He ignored the bait. "Have you thought about it?"

"I have."

"Second thoughts, Mistress Perrers?"

I inclined my head in a parody of regal dignity that I knew he would appreciate. "No, Sir William."

"Let me know when you do."

"I will not."

He grinned. "I think you will."

On our return, as the falconer retrieved his birds and carried them off to the royal mews, there he was again at my shoulder.

"Think of the advantages."

"There are none."

"I say there are." His gaze, forthright, lingering, drove a shaft of heat through my body. I felt it color my cheeks and quickly turned away.

"You are presumptuous, Sir William."

"I am indeed. Would you cast my offer into the flames without giving it due consideration? You would do as much for an offer on the feudal rights of a manor."

So I would, damn him!

"A woman would enjoy some words of courtship, Sir William." I was atrociously demure, studying the gold embroidery-work on my new gloves.

"I am not a man of soft words, Mistress Perrers." It was a statement of fact, not an excuse, and I could not resist abandoning the stitchery to search his face. There was no subterfuge in the man. He said what he meant, both fine wine and bitter lees of sediment in the cup. If I drank, I would have to accept both. . . .

"You might try." Still I hoped for something that might have a leaning toward courtship. "If you truly want my hand in marriage."

"I have no poetry in my soul."

Neither had I—but I would have liked to hear some from him. I think he saw my disappointment, for, stretching out his hand, he drew the tip of his finger along the curve of my cheek.

My heart turned over, a little leap of pure delight.

I thought about it again. I thought about Janyn Perrers. I thought about Edward. I worried the subject to death in the early hours. What would it be like to be tied to a man who did not need my care? A man whom I was free to choose or reject. I had no experience of such freedom. What would it be like to love a man of my own free will? I had no idea.

It would be far better for you if you loved no one!

As for that . . .

Discreetly I watched Windsor fit seamlessly into the daily pattern of the Court. His agility with horse or sword in mock combat, his merciless single-mindedness in hand-to-hand conflict, the tip of his sword resting against his opponent's throat—until he put it aside to grasp the man's hand in mutual congratulation. The arrogant lift of his head. The proud knightly stance. *Stop it, Alice!*

He was not a handsome man, but he took my eye.

I felt again that unexpected caress of his fingertip that made my face burn.

And I watched Edward slip further and further away from me, until the morning he demanded in a querulous manner as I curtsied before him, "Philippa? Where have you been? Have you persuaded Isabella not to wed de Coucy? Tell her I'll not have it. . . ."

It tipped me over the edge.

He saw me coming, and immediately stepped away from where he was loitering by a huddle of equally dissolute idlers who were casting dice to pass the time. Inactivity did not suit him. I kept my expression stern.

"Change of heart, dear Alice?"

"Yes."

His brows climbed infinitesimally, but at least he did not allow victory to descend into smugness. "Are you sure?"

"Yes."

"Good—I like a woman who does not mince her words."

I left the arrangements to Windsor, for he had the freedom from the public eye that I did not. Still it was a simple matter for me to make the excuse of visiting my little girls at Pallenswick. I was free to travel, had been so since the birth of John, and after a brief halt at Pallenswick I would make my way to Gaines near Upminster, a manor we had bought in partnership, and in Windsor's name. Edward stared vaguely at the wall beyond my shoulder and gave no recognition when I touched his hand in farewell.

I did not try to explain. John Beverley would care for him. My absence would not be a long one.

Windsor traveled separately. I was seated alone in my barge, rowed swiftly by the oarsmen who made easy weather of it with the pull of the tide. With every mile my nerves leaped like crickets in the summer heat. There in Upminster we were wed in a simple service in the village church with no fuss and no guests, no bridal ring for me or gifts exchanged between us at the altar. There was nothing to mark the occasion but for a solemn taking of vows; Windsor's steward and William Greseley were stolid witnesses. Greseley, perhaps recalling a previous marriage, managed what might have passed for a smile.

"I always knew you would have an adventurous life, mistress."

"And I have you to thank for much of it." I knew what I owed him.

"I have a manor in mind to purchase, not too far from here. . . ."

I stopped him with a hand to his arm. "Tomorrow, Greseley. That will keep for tomorrow. For today—I am busy."

It had been many years since acquisition of property had not been my prime concern. But not today. Today was for my marriage. Today was for the man who stood at my side and was now my husband.

I stood in the porch of a house I did not know, feeling nothing but shock, blind to the assets of the little wood-and-plaster manor of which I was now joint owner. I had done it. I had married him. And there he was, throwing back the door, gesturing for me to walk into the entrance hall, smiling at me.

Words would not come. In all that I had done in my life, I had no experience of such a relationship, stepped into at my own behest. It was like hopping from familiar territory into a strange land, all subtle shadows and traps for the unwary. As I entered, my heels echoing disconcertingly on the wide oak floorboards patterned with their whorls and knots, I was afraid.

"Well, Lady de Windsor?"

I shivered a little. Then laughed at how easily it had all been achieved. Yet perhaps it was not easy at all. How much did I really know about the man who stood regarding me? It was not easy to untangle my feelings for him.

"I suppose I am lady of the manor."

"You are indeed." He took my hand to lead me through the nearest doorway, rubbing my fingers between his. "You're cold. Come in— there should be a fire lit in here. Can't have my wife being cold." Then on a thought: "Did I actually say that?"

"I think so." I hardly registered the small paneled parlor, the pleasurable warmth, the polished furniture. Every sense was fixed on this man who had swept me off my feet. And had I not allowed him to do so? I removed my hood and mantle and placed them on a gleaming settle. "I suppose you intend to consummate this business arrangement in the proper manner?"

"Of course."

"A cup of wine and a signature on a document?"

He was already pouring the wine with solemn concentration, the flagon and cups having been made ready for us. His preparations had been meticulous. I took the one presented to me, raising it to my lips.

"I had a more energetic consummation in mind!"

And I laughed again. How easy he was to talk to, to laugh with. And how much my body desired that consummation. And then a thought wormed its way into my mind, for no apparent reason.

"Have you shared a bed with many women?" I asked bluntly.

"Yes." He lifted his cup in a silent toast. "Does it matter?"

"No."

"I won't ask you the same."

"No." I sighed a little. "But I was a virgin when I went to Edward's bed." And wished I had not brought the specter of the King into the room. I grimaced mildly. "Forgive me. . . ."

"It's not easy, is it, Alice?" He touched my hand with such understanding that my heart lurched.

"No. It is not." Nothing in my life had been easy.

"We knew it would not be. This day is ours. We'll not let others intrude."

We consummated our union in time-honored fashion, between the lavender-scented linen of Windsor's bed—what an efficient housekeeper he had acquired. How thoughtful he had been of my comfort—and for a soldiering man, astonishingly so. And how careful he was with me, an unexpected gentleness. Until his energies got the best of him, and he approached the task of disrobing me like initiating a campaign against the Irish: with a wealth of cunning and stealth to destroy all barriers. Not that there were any real obstacles to overcome between us. Were we not both experienced? Only my own unusual, unsettling reticence held me back.

"Alice . . . !" I had felt my muscles stiffen as he unfastened the lacing on my gown, letting his fingers trail across my nape. "You are allowed to enjoy this."

"I know. It's just that . . ."

"I know what it is. . . . You think too much. Let me seduce your mind as well as your body." His breath was warm, his lips soft along the line of my shoulder.

"You don't know any poetry," I managed on an intake of breath as he kissed the sensitive skin below my ear.

"But I do know how to use my lips for other purposes than mouthing meaningless sentiments. Like this . . ."

He was inordinately successful.

I did not compare him with Edward. I did not. I would not. There were no ghosts there with us, not Edward, certainly not Janyn Perrers. As for the nameless, faceless wraiths of Windsor's ghostly amours, I did not feel even one of them treading on my hem as he led me to the bed.

And then Windsor filled my entire mind. He was a new lover, with new caresses and heart-stopping skills, a resourceful lover whom it would take time to get to know.

As things were, I did not think I had that time.

On a practical note—a very necessary one—I took care to protect myself with the old wives' nostrum of a carefully positioned fold of wool soaked in cedar gum, messy but essential. It would not do for Windsor to get a child on me, and I bred easily. Were we not, even through our marriage, opening Pandora's box, allowing the escape of a multitude of dangers? A child would put weapons into the hands of those who did not love me. Besides, I was in no doubt: Whatever censure might be leveled at my own actions, Edward must be protected. I would not carry another child. I would never foist another man's child on Edward, or brand him as a cuckold.

And Windsor? He understood, and accepted. We both saw the yawning perils of our position, the strange delicacy with which our marriage must be conducted.

I received no bride gift after my wedding night. I did not care. For the first time in my life I had been given a gift that was far more precious than monetary value. I could not yet put a name to it, but I knew its value.

A strange happiness settled within me, like a bird come home to its nest. Physical delight made me languorous. A meeting of minds, as equals—for were we not equal in ambition and talents?—satiated me with pleasure. And so we lived out a little idyll at our manor at Gaines, far from enemies and Court intrigues and the pressures of the world. The few days we snatched away were long and warm, perfect for new lovers.

For that short time I was able to set aside my nagging fears for the future. I laid aside my anxiety over Edward in my absence. He was well cared for. My children were safe and lacked for nothing: I had enough wealth in land to protect them. Why should I not allow myself these few days for my own enjoyment? When had I last done that? I could not recall. Without guilt I wallowed in sheer self-indulgence, as we spoke of the inconsequential things that come to those who share a bed and a creeping, blossoming contentment in each other's companionship. Certainly nothing of our lives outside the walls of the manor was allowed to intrude. We sat or strolled as the mood took us, rode out in the meadows, ate and drank. Made love, like the young lovers we were not.

Did I regret my precipitate decision? Not for a moment.

Did Windsor? I think not.

When, as it must, my mind began to escape the confines I had set it, to reach out to that other life, there remained a fine solace to my very soul, wrapping around me like a fur on a winter's morning. When Edward died, God rest his soul, I would not be alone. I would be with this man whom I . . .

My careless thoughts slammed up against a barrier like a battering ram against a stone buttress. Uninvited, horribly intruding, fear bit deep. The words refused to form in my mind, although my heart urged them on.

With this man whom I had an *affection* for. That was enough.

Windsor's caresses awakened my body to an awareness of him that I had not anticipated. As all my earlier reticence was swept away by his experienced touch, I used my skill to make him shiver.

"I told you, you would not regret your decision," he whispered against my throat. "Why are you always so reluctant to believe what I tell you?"

"Because I know you for a devious man. And you, Will? Do you wish you had never made me that offer?"

"I knew I wanted you from the first moment I saw you. It was merely a matter of timing."

"Long-term planning."

"I am a master at it. And I am content."

I believed him. So was I too content. I would change nothing. But did I wish to commit myself in similar words? *It is dangerous to open yourself, body and soul, to a man you barely know and whom you suspect of less than altruistic motives.* And yet I did speak them.

"I am content."

And what did I do? I destroyed this new contentment.

Willfully, wantonly.

Because I was afraid.

Every day I was conscious of the moods of my new husband, learning to read them, learning his interests, learning the workings of his mind. I grew to know his care for me, the tenderness that sometimes undermined all my determination to remain a little aloof, and the fire of passion when we came together within the curtains of his bed. And throughout our rural sojourn, I was conscious of an energy burning deep within him, to be, to do, to act, to be engaged with the world beyond our bedchamber. It burned quite as strongly as the passion. He never spoke of it. He never said a word of his ambition to be elsewhere. And I loved him more for that. . . .

Love?

My realization of it stole my breath. Too soon, too reckless. Too hazardous. Why would I seek an inner fervor that robbed me of my freedom? I feared it like the plague. I would flee from it if I could.

In the end, honesty took me in hand and I could no longer deny the murmurings of my heart, but it was only to my own innermost thoughts that I spoke the word, savoring it on my tongue. I had hidden my emotions for so long, I was incapable of baring my soul to anyone. I had never done so to Janyn, to whom I was a means to an end. Nor to Edward, who was not interested in my soul. Before God, I could not expose my vulnerability to William de Windsor, who seemed against all the laws of nature to hold my heart in his hands. For if I did, would not that double, treble, quadruple my weakness? Better that I kept my own counsel. Better that I did not give him the power to hurt me. He did not love me. I would not put the power to wound into his hand.

So what did I do to our magical sojourn together? I destroyed it.

Here was my inarguable logic. If I did not destroy it, it would destroy itself, imploding on its inward-turning sweetness. A delight it might be now, but its honeyed intensity would soon rot our teeth. We could not stay together away from the world of the Court, where our ambitions must be played out. Windsor could not; and I had a duty elsewhere. At least this destruction was on my terms, with the hope of a renaissance, a reconciliation at some point and time in the future. My love was not on my terms, because I did not want it, but this decision would be. I would claw back control. Simply to preserve what we had, frozen in that sweet ice, would kill it slowly, for neither of us was made for domesticity, for happiness confined within four walls.

And yet in my heart I yearned for it. What I *wanted* and what I knew I must *not* want warred within me. And the victory of common sense near broke my heart.

On our return to Court, separately, discreetly as we must, I went immediately to Edward.

"Alice! Come and play chess with me. . . ."

He recognized me, welcomed me, defeated my wayward manipulation of my knight against his bishop with a few clever moves that I had been too preoccupied to follow, but I think he did not know that I had been absent for more than a few hours. I talked to him and explained what I wanted him to do. And he did it, accepting the rightness of my advice, signing and sealing the document.

My heart wept and my mind rejoiced at my success.

I took it to Windsor's room, little more than a passageway, in one of the distant wings. Going there was indiscreet, perhaps, but I chose my time and closed his door at my back, wishing there were another way as I offered the document, stepping no closer. If I did, I might be seduced by the strength of his arms. And if he kissed me . . . I thrust the document forward between us. "This is what you want, Will."

He took it, his eye traveling down, then up, his face illuminated with this victory, and I knew that I had done the right thing.

"Ireland!" he said.

"Yes. Ireland."

"King's Lieutenant."

"A valuable office."

"So you will be rid of me sooner than we thought."

"Yes."

He folded the document carefully, his mind suddenly arrested, as I knew it must be. "Is this your doing?"

"No." I perjured myself without regret.

His glance was sharp. "What made him change his mind?"

"Who's to say?"

So great was my sense of impending loss that I actually turned to leave him to enjoy his achievement alone.

"Is this difficult for you?" His question stopped me.

To persuade Edward, or to let you go?

And I knew he suspected my hand in it, despite my denial. Our knowledge of each other had grown apace.

"No." My voice was steady. "Edward needs a man of ability, not a young man barely out of adolescence—and as you so frequently say, who is there but you?"

"You knew it would be like this, Alice."

"Yes."

Still, the space yawned between us. He was the one to close it, to kiss me with a familiar echo of the passion I had come to desire.

"It's what I want, Alice." Did he think I did not know it? For a brief moment it grieved me that he should desire that distant office more than he desired me, but with his words, the sorrow passed. "I'll miss you more than I ever thought I could miss a woman." The wound healed a little, and I pressed my forehead against his shoulder. Until he lifted my chin so he could look at my face. "I'd ask if you'll miss me . . . but you'll never admit to that, will you?"

"No. How can I?" I frowned, caught in the toils of the dilemma I had helped create. He rubbed at the groove between my brows with his fingers.

"What's this? Guilt?"

"A little," I admitted. "Perhaps the King's Concubine is not free to miss you. Perhaps she is not free to have her emotions engaged."

"Does the King engage them?"

"With friendship. Compassion. Respect. All of those. I will not leave him, Will. I am not free to do so until his death."

At last the document that would take him from me was cast aside. Windsor's voice was tender. "Then I would say that the King could have no more loyal subject. And still I say you are free to miss me."

"Then I will." I would give him that, at least, and I thrust my guilt away.

His lips were soft on my brow. "Write to me."

"And risk interception?"

"You don't have to admit your undying love. Not that you would anyway!"

I laughed softly. We understood each other. "I'll write."

We made use of that one snatched opportunity to be together, in

Windsor's sparely furnished room. Our coming together was unsatisfactory, all in all, both of us with our senses stretched against possible discovery, struggling to make the best use of the narrow pallet. Little clothing removed, a hasty coupling—it was a reaffirmation of our commitment to each other rather than an outpouring of passion. And yet I would not have him leave me without experiencing that intimacy once more. How many months would it be before I saw him again?

We exchanged few words. What was there to say?

"Keep safe," he whispered.

"And you."

"I'll keep you in my thoughts, Alice."

"And you in mine, Will."

He was gone within the week. I could not put my loss into words; it was too great. He had said he would think of me, which was as much as I could hope for. For the first time in my life I knew what it was to have a broken heart.

How can it be broken! I upbraided my foolishness. *It cannot be broken unless you love him. And, of course, you do not!* And William de Windsor? I received an unexpected communication from my absent husband within the month. After a brief summary of events in Dublin, he added:

> *I said that I would miss you, Alice, did I not? I do. You belong to me, and it seems that I belong to you. Keep in good health. I need to know that you are safe for my return, whenever that might be.*

It was the closest to poetry that I would ever get from him. It was a precious thing. And yes, I wept.

Chapter Thirteen

*H*ow could I have been so disastrously shortsighted? I was terrifyingly, inexcusably complacent, unforgivably blinkered, and with no excuse to offer except that the normality of affairs lulled me into believing no change was imminent. Why worry? There was nothing to suggest that the long, warm days in the summer of 1375 held any danger. Edward was strong enough to host a tournament, and the spectacular Smithfield festivities in which I played a role left a sweet taste on the palate. So did Windsor's assertion that he would miss me.

There was no obvious cause for concern.

Why is it that we never see disaster approaching until it overwhelms us, like failing to foresee a winter storm lashing onto a lee shore, crashing down with terrible destruction and heartbreak? I never saw it, but it broke over our heads with disastrous force.

Looking back I realize that I could not have foreseen what happened. The yearlong truce with France was drawing to its close with the prospect of new hostilities, but not for a while. Perhaps another truce could be cobbled together. Certainly neither side was urging the other to a further bout of bloodlust.

Edward's health tottered on a knife's edge but did not fall. Some days were good, and on others he drowned in melancholy that I could not lift from him, but death did not approach. To tell the truth, the Prince was far beyond help. He would be ordering his shroud within the year, if I knew the signs. Joan, her eye to her son's future, was wound as tight as wool on a beginner's distaff. Her temper, ever unpredictable, was dangerously short. But the King held on to life, and he had his heir in young Richard.

Windsor was in Ireland, and although our communication remained erratic, I knew that one day he would return to me. I refused to admit my longing to see him again.

In the early months of the new year, a Parliament was summoned. The upkeep of an army being paramount, taxation was essential to raise the revenue: The royal Treasury needed a substantial input of gold. All in all, it was nothing out of the way. Even the Prince rallied to be present beside Gaunt and the King at the ceremonial opening, an impressive trio of royal blood adorned in their ceremonial robes of scarlet and ermine hiding the frailty of life beneath.

Joan stayed away from Court. No one mentioned witchcraft.

And so the days passed inexorably into the summer of 1376. Who could have foreseen the outcome of Edward's calling that thrice-damned Parliament? There was no intimation of danger as magnates, clergy, and commons came together in the Painted Chamber at Westminster with formal greetings and dutiful smiles on all sides. There was no undue restlessness in the ranks. Why would there be any barrier to fulfilling the royal demands? Parliament would act as it had always acted, to give its consent to raise revenue. The Commons retired, as they would, to the Abbey chapter house to elect their leader and consider the proposals to raise coin for the royal coffers. The debate would be brief and productive.

God's Blood! It was neither. And I learned of it soon enough.

Gaunt, driven by pent-up anger, divested himself of gloves and hat and thrust open the door of Edward's private parlor, where I sat. Shouldering Latimer aside, he slammed the door before striding across the room, where he halted in front of me.

"Where is he?"

Gaunt rarely lost control. Stark fear entered the room with him. Sweeping together the papers I was studying into a rough pile, then tucking them under the edge of a chest that held my pens and ink, I stood, my heart beating with sudden apprehension.

"The King is resting." I stepped before the door to the bedchamber. Edward was prostrate with exhaustion.

Gaunt took a turn about the room, unable to remain still. "The Commons! They've elected Peter de la Mare as their Speaker."

"Ah . . . !"

"De la Mare, by God!" Gaunt's teeth were bared in a snarl. "That name means something to *you*, of course."

I allowed my raised brows to make my answer. Every man and woman at Court knew of my recent confrontation with a member of the de la Mare family. It had been a regrettable little incident. Wisdom said that I should not have stepped into the argument, but when does wisdom count against a denial of justice toward an innocent man? I had become involved in a dispute that was not mine, and truth to tell, the outcome, mercifully to my advantage, had given me much pleasure.

"Our new Speaker is no friend to either of us," Gaunt remarked, twitching a curtain into shape, then punching it so that it billowed again into disarray. "I'm not sure which of us he despises most."

"I could hazard a guess."

Considering that Edward's privacy was relatively safe from invasion, I abandoned my stance and sat so that I could keep Gaunt in view as he continued to prowl. My recent adversary was a cousin of this Peter, now Speaker of the Commons: Thomas de la Mare, Abbot of St. Albans, a man with a famous reputation for erudition but none at all for charity or compassion. And not a man open to compromise.

Our clash of wills was all to do with the ownership of the insignificant little manor of Oxhay. Fitzjohn, a knight living there, was ejected from his property by the Abbot, who claimed ownership. So what did Fitzjohn do? Before marching once more into the manor to take hold of it, with worthy cunning he enfeoffed the property to me. And the Abbot, all prepared to summon the local mob to seize the manor in Saint Albans's name and force Fitzjohn out, decided at the last moment that Alice Perrers was not one to tangle with.

The consequence? I kept the property with Fitzjohn as my tenant for life, and the Abbot called down curses on my soul. Unfortunate, all in all, given the choice of the new Speaker, cousin to the Abbot.

"So where does that put us?" I asked, surveying my loosely linked fingers. Still, I did not see the true danger. Could Gaunt not use his influence against an upstart leader of the Commons?

"Under threat," Gaunt ground out through clenched teeth.

I frowned. "What possible mischief can he and the Abbot make, even if they combine forces?"

"Think about it." Gaunt swept across the room and gripped the arms of Edward's chair in which I sat, trapping me. His eyes were a bare handsbreadth from mine. I refused to allow myself to blink as I saw myself reflected there. "Who is Peter de la Mare's noble employer?"

"The Earl of March . . ."

"So, do I have to spell it out?"

Gaunt reared back and stalked to the window to look out, although I swear he did not see the scudding clouds. No, he did not have to spell it out. Finally I saw the connection. Peter de la Mare was also steward to Edmund Mortimer, Earl of March, the husband of Edward's grand-daughter Philippa. A man who was not lacking in influence as Marshal of England, he would be more than happy to see his infant son become the next ruler of England.

"And March is involved . . . ?"

"I'm sure he is!"

"Because of the succession . . ."

"Exactly! The whole lot of them are shackled together with my own princely brother in a plot against me."

My fingers tightened together, white-knuckled. Had I not always wondered how loyal Gaunt would be to the true succession to the English crown?

Gaunt turned his head to stare fiercely at me over his shoulder. "It's a conspiracy against me and those who stand as my friends. A neat little plot concocted by the Abbot of St. Albans and the Prince. Did you know they had long conversations together when the Prince stopped on his way from Berkhamsted to Canterbury earlier this year?"

No, I had not known.

"The Prince was not too ill to spend time putting weasel words into the ear of the Abbot. So there it is. March, the de la Mare cousins, and the Prince, all tied into a stratagem to keep me and my heirs from the throne."

Never had Gaunt spelled out his ambitions so clearly. Not to me. Not, I surmised, to anyone. For it was dangerous talk. Treasonous, in fact, for it all came back to the problem of the future succession. If the Prince's son Richard died without issue, the son of March and Philippa would rule England through order of descent, for Philippa had carried a son, a lad of three years old now. Not Gaunt. Not Gaunt's boy, Henry Bolingbroke. Would Gaunt be vicious enough, ambitious enough, to destroy the claim of his nephew Richard, or that of the infant son of March? Watching his fist clench hard against the window ledge, I thought he might. But thought was not proof. . . .

Whatever the truth of it, rumor said that the Prince lived in fear that his son might never rule if Gaunt had his way. And the Prince from his sickbed was using the allies he had: the de la Mare cousins and now March, who had apparently discovered he had much to gain in opposing Gaunt.

I forced my mind to untie the knots. I still couldn't quite see where this was leading. Unless the new de la Mare Speaker of the Commons intended to use the one weapon he had to get what he and his coconspirators wanted. My mind began to clear. The one weapon that would give him much power . . .

"Do you think that the Commons will grant finance for the war . . . ?" I queried.

"At a price. And I wager de la Mare has it all planned to a miracle of exactness. He knows just what he will ask for, by God!"

"What?"

"I scent danger on the wind. They're planning an attack. On me, on my associates in government. Latimer and Neville. Lyons. The whole ministerial crew, because I helped them into office. De la Mare and March will plot and intrigue to rid Edward of any man who has a connection with me. Gaunt will be isolated; that's the plan. Brother warring against brother." Gaunt's smile was feral, humorless, as his eyes blazed. "And they will declare war on you too, Mistress Perrers, unless I'm way off in my reading of de la Mare's crafty mind. Any chance that I might step into my brother's shoes will be buried beneath the crucified reputations of royal ministers and paramour alike." He folded his arms, leaning back against the stonework. "I did not think March had such ambitions. I was wrong. Being sire to the heir to the throne obviously appeals to him."

Sire to the heir? But only if Richard were dead . . . Or perhaps Richard did not need to die. . . . The complications wound around my brain like a web spun by a particularly energetic spider. March—and even Gaunt—might challenge the boy's legitimacy because of Joan's scandalous matrimonial history. They would not be the first to do so, but . . . I could not think of that yet. There was a far more urgent danger.

"Can you hinder Speaker de la Mare?" I asked.

"What can I do? The Commons are elected and hold the whip hand over finance," Gaunt responded, as if I were too much a woman to see it. "I'd look a fool if I tried and failed." When he rubbed his hands over his face, I realized how weary he was. "You have to tell the King."

My response was immediate and blunt. "No."

"He needs to know."

"What would be the point? If *you* can do nothing, what do you expect from an old man who no longer thinks in terms of plans and negotiations and political battles, who cannot enforce the authority of royal power? You've seen him when he is as drained as a pierced wine flask. What could he do? He'd probably invite de la Mare to share a cup of ale and discuss the hunting in the forest hereabouts."

"He is the King. He must face them and . . ."

"He can't. You know he can't." I was adamant. I watched as the truth settled on Gaunt's handsome features, so like his father's. "It will only bring the King more distress."

Gaunt flung his ill-used gloves to the floor. For a moment he studied them as if they would give him an answer to the crisis; then he nodded curtly. "You're right, of course."

"What will you do?" I asked as he recovered his gloves and walked toward the door, his thoughts obviously far away. My question made him stop, slapping his gloves against his thigh, searching for a way forward.

"I'll do what I can to draw the poison from the wound. The only good news is that the Prince is too weak to attend the sitting in person. It might give me a freer hand with Speaker de la Mare. If we come out of this without a bloody nose, it will be a miracle. Watch your back, Mistress Perrers."

"I will. And I will watch Edward's too."

"I know." For a moment the harshness in his voice was dispelled. "I detest having to admit it, but you have always had a care for him." Then the edge returned. "Let's hope I can persuade the Prince to have mercy on his father and leave him to enjoy his final days in peace."

He made to open the door, clapping his hat on his head, drawing on his gloves, and I wondered. No one else would ask him, but I would.

"My lord . . ."

He came to a halt, irritably, his hand on the door.

"Do you want the crown for yourself?"

"You would ask that of me?"

"Why not? There is no one to overhear. And who would believe anything I might say against you?"

"True." His lips acquired a sardonic tightness. "Then the answer is no. Have I not sworn to protect the boy? Richard is my brother's son. I have an affection for him. So, no, I do not seek the crown for myself."

Gaunt did not look at me. I did not believe him. I did not trust him.

But who else was there for me to look to? There would be no other voice raised in my defense.

Gaunt was gone, leaving me to search out the pertinent threads from his warning. So the Prince was behind the Commons attack, intent on keeping his brother from the throne. Every friend and ally of Gaunt would be dealt with. And I saw my own danger, for I had failed to foster any connection between myself and the Prince. But perhaps I was a fool to castigate myself over an impossible reconciliation. Could I have circumvented Joan's loathing? I recalled her vicious fury over the herbs, her destruction of the pretty little coffer. No, the Prince would see me as much a whore as his wife did.

Could I do anything now to draw the poison, as Gaunt had so aptly put it? I could think of nothing. Edward was not strong enough to face Parliament and demand their obedience as once he might. He needed the money. And what would the price be for de la Mare's cooperation to keep the imminent threat of France at bay? Fear was suddenly perched on my shoulder, chattering in my ear like Joan's damned long-dead monkey.

Watch your back, Mistress Perrers!

I considered writing to Windsor, but abandoned that exercise before it was even begun. What would I say? I could expect no help from that quarter before the ax fell. If it fell. All was so uncertain. I shivered. I would simply have to hope that its sharp edge fell elsewhere.

In those days following Gaunt's warning, while I sat tight in Westminster and rarely left Edward's side, the name of Peter de la Mare came to haunt my dreams and bewitch them into nightmares. I gleaned every piece of information that I could. Neither Edward nor the Prince attended any further sessions, so all fell into the lap of Gaunt, who tried to chain de la Mare's powers by insisting that a mere dozen of the Commons members should present themselves to confer privately with Gaunt in the White Chamber. De la Mare balked at the tone of the summons. How clear was the writing on the wall when he brought with him a force of well over a hundred of the elected members into a full session of Parliament? There they stood at his back, as their Speaker put forward his intent to the lords and bishops in the Painted Chamber.

He called Gaunt's bluff, and it put the fear of God into me. This was a dangerous game de la Mare was playing, and one without precedent, as he challenged royal power. I would not wager against his victory.

Oh, Windsor. I wish you were here at Westminster to stiffen my spine. I must stand alone.

Gaunt's description of events during that Parliament, for my personal perusal, was grim and graphic. *Thud!* Speaker de la Mare's fist crashed down against the polished wood. *Thud!* And *thud* again, for every one of his demands. Where had the money gone from the last grant? The campaigns of the previous year had been costly failures. There would be no more money until grievances were remedied. He flashed a smile as smooth as new-churned butter. Now, if the King was willing to make concessions . . . It might be possible to reconsider. . . .

Oh, de la Mare had been well primed.

There must in future be a Council of Twelve—*approved* men! Approved by whom, by God? Men of rank and high reputation to discuss with the King all matters of business. There must be no more covens—an interesting choice of word that clawed at my rioting nerves—of ambitious, self-seeking money-grubbers to drag the King into ill-conceived policies against the good of the realm.

And those who were now in positions of authority with the King? What of them?

Corrupt influences, all of them, de la Mare raged, neither loyal nor profitable to the Kingdom. Self-serving bastards to a man! Were they not a flock of vicious vultures, dipping their talons into royal gold to make their own fortunes? They must be removed, stripped of their power and wealth, punished.

And when Parliament—when *de la Mare*—was satisfied with their dismissal? Why, then the Commons would consider the question of money for the war against France. Then and only then.

"Do they think they are kings or princes of the realm?" Gaunt stormed, impotent. "Where have they got their pride and arrogance? Do they not know how powerful I am?"

"You have no power when Parliament holds the purse strings," I replied. The knot of fear in my belly grew tighter with every passing day, as we awaited the final outcome.

And there it was.

Latimer, Lyons, and Neville were singled out as friends of Gaunt. And the charge against them? De la Mare and his minions made a good legal job of it, ridiculously so. Not one, not a score, but more than sixty charges of corruption and abuse, usury and extortion. Of lining their pockets from trade and royal funds, falsification of records, embezzlement, and so on. I had a copy of the charges delivered to me, and read them with growing anxiety. De la Mare was out for blood; he would not be satisfied with anything less than complete destruction.

I tore the sheet in half as the motive behind the charges became as clear as a silver coin dropped into a dish of water. Guilt was not an issue here. The issue was their tight nucleus of control, a strong command over who had access to the King and who had not. Latimer and I might see our efforts as protection of an increasingly debilitated monarch; de la Mare saw us as a blight that must be exorcised by fire and blood. What did it matter that Latimer was the hero of the nation, who had excelled on the field of Crécy? What did it matter that he ran Edward's household with superb efficiency? Latimer and his associates were creatures of Gaunt. De la Mare was delirious with power and would have his way. Gaunt was helpless.

Throughout the whole of this vicious attack on his ministers, Edward was ignorant.

For what was I doing?

Trying to keep the disaster from disturbing Edward, whose fragility of mind increased daily. And I would have managed it too, having sworn all around him to secrecy, except for a damned busybody of a chamber knight, a friend of Latimer and Lyons, who begged for Edward's intercession.

I cursed him for it, but the damage was done.

After that there was no keeping secrets.

"They'll not do it, Edward," I assured him.

Dismissal. Imprisonment. Even execution for Latimer and Neville had been proposed.

"How can we tell?" Edward clawed at his robe, tearing at the fur so that it parted beneath his frenzied fingers. If he had been able to stride about the chamber, he would have done so. If he had been strong enough to travel to Westminster, he would have been there, facing de la Mare. Instead, tears at his own weakness made tracks down his face.

"This attack is not against you!" I tried. "They will not harm you. You are the King. They are loyal to you."

"Then why do they refuse me money? They will bring me to my knees." He would not be soothed.

"Gaunt has it in hand." I tried to persuade him to take a sip of ale, but he pushed my hand away.

"It is not right that my ministers be attacked by Parliament. . . ."

Did he realize that I too was not invulnerable against attack? I don't think he did. His mind, besieged by all manner of evils, could not see the full scope of what de la Mare was planning. I enfolded Edward's icy hand, warming it between both of mine. "I want to see the Prince . . ." he announced, snatching his hand away.

"He is not well enough to come to you."

"I need to listen to his advice." He was determined, struggling to his feet. I sighed. "I want to go today, Alice. . . ."

"Then you shall. . . ."

I could not stop him, so I would make it as easy as I could, arranging everything for Edward's comfort for a journey to Kennington. I did not go with him: I would not be welcome there, and it would do no good to add to Edward's distress by creating some cataclysmic explosion of emotion between myself and Joan. I prayed that the Prince would be able to give his father the comfort that I could not.

And so I made my own preparations. No longer could I delude myself that Latimer, Lyons, and Neville would escape without penalty. And when they fell . . .

So far my name had not been voiced in de la Mare's persecutions. I had remained unremarked, but that would not last; I saw retribution approaching. I had myself rowed up the Thames to Pallenswick— thereby removing myself from Westminster and from any of the royal palaces. Discretion might be good policy. What effect would it have on Edward's failing intellect and body if the one firm center of his life was gone? For once, the prospect of Pallenswick, the most beloved of all my manors, and reunion with my daughters, did not fill me with joy. Rather a black cloud of de la Mare's making settled over my head.

Storm clouds. Storm crows.

The words came back to me, Windsor at his most trenchant. The presentiments of doom were gathering.

I shivered with fear as the days passed, heavy with portent. Even though I was isolated from the Court, could I not see the future danger, its teeth bared like a rogue alaunt? I needed no recourse to a fortune-teller, or to my physician, who had something of a reputation for the reading of signs. I could read them for myself while sitting watchful at Pallenswick, every nerve strained. Braveheart slept at my feet, unconcerned, lost in a dream of coneys and mice. The blade Windsor had given me lay forgotten in a coffer upstairs. The threat to me came not from an assassin's dagger but from the heavy fist of the law.

The three royal ministers were dealt summary justice, their offices and possessions stripped from them. They were confined to prison, but the demands for execution died. Not even de la Mare could make the charge of treason stick. There was no treachery in these men to endanger King or state, unless acquiring a purseful of gold was treason. And if it was, then every man in government employ was guilty. But imprisonment was considered a just punishment. This was the price Latimer and Neville and Lyons paid for their association with John of Gaunt and Alice Perrers!

Holy Virgin! Would I be next? Gaunt, a royal son, would be safe, but the royal Concubine would be a worthy target. I too might end my days in a prison cell.

My mind leaped to Ireland, as it often did in those days.

Did Windsor know of my plight? It gave me some foolish comfort to think of him riding to my rescue. But of course he would not, and he was too far away to stretch out a hand to me. I shut out the image of his arms protecting me, his strength resisting any attack. It was too painful to imagine when I had no weapon that I might use. I had given Edward all I could—my youth, my body, my children. My unquestioning allegiance. Now I was truly alone.

And then, as expected, the charges against me arrived, ominously red-sealed. I had to sit, my legs suddenly too weak to hold me upright, as I read de la Mare's accusations, a pain hammering at my temples as I absorbed the horror of it. What had they concocted to make my freedom untenable?

Ah . . . ! As I read the first charge, the pain lessened. My breathing steadied. Predictable, nothing outrageous to shock me. I could answer this. I could state my defense. This was not so very terrible after all. . . .

She has seized three thousand pounds a year from the royal purse!

From where had they conjured that sum? Any monies I had taken were gifts from Edward. I had stolen nothing. It was his right to give gifts where he chose, and when I had borrowed to purchase some manor or feudal rights, it had never been without Edward's consent. Except for the purchase of the manors of Hitchin and Plumpton End that very year, when Edward's mind had slipped into some distant territory. And the borrowed sums had been paid back. For the most part, anyway . . . And if I had not repaid them through some oversight—well, I defied Parliament to find me guilty of fraud or embezzlement in that quarter.

She has seized Queen Philippa's jewels. She wears them. She has no shame in proclaiming her immorality with the King.

Yes, I wore them. Yes, I had no shame. Had Edward not given them to me? There was no illegality here. I read on.

She has shut the King away from his people. The only influence over him is hers, so that she might squeeze him dry of wealth and power.

True. I had kept him apart, protected. If it was a crime, I must answer for it, but it was not treason.

Ah! And then a charge with more than a snap of teeth. My heartbeat jumped again.

She has made use of the King's Court in her acquisition of land. She has been so bold as to sit beside the judges, influencing their verdicts in manorial disputes to her own ends.

I had. If I had been a man, intent on urging my interests in the courts, there would have been no accusation made. Was it a crime to do so? Windsor's harsh warning came back in a flood. They would seek to punish me for overstepping the boundaries suitable for a woman—but it was not treason.

My heart settled again. It would all come to nothing. By the end of the year there would be some new scandal to stir Parliament's ire. Edward need not be troubled, for the threats against me were empty ones and would die on their feet. My mind was more at ease, and, reassured by the power of my logic, I returned to Westminster and from there, as the heat of June began to press down on us, I wrote to Windsor.

> *Latimer and Lyons and Neville languish in prison, for which*
> *I am sorry. I have no power to help them. Gaunt is furious.*
> *Edward is inconsolable for reasons that will be known to you.*
> *De la Mare is frustrated that he can find no evidence of treason*
> *against me. I think that they might be content to let me go.*
> *There is no need for your concern about my safety.*
> *Of late I have wished you here with me.*

Edward is inconsolable, I had written, but not in reaction to my own predicament, because I told him nothing of the accusations leveled at me. How could I? The loss of his beloved son, in the same month that Parliament delivered those accusations, was too much for him to bear.

The Prince was dead.

I was with the King in those final days of his son's life, as were many from London and far beyond who traveled to see the end of this great warrior, struck down before his allotted time. At Westminster, men and women filed before the Prince's bed and wept openly as he wavered between sense and delirium. Joan remained beside him, rigid and tearless in her grief.

I did not weep for the Prince, but I did for Edward. For it was Edward's burden that he must watch the Prince die, his favorite son, his firstborn, his hope for the future and the protector of England. What hope could Edward have in Richard, the nine-year-old child who was ushered into the death-ridden chamber to make his nervous farewell and be recognized as the future King of England? The Prince slid in and out of consciousness, the pain great enough to disfigure his noble face, and Edward remained throughout to witness his passing. The outpouring of grief was too much for the King's spare frame. His face was gray with fatigue.

When it was over, I helped Edward to turn his stumbling steps back to his rooms and lie down on his bed, unseeing, unmoving, as if the Prince's death had drawn some of the life from his own body. Sitting beside him well into the night hours, I knew that I would not tell him of Parliament's attack on me. I told myself, willing myself to believe, that the Commons had slaked its thirst for blood on Latimer and Lyons; that the evidence against me was weak, and they would abandon me as not worth their effort.

Wrong! How desperately wrong I was. De la Mare would conjure the evidence from the ashes in the fire grate if he had to. I should have known he would not let me be, yet if I had, what could I have done?

I soon learned the depths to which de la Mare could sink in his desire for revenge.

We were at Sheen, where I hoped that the superb quality of the hunting and the comfort of tiled courtyards and newly glazed windows would give Edward's mind a more optimistic turn. Wykeham, restored to earthly glory as one of the newly appointed twelve high-minded men to counsel Edward in place of his scurvy ministers, arrived at the same time as a group of merchants representing the City of London, who had come to petition the King. Complaining bitterly over the precarious state of law and order in the capital, they were determined to be heard, though I would have preferred to send them away. They had been invited to send a delegation, so here they were to see the King and beg his intervention. Accepting the rightness of their cause, and perhaps conscious of the hate-filled de la Mare breathing his fetid breath down my neck, I allowed it. I had no intention of adding fuel to the fire by keeping Edward shut away from his people. We worked hard to make the best show we could, not in the great audience chamber, but in a smaller one, where the King was already seated when the petitioners arrived.

They bowed before him. Edward made no gesture of recognition.

Forgive me, Edward! Forgive me! I could have wept again for him. How close my tears were in those days, when for most of my life I had been dry-eyed. Could de la Mare, in rare pity for his King, not acknowledge the truth of why I had kept Edward from the public eye?

We had swathed him in cloth of gold and tied him as well as we could into his chair so that at least he gave the appearance of normality, but it was as if a statue filled the royal throne, not a living, breathing man. He looked vacantly at the merchants when they complained that the peace of the realm was in jeopardy. And when they went on to describe the lawless behavior of the mobs and John of Gaunt's troops, and the scandal of an attack against the Bishop of London himself, Edward, uncomprehending, replied with a mumbling of incoherent words that no one could hear, let alone understand.

"This is a travesty," murmured Wykeham in my ear where we stood a little removed from the audience.

"But I must allow it," I stated.

"Why?"

"Because de la Mare accuses me of standing between the people and the King, and—before God!—what he says is true. I have done exactly that." I could hear despair building in my voice. "You can see why. . . ."

"Yes . . ." Wykeham looked back to where Edward remained engraved in stone. "The commons should not have to see this."

"Nor should the King have to endure it," I added more curtly than I had intended. "To put him on show in this manner is . . ." I recalled having had the same argument with Windsor. Suddenly I felt very tired.

". . . is cruel." Wykeham finished my train of thought with a sigh.

One of the knights standing beside Edward leaned over to grasp his shoulder and keep him upright.

"End this, Alice," Wykeham murmured. "It can't go on."

The delegation stood uncertainly, a mix of horror and pity on their faces, and I hurried forward.

"The audience is at an end, gentlemen. . . ." And as the merchants bowed themselves out, gestures that Edward did not see, I touched Edward's hand. He did not respond. "Take the King to his chamber," I instructed. "I will come to him."

"I doubt he will know whether you do or not. I had not known he had faded so quickly," Wykeham said.

"The Prince's death was the final blow."

"Before God, it's pitiful."

"It's more than that. . . ." I could not watch as the knights lifted Edward from the throne and led him stumbling away. "Now, why are you here, Wykeham? I hope it's good news." I did not need to ask, now that I had time to read his expression.

"No."

"Then tell me. It can't be worse than what we have just seen."

"I think it can, mistress. Let us find someplace where you can be emotional."

"Emotional?"

"You might feel the need to throw something."

The words sent a bolt of fear through my body.

"I thought you should know, mistress, what de la Mare is saying to stir the Commons against you."

I was in no mood for guessing games. "What now? That I have se-creted the whole of the crown jewels—including Edward's crown—in a cache to ward off future poverty?"

"It's far worse." He waited until there was no one within earshot, and whispered, "De la Mare is citing necromancy."

I came to an abrupt halt, my hand fastening like a claw around Wykeham's wrist.

Necromancy? *Witchcraft!*

I think I laughed at the absurdity of it—until my throat dried, my thoughts tumbling as I tried to recall. This was no time for laughter. I could think of no possible evidence of necromancy that could be laid at my door . . . unless . . . Joan's accusations and the box of remedies. Surely her impassioned words would have no bearing on de la Mare's attack. My notions had been what any goodwife could have produced.

"He can't accuse me of that!" I retorted.

"Don't be too quick to judge! You might listen first, mistress, to what I know."

I took him into the garden, where we could walk or sit without eavesdroppers. Onlookers might wonder at a conversation between the King's Concubine and the Bishop of Winchester, but, under the cir-cumstances, they might consider my need for confession to be urgent.

Confession, by God!

"I am no witch!" I could barely wait until we were secluded, apart from the bees enjoying the heady flowers of lavender and thyme.

"That's not what your physician is saying!"

"My physician?" Father Oswald, a gentle, unassuming Benedictine monk, had been attached to my household for many years now. I would have thought him to be unswervingly loyal. "What has he said?" I racked my mind for anything that could be construed as dealing with the devil. A few foolish love potions for the damsels—but they were far in the past. As were the salves and drafts I'd given Philippa to ease her pain. There was no witchcraft there; nor would Father Oswald have any intelligence of them.

"Your physician's been put under some . . . pressure . . . to speak of what he knows." Wykeham was deadly certain. "His accusations against you ran like a stream in spate."

"Torture?"

"So I understand."

This was dangerous stuff. How many times had a difficult woman been accused of being in league with the devil, ultimately to face death by drowning or the excruciating pain of fire . . . ? I shuddered in the warmth of the parterre.

"I am no witch," I repeated stalwartly.

"Then let me tell you what's being said, mistress."

Wykeham pulled me farther along the pathway until we stood in the very center, facing each other on either side of the sundial. It was a magnificent tale, as old as time, told with remarkable—and frightening—exactitude. There we were, whore and priest, standing in a summer landscape, and I felt the jaws of death closing in around me. "So that you should be clear about it," Wykeham said dryly, his face severe but not without compassion, "they'll hound you to death if they can, Alice." Wykeham always had a way with words, probably from preaching so many sermons to the damned.

"Where did the evidence come from?" I asked.

"John de la Mare, brother to the Speaker of the Commons—how fortunate," Wykeham explained with blistering brevity. "He visited Pallenswick with a chamber pot of urine, asked for help to have his entirely fictitious malady diagnosed—and in pious charity Father Oswald agreed."

"Father Oswald always was a gullible fool when it came to judging others," I observed irritably. "Had he no suspicions?"

"Apparently not. He was brought to London and questioned. I've no doubt force was used." Wykeham eyed a lively flight of goldfinches in the adjacent bushes. "Your admirable physician admitted to a remarkable range of activities on your behalf."

"The last thing he did for me was mix a salve to calm my chilblains."

Wykeham grunted. "It's far worse than that. By the by, they said you were there, at Pallenswick. And that you grew pale with fear when you saw your man under restraint."

"By God! I was not!"

"I think God has no role in this. Rather the devil. This is what your man did for you, if he is to be believed."

Wykeham ticked the charges off on his fingers while I absorbed the depth of my supposed guilt. This was far worse than fraud and embezzlement. The accusations smeared the soft air in that pretty spot with the filth of necromancy. All of it false, yet its falsehood impossible to prove.

"Your physician claimed that upon your order he created two images, of yourself and His Majesty, and bound them together to make an indissoluble bond. Thus he explained Edward's infatuation with you. Their words—not mine. Your physician made two rings with magical properties for you to put onto Edward's finger, one to refresh the King's memory so that you would always be in the forefront of his thoughts, the other to cause forgetfulness of all else but yourself. And he made love potions and spells suffused with herbs picked at the full moon, at your request, to work your magic to bewitch the King into infatuation." He paused, eyeing me. "You have been very busy, it seems, Mistress Perrers."

"Have I not? And do you believe all this?"

Wykeham shrugged. "He also said he made a spell so that you could charm Gaunt and the Prince to your own ends."

"Both of them?" My voice was no more than a croak.

"Yes. I think he added both for good measure."

"It says little for Father Oswald's skill." Should I laugh or weep at the outrageousness of it all? "I failed singularly to win the Prince to my favor, and Gaunt's allegiance is unpredictable, governed by self-interest."

A silence fell between us. I had nothing at hand to throw.

"The Speaker is making much of it," Wykeham said.

"He would, of course." I tried to predict the next step in this battle, for surely that was what it was. "What have they done with my poor physician?"

"Sent him to St. Albans, in a sorry state, to face his superiors. They've done with him, mistress. It's you they want." Wykeham's gaze was cool and direct. I waited for his condemnation, but it did not come. So . . .

"You were kind to come here to inform me," I said over the chased metal of the sundial that showed the passing minutes. It seemed hours since Wykeham had first breathed the word *witchcraft*, since my world had become a thing of terror, but the line of shadow had barely moved. Now encroaching clouds blotted out the sun. "You still haven't said whether you believe the charge or not."

"The sin of avarice, perhaps. Of pride, certainly . . ."

"Oh, Wykeham . . . !" Would he list all my failings?

"But witchcraft? No, not that. I believe you have a deep affection for the King. I don't believe you would ever do him harm."

"My thanks. You are one of very few." It gave me some comfort, but not much. We began to walk back toward the palace, driven in by a sharp little breeze that had chased away the bees and promised rain. Here was blatant propaganda of the worst kind to blacken my character. I stopped, regardless of the spatter of heavy drops.

"Will they find me guilty?" And when Wykeham hesitated: "Don't give me a soft answer. Tell me what you think!"

"I'd no intention of hiding the truth. I think they might. De la Mare is slavering for the kill." I flinched when Wykeham did not temper his words. "With Latimer and Lyons under his belt, his confidence shines like a comet. I find it difficult to meet with him without addressing the sin of pride. Damn him!"

"What a handful of unpriestly expressions." I smiled bleakly. "And if the punishment is proven? Will it be death?"

He thought for a long moment. "Unlikely. Penance and fasting probably. You haven't killed anyone. Imprisonment at the worst."

My throat was dry and I barely felt the rain on my face. "Then I'll plan for the worst. I don't see de la Mare being content with a few missed meals and a paternoster." The thought of imprisonment was bad enough to me. I closed my mind to it. "What do I do, Wykeham?"

"You could take refuge at Pallenswick."

Inwardly I recoiled at the implication, that making a defense against the charges would be a waste of his breath and mine. But flight? "No." I wouldn't even consider it. "I cannot. You've seen the King. He needs me."

"Then you remain here and do nothing. Just wait. The Speaker might abandon it . . ."

I completed his sentence when he hesitated again. ". . . if he finds something worse to pin on me."

Wykeham looked 'round sharply. "Why? What else have you done?"

I shook my head and looked away, across to the trees that were now shivering in the wind. There was one secret I prayed would remain hidden from public knowledge for a little time yet. It would bring too much pain to Edward.

And if it didn't?

Back in my room, where I retired to change my muddied skirts, I hurled a handsome glazed jug at the wall, and then regretted it. I felt no better for it, and one of the serving maids had to clean it up.

Once Wykeham was gone, I returned to Edward's side in his great chamber. He was now wrapped in a chamber robe, the scarlet and fur at odds with the wasted figure it contained. Before the fire—he always felt the cold even on the warmest day—he slept in his chair, his head forward on his chest, a cup of ale at his side. John Beverley, his body servant, stood close by if he should wake and lack for aught. I gestured that he should leave, and sat on a stool at Edward's feet, as I was wont to do when he was still in his prime and I was a young girl. But my thoughts were not of past memories. As I leaned my head against the chair, Wykeham's warnings echoed shockingly in my mind. He might be sanguine about my punishment, but I was not convinced. Prison walls seemed to hem me in.

When Edward moved, I looked up, grateful for the distraction. His eyelids lifted slowly and gradually his eyes focused on me. They were lucid and aware. My heart leaped with joy.

"Edward."

"Alice." Even his voice was stronger. He could still surprise me. "Dear girl. I have missed you."

"I have been here with you while you slept. You had an audience with some of the worthies from London."

He sighed a little. "I don't remember. Bring me a cup of ale."

I reached to pick up the forgotten cup beside him and placed it in his hand, curling his fingers around it. Sometimes he was still very much the King.

He sipped, then handed the cup back to me. "Will you sing to me?"

How little he remembered! "I would, but it would not be to your pleasure. I'm told I have a voice like a creaking door hinge." I smiled as I recalled one of Isabella's more vulgar remarks and saw an answering gleam in Edward's eyes. "But here is a verse I have found and liked, because it speaks of old lovers, as we are. . . ." I sank back against his chair, arranging my skirts, drawing the little book from the purse at my belt. "It is about the cold of winter, and the warmth of enduring love. You will like it too." I began to recite, slowly, gently, forming the words clearly so that he might follow.

> *"The leaves are failing; summer's past;*
> *What once was green is brown and sere;*
> *All nature's warmth has faded fast and gone from here;*
> *The circling sun has reached the last house in its year."*

"You have it right, Alice. Winter has me in its thrall even in the heat of summer." Edward dragged in a breath, as if it were painful for him to speak it. "I am no use to you as a man. I regret it, but am unable to remedy it."

"No, but listen, Edward. It is not sad at all.

"The world is chilled in every part:
But I alone am warm and grow
Still warmer. It delights my heart to feel the glow:
My lord made the burning start—I love him so."

"Alice . . . You have a beautiful voice." The slight slurring of his words that always returned when he grew weary was very evident. "I think that was one of the first things I noticed about you."

"I doubt it!" I laughed a little at the memory. "I think I was shrieking like a fishwife in the chapel at Havering when I was accused of theft! And you were tied up with your clock."

"I had forgotten. . . ." He sought my hand and his fingers tightened around mine. I could feel his eyes on my face, on my lips, as I read the final tender lines.

"This fire in my heart is nourished by
My lord's kisses and his gentle touch;
And shining from his radiant eye the light is such
That neither earth nor brilliant sky can show as much."

"There, you see." I closed the little book. "Love remains even in the depths of winter and the fullness of years."

Silence settled around us. He was asleep again, and my heart was full of sorrow that he should mourn the loss of virility so keenly and above all else. We might no longer be lovers, but we were bound together by our past that stretched over well-nigh thirteen years. Even in sleep, his fingers held mine and I knew he was pleased.

For a little time my fears of witchcraft were banished. I would allow nothing to separate us. Not until death released Edward from his present sufferings.

"Is it true?" Wykeham demanded, his voice raw and positively vibrating with disbelief. He had come to Sheen again in a towering fury.

"Is *what* true? If it's more empty mouthings of de la Mare that you've come to report, then don't! Just go away!"

I reacted without patience. I was weary beyond my soul. There was no royal audience to distract us this time. Lost in the past, Edward was dictating orders to mark the occasions of the deaths of both his mother and Philippa. And this was after a week when he had spoken not one word to anyone: not to his servants, not to God. Certainly not to me. I had made myself scarce until the doleful ceremony of remembrance was done.

"Is it true?" Wykeham bellowed.

I stood in the center of the Great Hall. "Is what true?"

When Wykeham shouted back, careless of who overheard, I knew my fate was sealed. When he had come to warn me about the charge of necromancy hanging over my neck, he had been the concerned and courteous priest. Now he was the dread harbinger of doom, the executioner. There was no escape for me.

"You actually *married* him?"

Holy Mother! "Who?" I asked, playing desperately for time.

"You know who!"

Wykeham watched me. He was waiting for me to deny it, while knowing that I couldn't.

"Yes." I raised my chin. "Yes, I did."

"I don't believe that you would do anything so . . . so"—he groped for self-control—"so ill-advised!"

"Well, Wykeham! How mealymouthed!" There was nothing genial about my smile. "And how did de la Mare mine that little gem?" I asked. "I thought no one knew."

"Does it matter?" His voice had dropped to a hiss. *"When?"*

"Just before he returned to Ireland."

"That was when? Two years ago? You've been wed for two years?" The volume grew again to echo above us. "In God's name, Alice! What were you thinking?"

I did not want to explain. I did not think I could.

"Does Edward know?" Wykeham threw up his arms as much in despair as anger.

"No."

"Don't you realize what you've done?" At least Wykeham now had the sense to lower his voice. "You've made him an adulterer!"

I lifted a shoulder. "And so were we both when Philippa was alive.

Edward did not step back from it then, when he had all the knowledge. What's the difference?"

Wykeham kicked a foot into the ashes of the open fire, sending up a shower of sparks.

"Why, Alice? Why do it? If it was a roll between the sheets you wanted, why not just do it without the sanction of Holy Mother Church? As for the man you chose! God's Blood! A more self-interested, unprincipled bastard I have yet to meet. . . ."

Because . . . because . . . I watched the sparks die as they fell into gray dust. Because I loved him. Because beneath the hard-edged ambition and ruthless temperament there was in Windsor a man of rare honesty who actually cared for me. But I would not say this to Wykeham. He would not have believed me.

"I wed him because he asked me."

"Alice!"

I abandoned the flippancy. "Don't lecture me, Wykeham. You of all people should know that I must make my future secure. I come from nothing and will return to nothing if I don't make provision. I will not have my children live in penury or on the charity of others, as I did."

"Surely you have enough property by now to keep shoes on their feet!"

"Perhaps I need a man to stand for me."

"But to *wed* him."

"He offered when no one else would. It is not adultery. Not in the letter of the law. The King and I are no longer intimate." The priest in him flushed to his hairline. "Don't be prudish, Wykeham. It can't be a surprise to you that the King is incapable."

"But the King recognized the children you had together. They will never suffer."

"Yes, he made provision. But will Princess Joan allow the provision to continue when her son is king?" It was a half-buried fear that was quick to resurface. "I dare not risk it. If marriage to Windsor secures my daughters' dowries and marriage, then I'll not regret it."

"What will Edward say?"

Which brought me up short, as he intended. I replied slowly. "He will be hurt, of course."

"You must tell him. Unless he knows already."

"Pray God he does not."

As Wykeham left me alone in the Great Hall, all its spaces empty around me, I thought of the one thing I had not said. I had wed Windsor—a name that had not once been voiced between us—because I loved him. How weak did that make me?

How swiftly gossip flew. Edward knew. There were always those at Court who would make mischief, and Edward's mind was clear enough.

"You betrayed me, Alice. You betrayed my love for you."

He rubbed his hands together in incessant repetition, one over the other, his fingers tearing, his nails marking his skin. Guilt-ridden, I fell on my knees, trying to still his fretful clawing, but he would not stop. Edward turned his face from me as he had never done before.

"I don't want you here."

I deserved it. All my senses were frozen.

Did the Commons have mercy on me? By God, they did not! In a mood of vengeful exuberance they ordered me to appear before them in the Painted Chamber at Westminster. And I obeyed—what choice did I have?—seeing nothing but the lugubrious face of de la Mare gleaming with unholy virtue as I set my mind to hear and accept my punishment for bringing the King of England into adultery. By now I feared the worst, gripping my hands together as I sat on the low stool provided for me. At least they allowed me to sit.

I sat straight-backed, determined to hear my fate with dignity. I would never bow my head before de la Mare. Whatever punishment they meted out, nothing could be worse than Edward's rejection of me.

Nothing?

Ah, no! There was worse, much worse. What had they done? The door to the magnificent Painted Chamber opened and there was Edward, brought to appear before his own Parliament for my sins and his, and I saw the panicked fear in his gaze as it skittered over the vast assembly. I stood abruptly; I even think I reached out to him in my guilt and misery, but he did not look at me, all his efforts fixed on walking to take his place on the throne. Slowly, one step after another, he dragged himself there, and pushed himself upright to face his accusers. And I prayed that they would turn their claws on me, not on Edward, who did not deserve this. I willed him to look at me. Whatever was asked of me, I would not betray him more than I already had done. I would not do or say anything to increase his humiliation. Was it not terrible enough that he must be here?

De la Mare bowed. "We are honored, Sire."

And I sank back to my seat as I waited for the blow to fall, as de la Mare faced Edward.

"Majesty. We are concerned that Mistress Perrers has acted toward you with a degree of insincerity that is beyond belief."

How smooth he was. How terrifyingly, horrifyingly respectful before plunging the metaphorical dagger into Edward's unsuspecting heart.

Edward blinked, hands clutching.

"We believe she has put Your Majesty's soul in mortal danger."

Would he dare to accuse Edward of being complicit in adultery? My nails dug deep into my palms.

"Were you aware, Sire, that Mistress Perrers had entered into matrimony? That she has been married to the knight William de Windsor for two years or more?"

Bewildered, Edward shook his head.

"Were you so aware, Sire?"

"No . . . !" Again I was on my feet. How dared they question him! This was my guilt, not his.

"Be seated, Mistress Perrers."

"It is not right. . . ."

"It is very right." De la Mare swung back to the King. "Did you know, Sire?" I sat again, forcing myself to look at Edward in his extremity and accept that this was all my doing. "Were you aware, Sire, that the woman who is acknowledged as your mistress is married?" The question was hammered home once more.

And I heard Edward reply. Calm and clear. Unemotional. "I was not aware."

"Would you swear to that, Sire?"

The Speaker would dare to ask the King of England to swear an oath? Edward's face was ravaged, but he replied, "I swear on the name of the Holy Virgin. I did not know."

"So she tricked you, Sire."

"I don't know. How could I know . . . ?"

Oh, Edward! How could I have put you in this position?

It was all de la Mare needed. Facing me now, he flung out an arm in a dramatic all-encompassing gesture.

"You are guilty. You have willfully put the King into the state of adultery. You tricked him with your lies and deceit. The fault is yours."

I waited for the noxious taint of witchcraft to fill the chamber.

"What is the punishment for your crime? There are those here who demand your execution. The means you have used are unholy, disgusting in the sight of God. We have evidence of . . ."

I tensed. This would be the moment. *Maleficium!*

"Sirs . . . !"

I looked across the chamber. It was Edward. De la Mare hesitated.

"I beg of you," Edward said, each word carefully formed as he looked at me at last, his eyes weighted with sorrow, confusion, and, astonishingly, a hard-won determination. My heart was wrung. "Show her mercy, sirs. I beg of your compassion. She does not deserve execution. If you have any loyalty to me, your King, you will show this woman leniency in your judgment. She has done wrong, but she does not deserve death."

I held Edward's gaze. In that final sentence he had both betrayed and upheld me. All hung in the balance.

"Mistress Perrers deserves a lesser punishment than death," Edward repeated. "I beg of you . . ."

And grief all but overwhelmed me.

"We honor your request, Sire." De la Mare could not disguise his self-congratulation, so smug that I felt an urge to vomit. "Stand up, Mistress Perrers."

I did so, bracing knees that refused to obey me.

"We are decided. . . ."

De la Mare spelled out the terms of my punishment. As it flowed from his lips, detailed, thorough, I knew that it had been decided all along. There had been no need to put Edward through this pretense. Grief was transmuted into an anger that shook me as I absorbed the extent of de la Mare's revenge. Even Princess Joan could not have thought up any better.

Banishment!

The single word hung in the air with all the heaviness of its meaning. I was banished. Never to see Edward again.

"You will live at a distance from the royal Court. You will not return. If you disobey, if you make any attempt to approach the King, you will lose everything you own and suffer permanent exile overseas." The Speaker's lips widened into a rictus of a smile over his discolored teeth. "If you break in any way the terms of this banishment, all your property, your goods and chattels will be seized and confiscated." His pleasure disgusted me, but I stood unmoving, unresponsive. I would never give him the satisfaction of seeing how much this penalty wounded me.

Glancing at Edward, I knew that he did not understand. His eyes were closed, his mouth lax. He had no inkling of what they had just done. If I walked across the chamber to him now, I would be left with nothing and banished from England.

With blood drained from my face, my hands as cold as ice, I did what they wanted. My lips pressed to the crucifix presented to me, and I swore that I would never return to the King. I would live apart, away from the royal Court. I would never see Edward again.

Thus I abandoned him, or so it felt in my heart.

Where to go? I collected my immediate possessions and went to Wendover, Wykeham's old manor that Edward had gifted to me. My sore heart urged Pallenswick, but I knew Parliament would consider it too close to Sheen, or the Tower, or Westminster, wherever Edward might be, and with too easy a route along the Thames. So I went to Wendover, a good three days' journey, to lick my wounds, after I had risked seeing Edward for the last time. Surely a final farewell would be allowed.

He did not know me. When I stood before him and spoke his name, he did not answer. His eyes made no contact with mine.

"Edward!"

There was no flicker of acknowledgment in his empty gaze.

"I have come to say farewell."

Nothing. I was not pardoned. His wayward mind could not encompass me or what I had done. I kissed his forehead and curtsied deeply.

"Forgive me, Edward. I would not have it end like this. I would never have left you."

At least he was spared the pain of parting. I closed the door of his chamber, swallowing my tears. I was Alice Perrers, King's Concubine no longer, humiliated, repudiated, maliciously destroyed.

Who was not in the Painted Chamber to witness my downfall?

Gaunt.

Who made no attempt to see me, to stand for me?

John of Gaunt.

He too had abandoned me. The alliance, tenuous at best, did not bring him to my side when I most had need of him. I was no longer of any value to him. He'd been refused the position of regent for his nephew Richard by the magnates who feared his power, and I had no means of helping him. It would do no good for Gaunt's name to be coupled to any degree with mine.

He turned his back on me.

And my poor, lost Edward? I had Wykeham tell me how he fared. On the days when he was driven by anger, he accused Windsor far more harshly than he accused me. And then there were times when old loyalties returned to Edward, when he looked for me, asked for me, and was told that I could not come. Days when his senses deserted him. I knew of the hours when he sat in uncomprehending gloom with tears on his cheeks. The King was nothing but a lonely, forgotten old man, with no one to stir his spirits to life. Who would reminisce with him? Who would talk to him of the glory days, as I had done?

No one.

Gaunt was too busy plotting revenge against de la Mare and the

Earl of March, who now stood with Wykeham as one of Edward's councilors. Isabella was back with her husband in France. There was no one to remember the past.

I also knew of the increasing number of days when Edward's thoughts turned inward.

"I will bury my son, my glorious Prince, and then I will die."

I wept for him. I did not write to Windsor. I could not find the words; nor could I bear his pity.

Chapter Fourteen

For the first days at Wendover I grieved until hot rage blew through me like a wind before an August storm. It shook me by its virulence as I heaped my hatred on the absent, crowing, self-satisfied Master Speaker.

"May Almighty God damn you to the fires of hell! May your vile body be gnawed on by worms, your balls roasted in everlasting flames and . . ." I was not circumspect in my choice of language, but it brought no release.

Never had my life stretched so emptily, so helplessly before me, my hands so idle and without power. My knowledge of the outside world in those terrible weeks was reduced to what was common gossip, brought into the house by my servants and passing peddlers. Poor stuff! The Prince's body lay embalmed in state in Westminster Abbey week after week. There were no moves to bury him, Edward unable to make a decision. Princess Joan and the young heir were at Kennington. Gaunt was biding his time, but furious with events. The Good Parliament had ended its days, preening over its success in holding the King to account.

"And I am banished, by God! How dare they! How dare they!"

With a need to occupy my hands and my mind, I swept through the manor, stirring up steward and servants to clean and scour and scrub every surface, every nook and cranny. There was absolutely no need for me to disturb their perfectly adequate daily routines, but I could not rest. They would have to suffer me, perhaps for the rest of my life. God's Blood! At thirty-one years I could not contemplate it.

Braveheart slept at my feet, oblivious to my mood, uncaring of whether we were at Wendover or Sheen.

I stalked from room to room, my pleasure in my surroundings and my acquisitions dimmed. Even the magnificent bed—a gift from Edward—carved and swagged with deep blue damask hangings, the oak tester and pillars polished to a rich gleam, did not satisfy me. I saw far too much of that fine weaving that closed me in, for my nights were troubled. If I had had a looking glass, I would have abjured it. It would have shown me all too clearly the effect of my lack of appetite and restless thoughts. My collarbone pressed against the cloth of my gown, and my girdle must be tightened or it would fall around my ankles. As I pressed my fingers against my sharp cheekbones, I grimaced, suspecting that the dark thumbprints of weariness would not enhance my looks.

Lured by the soft warmth of autumn, I took the side door out into the orchard, where the apple trees hung heavy with the fruit and doves preened in the dovecote, a lovely scene if I were of a mind to admire it. But before I could take a breath, an unbidden image leaped into my mind, so that I sank down on the grass, helpless, enclosed in that one moment of the past.

"Today you are my Lady of the Sun," Edward says as he hands me into my chariot.

And there I sit, garlanded with flowers, swathed in cloth of gold, pulled by four shining bay horses. I am no less superb. A cloak of shimmering gold tissue, opulent in its Venetian style, is spread around me, so disposed to show a lining of scarlet taffeta. My gown too is red, lined with white silk and edged in ermine. Edward's colors. Royal fur fit for a queen, no finer than the myriad of precious stones refracting the light: rubies as red as fire; diamonds; sapphires, dark and mysterious; strange beryls capable of destroying the power of poison. Philippa's jewels. My fingers are heavy with rings. "Today you are the Queen of the Ceremonies, the Queen of the Lists," Edward says. He is tall and strong and good to look upon.

I am the Lady of the Sun.

I blinked as a swooping pigeon smashed the scene, bringing reality back with a cruel exactitude. How low I had fallen! I was caged in impotent loneliness, like Edward's long-dead lion. Powerless, isolated, stripped of everything I had made for myself.

I was nothing.

Impatient with myself, I rose to go back inside and harry someone into doing something, but was stopped by my two daughters, Joanne leading her younger sister in their escape from their governess. Joanne, six years old, was fair and strong limbed like her father. Jane, two years younger, was a shy child, not like me at all, despite her dark hair and plain features. They ran laughing through the orchard, shouting to each other in their joy of freedom. And my heart tripped a little at their innocent pleasure. I did not remember running or laughing in my childhood. I recalled very little joy. God help me to keep their lives safe.

Seeing me, they ran to jump and caper, full of chatter and news. With promises that we would ride out in the afternoon, I dispatched them back to their lessons. They would read and write and figure. No daughter of mine would lack for such skills, and nor would my sons. I wanted no ignorant, untutored gentlemen with the King's blood in their veins and nothing between their ears. John, as befitted a lad of royal birth, learned the lessons of a page in the noble Percy household. Nicholas, at eleven, was taught his letters by the monks at Westminster. I had such a pride in them. As for my girls—they would each have an advantageous marriage as well as an education. I smiled a little as I stooped to pick up a much-worn doll that Joanne had dropped on the grass. Combing my fingers through its disordered hair, I vowed that I would ensure that my daughters were capable, even without a husband.

A movement caught my eye. A robin flew up into the boughs of the apple tree, making me look up.

"Is this you?"

I hadn't heard, neither the approach of horses nor the soft footfall. Nor even felt the movement of air. Startled for a moment, the fear still lively that Parliament might not have finished with me, I took a step back. And then I clutched the doll to my breast, because I knew the voice and the solid figure outlined by the sun through the branches.

The years rolled back and away to the day I first set eyes on Edward in the great hall at Havering, his body backlit by the low rays of the afternoon sun, the hounds at his feet, the goshawk on his wrist, a corona of light around his head and shoulders. He'd been crowned with gold. I had simply stared at such an aura of power.

But this was another time, another life.

William de Windsor stepped forward, and the moment passed as he was enclosed in dappled shadow. I suddenly felt an upheaval in my belly, my mouth dry with nerves, my whole body weak with longing. I would run to him, cast myself into his arms, press my mouth against his, and feel the solid beat of his heart under the palm of my hand. It was three years since I had seen him last. Three long years! I could cover the distance between us within the space of one heavy beat of my heart and . . .

No, no. I must guard my response. I must be measured and calm. Lightly controlled . . .

Why? Because it was never wise to give weapons into the hands of others, even the man I loved with a physical desire so strong that it shivered through me like an ague. How terrible it was to fear putting myself under the dominion of a man whose affection I craved. But if my life had taught me one indisputable fact, it was the need to be resilient, self-reliant. I must not show my husband how afraid I was of giving him power over me, power to hurt and wound and destroy.

But he will not hurt and wound and destroy. You know him better than that.

No, I do not know him at all!

But I could not stop my mouth from curving in a smile when my eyes lifted to his.

"William de Windsor! By the Virgin!"

"Alice Perrers! As I live and breathe!" The familiar goading tugged at my heart. "Picking apples?"

"No." I held up the doll. "And I thought I was Alice de Windsor, your wife."

"So did I. But it's so long since our ways met. . . ." He took off his hat, sweeping a splendid bow. "I didn't recognize you in this rustic garb. It took me some days to find you."

"I suppose you thought I was a servant."

"Impossible!" His voice was warm, but he did not approach me. A tension in his stance warned me that all was not well. The skin was stretched taut over his cheekbones, and the habitual cynicism touched his mouth with what was barely a smile. Momentarily I wondered why, but my own anxieties prevailed. I took another step away, thoroughly irritated with myself and with him as he observed: "I hear you're banished from Court by the great and the good."

"Yes, as you can see. The Good Parliament—good, by God!—in its wisdom decided to sweep the palaces clean of all unwholesome influences. Latimer, Neville, Lyons . . . all gone."

"And you."

"And me. They left me until last, to savor the moment. They cast me into outer darkness." All my pent-up frustrations overflowed. "And if I set foot within a yard of Edward, they'll rejoice in taking every last inch of my property and packing me off even further into oblivion. Your wife will be living somewhere in France for the rest of her life, so you'll never see her at all!"

"They've got your measure." Windsor's teeth showed with a wolfish grimace. "Is that why you're holed up here, not a silk ribbon or a jewel to be seen, rather than banging on the door at Sheen for admittance?"

"Yes." I smoothed my hand over the plain russet kirtle beneath the unfashionable open-sided cotehardie, miserably unadorned even if the wool was a good weaving. "My new role in life. Rural seclusion."

"Perhaps we'll both grow to enjoy it."

"I doubt it!"

"So do I. But we are no longer invited to dine at the royal table, and so must make do with the scraps dished out to us."

It was almost a snarl, enough to give me thought, to snatch my mind from my own ills. How could I not have *seen*? I should have asked him the moment he stepped into my orchard.

"What are you doing here?"

"You haven't heard? Summoned—again! In disgrace—again! Relieved of my position." The words were clipped, every vestige of edgy banter gone under a layer of black temper.

"Edward has dismissed you . . . ?"

"Yes. My services are no longer needed. There will be no further reinstatement. I shouldn't be surprised, should I?"

"Oh, Will!" And I held out my hands to him. Of course he was aggrieved. The ultimate courtier and politician, he would hate as much as I to be thrust into this powerless obscurity. I could remain distant from him no longer. I crossed the grassy, apple-strewn divide in easy strides. "I'm so sorry, Will. Oh, Will—I am so very glad to see you."

Even his name on my lips was a soft pleasure. All my intentions scattered in the face of his dismissal, and I stepped into his arms as they closed around me.

"That's better," he said after a moment when he almost resisted the intimacy. "It almost makes it worth my while returning."

For a moment we stood silent and unmoving, savoring the shifting patterns of light and shade, my forehead pressed against his shoulder, his cheek resting on my hair, the doll still clutched in my hand. I felt him relax, slowly, gradually, beneath my hands. The robin trilled above us, but we let the deeper silence enfold us.

"So what's the King doing?" Windsor asked eventually when the robin flew away.

"He's not doing anything. He's old and lonely. I don't think he understands." I placed my fingers against his mouth when he opened it to deliver, I supposed, some sharp comment on the King, who had accepted my banishment without redress. "He deserves your compassion, Will. Did he not plead for me? And Edward needs me—he is helpless. Who will know how to care for him?" And tears began to slide down my cheek into the damask of his tunic.

"I've never seen you weep before! For sure you've never wept over me! I think you had better tell me all about it." Windsor led me to a grassy bank set back near the perimeter hedge and dried my tears with the edge of my cotehardie. He took the doll from me, sitting her down between us as a quaint chaperone, and held my hands between his, his eyes narrowed on my face as I sniffed. "I see you, Alice—before you even think to hide the truth. You're too thin. When did you last sleep through the night? Your eyes are so very tired." When he ran the edge of his thumb under my eye, it took my breath away, and then his mouth was warm against my temple. "What terrors have you had to face on your own, my brave girl?"

His compassion all but undermined my self-control. "I am not brave. I've been terrified out of my wits."

"Why didn't you send for me?"

"What could you have done?"

"Perhaps nothing. Except be here to make sure that you eat and sleep and don't malinger. You've always stood on your own feet, haven't you?"

"There is no one else."

"I see." As his brows snapped together, I thought I had hurt him. But what could he have done at so great a distance? "I'm here now, but you fought your enemies alone. I admire you for it. So tell me what terrified you." His earlier sharpness crept back. "Unless you prefer to keep it all to yourself."

Yes, I had hurt him. But that was the life we led.

"I will tell you."

And I did, with a strange relief, even though I had determined not to. I told him of Parliament's vendetta. The accusation of necromancy and Joan's probable involvement. My ultimate banishment. Edward's brave defense of me at the last, when his heart was split in two.

I sighed. "It's been quite a month," I finished.

"So Edward knows about our marriage. And blames you."

I nodded and sniffed again. "Yes. But he blames you more." I would tell him the truth. What harm would it do? "Edward damns you for the whole. He blames me for the hurt I caused him, but in his eyes you were the instigator. He thinks you have corrupted me. He even purchased a chest to lock away all the accusations made against you for his future reference. He sits and looks at it and plots his revenge, so I'm told." I touched his hand. "I don't think it can ever happen. He no longer has the will to carry it out."

"Perhaps not, but I am relieved of my position," Windsor responded, a bright spurt of anger erupting again. "For fraud. What is fraud? A mark on a line of necessity. I have taxed them heavily. I have made my own fortune. But I have kept the peace and the government is at least efficient. I have kept those arrogant lords on a short rein. And all I get is dismissal." He shrugged and I saw the fire die in his eyes, to be replaced by resignation. "It's out of my hands. A man who wields authority must always risk losing it."

"And a woman who has power, unless born to it, makes enemies."

"So both our names are to be trampled in the mud." He dried my tears again with his own dusty sleeve—I think I no longer cared if he left smears on my cheeks—and kissed me, a demanding assault on my lips, a little rough, as if he had missed me.

Windsor raised his head and looked at me, his dark eyes holding mine, his thoughts beyond my imagining.

"Don't weep, my resourceful wife. We shall come about. Is there anything for a much-traveled man to eat and drink in this pearl of a manor?"

Mentally I shook myself into the reality of my orchard at Wendover and the practicality of a long-absent husband returned to me. This was no time for dreams. "There is," I said. "I've been an unthinking hostess."

"And hot water to remove the filth of travel, perhaps?"

"I could arrange that."

"Even to remove the odd louse? By God, I've stayed in some miserable inns. . . ."

"Definitely, I can arrange that!"

"And perhaps a bed?"

"I expect so."

I led him into the house, some semblance of good humor restored between us. After he'd eaten and washed, we banished our concerns to some distant place beyond our bedchamber door and made of our reunion a private celebration. I had forgotten how resourceful he was. His hands and mouth woke my body to a depth of desire that consumed me. Even the worries that had stalked me vanished. How could they exist when he was intent on possessing my body, and I was equally intent on allowing it?

Next morning Windsor was up at dawn. I awoke more slowly, my mind full of spending the day with him and renewing the tentative bonds that we had first created so long ago. But I saw that his sword was gone from where he had dropped it beside the door, and I could hear the sound of the house astir and busy between kitchen and parlor. I dressed rapidly, knowing what I would find before I entered. Windsor, dressed for riding, was already breaking his fast. On the coffer by the door was a leather wallet topped by his gloves, sword, and serviceable hood.

All my bright anticipation fell to earth with a crash. I should have known, should I not? The pleasures of the bedchamber would not keep Windsor from what must be faced and challenged. For a little while I stood on the threshold, studying the stern lines of his face, the quick movement of his fingers, strong and capable, as he sliced and ate, my mind reliving the recent dark hours when he had ignited a flame in me. Then I stepped in.

"Are you abandoning me, Will?" I asked, producing a bright smile despite the chasm that his imminent departure had opened up before me.

"Yes, but not for long. I'll look at my estates. In spite of an excellent steward, the mice will have been playing while the cat's away in Ireland, and you, I think, have been preoccupied," he said around a mouthful of home-cured ham. "But I'll return by the end of the week."

I would not have wagered on it, but it had to satisfy me. I came to sit across from him, resting my elbows on the board, taking a sip from his mug of ale. "Will you find out what's happening at Court for me?"

"If it pleases you. What's Gaunt doing? Do we know?" Windsor stood, snatching the small beer back again and finishing it, brushing any trace of crumbs from his tunic.

"I don't know. But he'll not be content. Parliament humiliated him."

"Hmm! So he'll be looking around for opportunities for revenge." He smiled thinly, as if on a new thought, his hands busy tucking documents into the wallet. "Life might become interesting. I might even become acceptable again."

I followed him out, deciding to allow him his enigmatic statement. I doubted he would explain, even if I asked.

"Will you try to get news of Edward? Wykeham is a good correspondent, but . . ."

"I will. He might wish me to Hades, but I'll do it. God keep you,

Alice." He strapped the wallet to the saddle, whilst I stood like a good wife to wish him Godspeed. Then he turned and surprised me by cupping my face in his hands.

"I'll do what I can. Don't fret. I can't have your sharp wit and intelligence wasting away to a shadow. What would I have to come home to?"

"An amenable wife?"

"God preserve me from such!" A kiss and he was gone. Less than twenty-four hours after he had arrived, with not one word of affection. Or love.

I raised my hand in farewell, retreating smartly into the house as if I did not care. Oh, but I did, and when Windsor did not return within the week I mourned his loss beyond all sense, as if it were a death.

During his absence, Windsor did not forget me or my need for news, sending a courier with a hastily written note. I read it again and again, finding it a lifeline to Windsor, as well as to Edward and the Court. Gaunt, magnificently vocal and brimful of revenge, had declared war on the actions of the Good Parliament.

You will be interested to see how busy he has been in your absence from Court.

And I was, reveling in the details, admiring Gaunt's ruthless efficiency. He announced that the Good Parliament had proceeded contrary to Edward's commands, thus rendering its actions null and void. Edward's new body of twelve councilors was summarily dismissed.

Poor Wykeham was once more deprived of royal office. As was the Earl of March. Gaunt would relish that dismissal, holding the young man wholly accountable for the clever plot with the de la Mares to undermine Gaunt's own power.

Latimer is released from his imprisonment. I know this will please you.

And then Gaunt began hunting in earnest, his own forces taking Peter de la Mare prisoner.

He is held fast in a cell in Gaunt's castle at Nottingham. Word is that there is no prospect of a trial. The Earl of March has been forced to hand over his Marshal's staff in the face of Gaunt's threats. Gaunt is nothing if not thorough. Try not to be too overjoyed. It is unseemly in Lady de Windsor.

I laughed aloud. I had no sympathy for the man who had forced Edward to plead for me in public. Ah! But I did not enjoy the next paragraph. I think Windsor must have known I would find it hard, because it was written plainly, without comment.

Gaunt has charged Wykeham with fraud as Edward's Chancellor. I am told that the evidence was thin, but Wykeham is deprived of all his temporal appointments and forbidden to come within twenty miles of Edward's person. He has retired to a monastery at Merton. . . .

I regretted it. Once again Wykeham had suffered political isolation for his loyalty to Edward.

And the one name omitted in Windsor's comprehensive summary?

Alice Perrers. What of *me?*

Well into the third week, at the end of a sultry day that weighed us down with damp heat so that even taking a breath was wearying, Windsor returned. I was out of the house, dashing into the courtyard, the instant I heard the approach of a horse. I hardly allowed him to swing down from the saddle before I was at his shoulder, pulling on his sleeve.

"What's happening?"

"Good evening, my wife!"

"What about me?"

"Ah! No one is mentioning your name, my love!"

"Is that good or bad?"

"Impossible to tell."

"And Edward?"

He shook his head. "He's ill. It's thought to be only a matter of time. . . ."

He looked tired, on the edge of a short temper, as if he had ridden long and hard. As if business had not gone entirely as he would have liked. I sighed. "Forgive me, Will. What of you? I've been selfish. . . ."

"Let us say single-minded."

Tossing his reins to a groom, he walked with me into the house. He drew my hand companionably through his arm.

"You sent me no word of your fate," I accused as we moved into rooms dim with evening light.

"What's to write?"

I saw the glint of anger in his eye despite the shadows. I had been selfish. After a lifetime of major and minor selfishness, I was learning that there were others who needed my compassion and comfort. Windsor seemed an unlikely man to need them—and he would never ask them of me—yet I was beginning to know he might actually value a solicitous welcome from me. So I applied myself to the wifely skills that still came unhandily to me with Windsor, relieving him of his gloves, hood, and mantle, dispatching a servant to bring ale, and pushing him to sit on a settle beneath an ancient oak tree at one side of the house, where we would enjoy the blessing of any movement of air. Conscious of how weary he was, I sat beside him, and leaned to push wayward strands of hair back from his brow where they had stuck with perspiration.

"Very wifely." He smiled. But the usual mockery was missing.

"I'm practicing. Allow me to try my skills." I poured the ale when it was brought to us, and gave it to him, waiting until he had drunk deep. "You have been to Court."

"Yes. To Sheen."

"And?"

"My dismissal is confirmed. I've been rewarded a pension of one hundred pounds a year for my past services. And should be grateful for it. The King wouldn't see me. He sent a thin-lipped lawyer with the message!"

"Perhaps he couldn't see you," I suggested, to lessen the slight.

"Perhaps. I doubt the message would have been any different." He sat and brooded, staring at the scuffed toes of his boots. "It was strange." He looked up at me. "As if the heart had gone out of the palace. Everyone waiting for the King to breathe his last."

I could not reply. We sat in our own little silence.

"What will you do?" I asked eventually.

Windsor hitched a shoulder. "Administer my estates." His smile was wry. "Much as you will, I expect."

I knew what I wanted. I had thought of this. I knew what I wanted more than anything. I said it before I could tell myself that it would be better not to.

"Stay with me, Will. Stay here. Don't go back to Gaines."

His brows rose. "How conventional. Set up home, like husband and wife?"

"Why not?"

"I can think of worse things."

"I wasn't sure you wanted it," I said. For, apart from the brief early days after our marriage, we had never lived together. Secrecy and Ireland had kept us apart out of necessity, and since our union was of a practical nature, perhaps he envisioned us always living apart. But now there was no need for pretense. . . .

"I admit I had not seen us living in connubial bliss," he said. "But since we are both here, both outcasts . . ."

"Could you think of any better outcome?"

"I don't know that I could." He leaned close and pressed his lips against mine, a very soft caress, as if he were unsure of my response—or even his own. I returned the salute, my lips warm and inviting. Suddenly I wanted him deep within me, a stroke of heat.

"Take me to bed, Will."

We looked at each other. And smiled.

"Will . . . ?"

"Go on. Say it."

"Do you have any affection for me?"

"Is that in doubt?"

"Everything is in doubt."

"Then I do."

"That sounds as if you are placating a child."

The harsh lines softened in wry amusement. "Hard questioning, Alice. Worthy of Gaunt himself."

"You can tell me the truth. I won't weep on your shoulder."

"I wouldn't mind. I have a very handy shoulder, and it's yours for your use."

"Will . . . !"

"Do I have an affection for you . . . ? Who did I seek out first when I returned to England?"

"Me. I think."

"Who did I write to, most inconveniently?"

"Me."

"There you are, then. I think I even told you I missed you. Now, that's a first. . . ."

I punched his shoulder with my fist, my heart already lighter. "Is that all I'm getting?"

"Yes. I'm tired. Come and be wifely in the bedchamber."

Not love. Affection. But enough—it would have to be enough. And later, when we were entwined, sweat cooling on naked limbs, he said, "Alice. Do you have an affection for me?"

So he had noticed that I had not reciprocated. Of course he had. I made him wait as I always did.

"Yes, Will. An affection." Only my heart knew that I could lie as well as any man.

Later, I sat and combed my hair at the open window, my husband still a heap in the bed. I heard the eventual upheaval but did not look over. My thoughts were not at ease, despite the pleasure of the last hours.

"What's going on in that marvelous brain of yours?" he asked, soft-voiced.

"Edward."

"I should have known."

There was no judgment in his voice, though I had brought the King into our bedchamber. I turned my head.

"Do you think I'll see him again before he dies? I don't want him to die alone, the hard words still standing between us." It was not easy to recall the last time I had seen him. "He never pardoned me, you see. I would like to see him once more."

"Don't set your heart on it. Who's to say you'll ever be given leave to return. It's in the hands of the gods."

"More like Gaunt's."

Windsor's silence spoke for itself—and gave me little comfort.

*　　*　　*

I was difficult to live with. I knew I was, and could make neither excuses nor amends. After the years as Edward's lover, confidante, and soul mate, and recently his solace, I found the distance insupportable. He had made me all that I was, all that I could ever be. To be separated from him now at the end was beyond tolerating. If Windsor regretted moving his household to join with mine, he gave no indication of it, although I think that a less confident man would have washed his hands of me, miserable creature that I was, and packed his bags. He gave me space in which to mourn the King, who was not yet dead, a silent but compassionate space. At night he held me in his arms when he knew I did not sleep. He did not chide me as I deserved, even when I snapped and snarled at him because he was the only one I could snap and snarl at.

And when it became too much for any man, he challenged me in a typical peremptory manner.

"What are you doing?"

I was staring out of the window. "Nothing."

"Which is patently obvious and useless. Go and interfere in one of your estates. Just how many do you have?"

"Fifty-six at the last count," I replied without thought.

"*What?*"

"Fifty-six." He looked stunned. "And before you ask, only fifteen of them were gifts from Edward. I was quite capable of purchasing the others for myself."

"By God!" He paused, as if he could not believe what Greseley and I had done over the years. "I didn't know I'd wed a woman of such means . . . ! No wonder they've got you in their sights! If you were a man, it would qualify you for an earldom." And he gave a sudden loud roar of laughter. "And you do realize, my dear one, that all your fifty-six estates now belong to me, as your husband?"

That got my attention fast enough.

"Only in name!" I snapped. Which was not true, but I was in no mood for legalistic banter.

"Now, why do I think I might find some noxious and fatal substance flavoring my ale if I lay claim to them?"

"Hemlock, I was thinking . . . !"

But he had defused my quick anger. I managed a smile, if a pale travesty of one. And Windsor's voice became gruff with an underlying concern.

"But that's by the by. Sitting there will not help. Take the girls and . . ."

"Edward has made his will."

"Oh. Are you sure?"

"It's the talk of the market. He's dying, Will. He must know it."

I heard him exhale, and he abandoned any argument he might have made. Rejecting words as a lost cause, he took my hand to lead me into the parlor that he had taken over for his own business affairs, and sat me down before a pile of accounts.

"Check the figures for me, Alice. If that won't distract you, nothing will."

"Who are you? Janyn Perrers?"

"Why?"

I smiled, really smiled, for the first time in days. I had never spoken of the details of that marriage. "It's how I passed the nights of my first marriage."

"God save you!" He kissed the top of my head. "But I'll still crack the whip. To work, woman!"

Holy Mother! It was dull work at that.

"And if you could finish them before the end of the day . . ."

"Am I your clerk?"

"No. You're my wife and you are suffering."

I felt another light kiss on my hair before he left me to it. And through those dreary November days I concentrated on Windsor's finances and my own. I was grateful, even through the fear that this might be all that my future life held for me.

One morning, when the frost was white on the hedges, and I was so bored as to be near to ripping the pages from the ledger, Windsor entered the room and took the pen from my hand.

"What now?" I complained. "I refuse to look at one more document of tenure or . . ."

"There's a man on a horse just ridden into the courtyard."

"A peddler?" I yawned. I supposed I would value the distraction.

"More official than that. A royal courier, I'd say." I was out of my seat. . . . "Alice! It could be to your danger. . . ."

"How can it? I've obeyed them to the letter in their damned banishment!"

"But still . . ."

"They would have sent a force to arrest me . . ." I shouted back, and was down the stairs into the hallway before the man had climbed the steps to the porch.

"Mistress Perrers . . ."

Not another nail in the coffin that the lords had constructed for me! Far less confident than I might have seemed, I snatched the missive from his hand, tearing it in my urgency. "Fetch him ale. . . ." I had time for nothing but the contents. For a moment I closed my eyes, then opened them and read. . . .

I skimmed over the word *banishment*, flushed with the heat of panic despite the chill of the morning. Then forced myself to read more slowly.

And the fear began to drain away. For there it was. Written by a palace clerk in the name of Gaunt.

My banishment was no more. I was free to return to Court, to Edward. So much in so few lines. My head felt light, my senses adrift, and I sank to the settle at my side.

"Will?" I called.

He was standing in the doorway looking at me, reading my face before I spoke.

"You are free?"

"Yes." I sighed. "Oh, yes."

And I had Gaunt to thank for it, for what reason I knew not. Past loyalties? Sympathy for his dying father? To spite Parliament, more like. I cared not. He had had the banishment revoked by the Royal Council. I was free to travel, free to return to Court. To see Edward again.

"Well?" Windsor still waited.

I stood, feeling stronger, and walked slowly across to him. I think my words surprised us both. "You are my husband. I need your consent."

"And that's the first time in your life you have asked for it."

I flushed. "I need your approval."

His gaze was quizzical. "Would you go if I did not give it?"

I hesitated.

"There has always been honesty between us, Alice."

"Then yes, I would go with or without your permission. If I did not see him, it would be on my soul."

He closed his hands on my shoulders, kissed my forehead and then my lips. Our final embrace was strained with unspoken words and longings.

"Do you want me to come with you?" he asked, his arms banded 'round me.

"No."

"I suppose I must find a clerk to finish the accountings." I heard the smile in his voice.

"He won't be as accurate as I am." And I laughed softly into the fine wool of his tunic as the endlessly nagging fears of the past weeks loosed their grip.

"Go to Edward." His compassion for me struck deep. "And then you will come back to me when you can. When it is over."

I allowed myself to look at him, rubbing my knuckles over his jaw, running a finger over the hard line of his mouth. I knew him well enough to read the concern for me behind those austere, resolute features. I pressed my lips to his.

"Yes. I will return."

Within hours, my belongings were packed and loaded onto two horses, a groom and one of Windsor's household mounted to accompany me. I kissed my daughters and rode like the wind to Eltham, to Edward. And the official document authorizing my release? What happened to it? I had no recollection. With unusual carelessness I did not keep it.

Afterward I wished I had.

Chapter Fifteen

*L*eaving my baggage to be unloaded, I stepped into Eltham's Great Hall, good memories of this palace, which Wykeham had renovated, sweeping back and lifting my spirits. But as I walked purposefully, absorbing the atmosphere, I was forced to accept that much had changed. It was, as Windsor had said, as if the heart had gone out of the Court. It had, as I had imagined, the still, dust-laden quality of a stone coffin. The servants I passed looked at me askance. All bowed or curtsied as they had in the past, and no one stopped me, but one man, his hand half-hidden against his hose, curled his fingers against the power of the Evil Eye. I saw it. My reputation as a witch had sunk deep.

That was not all. It would be no easy task to return to my old position. Legs braced, arms folded as if to repel a troop of invaders, Roger Beauchamp, Edward's new chamberlain who had replaced Latimer, stood foursquare before the door to Edward's accommodation, drawing himself up as his eye lit on me. I had come so far and so fast, and now this paid minion would keep me from Edward's side. I knew from the set of his mouth that it would take little for him to draw his sword and drive me from the palace. *I* might know that my banishment had been lifted, but the speed of my arrival had preempted the news. The word had not yet reached Eltham. Or perhaps it had and he would still deny me.

Here I would discover how much power remained to me. Not much, I thought.

Beauchamp regarded me like one of the vermin that could never be exterminated from even the public rooms of the palace. "You should not be here! The law forbids it." No respect, all denial, Beauchamp's challenge confirmed my fears.

"I wish to see the King," I replied without heat.

"I say you will not."

"And will you stop me?"

"I will, madam!"

"My banishment is lifted."

"And you have proof?"

No, I had not. I had not brought the letter. In my urgency I had not seen a need. Not that Beauchamp would have accepted anything less than a royal declaration, stamped and sealed.

"The decisions of the late Parliament have been declared null and void," I stated calmly. "By his grace of Gaunt himself." Surely the name would have some power.

"I have no knowledge of it." Beauchamp's stance and reply remained implacable.

How I wished for Latimer's return. And how had this monster escaped Gaunt's purging? I gestured to the door at his back.

"Let me pass. The King will see me."

"The King will not." Beauchamp drew his sword.

I retreated not one inch. "If you intend to stop me, you will have to use that, sir." I pushed the flat of the blade away with my hand. "I wear the Queen's jewels. I have borne the King's children. Will you deny me?"

And I hammered with my fist on the door to Edward's chambers.

No reply. However confident I appeared, I was far from it. I hammered again, anxiety building layer upon layer so that I could barely breathe, as Beauchamp's fingers clamped peremptorily, unforgivably, around my wrist. I thumped again on the door with my free fist, raising my voice.

"Sire! It is Alice." I tried to wrench my wrist free, but Beauchamp held on, and in that moment all was blackness in my mind. I would be cast out. Gaunt's promise was nothing but a charade. . . .

"Majesty . . . !" I heard my voice, harsh with terror.

The door opened.

"What's all the noise and fuss, Beauchamp? It's enough to wake the dead. Be still, man. . . ."

My wrist was released.

Once, I would have gone to him, touched him, spoken with him, no matter who stood between us. But now—considering our parting words, I could not. Yet, to see him standing alone, unaided, to hear him speaking without difficulty, his words with clear meaning—the impact clenched around my heart. Edward, still King, still regal even with the stooped shoulders and hollowed cheeks of old age, was standing in the doorway. Not robust but steady enough with one hand clawed around the edge of the doorjamb.

I sank into a deep curtsy.

"My lord. I am here." I waited until the faded blue eyes tracked across my face; only then did I rise to my full height. "It's Alice. I have come to you. Let me in, to be with you."

Would he turn his face away? Would he reject my return? Would his wayward mind recognize me? The moment when Edward looked at me seemed to last a lifetime. And to my relief the focus sharpened with recognition. And there in that acknowledgment was an astonishment that held unmistakable joy.

"Alice . . . I asked for you. I was told that you could not come to me. . . ." And then he held out his hands to me and I placed mine there.

"Now I am here. Let us go in," I said, my confidence surging back. And I stepped inside the room.

Moisture glistened in Edward's eyes, but his command was still strong, and so were his memories. As he would have done in the past, he bowed and raised my fingers to his lips, first one hand, then the other.

"I have missed you."

"I couldn't bear that you should be alone."

"They kept you from me. . . ."

"It was not my choice. But your son has rescued me. I am free to be here with you."

"Then come. . . . We will talk."

And it was impressed on me how harrowing the intervening months had been for him. We were forced to walk slowly, Edward's right foot dragging a little with every step, his arm beneath my hand tense with the effort to walk unaided. But he was determined, and we reached the great chamber.

"Alice . . ." Before he could say more, I sank to my knees before him. "What's this?"

"I need to ask your pardon, Sire."

"A minute ago you called me Edward and demanded admittance. Now you are on your knees. This is not the Alice I recall." The ghost of a laugh was tragic on the once-fine features, the muscles on the right side of his face refusing to obey the demand to smile.

I bowed my head. I could not laugh. "I hurt you. I betrayed you."

"So you did. You should have told me. I think I would have understood."

"What man could understand that I had married another in secret?"

"Ah, well . . . What I don't understand is why Windsor? Why such a man?"

I could think of no reply that would explain the call of blood, one to another. "He will care for me," I managed.

"Yes. I expect he will."

"My loyalty to you has not changed, my lord."

"But you are a young woman, and I . . ."

"My lord . . . I am so sorry. . . ."

"We must have the courage to face our limitations. My flesh ignores the demands of my heart." Again that heart-wrenching smile. "How many old men have said that when their young lover looks elsewhere? I am not the first. I won't be the last."

His candor overwhelmed me. Nor could I explain that my attraction to Windsor wasn't solely physical, but a meeting of minds.

"It was not my choice to leave you, my lord. Will you forgive me?"

"You know I will. But only if you call me Edward again. Come; stand. It's too exhausting looking down at you." And he raised me to my feet with a remnant of his proud grace. "Have you come to stay?"

"I have. If you want me."

"Do I not want the sun to rise tomorrow? You are mine and I have a need of you, if you can tolerate the weakness of an old man."

"This is where I wish to be."

Edward's brow creased, for which I was sorry. "They—those who have no love for you—say you have no heart, Alice. That you are as cold as stone. As hard as flint. What do *you* say?"

I regarded him gravely as I swallowed against the press of tears. "What I say has no weight. What do *you* say, my lord?" Enclosing his cold hands between mine, in a deliberately intimate gesture, I placed them, flat-palmed, between my breasts where my heart beat. "What do *you* say?"

"I say that you are never cold to me." Leaning a little, he pressed a kiss between my eyebrows. "You are as gentle as a blessing, as warm as the sun in summer."

We both knew that Windsor would not be spoken of between us again. It was a tacit agreement that for the length of Edward's life, my husband did not exist. Edward turned from me to shuffle toward his bed with its embroidered heraldic hangings. "I am weary, Alice. I have not slept well since you went away. Or at least I don't think I have. . . . Memory plays tricks on me. . . ."

"Then you must sleep now. I'll stay with you."

I helped him to lie down on the magnificent bed that we had shared. And I sat beside him, curled against the pillows, his hand in mine as his eyelids began to droop.

"Do you know?" he murmured. "When they told me that you were not allowed to come to me, that we would be parted forever, I was destroyed. Not an emotion appropriate for a king, is it?"

"No. But it is the emotion of a man of honor and courtesy. Of a lover." I folded his hand between mine.

"I thought I would never see you again. . . ."

"But I am here now."

"And all will be well."

"All will be well."

I sat with him until sleep claimed him. I would have liked to have told him that he would grow strong, that he would resume the mantle of kingship. I would have liked to assure him that his present clear understanding would remain; that he would know my love and care of him for all the remaining days of his life. But I could not. This lucidity, I suspected, was transient. I tucked the memory away for the difficult days.

Did I weep for him?

Not now. He would not have wished it. I would do what I could for him. I would stay until the end. Windsor would understand.

For that I was surely blessed.

Despite my fears, Edward's grip on life proved to be ferocious, his mind set on one final magnificent gesture. He was in no fit state to travel, but his resilience was a fine thing.

"I will do it. I will not be gainsaid in this! Do you hear me, Alice?" I heard him. Saw the flash of the old imperious Plantagenet regality. But so brief, so painfully brief. His head lolled forward, his chin against his chest, and he dozed. But on his awakening, the thought was still firmly lodged in his unsteady mind.

"I will sit at the table in Wykeham's Round Tower at Windsor, even if I have to be carried into the chamber in a litter."

This would be the last St. George's Day that Edward would ever see, whether he went to Windsor or no. His physicians warned against the exertion. I shrank from the bathos of the scene that would ensue if I consented. I could not bear it for him.

"Arrange it for me, Alice." His twisted mouth could still issue orders. "Would you stop me from doing something that will bring *you* such personal joy? I don't think you'll refuse me."

I flushed at the accusation, but held my ground. "Your health is of prime importance to me, Edward!"

"I know. But I also know you'll allow me to see this through." His speech was slurring as his energy waned, but he could still grip my hand. "Do it, Alice!"

How could I not? Edward dragged himself through the days with sheer willpower. He wanted to do it—and so he would.

"I will arrange it. But you know what I will ask," I said.

"Yes." His sigh acknowledged the burden I had put on him. "Do I not know you like I know my own soul? A difficult request, Alice . . ."

"Simply to be there, to watch? Is it so difficult?"

"Unorthodox . . ." His tongue struggled a little over the word.

"You have the power to make the unorthodox the most acceptable thing in the world."

Oh, I wanted to be there more than I could express. This occasion to mark St. George's Day meant as much to me as it did to Edward. I did not expect the flood of vitriol that was to be unleashed against me. Or perhaps I did. . . .

"It is not appropriate, my lord! She will not be admitted!" Princess Joan, whose nose for Court intrigue had sharpened with her widowhood, was haranguing Edward before the week was out.

"But on this occasion . . ." Edward might regret the onset of a battle royal with the Princess, but he was still prepared to argue my case.

Except that Joan rolled over him like the English cavalry destroyed the French at Poitiers. "She is not a Lady of the Garter. Only those of royal blood qualify for such high recognition. Only Philippa and Isabella. You yourself would have it so, my lord. Would you put a lowborn woman on the same footing as your wife?" She willfully ignored my role as Lady of the Sun, when Edward had done just that. "Even *I* am not allowed. . . ."

"I hear you, Joan." Edward raised a weary hand. "Tradition weighs heavy—and since I was the one to create it . . ." He smiled apologetically at me.

Since you created it, you could claim the right to change it! But seeing the fretfulness in him, I closed my mouth on any counterargument I might make. I allowed Joan her little victory, for did *I* not have one that was even greater? It would be for me a moment of pure joy.

"You will come with me," Edward ordered, gripping my hand.

"I will come to Windsor with you," I agreed.

"But not to the ceremony," Joan added for good measure.

Well, we would see what we would see.

We arranged it most carefully, traveling by river to arrive on the day before the ceremony so that the inhabitants of Windsor would not see Edward lying on a litter rather than riding on a warhorse to their gates.

I would at least guard him against that ignominy. But would he be able to walk into the chamber? Would he be able to lift the great sword of state?

It was in God's hands.

And so the day dawned. Edward broke his fast, a cup of wine driving color into his cheeks and strengthening his sinews. I withdrew into the background as his servants clothed and prepared him for his celebration and his ordeal. With lambskin and fur to protect him, fine robes covered his wasted body, giving him a semblance of majesty. I stood aside as he lifted his head and walked slowly into the chamber, his hand pressing hard on the shoulder of one of his knights, to take his seat at the vast circular table.

What was he thinking? I knew the answer. Of his first inaugural ceremony, more than thirty years ago, when he was in the full strength of his youth, attended by the flower of Europe's chivalry and Philippa, who presided over the subsequent festivities. There would be no festivities to preside over this year—Edward could not maintain his strength for more than an hour. At least Joan would not have the excuse to lord it over the proceedings. And I, the whore, the mistress, would be shut out of the sacred ceremonial. The solemn rituals had no role for the King's Concubine, and unlike my splendor as the Lady of the Sun, Edward could not make one for me. All I could do was imagine. . . .

My eye was taken by the approach of young men clad in scarlet robes at the end of the procession, and all my desire was centered on the one fair face in their midst.

I would not be shut out! I would not be absent from this most glorious acceptance of what I had done in my life. I slipped inside the door and stood to the left in the shadow of a great curving tapestry, unmoving, my breathing shallow. I would simply be there. A silent witness.

There were twelve youths, the new generation of England's rulers, royal blood flowing through an impressive number of veins. I recognized them all. Edward's two grandsons were the first to kneel and feel the kiss of the sword on one shoulder, then the other: Richard of Bordeaux, slight and fair at ten years, and Edward's heir; Henry Bolingbroke, Gaunt's son of similar age; followed by Thomas of Woodstock.

Then the young men: Oxford, Salisbury, and Stafford. Mowbray, Beaumont, and Percy. All the great names of the kingdom receiving Edward's final gift of a knighthood. I had been right. So weak was his arm that the great sword of state quivered, but his will was as strong as ever. I knew he would see it out to the bitter end.

They knelt to receive the honor of knighthood, stood, stepped back. There was only one face I looked for, only one who made my heart bound. And there he was at last. The final youth to kneel before his King—and his father.

John. Our son. *My* son!

Pale, with nerves chasing across his features, John sank to one knee, his hair bright in the light through the high windows. At thirteen years, he still had the uncoordinated limbs of youth, but he had been well schooled for this day. I held my breath as Edward raised the great sword for the final time, and our son lifted his head to receive the accolade. Pride warmed my blood. Such public recognition of what had been vilified—my place in Edward's life. I slipped out. I had seen all I needed to see. My son, a Knight of the Garter. Emotion choked me.

"Take me to Sheen," Edward ordered when the young men, released from their ordeal, had toasted themselves with relieved laughter. "I'll die there."

I was afraid that he would.

"What is it?" I asked, seeing the shadow of grief on his face as we began the journey.

He shook his head.

"I shall nag at you until you tell me!"

"There's one regret I have. . . ."

"Then it can be remedied."

"No. It cannot. I allowed matters of state to step in front of friendship. It was a grave misjudgment, and I don't think it can be forgiven."

He closed his eyes and would say no more. And however much I worried about it, I could not think what it was that disturbed his rest. And if I could not decipher it, how could I put it right?

And then in the night it came to me. I knew what I must do. And quickly.

*   *   *

Edward lay on his bed, his chest barely moving, his skin so thin and pale as to be almost translucent, like a pearl from the Thames oyster beds. Occasionally his breath fluttered between his lips, but that was the only sign of the life that remained to him. The day had come. That long, courageous life, lived to the full for the glory of England, was drawing quietly to its close.

The last time I had kept vigil beside the dying had been with Philippa. I smiled a little at the memory of her amazing duplicity born out of compassion. Then my smile faded, for who could have believed it possible that Edward's loss of his most dear wife should place his feet firmly on the path to deterioration. Every day for the past eight years he had missed her keenly, until his mind could bear it no more. I was second-best. So I had always been. I had known it and accepted it. Today Edward would lay the burden aside.

And so would I.

At the foot of the bed knelt Edward's confessor, Father Godfrey de Mordon, a man of crudition and superior oratory, of morals as narrow as his unfortunate ferretlike features. I disliked him as much as he disliked me, but I let him pray. I did not pray, but simply sat and watched as Edward's life ebbed, until the priest's voice broke into my thoughts.

"His Majesty needs to repent."

"Later."

A pause.

"It would be better if you were not here."

I turned my gaze on him, noting the deliberate absence of respect in his address. "Yet I will stay."

"You have no place in this final confession of the King's sins." The priest's scowl informed me that I was the source of the most virulent of them.

As he made the sign of the cross and launched into yet another Ave, I reflected how Father Godfrey had revered Philippa as a saint, while he regarded me as the worst of Eve's daughters. I folded my hands, one over the other in my lap. What would this priest say if I announced that I *was* innocent once? Who did he think had arranged that the King of

England should take a girl with no background, no beauty, and no breeding as his mistress?

Edward sighed, his hand clutching convulsively against the bed-cover. That was all in the past. This priest would not want to hear my justifications. Here we were at the end of that supremely difficult road. It was in my heart to pray that Edward might keep hold of the thread that bound him to me, but I could not. He wanted to let go. He had had enough of weakness and forgetfulness, of lack of dignity. So I prayed that death would be quick now, and painless, that he would slip away into soft oblivion.

And when it was over?

I would go to William de Windsor, of course, but with the King's death, the wolves might be howling at my door again, and Gaunt might not consider it politic to hold them at bay. The thought of Windsor settled me. He would strengthen me. He would hold me in his arms and keep the nightmares away by the force and heat of his body against mine.

In the shadows beyond the bed, John Beverley tidied and arranged with his usual quiet competence, having done all he could to make the King comfortable.

"Go now," I murmured. "You can do no more."

We were alone, the priest and I, and Edward was sleeping, the precursor of death. I closed my eyes, suddenly very weary.

The priest's voice scraped along my nerves as he stood. "Mistress Perrers! His Majesty must confess before God. . . ."

"Of course." It would be necessary, but my eyes gleamed. It was in my mind to reduce this pompous cleric who despised the ground I trod on. "Now that you've got up off your knees, make yourself useful and light more candles. It's too dark in here."

The palace might be silent, but Edward would die with light and power surrounding him.

"It's not fitting. . . ."

"Do it. Why should he not die in the light? He lived his whole life in it."

Reluctant to the last, Father Godfrey obeyed, until the chamber shone as if for a royal feast. I touched Edward's hand, unsure even now that he would wake, but his lids lifted slowly. He turned his head toward me. "I'm thirsty."

His voice was labored and low, his breathing heavy. I poured a cup of wine and held it to his lips so that he could sip, then banked the pillows behind him, lifting him so that he might be aware of his surroundings. And his eye fell on the crown that rested, by my orders, within his vision on the bed beside him. "Thank you." Stretching out his hand, he touched the jeweled gold.

The priest stepped up to the bed. "There are more important things for you to face now, Sire." He held up the crucifix around his neck. "Your immortal soul . . ."

"Not yet. My soul can wait."

"Sire—I urge you to make your last confession."

"I said not yet. Talk to me, Alice."

So I would. Without sentiment or pity. We would pretend that there was all the time in the world, and I would entertain the King as I had always done. Edward would die as he wished. I sat on the edge of the bed, turning my back on the priest. It was as if we were alone, as in the days of our past together.

"What do we talk about?" I asked.

"The glory days. When I was the mightiest King in Europe."

"How can I? I didn't know you when you were the champion of Crécy."

"Ah . . , ! I forgot. You were a child. . . ."

"Not even born."

"No . . . It was Philippa who was with me then."

"So she was. And loved you for every moment of your marriage."

"Sire . . . !" The priest hovered at my side.

"Let him be . . . !" I snapped.

"Talk to me about the last day we hunted the deer at Eltham," Edward said.

"Your hounds brought down a tined buck. You had a good horse and rode as well as any man." It had been one of his better days. My throat clenched hard.

"I did, didn't I? Despite the years . . ."

"No one could match you."

"It was a good day." Edward closed his eyes as if he could see imprinted there the memory of his greatness.

"It is sacrilege that you speak to him of hunting," Father Godfrey hissed at me. "That you encourage him." He turned to Edward. "Sire . . . !"

The tired eyes opened. "I'm not dead yet, Godfrey."

"You must make your peace with God!"

"For what?" Suddenly those eyes were unnervingly keen. "For all the dead on the battlefields of France? Will He forgive me for those I sent to their deaths, do you think?"

"He will if you repent." The priest held his crucifix higher.

"How can he repent of the deeds that made him the great King he is?" I challenged the priest.

"Leave it, Alice!" As ever, Edward was more tolerant than I. "Do you remember the day we flew the falcons from the battlements at Windsor? Now, there was a sight. . . ." Edward breathed laboriously through a long silence. And then: "Alice?"

"I'm still here."

"I'm . . . sorry it's ended."

Father Godfrey swooped in like some form of venomous insect. "He's slipping away. Get him to repent. He mustn't die unshriven."

"He'll do as he wishes." I stroked Edward's hand, careful of the fragility of his skin. "He always has. He has enough favor notched up with the Almighty to get him into heaven whether he dies unshriven or not."

"Blessed Virgin! Get him to make confession!"

It was too much. I stood, making the priest step back. "Get out!"

Father Godfrey held his ground, but his eyes slithered away from mine. "I will not."

I strode to the door and opened it. "Bring Wykeham as soon as he arrives," I ordered the nameless squire outside, and saw Edward's face light with joy. Edward's one regret, his alienation from Wykeham. I had been right to send for him. If anyone was to shrive Edward, it would be Wykeham.

Father Godfrey stalked out. "When the King is dead, who will save you then, Mistress?" he snarled.

Which unfortunately echoed my own thoughts.

Wykeham arrived and Edward rallied, with ill grace and a delicious levity that completely failed to rile the imperturbable Wykeham.

"Wykeham? Is that you? You were almost too late! Let's get it over with. . . . I ask your pardon for a dismissal you did not deserve. And I repent of all my sins. Will that do?"

"For myself, I'm deeply grateful." There was the shine of unshed tears in Wykeham's eyes. "As for the Almighty, I think He might need rather more than that, Sire."

"Intercede for me, damn it." A spark of the old fire. Edward's lips attempted a smile. I stood, silent, content with the much-desired reconciliation. "Why did I make you bishop if you won't speak for me at the feet of God?" Bold words, but his voice was failing.

"I doubt God will accept intercession by a third party for fornication." Wykeham's harshness surprised me, but then, he was a priest, after all. "And adultery," he added. "You must confess your sin if you hope for forgiveness."

"Then I'm condemned to the fires of hell. I'll not betray Alice in repentance. Nor will we argue witchcraft. I was not bewitched. The decisions and actions were all mine, and I'll answer for them." Edward's hand closed around mine as his breath caught. "Sooner rather than later. I can see death waiting beside the door." Edward looked up at me, but his sight was blurred now. "Do you suppose Philippa will be waiting for me?"

"I expect she will."

"Yes . . . It will be good to see her. . . ." It hurt me, a blow delivered without intent, but one I should have expected. But still it hurt. "Hold me, Alice."

I knelt on the bed and stretched to put my arms around him, horrified at how thin and insubstantial he had become.

"You never were a witch, were you?"

"No. I never was. You knew what you wanted without my intervention."

"So I did." He drew in a breath. "Take them. . . ." A ghost of a laugh shivered under my palms. "Take them, as I said you must. I can't do it . . . but you can. They're yours . . . your final insurance against dreaded penury. . . ."

"I will."

"You were the light of my final years. The joy of my old age." His breath caught again on a harsh intake. "Do you ever have any regrets, Alice? For what we did?"

"No. I regret nothing."

"Nor I. I love you. . . ." His voice died away. Until the final whisper: "Jesu, have pity."

Then his breath was gone.

So England's great King died in my arms, his head on my breast, light blazing around him as if he were already in heaven. And I had perjured my soul, denying any regrets.

"God have mercy." Wykeham, still on his knees, made the sign of the cross.

"Farewell, Edward. Philippa will stand beside you when you approach God's throne."

I stood to perform my final tasks for him, removing the pillows so that he could lie flat. I combed my fingers through his hair, arranged his linen so that it fell gracefully against his neck before placing his hands palms-down at his sides.

And then . . . because he had remembered . . . I began to take the rings from his fingers. A cabochon ruby. A sapphire flanked with diamonds, heavyset with pearls. A trio of beryls. A magnificent amethyst, set alone. I took them all.

With a sharp oath of distress Wykeham sprang to his feet. "In God's name! What are you doing?"

And I turned to look at him. The bright light illuminated the expression on his face, every deeply marked line making it clear exactly what he thought of my actions, and over all a contempt of me so deep as to coat me from head to foot. For a moment it shocked me into immobility. Did Wykeham, the best man of God I knew, truly believe me capable of robbing the dead? Of stripping Edward's corpse of everything of value out of pure avarice? Would Wykeham of all men con-

sider me guilty of such a final infamy? *Do you have any regrets?* Edward
had asked, and I had denied it. But sometimes the reputation I had
achieved was a heavy burden. Why should I alone be the one to deserve
the world's scorn?

Emotion raced across my skin to match Wykeham's, and far more
deadly. Combined with my anguish, bright anger melded to create a
vicious brew. So Wykeham believed the worst of me, did he? He would
damn me just as readily as Father Godfrey for my sins. Then let him.
In my torment, a desire to hurt and to be hurt was born within me, a
vehemence that would not be restrained. Fury was there, but also self-
loathing. And an urge to destroy.

So be it!

I would destroy Wykeham's so-called friendship. I would destroy
any good standing I had with him. I would live up to the worst of my
reputation. For who would care? The only man who had cared was
dead.

Windsor cares!

I slapped the thought away.

Oh, I had an enormous talent for dissimulation. For self-mockery.
I held up the rings on my palm so that they glimmered with a myriad
of reflected candle flames.

"Don't I deserve this for giving my youth to an old man?" I demanded. Never had I sounded so cold, so unfeeling.

"You are robbing the dead." Wykeham was aghast, as if he could
not believe what he saw. I drew a ring set with opals from Edward's
thumb, feeling the force of Wykeham's stare as I did so. "It is an abomination!"

"Hard words, Wykeham!" I placed the ring with the others on my
palm.

"Once, I thought you almost worthy of my friendship."

Friendship? I had just seen the limits of friendship, to be condemned without trial.

"Foolish Wykeham. You should have listened to the common gossip." I raised my chin, praying that the tears that had formed a knot in
my throat would not betray me. "What do they say about me? What do
the courtiers and the Commons say?"

"You know what they say."

"But *you* say it. Humor me. Let me hear it spoken aloud." How I wished to lash out, to cut and wound. And be wounded. I would hear anew the dregs of my reputation. In my grief and anger I had no control.

His lips were a thin line of disgust. "They say you're an unprincipled slut . . ."

"Well, that's true."

". . . and without shame."

"Is that all?" I think I tossed my head. "I'm sure it's worse than that."

His eyes blazed as bright as the candle flames. "You're a grasping, self-seeking whore."

"That's closer to the truth, forsooth!"

"Will nothing shock you?" His rage was suddenly as great as mine, his tongue unbridled. "They say you fucked the King to drain him of his power. You're nothing but an adulterous bitch who betrayed Queen Philippa and—"

I struck him. I actually struck him, the hand that did not clasp the rings hitting flat against his cheek. The man who had stood as the closest I had to a friend at Court in recent years, who knew the truth behind all the Court scandals.

"My lord bishop!" I mocked. "So shocking! And for you to repeat such vulgar language!"

And I began to laugh.

Cheek aflame, he snarled, "You don't like the truth, do you?"

"I didn't think you'd actually say it to my face. I really didn't. . . . But there's your answer: Always believe the gossip of the stews and the whorehouses. Always believe what's said of a woman who makes use of the talents God gave her." I poured all the scorn I could into my voice.

For a moment he was speechless. Then he gestured to the rings in my hand.

"Are you *proud* of what you've done?"

"Why not? I'd be living in the gutter in London if I'd been less than an unprincipled slut. Or I'd be dead. Or a nun—which is probably worse."

"God have mercy on you." He flung out his hand, stabbing me with his finger. "You've missed one! He's still wearing the emerald. Don't let that one escape. It's worth more than all the rest put together. It will keep you in silk and fur until the day of your unworthy death!"

The emerald. I made no move to take it.

"Why stop now? Have you suddenly developed finer feelings? You squeezed him dry of everything you could get out of him. You took what should have been Philippa's. His company, his loyalty, his devotion into old age . . ." I flinched at the hard words, but recognized them for what they were. Wykeham's own grief, lashing out at me. "Take it!" he hissed, and drew it from Edward's finger, holding it out to me.

"I can't. . . ."

"Oh, I'm sure you can!"

"It's the royal seal. . . ." I took a step away.

"Since when would such niceties stop you?"

"The coronation ring . . . It belongs to Richard. . . . It's not for me. . . ."

It was a mistake. I knew it as soon as I had opened my mouth. My deliberate construction was destroyed with those few careless words. Wykeham simply looked at me, the emotion draining to leave his face white and drawn except for the print of my hand. His hand with the emerald ring dropped to his side.

"Oh, Alice!"

All the fury leached from the room, leaving it still and cold despite the constant shimmer from the burning flames.

"Alice . . ."

"I don't want your pity, Wykeham." I turned my face away. "Goodbye, Edward. I hope I made you happy when you thought there was no happiness left in life." For a final time I knelt and kissed his hand. "I loved him, you know. In spite of everything. He was always kind. I think he loved me a little. I was not Philippa—but I think he loved me. . . ."

"Where will you go?"

"To Pallenswick."

"To Sir William?"

"Yes."

"Let him take care of you."

"I don't need him. I don't need anyone. . . ." Still I would punish myself.

"Alice . . ."

"Don't—just don't! If you're about to bless me, don't think of it!" I rubbed the sudden moisture from my cheeks with my sleeve. "Your God will rejoice at my sufferings. Perhaps you should offer up an extra Ave and a *Deo Gratias* for my ultimate punishment."

Tears were streaming down my face.

"You can't go like this. . . ."

"What will you do? Put the record straight? Paint me as a virtuous woman? No one will believe you. I will always be the King's whore. And I was—I think I filled the role with superb competence." I opened the door, looking back over my shoulder to the shining crown on the bed beside Edward's hand. "Do you think the boy will wear it as magnificently as *he* did?"

"No. No, I don't think he will."

"Good-bye, Wykeham." I knew I might never see him again. "He said I should take them, you know. . . ."

"I expect he did." Wykeham bowed low. "Take care."

I laid my hand on the latch, suddenly without the strength to lift it. I felt as empty as a husk. I knew there were things to do, but at that moment, I had no very exact idea of what they were.

All I knew was that I wanted to be with Windsor.

The horrors of that day were not at an end. Could they get any worse? They could. They did. When all I wanted was to escape from my own grief, from the unbridled excess I had indulged in to justify Wykeham's censure, there in the Great Hall stood two figures just arrived. One had a high, piping voice, the other the mien of a public executioner.

The child King and his mother.

In a moment of sheer cowardice, I considered disappearing through the maze of rooms and corridors before Joan could notice me. She now had the power to draw my blood. In the aftermath of what had happened, I felt that I might bleed all too readily.

No! No! You will not retreat!

I had never avoided confrontation, and I would not start now. Gathering my resources, I took on a hard-edged veneer of arrogance, as if Edward had not just died in my arms. Thus I descended the staircase with a swish of my velvet skirts and swept a magnificent curtsy to the ten-year-old boy who now wore my lover's crown.

"Your Majesty."

Richard, God help him, clearly did not know what to do or say. His forehead furrowed and he gave me a nervous smile. "Mistress Perrers . . ." He looked up to his mother's face for some idea of what he should do next. Then he bowed to me with quaint solemnity.

"There is no need to bow, Richard." Joan's painted face was brittle, cold as a winter's frost. And unbearably calculating. "So Edward is dead, is he?"

"He is, my lady." How scrupulously polite I was. She would never accuse me of ill manners.

"Mama . . ." The boy tugged on his mother's sleeve.

"You are King now, Richard," she told him.

Still, it meant nothing to him. He turned back to me, his pale face alive with anticipation. "Will you take me to the royal mews, Mistress Perrers, to see the King's falcons?"

Your falcons!

The realization nipped at my heart. "No, Sire," I replied gently, although my greatest wish was to be away from there, away from Joan and her son. "It is too late tonight. Shall I send for refreshment, Majesty?"

"Yes. If you please. I'm hungry. . . ." He almost danced on the spot with impatience. "*Then* can we go and see the hunting birds . . . ?"

Joan's hand descended on her son's shoulder like a metal lock. "Mistress Perrers—or is it Lady de Windsor? How does one know?— Mistress Perrers will not be staying, Richard." And to me, her lips curled with vicious pleasure, her eyes suddenly hot with satisfaction: "You have no role here. Your reign, Queen Alice, is over." She had the upper hand at last and would revel in it. "I will give orders for your chambers to be cleared forthwith. I expect you to be gone before—let me see, I suppose I can afford to be magnanimous—before sunrise."

Smoothing her hand over the fair hair of her son, she tilted her chin in a smile that showed her teeth. "You will ensure that you take nothing with you. If you do"—her teeth glinted—"you may be sure that I will demand recompense."

So, she would strip me of all my personal possessions—it was not unexpected. Nor, I suppose, could I blame her after a lifetime of disappointment. But I would fight back.

"I will take nothing that is not mine, nothing that was not given to me," I replied as I clutched the rings tightly in my hand so that the settings dug into my flesh.

"By an old and besotted man who could not see you for your true worth."

"By a man who loved me."

"A man you bewitched by who knows what evil means."

"A man I respected above all others. Anything he gave me was of his own free will. I will take what is mine, my lady."

So I curtsied to her, a deep obeisance, as if she were herself Queen of England.

"Get out of my sight!"

I turned and walked away, the clear voice of the child carrying down the length of the hall. "Can we go and see the falcons *now*? Why will Mistress Perrers not take me . . . ?"

It would be hard for him to be King. It would be impossible for him to step into Edward's shoes.

I left Sheen. It was in my mind that I would never return there, or to any of the royal palaces that had been my home. Joan was right, however malicious the intent behind her words. My reign, if that was what it was, was over.

Chapter Sixteen

*E*very living soul in London could claim to have rubbed up against the closing minutes of Edward's final journey to his burial on the fifth day of July in Westminster Abbey, close to Philippa's final resting place, just as he had promised her. Did the worthy citizens not crowd the streets to watch the passing of the wooden effigy with its startlingly lifelike death mask? Even the wooden mouth dragged to the right, memento of the spasm of muscles that had struck him down. Edward's people stood in dour silence, remembering his greatness.

This is what I was told.

Edward was clothed in silk, his own royal colors of white and red and cloth of gold gleaming, his coffin lined with red samite. He was accompanied to his tomb with bells and torches and enough black cloth, draped and swagged, to clothe every nun in Christendom. A feast celebrated his life, the food valued at over five hundred pounds, at the same time that the gutters were filled with the starving. Such wanton extravagance. But he was a good man and the citizens of London would not begrudge the outward show. Why should their King's life not be celebrated? The isolation and failure of his last years—when was the last time any of them had set eyes on him?—were pushed aside by those who bore witness to this final journey.

But what of me?

Should I not have been allowed to say my final farewell? So I think, but it was made very clear to me that my presence was not desired. Was not appropriate. It was made more than clear by a courier from the mother of the new child-monarch, who announced the news with a set face, speaking by rote.

Could the despicable Joan not have written her orders? Of course she could have, but that would have meant treating me as an equal—and that she could never do. Even on her deathbed, if I held out to her the gift of life, I swear she would have spit in my face.

"You are not to attend, mistress." The messenger at least dismounted and marched over to where I waited for him. I had thought he might shout from beyond the courtyard arch. "It is unseemly for one who is not a member of the family to accompany the coffin. His Majesty King Richard has ordered that you remain outside London during the ceremonies."

"His Majesty?"

"Indeed, mistress." He revealed not a flicker of an eye, not a quiver of a muscle. But we both knew the truth.

"I will consider the request."

The courier looked askance but presumably carried a more suitable response back to Westminster, while I called down curses on Joan's malevolent head. But she had the power now in the name of her son, and I was banished. I must remain at Pallenswick, where I had been reunited with Windsor. I watched the courier gallop from my land, watched until his figure was swallowed up by distance. Then I leaped into action.

Ordering my barge and an escort to be made ready for the following day, I sped up the stairs to my chamber in search of suitable garments in which to mark Edward's passing. I had discarded no more than three gowns as too drab or too showy before Windsor appeared in the doorway.

"I didn't know you were here," I said, engrossed. "I thought you were riding over to inspect the repair of the mill wheel."

"To hell with the mill wheel! Don't do it!" he ordered, without preamble.

"Do what?"

"Don't play me for a fool. Alice! I can see inside your head!
Don't go!"

So he had the measure of me. How could he read me so well? He
was the only man who could. I kept my eyes on my busy hands, match-
ing a fur-trimmed surcoat to an underrobe of black silk.

"Why should I not? Do I obey the directives of Joan?"

His stare was intimidating enough. "Don't go because I don't want
to have to visit you tomorrow night in a dungeon in the Tower!"

"Then *don't* visit me. I won't expect you." Crossly, furious at Joan
and at my own weakness that I felt the hurt of it, I spread the garments
on the bed, then began to search for shoes in a coffer.

"So you admit you might end up there?"

"I admit to nothing. I only know that I must go!"

"And you were never one to take good advice, were you?"

"I took yours, married you, and look where that got me! A whole
fleet of enemies. And banished, forsooth!" The accusation was entirely
unfair, of course, but I was not concerned about being dispassionate. I
stood and looked at him, daring him to disagree, my hands planted on
my hips.

And he did. Of course he did. "I think you made the enemies well
enough without me."

I took a breath, accepting his deliberate provocation. "True." And
I smiled faintly, the sore place beneath my heart easing a little just at
the sight of him, strong and assured, filling the doorway to my room.
But I turned my back against him. Suddenly I wanted to tell him how
much I loved him, but I dared not.

"You loved him, didn't you?" he stated.

I looked up, startled from my unwinding of a girdle stitched in
muted colors—I would pay my final respects with commendable discretion. "Yes. I did." I thought about what I wanted to say, and explained, as much to myself as to Windsor. "He was everything a man
should be. Brave and chivalrous, generous with his time and his affec-
tions. He treated me as a woman who *mattered* to him. He was loyal
and principled and . . ." My words dried. "You don't want to hear all
that."

"Quite a valediction!"

"If you like. Are you jealous?" Completely distracted now from the heavy links in my hands, I tilted my head and watched him. Without doubt, jealousy as green as emeralds in the ring I had refused spiked the air between us. "I don't think you are necessarily either loyal or principled. Only when it suits you."

Now, there was a challenge. What would he say to that?

"God's Blood, Alice!" The bitterness in the tone shivered over my skin.

"So you *are* jealous!"

He thought for a moment. "Not if you lust after me more!"

Which made me laugh. "Yes. You know I do." Impossibly forthright, Windsor always had the capacity to surprise me, and to confess to lust was far easier than to admit to love. The power would remain with me. "I had a love—a deep respect—for Edward, but I lust after you—just as you lust after me. Does that make you feel any better?"

"It might! Prove it!"

Abandoning the garments, my mood softening under his onslaught, I walked toward him and he took me in his arms. We understood each other very well, did we not?

"I want to be with no one but you, Will," I said, and pressed my lips to his.

I hoped he would be satisfied, and although I thought he might push me, to my relief he did not. What was it that made me love him so much? What was there to bind me to him? We did not hunt together, as I had with Edward. We did not dance—Windsor, I suspected, was as wrong-footed at dancing as I. There was not a poetic bone in his whole body to seduce me into love and longing. We did not even have the intricate and magical workings of a clock to bind us. What was it, then, except for naked self-interest? Was that all it was? I did not think so, but I could not tally the length and breadth of it as I might assess a plot of land.

But I loved him. And pretended I did not.

"Glad to hear it." He kissed my mouth, his desire evident. "Do I come with you?"

"No. I'll go alone."

"I still say you shouldn't. . . ."

I placed my fingers over his mouth. "Will, don't. . . ."

His teeth nipped at my fingertips. "Do you want me to stay to-night?"

"Yes."

So he did.

"I'll keep you safe, you know," he murmured against my throat, his skin slick, his breath short, when I had proved to him that his jealousy had no grounds.

"I know," I replied as I fought against the dread that threatened my contentment. The powers ranged against his protection of me might be too great. The royal hospitality in the dungeon in the Tower might not be a figment of my imagination.

"I'll not let any harm come to you."

"No."

His arms held the black fears at bay and we enjoyed each other; my heart was lighter with the rising of the sun.

"Don't go!" he murmured.

And still the dangerous word *love* had not been uttered between us. I was forced to accept that it never would be.

I ignored Windsor's advice and went to Westminster.

Anonymous in black and gray—posing as nothing more than a well-to-do widow, for I was not completely lacking in good sense—I took myself to Westminster, to the Abbey, with two stalwart servants, who forced a way through the crowds. I would be there. I would let the mysticism of the monastic voices raised in Edward's requiem Mass sweep over me, and would thank God for Edward's escape from the horrors of his final days. I would not be kept out—not by Joan, not by the devil himself. The crowds were predictably ferocious but no impediment to the elbows of a determined woman.

We approached the door. A few more yards, and then it would be possible to slip inside. A blast of trumpets brought everyone around me to a halt, apart from the usual haphazard pushing and jostling, until those at the front were thrust back by royal guards, each applying his halberd as quarterstaff. I edged my way as close as I could, and there, walking toward the great door, was the new King, not yet crowned, pale and insubstantial in seemly black, his fair hair lifting in the wind. What a poor little scrap of humanity, I thought. He had none of the robust presence of his father or grandfather, nor, I suspected, would he ever have.

And at his side? My breath hissed between my teeth. At his side, protective, self-important, walked his mother. Joan the Fair, her sour features unable to restrain her final triumph. Stout and aged beyond her years, wrapped around in black velvet and sable fur, she resembled nothing less than one of the portly ravens that inhabited the Tower.

Damn you for standing in my path to Edward's side!

She was so close I could have touched her. I had to restrain myself from striking out, for in that moment of blinding awareness, I resented her supremacy, her preeminence, the power that she had usurped, which was once mine. A power against which I had no defenses.

I hope your precious son rids himself of your interference as soon as he's grown! I hope he chooses Gaunt's influence over yours!

Did she sense my hostility? There was the slightest hesitation in her footstep, as if my antagonism gave off a rank perfume, and she turned her head when she had come level with me. Our eyes met; hers widened; her lips parted. Her features froze, and I was afraid of the threat I saw writ there. It was within her authority to bring down the law on my head, despite the solemnity of the occasion. My future might rest in those plump, dimpled hands. What had possessed me to risk this meeting? I wished with all my heart that I had heeded Windsor's caustic warnings.

Joan's mouth closed like a trap and her hesitation vanished. How sure she was! With a little smile, she placed one hand firmly on her son's shoulder, all the time urging him forward into the Abbey. So much was said in that one small gesture. And then they had moved past me, so the frisson of fear that had touched my nape eased. She would let me go. And I exhaled slowly.

Too soon! Too soon! Joan stopped. She spun swiftly on her heel. The men-at-arms lining the route stood to attention, halberds raised, and fear returned tenfold, flooding my lungs so that I could not breathe. Would she?

Our eyes were locked, hers in malice, mine in defiance, for that one moment as immobile as the carved stone figures that stared out with blind eyes above our heads. Would she punish me for all I had stood for, all I had been to Edward? For this ultimate provocation in the face of her express orders?

Joan's smile widened with an unfortunate display of rotted teeth. Yes, she would. I almost felt the grip of hard hands on my arms, dragging me away. But she surprised me.

"Close the door when we are entered. Let no one pass!" Joan ordered. "The proceedings will begin now that the King is come." She turned away as if I were of no importance to her, yet at the end she could not resist. "Your day is over," I heard her murmur, just loud enough so that I might hear. "Why do I need to bother myself with such as you . . . ?"

For the briefest of ill-considered moments, spurred by brutal insolence, I considered following in the royal train, slipping through before the great door was slammed shut, and taking my rightful place beside my royal lover's tomb. I would insist on my right to be there.

Ah, no!

Sense returned. I had no rightful place. Sick at heart, I fought my way out of the crowd and back to my water transport, where I was not altogether surprised to find Windsor waiting for me. Nor was I displeased, although furious with Joan, but mostly with myself for my impaired prudence. In true woman's fashion, I took my embittered mood out on him.

"So you've come to rescue me!" I said with a nasty nip of temper.

"Someone had to." He was suitably brusque under the circumstances. "Get in the barge."

I sat in moody, glowering silence for the whole of the journey; I had been put very firmly in my place, more by Joan's final words than by anything else. Windsor allowed me to wallow, making no attempt at conversation to discover what had disturbed me. He simply watched life on the riverbank pass by with a pensive gaze.

Why do I need to bother myself with such as you . . . ?

I had always known that the days of Edward's protection would end, had I not? But to be cut off quite so precipitously . . . It had been frighteningly explicit. There was a new order in England in which I had no part. I must accept it, until the day of my death.

My personal mourning for Edward was far more satisfying, to my mind, and what he would have wished me to do. On my return, I did what he had loved, what he had reminisced over even when he could barely sit upright against his pillows, much less climb into the saddle. I took a horse, a raptor on my fist, Braveheart at my heels—older but no wiser—and hunted the rabbits in the pastures around Pallenswick. The hunting was good. When the falcon brought down a pigeon, my cheeks were wet with tears. Edward would have relished every moment of it. And then, retired to my own chamber, I drank a cup of good Gascon wine—"dear Edward, you will live forever in my memory"— before I turned my back on the past and looked forward.

But to what? Isolation. Boredom! They were better than being hunted down by a bitter woman bent on vengeance, despite her words that I was nothing to her. I knew it was not in Joan's nature to abandon the chase. Thrusting myself under her nose had not been one of my wisest choices.

"I shouldn't have gone, should I?" Wrapped in a heavy mantle, unable to keep warm, I huddled over the open fire when the weather turned unseasonably wet and wild.

"I told you not to," Windsor remarked, entirely without sympathy, except that his hands were astonishingly warm around my freezing ones.

"I know you did." I was moody and out of sorts, much like the high winds and sudden squalls of heavy rain that arrived to buffet us.

"Don't worry. They can't get to you, you know. Your banishment was rescinded by Gaunt himself."

"Do you believe that she'll forget?" His optimism was unusual.

"No." So much for optimism! He scowled down at his fingers encircling my wrists, with the cynicism I appreciated in a world of flattery and empty promises. "How much did the King leave her in his will?"

I answered without inflection. "A thousand marks. Not enough to crow about. And Richard gets Edward's bed with all the armorial hangings."

Scowl vanishing, Windsor guffawed immoderately. "Far better that *you* should have had the bed!"

"Joan will probably have it burned to rid herself of the contamination of my presence. She'll not let the boy sleep in it."

"Are you mentioned?" he asked.

"No." I had not expected it. I had no place in Edward's will. He had given me all that he could, all that he had wished to give.

"At least that should give her cause for rejoicing."

"I doubt it! When I left Sheen I made sure I had Philippa's jewels packed in my saddlebags and Edward's rings safe in the bodice of my gown. Short of searching my body in full public view, she couldn't get her hands on them!"

Windsor laughed again, then sobered. "Enough of Fair Joan. We can't spend the rest of our lives worried out of our minds, can we? So we won't."

Which I had to admit was the best advice I could get.

Windsor released my wrists and raised his cup of ale in a toast.

"To the storms. Long may they last. May they flood the roads and riverbanks between London and Pallenswick until Joan forgets."

"By the Virgin! Until hell freezes over!" But I took his cup, finished the ale, and echoed the sentiment. "To the storms."

The rain and winds abating, the roads were soon open again, and the Thames was once more busy with river traffic, so we heard of events in London and elsewhere. Some of them encroached on my existence not at all. How strange that was.

The boy Richard, clad in white and gold, was crowned on the sixteenth day of July. A Thursday, forsooth! Unusual, but chosen as the auspicious Eve of St. Kenelm, an undistinguished but martyred child King of the old Kingdom of Mercia.

"Doubtless Fair Joan thought the lad needed all the happy auguries he could get," Windsor growled.

Which was a sound assessment. There were troubles afoot. In the absence of a strong English army with a king at its head, the French had seized the initiative with numerous incursions along the south coast of England, burning and pillaging all they came upon. The town of Rye became an inferno. Some French marauders even reached Lewes. In Pallenswick we felt safe enough.

How strange to have no association with such momentous events, to be entirely divorced from the King's plans to drive the French out. Who would take on the direction of foreign policy? Gaunt, I supposed. I closed my mind to it, for it no longer touched me.

But some events, through association, touched me closely.

Wykeham, my dear Wykeham, was formally pardoned, thus confirming the healing of the wounds between Edward and his former Chancellor. At least I had been able to achieve that much for an old friend. Wykeham wrote:

I am restored to grace, but not to political office. I shall turn my mind to the matter of education at Oxford with the building of two new colleges. I know that will appeal to you—although no woman will set foot within their doors! I might owe you that— but we must both accept that it cannot be done.

It made me smile. How difficult for a priest to acknowledge a debt to a sinful daughter of Eve, but he had done it, and with such elegance. I wished him well. I thought we were unlikely to meet again.

Finally, there came some unsettling news that made me laugh—and then frown. With the meeting of Parliament, Gaunt was invited to join a committee of the Lords to deal with the threats from across the Channel.

"So, Gaunt's star is in the ascendant," Windsor remarked, reading Wykeham's letter over my shoulder.

"To be expected," I replied. "He has the blood and the experience."

"Unfortunately no reputation for success!"

Windsor's contempt did not disturb me. What would Gaunt's waxing power mean for me now? Our ambitions no longer ran in parallel lines. But Windsor was thoughtful, taking Wykeham's letter to reread at his leisure. It always worried me when he felt the need to brood over a cup of ale.

But I laughed when I read of Parliament's outrageously high-handed petition to young Richard. How predictable of them! In the future, only Parliament should have the right to appoint Richard's Chancellor, Treasurer, and every other high office of state they could discover. Parliament would control the King at every step. No one was ever to be allowed to do what *I* had done when Edward was too ill to do it for himself. There would never be another Alice Perrers, ruling the royal roost.

Yes, I laughed, but there was not much humor in it.

I found nothing to laugh at afterward. A heavy hammering on my door at Pallenswick, much like the thump of a mailed fist, brought me hotfoot from my receipts and estate records. Windsor, I knew, was engaged in draining water meadows over at Gaines. Nor would I expect him to knock on my door when he returned—we still led a strange peripatetic life, in no sense a united household, as if our marriage were still some unshaped business entity that sometimes demanded our intimacy and sometimes did not. No, Windsor would not knock. Rather he would fling the door wide and stride inside, his voice raised to announce his arrival, filling the house with his formidable, restless presence. This was not Windsor. My heart tripped with a fast rebirth of the fear that always lurked deep within me, but I would not hide. . . . I strode toward the repeated thud.

"A group of men, mistress." My steward hovered uncertainly in the entrance hall. "Do I open to them?"

"Do so." If this was a threat, I would face it.

"Good day, mistress."

Not a mailed fist, but a staff of office, and potentially just as forceful. The man at my door was clothed in the sober garments of an upper servant: a clerk or a gentleman's secretary. Or, a breath of warning whispering over my neck, a Court official. I did not know him. I did not like the look of him, despite his mild expression and his courteous bow, or the dozen men at his back. My courtyard was crowded with pack animals and two large wagons.

"Mistress Perrers?"

"I am. And who are you, sir?" I asked with careful good manners.

All had been quiet on the London front over the past months, Richard getting used to the weight of the crown and Joan queening it over the Court. I had not stirred from my self-imposed exile.

"Keep your head down," Windsor had advised after my previous flirtation with danger. "They've too many problems to be concerned about you. Defense of the realm has taken precedence over the old King's mistress. Another few months and you'll be forgotten."

"I don't know if I like that thought." Obscurity did not sit well with me. "Do I want to be forgotten?"

"You do if you've any sense. Stay put, woman."

So I had, and as the weeks had passed with no further evidence of Joan's malevolence, my dread had abated. But if Windsor was well-informed, as he usually was, what was this on my doorstep? It did not bode well. Mentally I cursed Windsor for his overconfidence, and for his absence. Why was a man never around when you needed him? And why should I need him, anyway? Could I not deal with this encroachment on my own property? I eyed my visitor. This man in his black tunic and leather satchel carried far too much authority for my liking. My throat dried as his flat stare moved over me from head to toe.

But they cannot arrest you. You have committed no crime. Gaunt stood for you! He rescinded the banishment!

I breathed a little more easily.

The official bowed again. At least he was polite, but his men had an avaricious gleam.

"I am Thomas Webster, mistress." From the satchel, he took a scroll. "I am sent by a commission appointed by Parliament." Soft-voiced and respectful despite those assessing eyes, he held out the document for me to take. I did so, unrolling it between fingers that I held steady as I scanned the contents. It was not difficult to absorb the gist of it within seconds.

My breathing was once more compromised. My hand crushed one of the red seals that spoke of its officialdom, and I pretended to read through it again whilst I forced a deep breath into my lungs. Then I stood solidly on my doorstep, as if it would be possible for me to block their entry.

"What's this? I don't understand." But the words were black and clear before my eyes.

"I am given authority to take what I can of value, mistress."

The beat of my heart in my throat threatened to choke me. "And if I refuse?"

"I wouldn't if I were you, mistress," he said dryly. "You've not the power to stop me. I have a list of the most pertinent items. Now, if you will allow me . . . ?"

So they came in with a heavy clump of boots, Webster unfolding his abomination of a list. It was an inventory of all I owned, everything that Pallenswick contained that belonged to me.

Panic built, roaring out of control.

"The house is mine!" I objected. "It is not Crown property. It was not a gift from the King—I bought it."

"But bought with whose money, mistress? Where did that money come from?" He might have smirked. "And whose are the contents? Did you buy those too?" He turned his back on me, beckoning to his minions to begin their task.

There was no answer I could give that would make any impression. I stood and watched as the order of Parliament's commission was instigated. All my property was hauled out before me into the courtyard and stowed in the wagons and on the pack animals. My linen, my furniture, even my bed. Jewels, clothing, trinkets, and through it all Webster reading from his despicable list.

"A diadem of pearls. A gold chain set with rubies. A yard of scarlet silk ribbon. A pair of leather gloves, the gauntlets embroidered in silver and . . ."

"A yard of ribbon . . . ?" A cry touching on hysteria gathered in my throat.

"Every little helps, mistress. We have a war to fund," he replied caustically. "Those jewels will fetch by our reckoning close to five hundred pounds. Better a well-armed body of men to defend English soil than these pretty things 'round your neck!"

It was useless. I watched in silence as everything was carried out of my house. When I saw the robes clutched in the arms of a burly servant, a heap of fur and silk and damask in rich blue and silver, the robes that Edward had had made for me for a second great tournament at Smithfield, I choked back the tears. They had never been worn; that second tournament was never held. The robes were cast on the wagon with all the rest.

And there I was, left to stand in the empty entrance hall of my own house.

"Have you finished?"

"Yes, mistress. But I should warn you: Parliament has taken on the burden of your creditors. Any man with a claim against you is invited to put forward his demands."

"My creditors?" It grew worse and worse.

"Indeed, mistress. Any man with a grievance for extortions or oppressions or injuries committed by yourself"—how he was enjoying this!—"can appeal to Parliament for redress."

"Where . . . where did this order come from?" I demanded. Oh, I knew the answer!

"From Parliament, mistress."

Inhaling slowly, I clenched my fists against the shriek of anger in my head. This was not from Parliament. I would wager the pearl diadem that had just disappeared into the pack on the back of a mule. I knew whose fingers were in this pie. So she was not content to allow me to live in obscurity! I knew from whence this campaign of retaliation had stemmed and it was vicious! I could see her rubbing her hands with the satisfaction of it.

God's Blood!

I forced myself to think coldly and logically. If this was all she took . . . I had other manor houses, each well furnished. I would allow her this, however furious it made me.

And then I saw Webster removing yet another scroll from his satchel.

"Have you not taken everything you can?"

"This is not a reclamation order, mistress. It is for you to present yourself in London."

I snatched it from him. Read it. I was to appear before the House of Lords.

"A trial?" I gasped. He stood unspeaking, stony-faced. What possible charges had they discovered now? "Tell me!" I demanded. "Is this a trial?"

"It is written there, mistress." Webster indicated the document crumpled in my hand. I must appear before the House of Lords on the twenty-second day of December. And the charge against me? Fraud. Treason!

Treason? That was not possible!

But I knew that anything was possible. Fury was replaced by terror. This was to be no political slapping of my knuckes: This was to be a trial with legal consequences. How far would Joan go in her desire for revenge? The penalty for treason was death.

Windsor returned from a damp morning in the flooded meadows around Pallenswick to find me sitting mindlessly on the floor in the now empty parlor. No furniture, no tapestry; even the log basket beside the fireplace had been taken. . . . I was stunned, as if Joan had struck my face with the flat of her hand—as she had once so long ago. When I failed to register the echo of his boots on the polished boards, he knelt and lifted the document from my unresisting fingers. Skimming down it, he swore fluently, threw his gloves and sword onto the floor, and sat down beside me.

"I see the vultures have been here."

"Yes." His boots in close proximity to my skirts were filthy with mud and slime and the odd strand of duckweed. I did not care.

"Where are the girls?' he asked.

"With Webster," I replied dully. "Being fed bread and small beer in the kitchen. If our visitors left us any . . ."

"Is every room as empty as this?"

Words failed me. I lifted my hands, let them drop. Misery engulfed me.

"What are you going to do?" He thrust the question into the silence.

"I think I'll sit here and wait for the ax to fall on my neck."

"Really?" Windsor stood. He gripped my forearms and with a flex of muscles stood, lifting me with him. "Stand up, Alice. You need to stand on your feet. You need to think!"

"I can't."

"Is the woman I love so easily intimidated?"

I stood rigid in his embrace, unable to think, unable to respond. Into which black hole had all my courage vanished? I was full to the brim with self-pity, and because I no longer felt brave, I wept for my own weakness, for all I had lost. That the gifts given to me by Edward out of love and gratitude should be snatched back in spitefulness, destroying the physical evidence of Edward's place in my life. And when honesty forced me to consider that I had not always been entirely without blame, I wept for that too. I had enjoyed my power as King's Concubine. I could not be completely absolved of using crown gold for my purchases, but I had always paid it back. Hadn't I? Well, for the most part I had paid my debts. And here was the day of reckoning. I wept into Windsor's shoulder.

"Is the woman I love so lacking in backbone that she will stand and weep rather than fight for what is rightfully hers?"

They were harsh words, but he tightened his hold and propped his chin on top of my head until I began to relax and take my own weight. The solid beat of his heart had a reassurance all its own. I eventually rested my forehead against his shoulder and could breathe evenly again. . . .

The word blazed in my mind. I looked up sharply, dislodging his chin, seeing myself reflected in his eyes.

"*What* did you just say?"

"Which bit of it? That you lacked backbone?"

I ran my tongue over dry lips, scrubbed at my face with a square of linen that Windsor obligingly offered me, and frowned. "I think you said that I am the woman you love?"

"You are. Didn't you know? You don't look very pleased with the idea."

My hands tightened on his sleeves. "Say it again. As if you mean it." In case he did not. Pray God he did!

"Dear Alice. I love you. You hold my sun and moon in your hands!"

"And that is poetic!"

I thought his answering smile was a little wry. I could not believe it! But I must, mustn't I? Windsor was not a man to say what he did not mean. An immeasurable joy rioted through me, as if to fill me with a shimmering light to disperse the shadows in my mind and heart. Until all the events of the morning flooded back . . .

I stared at him. "Why did you have to tell me now?"

"When should I tell you?"

Windsor was humoring me, distracting me. I pushed his hands

away so that I stood alone. "Tomorrow. Last week. Anytime but when my face is blotched with tears and my home stripped bare and my mind full of Joan's perfidy."

"I thought you knew."

"No, I didn't! How could I? You have never said it before." How could he be so obtuse? There he stood, solid and real and *difficult*! And infinitely loved. "I want to enjoy it, not have it outweighed by the fact that I might be staring financial ruin—even death, if they prove treason against me—in the face! And I think you should know"—I did not even hesitate—"I love you too."

Windsor grinned. "There you are, then!"

I plastered my hands over my mouth. "I didn't mean to say that!"

"I don't see why not." He had captured my hands again, humor still lurking in the curve of his mouth. "We'll celebrate our mutual love and worry about venomous Joan together."

His mouth was hot and sure on mine.

"Oh, Will . . ."

"What is it? I've just proclaimed my undying love for you. And you don't look very happy about it!"

I sighed. "I'll come about."

"Let me help." And he kissed me again.

My thoughts were all adrift as I sank into that embrace. But not for long. This was no time for amorous sighs and pleasurable longings. I was not yet free to enjoy them, as Windsor well knew. Framing my face in his hands so I must attend, concentrate, Windsor began to speak in a low, controlled voice that belied the emotion that pulsed beneath his skin. "Now listen to me. You need to be strong, Alice. Listen!" With his hand beneath my chin he made me look at him. "You will stand before the Lords and answer every question they put to you. There is no evidence of fraud against you. As for treason—they'll not make that stick."

"You are so confident." I frowned, not at all persuaded.

"No, I'm not. I am too realistic. But you need to show a confident face or they'll tear you apart."

"Why would they do it? Now, when my days at Court are over?"

"You know why. They'll destroy you for the days when you held power and they did not."

"Can we stop them?"

"I don't know. How can we know until we know their evidence? But we'll have a damned good try."

I took a deep breath, conscious at last of some of the despair sliding away, and I asked what I wanted most in the world. "When I have to go, will you come with me?"

"The devil himself wouldn't keep me away! Don't weep anymore. . . . Tears have no currency in the game we're playing!" His gaze was fierce, his hands steady as he took the linen and finished mopping my tears with a thoroughness he might use to dry his horse after a rainstorm. "Are you not my wife? Do I not love you? Be brave, Alice. You have been so all your life. We will go together to Westminster and confront the bloody scavengers in their den. As for now . . . I think we are owed some time of our own. In God's name, we haven't claimed much over the years."

"To do what?" My thoughts were still wayward, seeing the malevolent, sneering faces of Edward's Court ranged against me.

With a huff of impatient breath, Windsor clasped my shoulders and shook me. "Stop thinking! Come to bed—and I'll show your doubting mind that I truly do love you and that it's not a figment of your imagination. . . . On the other hand, we don't have a bed, do we?"

"No!" I felt ridiculous tears begin to well again, but managed a croak of a laugh.

"I swear it won't be a problem!"

In my bedchamber—our bedchamber—Windsor spread his cloak on the floor in a patch of sunshine, folding his tunic for my head. And in broad daylight he gave me a glimpse of what I had never known—a distilled essence of the magic of unencumbered love, freely given, freely received. I felt the chains of duty and expectation slip away, replaced with soft bonds of delight and passion and hot desire.

"Convinced?" he asked between kisses.

"Oh, Will . . ."

I could not string two words together, wrapped as I was in the moment. It was impossible not to admire his soldier's body, firm and well muscled, as he stripped off hose and boots. The sunshine softened the hard planes, highlighting the power of thigh and shoulder.

"Poitiers?" I murmured, pressing my lips to an old scar that ran along his ribs, angling from sternum to waist.

"Yes." He stretched, lifting me with him, inquiring, "Do you intend to kiss all my scars?"

"That would take far too long." He loosed my shift and I stood naked, exposed. "I am in lust and desire, Will. My knees are weak with longing. . . ."

"And with love?" His own lust and desire were as evident as the liquid heat between my thighs.

"Yes, and love."

The floor was hard, with no goose down, no linen, no lavender-scented coverings. It mattered not one tiny feather from the pillows we did not have. I let him take me as he wished. Or perhaps I did not exactly allow it at all. He was not a man to ask permission, and I would have it no other way. My mind was wiped free of everything but the two of us there together in a house that echoed with emptiness, the sun gilding breast and thigh. Two private people entirely absorbed in each other, attracting no interest from the outside world.

"Why do we love each other, Will?" I asked.

"I've no idea. Don't worry about it. Some things are granted simply to be enjoyed. . . ."

His enjoyment of me was balm to my soul, his weight solid, his possession thorough. I held on to him when every muscle and nerve shivered in response to his attentions, as I had never needed to hold on to any man before. My heart was full of joy, so much that I might weep again. But I did not. It was a time for rejoicing, and Windsor's clever hands pushed back the shadows.

But not forever.

When he slept, hair mussed, face buried in his tunic folds, I lay awake. A trial? Unknown evidence? I held Windsor's love for me close, a talisman to ward off the fear.

"Did they get Philippa's jewels, then?" Windsor asked when it became necessary for us to dress.

I fear my expression bordered on the smug. "What do you think?"

"God's Blood!" His laughter echoed strangely in the unfurnished room. "Tell me, then."

"It pays to be prepared and vigilant. But they will require a little polishing."

With some forward planning against the day when this might happen—had I not always been chary of just such an eventuality?—my steward had hidden them, together with Edward's rings, in a sack half-full of weevil-ridden flour. Webster, thank God, had considered the confiscation of the detritus of my cellars beneath his dignity.

Windsor was making headway with the laces of his tunic. "By the by—I have this for you. . . . I was distracted." He delved into the inner lining. "I don't think I've ever given you a gift before."

He took out a silver looking glass. It shone enticingly in the soft light, its engraved stems and leaves skillfully intertwining around the rim like the arms of lovers.

I frowned. "No!" I said stonily, ungraciously.

Windsor stared at the glass, and then at me with solemn astonishment, as if my female mental processes were beyond his understanding. "Alice, my love! I haven't stolen it. I came by it by fair means—and show me a woman who does not use a glass."

"She sits before you."

"But why? Why will you not?"

"I don't like what I see." This was the truth; I was not seeking compliments.

"Which bits?"

Was this the time for humor, when I still sat, disheveled, in my shift? "All of them . . . I'm not . . . Oh, Windsor!" Infuriated, for it was a pretty thing, I clasped my hands in my lap.

"At what age does a woman begin not to care about her appearance?" Windsor had no intention of allowing me to refuse. "I think she must be on her deathbed."

He fell to his knees beside me on his much-creased cloak, held the glass up, and with his free hand traced the line of one of my too-dark brows.

"I see no ugliness," he said softly, "for you are lovely in my eyes. I want you to see *Alice*. I want you to see the face of my wife and the woman I love."

His words took every refusal out of my mind. How could I not accept the gift without unforgivable churlishness? And my image was not as bad as I had feared. The face that looked back at me was no beauty, but the lack of symmetry was striking in itself. Even the brows were supportable. I tilted my chin and smiled, and my reflection did likewise; perhaps this unexpected happiness had given me a softening of feature. So I became an owner of a looking glass when I had vowed I would not, and was not displeased when Windsor kissed every bit of my reflected face.

We moved to Gaines, where we at least had a bed—so far.

I knew exactly the impression I wished to make for my appearance before the Lords. I had thought I would be edgy, apprehensive of the outcome, with mouth dry, heart pumping so that I must swallow against nausea. And I was, all of those, but more than that I was defiant! Since the visit of the deplorably efficient Webster, Joan—with the backing of the courts—had been encroaching step by poisonous step. My beloved manor near Wendover, Edward's gift, had been taken from me, my people turned out, my furnishings impounded, without my even being there to give my yea or nay. As I was informed, my ownership of the estate was not legal. It had reverted to the Crown, and was now the property of King Richard. Not that he had much use from it. On his mother's advice he granted it to his half brother, Thomas Holland, Joan's son by one of her earlier, dubious, probably bigamous marriages.

I'm sure it gave her inordinate pleasure.

I seethed with impotence, for disconcertingly, worryingly, Gaunt too made much of my inability to fight back. My house on the banks of the Thames hopped easily from my hand to his. All my London property along the Ropery was added to the total of the royal Duke's own wealth. Two of my choicest manors dropped neatly into the pocket of Gaunt's son-in-law. I was truly dispensable in Gaunt's eyes. He had no further use for me, and I learned a hard lesson: Never trust a man who puts power before loyalty.

So, to attend my so-called trial, I dressed not with circumspection but in a blaze of rebellion.

"There!" I smoothed my hands down my dress before fastening a loop of gold and opals around my wrist to match the collar lying snugly against my collarbone, addressing Jane, who sat on the floor of my bedchamber to watch the transformation from country wife to Court lady. Not all of my garments were stored at Pallenswick. "I'll show them I don't fear them!" I announced, and marched down to the parlor, where Windsor awaited me. For a long moment he remained slouched in a chair and looked me over.

"By the Rood, Alice!" His voice was belligerent.

"Is that good or bad?" I thought I looked very well for my summons to kneel before the overmighty Lords.

Lips tight pressed, without a word, Windsor marched me back to my chamber, picked Jane up off the floor where she still sat, and deposited her in the middle of my bed with an absentminded ruffle of her curls.

I clenched my hands into fists. "I don't like your high-handedness!"

"And I despair of your lack of perspicacity!" He faced me, his manner annoyingly imperious, his voice cracking like a whiplash. Nor did I appreciate his choice of words. "Are you stupid? You are on trial, Alice. For fraud and treason. How difficult do you want to make it for yourself? Do you really want to antagonize the misbegotten titled scum who'll sit in judgment over you before the first word is uttered?"

I felt my face flush with heat. "They are already antagonized. What does it matter what I wear?"

"Oh, it matters! You look like a concubine!"

"I was a concubine!"

"I know. We all know. But there's no need to slap them in their high-blooded faces with it. Look at yourself in all honesty."

He spread his arms to take in my appearance, and I forced myself to see through his eyes. Through the eyes of the Lords. It was, I suppose, on the edge of regally treasonable, as if I had usurped the power of the monarchy for myself. Not quite with the flamboyance of the garments I had worn as Lady of the Sun, but with enough éclat to take the eye, for I wore the same violet silk and gold cotehardie that had driven Isabella to wrath.

"You're fighting for your freedom here—perhaps even . . ."

"My life?" I snapped back, the flush fading to an icy pallor.

"Don't be melodramatic." He barely hesitated. "I can't say I see you on a scaffold, but you can't argue against it—there'll be more than one of those ranged against you who'll call for your death."

"Which seems to be a contradiction to me."

"And to me also, my combative wife." He pushed his hand through his hair and groaned. "You need to be careful; don't you understand? If they choose to resurrect the charge of witchcraft against you . . ." I saw the worry on him. "And you need to wear something less . . . challenging."

"If you say so." I knew he was right. Of course he was. I sighed and began to strip off the splendidly offending garments. "It's difficult when the mother of the King is sharpening her nails, isn't it?" He did not reply. As I stood with my outer robe crushed in my hands, I admitted, "I am afraid. Oh, Will, I am afraid." I needed his help and his fire in my belly.

Windsor's voice gentled at last. "I know." He took the garment from me and laid it on the bed, smoothing its folds with care. "It is very dangerous. But we know well how to manage hostile forces, do we not?"

"Oh, we do." The underrobe, unlaced by Windsor's nimble fingers, fell around my feet. I sighed again. "I'm sorry. I let my emotions run away with me."

"Of course you did. You're a woman. And a very dear one to me. I won't let them harm you, you know."

"I think you might not have a voice in the matter."

"How little faith you have in me." He thrust a pair of plain leather shoes into my hands. "Don't stand there thinking about it. If you're late, they'll sneer even more down their aristocratic noses. But remember: I will be with you. I'll not let you suffer alone."

"Suffer! My thanks!"

I dressed rapidly and circumspectly, going to my trial in sobriety and seemliness. No jewels! To wear even one of Philippa's jewels would be like putting a flame to dry kindling laid ready for the fire.

Thus I returned to London for the first time since Edward's funeral. It seemed to me a much longer stretch of time than the actual weeks since I had fled from the door of the Abbey with Joan's triumphant prediction resounding in my ears. Momentarily my spirits leaped at the familiar noise and bustle, the sight of wealthy merchants and their wives in as much finery as Edward's sumptuary laws would allow. The glimpse of the Thames between warehouses, opaque like gray glass in the winter air, drew me. I was not a natural country dweller and never would be—then I recalled with a cold squeeze of a hand around my heart that I was not here for the pleasures that London could offer.

I touched Windsor's arm for reassurance, grateful when he covered my hand with his own. If affairs went badly for me, I might spend my days in a dungeon or banished from the realm. Or worse . . . Trying to reply to some bland comment made by Windsor as we wove a path between beggars and whores and the dregs of the London gutters that milled by the waterside, I swallowed against a knot of pure terror.

Dismounting at the Palace of Westminster, Windsor took charge of our horses and I questioned one of the officials. Where were the Lords intending to meet? I was directed to a chamber that Edward had sometimes used for formal audiences, such as the visit of the three kings so many years ago. So this too was to be very formal. But then there was no time to think. Windsor was pulling at my mantle and we walked briskly toward my fate. Guards barred our way at the door; the lords were not yet assembled. Impatiently, I turned to see a man sitting on one of the benches usually occupied by petitioners, waiting for us.

"Wykeham." Windsor nodded briefly.

"Windsor," Wykeham reciprocated.

The two men eyed each other with little warmth. That would never change.

"I thought that you of all people would have kept clear of this place," I said, to hide my astonishment that the bishop should be here. "It's not politic for a sensible man to be seen in my company."

"You forget." His grimace as he kissed my fingers was a praiseworthy attempt at a smile. "I'm a free man, pardoned and reinstated. I shine with honest rectitude. Parliament in its wisdom has turned its smiling face on me, so nothing can touch me."

I had never heard him so cynical. "I hope I can say the same for myself after today, but I am not confident."

"I expect you can talk them 'round." His mordant humor had an edge. Warmed by his attempt to reassure me, however much an empty gesture it proved to be, I asked what I had never asked before.

"Pray for me, Wykeham."

"I will. Even though I'm not sure it matters to you. You spoke for me when I needed it." He pressed my fingers before releasing them. "I'll do what I can, lady. The Lords might listen if I speak for you. . . ."

The unusual term of respect from Wykeham almost brought me to tears, and I curtsied deeply to him, as I had never done before.

"You have some strange friends, my love," Windsor observed when Wykeham was gone. "The man—priest or not—is enamored of you. God help him!"

"Nonsense!" I replied, marshaling my scattered emotions. "I helped to get him dismissed."

"And you reunited him with Edward. You are too hard on yourself." He folded my hands in his and kissed my lips, my cheeks. "Remember what I told you," he whispered against my temple.

And then I was on my own.

Without any fuss or fanfare, I was shown into the chamber. There was no chair placed for me this time: I was expected to stand throughout. Before me and beside me, on three sides, the ranks of hostile faces stared their enmity, just as I had imagined. And in the end Windsor could not keep his promise to be with me—he was barred at the door. He did not bother to argue when faced with the point of the guards' halberds. I could imagine him pacing the chamber outside to no avail.

I looked 'round at those I knew and those I did not. Would there be justice? I thought not.

Be calm. Be reasoned. Be aware. Don't allow yourself to be tricked into any admission that can be used against you. Tell the truth as much as you can. Use the intelligence God gave you. And don't speak out of turn or with misplaced arrogance.

Windsor had been brutal in his advice.

But I was so alone. Even his love could not still the rapid trip of my heart.

"Mistress Perrers."

I looked up sharply. Their spokesman, a sheaf of pages in his hand, was Henry Percy, Earl of Northumberland, Marshal of England. A close associate of Gaunt. I did not like this. I did not like it at all, but I clung to my resolve and I inclined my head.

"My lord."

"You are summoned here to answer to charges of a most serious nature. Do you understand?"

So that was how it would be. Formal and legal, entirely impersonal. I still did not know what the charges were.

"Yes, my lord. I understand."

"We require you to answer questions concerning your past conduct. There are outstanding charges against you."

"And they are?" Fear bloomed against all my desires.

"Fraud, mistress. And treason. How do you plead?"

"Innocent," I replied instantly. "To both. And I question the validity of any evidence against me." I might be circumspect in my replies, but I would not be a fool. I knew what they were about, concocting some spurious occasion on which I had committed treason. Even fraud was a matter for debate.

"They are serious charges, mistress. Perhaps you should take time to consider. . . ."

"In what manner have I ever committed fraud?" I kept my voice clear and strong and confident, my spine straight as a halberd staff. "I have never used dishonest deception or trickery to benefit myself. I have never used false representations. If you are questioning my holding of royal manors, they were freely given to me by King Edward, gifts of his generosity, out of his affection for me." Let them accept that statement! "Those I purchased in my own name were done so openly and legally, through the offices of my agent. I utterly deny the charge of fraud, my lords."

My breathing, with great effort, was slow and controlled, my voice even and commanding. What evidence could they possibly have?

"But in the matter of treason, mistress . . ."

"Treason? On which occasion did I violate my sworn allegiance to my King?" I was on firm ground here. Not even this august body could find evidence of my bringing the state of the King into danger. "I challenge you to find any evidence of my being a danger either to the King's health or to the security of the realm." Perhaps not wise, but fear compelled me to state my case so bluntly. I appraised the faces turned toward me. Some met my gaze; some looked anywhere but at me. "Well, my lords? Where is your evidence?"

The Lords moved uneasily on their benches, whispered together. Northumberland shuffled his documents.

"We must deliberate, mistress. If you would wait in the antechamber?"

I stalked out.

"What's happening?" Windsor was immediately there, drawing me to sit on the bench recently vacated by Wykeham.

"They are deliberating."

"What, in God's name? You were barely in there for five minutes!"

"I don't know." I could not sit, but prowled across the width of the room and back.

"I presume it's not going well?"

"Nothing is going well. They charged me, but refused to produce any evidence against me. What do I make of that? If they have no evidence, why call me here? I am afraid, Will. I'm afraid of what I don't know."

"I wish I could be there with you." He rose to prowl with me.

"I know." I leaned into him. "But I don't think it would do any good. Even the Archangel Gabriel himself could not keep the Lords from my tearing out my throat."

Within the half hour I was called back.

"Mistress Perrers," Northumberland said, with a self-satisfied air. "The Lords have debated the evidence against you. That you did wantonly and deliberately disobey the orders issued by the Good Parliament."

What was this? A completely new direction? Fraud and treason had suddenly been abandoned, unless it was treason to disobey Parliament. In that moment I realized that the Lords had known from the beginning that these charges were untenable. But what was the implication here? I felt the ground shift under my feet. This was far more dangerous, a presentiment of it shivering along my spine. How I wished for Windsor's strength beside me.

"Which orders?" I asked, genuinely puzzled. Had I not obeyed them to the letter? Surely this could not be witchcraft again? Nausea gripped my belly.

"The orders that banished you from the person of the King and from living anywhere in the vicinity of the royal Court . . ."

But had I not done what they asked of me?

"I reject that accusation."

"Do you?" A complacent curve of Northumberland's mouth attested to his certainty that my denial would hold no weight. "You were banished—and yet you returned to be with His late Majesty in the weeks before his death. . . ."

Be calm! They cannot prove your guilt on this. . . .

"I observed the orders," I stated, choosing my words with care, whilst my heart galloped like a panicked horse. "I lived in retirement. I did not return to Court until my lord of Gaunt had the orders against me rescinded. I state this, a fact that must be well-known to all here present, as proof of my innocence."

"This Chamber knows nothing of that. It believes that you are guilty of breaking the terms of your banishment by Parliament. A most heinous crime."

"No! I did not! I was informed by the hand of my lord of Gaunt himself that I was free to return."

"And you have proof of this?"

"No. But the pardon must exist."

The letter. What had happened to it? My thoughts skittered like rats in a trap. There must be proof. . . .

"Furthermore"—Northumberland continued as if I had not

spoken—"you are charged that you used your malign influence on His Majesty King Edward in the final days of his weakness, to achieve the pardon of Richard Lyons, whom Parliament had condemned for his dire culpability in matters of finance. By your instigation, Lyons was released from the Tower."

It was simply not true. I considered the accusation, my mind racing over the facts. There was no evidence of my involvement. There was *none*! My spirits rose, and yet I was puzzled at this accusation.

"Lyons was pardoned on the authority of my lord of Gaunt, in King Edward's name, when the decisions of the Parliament were reversed," I replied, once more sure of my ground. "He and my lord Latimer were both released. It is no secret. It must have been known to your lordships."

Northumberland denied it. "This Chamber holds that you are guilty of effecting the pardon of this man, a man considered to be a threat to the realm."

"No . . . !"

"The scale of his embezzlement was an outrage. To grant him a pardon was an act against the authority of Parliament. . . ."

"There must be Court officials who know the truth. Gaunt himself . . ."

Northumberland's eyes met mine, horrifyingly bright with his supremacy over me. "We are aware of none. Not one has come forward in your defense."

"I can find them." How amazingly composed I sounded, yet the palms of my hands were slick with sweat. "The lawyers involved with the case will speak for my lack of involvement. I had nothing to do with Lyons's pardon. It must be on record that my lord of Gaunt had the legal papers drawn up."

Silence. Not even the habitual scuffling of my aristocratic judges. I found that my hands had curled into fists, the nails digging into soft flesh. Northumberland gave a curt nod.

"It must not be said that this Chamber is guilty of trampling justice underfoot. We will allow you time to find your witnesses, mistress. We will hear them and assess their evidence."

"How long?" I asked. "How long will you give me?"

"One afternoon and one night, mistress." His smile was a smirk, if I was not mistaken.

"But that's impossible. . . ."

"A committee appointed by us will meet tomorrow at ten of the clock to hear your evidence."

"I beg for longer, my lords. . . ." I looked 'round at the faces, but knew that my plea fell on willfully deaf ears.

"That is the best we can do."

I walked from the room, shoulders straight, head high. They knew I would lose.

"One afternoon and one night? By God! They're sure of themselves. And I don't like having a door slammed in my face!" Windsor struck his fist against the wall, then became fiercely practical. "So where do we start?"

"It was Gaunt's doing; he ordered Lyons's release. The evidence must exist," I fretted. "All I need is someone to unearth it from wherever it's filed away and stand beside me to put it before the Lords' Committee."

"Who? Who would know?"

We were walking rapidly through the corridors to the wing of the vast palace given over to Court business, a rabbit warren of clerks and lawyers.

"I don't know," I said. "One of the Court's legal men. There are enough of them."

"But will they?"

"Will they what?" My mind was already leaping ahead. Who could I pin down?

"Find the evidence. Present it before the Committee. Who in God's name can you find to stand before the Lords and challenge their rulings?"

I stopped in my tracks. "Why would they not?"

"If there's an interest to keep the evidence hidden . . ." He raised his hand as I opened my mouth to deny such an outcome. "*If*, I say . . . then retribution against any man who spoke in your defense could be sharp and swift. It could keep mouths firmly closed. Even if the evidence still exists . . . and I have my doubts!"

I blinked to hear it spoken so brutally. For was it not what I feared? The assurance of Northumberland had stirred my fear to hot flames.

"I can't do *nothing*! I can't just *accept* it!" I retaliated.

"No. And our time is slipping past." Windsor had redoubled his pace. "Let's see who we can track down to their legal lair. Who was the man who took all your property from Pallenswick? He might consider that he owes you the truth."

"Why is it, Will," I grumbled, "that you always think along the lines of debts that can be called in and gifts that need to be reciprocated?"

"Because I've spent my life calling them in or repaying them!" He strode on, pulling me with him. "Do you remember his name?"

"Thomas Webster."

"Go and talk to him." He pushed me through a door that would take me into the legal rabbit run. "I'll see if any of Edward's servants manage to have a memory that I can prick. With a dagger if I have to."

I tracked Thomas Webster down to a small, shabby room where he was surrounded by vellum, ribbons and seals, and the smell of ink and elderly documents. How evocative that smell was, with memories of past times. Safer times. Master Webster looked up impatiently as I entered, then, seeing me, instantly dismissed his clerk. Not, I decided, a good sign.

"Master Thomas Webster." I stood before his desk, arms at my sides, as he came slowly to his feet.

"Mistress Perrers . . ."

"Do they exist?"

He knew why I was here in his den. His eyes shifted beneath mine, and slid down to where one hand toyed with an inky quill. He knew exactly my meaning: the documents to prove that Gaunt had had the pardons drawn up.

"I am sure they do, mistress."

"Will you find them for me? Will you stand as witness for me?"

"No, mistress."

Well, that was plain enough. "Why not?"

Now he looked at me. "You know the reason. It's more than my position is worth to help you."

"Will you not even help me to prove that my banishment from Court was revoked by my lord of Gaunt?"

He did not even bother to answer.

"Then who will?" I demanded. "Who will help me?"

His face as bland as a baked custard tart, he cast the quill with its ruined nib onto the desk. He did not need to reply. As I discovered in further fruitless search for the whole of that afternoon, no one would help me. The Court lawyers became invisible. They vanished into the stonework and paneled walls like cockroaches at the approach of a candle. Those whom I cornered claimed an astonishing loss of recall.

"It's hopeless!" I met up with Windsor, who was looking unusually harassed, in the Great Hall.

"So Webster is intransigent?"

"Webster is a self-serving bastard!"

"Edward's servants are also less than cooperative," he remarked. "But there is one who might come up to the mark. . . ."

"How much did you pay him?"

"Best not to ask! I wouldn't wager on his appearing in the final shake-up, but at least he did not refuse outright."

I had little hope. If a lawyer would not stand for the truth, with all the legal documents to prove his case, how could I expect a page or servant to put himself forward against the will of Parliament?

"Don't give up hope, Alice," Windsor said, though his face was grim. "Not until the final judgment is given. There's always hope."

"I'm not so sanguine."

"Nor am I. But we can't both give up before we begin!" I balked at the unexpected harshness, but he drew my hand through his arm and led me toward the screened door at the end of the hall.

"What do we do now?" I asked.

"We stir up the kitchens to find us ale and something that passes for food. Then we keep my wavering witness under surveillance." His grin had a not altogether pleasant edge. "If he changes his mind, we do all we can to change it back!"

We had little sleep that night.

Ten o'clock. Edward's beloved clock at Havering would be marking the hour. The Committee chose a smaller, more intimate chamber in which to examine my evidence, one just large enough to hold a half dozen of their number and the accused. And a witness, if one were brave enough to appear. Or sufficiently foolhardy . . .

I entered. I curtsied to the chosen Lords seated before me behind a table, a solid barrier between accusers and accused. I looked from face to face to see who would determine my future.

The temperature in the room dropped to ice.

Seated in the center of my judges, presiding over the case against me, was Gaunt himself. My erstwhile supporter, my ally, who had striven to win my allegiance, who had annulled my banishment to allow me to return to Edward.

Sitting in judgment?

I inhaled slowly, deeply, trying to calm the terror that flared anew. Why had he chosen to do this? What effect would his weighty presence have on the judgment for or against me? The answer was as plain as the flamboyant black-and-red damask of his tunic. I looked directly at him. He looked at me. If I had hoped to find a friend amongst the Lords, I had been woefully mistaken. But then, I had never trusted him, had I? I was right not to. Gaunt's presence, I knew full well, would destroy the one solitary hope I had clung to, however hopelessly, through that endless night: that he might once again come to my rescue. He was here to punish me. He was here to destroy any evidence that we had worked together in the past by making an example of me. He was hunting, his eyes as hard and cold as granite, and I was the quarry. I would find no rescue here.

"Mistress Perrers . . ."

My attention was dragged back, my interrogator once more Northumberland. Not that it mattered. Gaunt might not personally undertake the examination of my evidence, but his authority would color the whole proceedings. The outcome was, I feared, his to direct.

"Mistress Perrers—we will weigh your evidence to support your innocence. Have you discovered any lawyer who will speak of the origin of Lyons's pardon? Have you discovered the documents?"

"No, my lords. I have not."

"Then the evidence against you still stands and you must be presumed guilty." How gentle his voice sounded. How venomous!

"I have found one who will speak for me," I stated.

"Indeed?" The disbelief in that single word was impressive, and chilling to the depths of my soul.

"I would call John Beverley," I said.

"And he is?"

"An attendant in King Edward's retinue. A personal body servant. A man whom the King—the late King—trusted implicitly."

"Then we will hear him."

The door at my back was opened. I prayed, I prayed as hard as I could, that John Beverley had not fled.

"Keep him here, whatever you do!" I had told Windsor that morning, "and stop scowling at him." John Beverley was the only man Windsor and I could locate who had a smidgen of courage and respect for the truth. Whatever effort it had taken from Windsor, we had brought Beverley at least as far as the door to the chamber. I thought perhaps the means employed by my determined husband had been physical: Beverley was nervous. I feared he was also untrustworthy. But what choice had I but to put my freedom into his hands? All I could do was pray that his past loyalties would hold true. He entered, thinning hair untidy, as if he had dragged his hands through it, his gaze flickering over the Committee. When he saw Gaunt, his nervousness changed to horror. The skin of his face became gray, and my heart fell.

"John Beverley," Northumberland addressed him.

"Yes, my lord." His hands were gripped ferociously, his broad features anxious.

"You were body servant to King Edward?"

"Yes, my lord."

"We are here to ascertain the truth of the pardoning of Richard Lyons. You recall the matter to which I allude? To your knowledge, did Mistress Perrers persuade His late Majesty to grant Lyons a pardon?"

"Not to my knowledge, my lord."

"Are you sure about that?"

"Yes, my lord."

I sighed. Beverley was a man of few words, his eyes those of a terrified deer facing the hounds. Pray God he would use those words on my behalf.

"How is that? How can you be so sure?"

"I was in attendance on His Majesty constantly in those last days, my lord." A few petals of hope began to unfurl beneath my heart. Beverley's voice grew stronger as his confidence grew. Here was something he could speak of with authority. "I never heard the matter of a pardon mentioned by the King or by Mistress Perrers."

"So neither of them talked of it."

"No, my lord. Neither King Edward nor his . . . nor Mistress Perrers. I swear the King never gave the order for a pardon for the man."

A dangerous statement, all in all. If the pardon had not come from Edward, it had been on Gaunt's own initiative. Thus, Gaunt had usurped a royal power that was not his by right to use. I held my breath as the tension in the room tightened. There was a shifting of bodies, the slide of silk against damask, a scrape of boots against the floor. And on Gaunt's brow a storm cloud gathered. If Beverley did not notice it, he was a fool. Would he stand by his word, or would he play the coward? Windsor's intimidation or monetary inducement suddenly weighed little against Gaunt's unspoken ire.

"You will swear to that? You will take an oath to that effect?" asked Northumberland. "That Mistress Perrers did at no time persuade the late King to issue a pardon for Richard Lyons."

"Well . . . yes, my lord."

"It would, you understand, be dangerous to swear to something of which you are to any degree uncertain. . . ."

"Ah . . ." And as I watched him, Beverley's eyes skipped from Northumberland to Gaunt.

"Do you claim, Master Beverley, that Mistress Perrers had *no* influence on the King's decisions? You say that you were with the late King constantly."

"Yes, my lord."

"But were there not times when Mistress Perrers was alone with the King, without your presence?"

"Of course, my lord."

"And during those times, could she perhaps have raised the question of Lyons and his pardon?"

"Well . . . she could, my lord." Beverley gulped.

"If that is so . . . are you free to say that Mistress Perrers did not undertake the pardon of Richard Lyons?"

I heard him swallow again, seeing the pit before his feet, a dark morass of claim and counterclaim that he had dug for himself. I too saw it, but forced myself to stand perfectly still, watching Gaunt's face.

"No, my lord. I suppose I am not."

"Then, by my reckoning, you cannot support Mistress Perrers with your testimony. Can you?"

"No, sir. By my conscience, I cannot." I thought Beverley sounded relieved at having the decision made for him.

"Thank you. We appreciate your honesty. You are free to go."

Gaunt's face was blandly tranquil; he appeared satisfied with a job well-done as he looked at me. It was as if we were alone in the room, and I knew that I would be judged without mercy.

The Committee conferred in low voices.

John Beverley left the chamber with not one look in my direction, keen to dissociate himself from any suspicion of connivance between us. I could hardly blame him. Not all men were given the courage to stand by the truth. Not all men were like Windsor, who I knew would stand by me to the death. Standing alone before Gaunt's handpicked lordly minions, I needed Windsor as I had never needed anyone before. Since Philippa's intervention in my life, I had struggled and maneuvered to keep my feet in the fast-flowing stream of Court politics. I had striven to make my future and that of my children safe. I was even proud of my success. Now all was brought to nothing. Here I stood, helpless and vulnerable, without friends.

Except for William de Windsor.

The strange sense of relief that I was not completely alone, whatever happened, was my only glimmer of hope in this moment of dread.

"Mistress Perrers!" There was Northumberland demanding my attention. Gaunt's expression was carved in stone. Northumberland stepped forward. "We have made our decision. This is our judgment. . . ."

And how little time it took to undermine all I had made of my life.

"We consider you to be guilty of obtaining the pardon for Richard Lyons."

Guilty!

"Therefore this Committee, in the name of the Lords of the Realm of England, confirms the original sentence delivered by the Good Parliament. The sentence of banishment remains against you. . . ."

Banishment! Again! The word beat heavily against my mind.

But Northumberland had not yet finished twisting the knife in my heart's wound.

". . . also we command the forfeiture of all your remaining lands and possessions obtained by fraud and deceit."

The enormity of it shook me. The illegality of my actions was simply presumed without any need to show proof. My own purchase of land and property was presumed to be through deceit, and so I was to be stripped of everything, whether illegal or not. I was *presumed* guilty, not proven to be so. So much for justice. How they must hate me. But had that not always been the case?

"Do you understand our decisions, Mistress Perrers?"

I stood unmoving, aware of all those eyes: some condemning, some sanctimonious, some merely curious to see how I would react. Gaunt's eyes glittered with triumph and avarice. My estates were open to his picking. From ally to enemy in that one sentence. I could barely comprehend it. And when I did, I despised him for it.

"I understand perfectly, my lords," I remarked. "Am I free to go?"

"We are finished here."

I curtsied deeply and walked from the room.

Am I free to go? I had asked. But where would I go?

Before my mind could fully grasp what had been done, I was standing in the antechamber. The judgment was passed; I was not restrained, yet banishment, a black cloud, pressed down on me. Blindly I looked for Windsor, waiting for me by the window. I think I must have staggered, for in three strides he was beside me, holding my arm.

"Beverley played the rabbit, I presume. He scuttled out before I could get my hands around his scrawny little neck."

I blinked, unable to string two thoughts together or find words to explain what had been done to me.

"Alice?"

I shook my head. "I . . . I can't . . . but I need to . . ."

One close look at my bleak expression was enough for him. "Don't try to speak. Come with me."

He lost no time, but led me out into the icy air. I shivered but was glad of the cold wind on my face. In the courtyard, horses were waiting with Windsor's servants. As if from a distance, I realized that he had feared this, and made provision even as he had encouraged me to believe that justice would smile in my favor.

"Thank you," I whispered. How dear he was to me. How much I had begun to lean on his good sense, his cynical streak of practicality.

He raised the palm of my hand to his lips, then, realizing how cold I was, stripped off his own gloves and drew them onto my hands, wrapping his own mantle around my shoulders. The warmth was intense, welcome, despite the cruel tingling of my fingers.

"You are very . . . kind to me."

"Kind, by God! Do I not love you, foolish one?" He peered into my frozen face. "I suppose you still don't believe me. But this is neither the time nor the place to beat you about the head with it. Just accept that it's true and that I won't desert you. Feel that?" He pressed my gloved palm to his chest. "It beats in unison with yours. Is that poetic enough for you? Perhaps not, but it's the best you'll get at this juncture." His kiss on my mouth was firm. "Now up with you. Before the vermin change their mind. I'll take you home."

"But where is home now?"

"Home is with me."

What a strange place and time for such an assurance. Beneath his harsh exterior was a sensitivity that always had the power to move me. His intuitiveness was a thing of wonder. And he must have known: I needed those exact words to bite through the paralyzing horror. Nor did he wait for any reciprocal response from me. Blasted by rampant shock and fear, I could not tell him what had occurred. By now I was shivering constantly, a reaction that was nothing to do with the whip of the wind off the river. I gripped the reins that he forced between my fingers, but sat there, unable to make the simplest of decisions, until he leaned from his own mount and grasped my bridle. With an impatient grunt he pulled my horse after him into a stumbling trot. It jerked me back into my senses, and I pushed my mount alongside his.

"Will they enforce the banishment this time?" I asked, even as I knew the answer.

"So that's what they did. I wondered what had reduced you to silence."

I could not smile at the heavy humor. "Yes, and worse."

"Who was it?"

"Gaunt. He was there. He sat in judgment on me." All I could see was his hard face, his furious desire to wash his hands clean of his association with me.

"Then we'll not wait around to find out." Windsor urged our mounts into a faster trot, our escort keeping pace.

"Where are we going?"

"To Gaines. Do you agree?"

Why not? Would I be safe anywhere? "Yes. To Gaines. It is our own. They cannot question my ownership of Gaines, since it is in your name too." I saw his quizzical look. Of course, he didn't know. "Oh, Will! They're going to take away all my property, my land. . . ."

He showed no surprise.

"Then I'll take you to one of my own manors, if you prefer. You and the girls . . ."

As I thought about it, the cold in my belly began to melt. He would take care of me, whatever happened. Yet, I decided that I needed the comfort of familiar surroundings. "No. Take me to Gaines. And, Will . . . ?" He looked across. His face was vivid and alive, strong enough to confront any danger. "I know you love me. And I love you too."

"I know you do. Now get on, woman. The sooner we're out of London, the better, before they find another crime to hang around your neck."

Chapter Seventeen

*I*t was not my neck the Lords had their eye on next. The Lords launched their new assault against Windsor, not against me, with a charge breathtaking in its audacity, its low cunning: the most obvious of charges that it would be impossible for him to deny. Windsor was accused of harboring a woman who was under sentence of banishment. He was ordered to London to appear before the Lords.

"How dare they," I raged. Anger can most assuredly take the chill from terror. "How dare they transfer my guilt to you?"

"They dare with no compunction whatsoever," Windsor remarked with astonishing nonchalance. "It's a perfectly pragmatic decision by Gaunt, or Joan, to make life unpleasant for you." Infuriatingly, unlike me, he seemed to have no concerns. He admitted his guilt openly to the official who brought the summons, with me standing at his side, my hand clamped to his arm as if to prove his culpability for all to see.

"I can hardly deny it, can I?" he remarked mildly, offering the courier a cup of ale before his return journey. "We've been sharing a roof and a bed, to the knowledge of everyone who cared to take an interest in our doings. It's no secret that we're married, is it, Lady de Windsor?" He bowed to me and smiled placidly at the startled official. Since when did the accused ever admit to guilt?

I growled my disapproval.

Windsor went to London to face his accusers.

"Look for me within the month. If I'm not back, I'm in the Tower. Send me a parcel of food and wine!" His mouth was warm but fleeting on mine, his mind already racing ahead. "Don't worry. And for your safety don't leave Gaines—or they'll have you clad in a white shift and crucifix before you can sneeze. We don't want that, do we?" I caught the spark in his eye. "What do I know about bringing up young girls? They need their mother here. I will not have you living barefoot on the seashore until some passing ship can be found to take you off and deposit you in some godforsaken spot in France. So stay put!"

What sort of advice was that? I sat at home and harried the servants as the days lumbered past, all my old fears surfacing, my body cold, my mind frightened and unbearably lonely. The weeks crawled.

Why is it that time allows us to ponder our gravest fears rather than our brightest hopes? Once, I had been certain that Windsor would stand by me, certain that I would never be alone again. I had been so sure. But now the doubts crept in. What if I was wrong? Would he betray me under Parliament's intimidation? Would he abandon me and leave me to Joan's mercies? Would he promise never to see me again, if that was what they demanded from him in return for his own freedom? No one could ever deny that Windsor had a streak of self-interest as wide as the Thames through his very bones.

The days were endless, and I felt increasingly bereft.

Thank God! Thank God! Four long weeks and Windsor returned.

"What did they say?" I demanded, standing at his horse's shoulder, looking up into his face, and making no attempt to hide the anxiety that had raged since the day of his departure. I had not even waited until he dismounted, but had run out into the courtyard from my bedchamber without veil or shoes. I now gripped his bridle so fiercely that his horse sidled and tossed its head. I held on, wincing at the stones beneath my feet.

"And good day to you too, my lady!" he replied as the animal snorted, sidestepping.

"Don't play with me, Windsor. . . ."

"Wouldn't dream of it. If you'll allow me to dismount . . ."

I stepped back. "Well?" He swung to the ground in a cloud of dust, beating it from his tunic and the folds of his mantle. "Now will you tell me? Why keep me waiting . . . ?" Fear was a hard knot in my throat, and my blood was laced with lead.

His stare was speculative. "They've dropped the charge against me."

As simple as that? "I don't believe you!"

"I can't think why not. I told you not to worry."

"So you did." I grimaced at his easy confidence, a confidence I might once have had. "I'm so pleased, Will . . . but I still can't quite believe . . ."

"There's more!"

Of course there was. The knot that had momentarily slackened tightened again, and my blood seemed to drain to my feet. "Tell me. What terms did they demand?"

"The members of Parliament, in their wisdom, have changed their collectively narrow minds on the little matter of your banishment."

"Changed their minds . . . ?"

"You are, as of yesterday, free. And so am I, from the charge of willfully consorting with a banished woman."

Still unsure, I watched Windsor's expression for any reaction, for confirmation, but there was none. It might have been chipped out of stone. He neither expanded on his news nor moved to touch me. There was something between us, much like one of Wykeham's formidable walls of stone blocks. There was something more that he was not telling me.

"There's a fly in this bowl of pottage," I said, hating to have to ask, fearing the answer. "What is it?"

"How do you know there is one?"

"I can tell by your face."

"And here was I thinking I was being inscrutable!"

I punched his arm, not playfully. "There is always a price to be paid by someone." I frowned. "I just can't see how it would work. . . . Joan would never want the banishment lifted." I was certain of it. So what had prompted this turn of fortune in my favor?

"Pour me a cup of ale, my love, to rid my mouth of the poison of

Court negotiations, and I might just tell you all." Windsor tossed his reins to a waiting groom and wound an arm around my waist in his habitual comforting greeting. "It's been a long few weeks. I feel in need of some home comforts."

He kept me waiting while he ate his way through a plate of beef and a flat loaf, by which time I was all but hopping with frustration, but I knew him well enough to keep my mouth closed and my impatience to myself. I sat opposite, eyes fixed on his every move, every damned mouthful of bread and meat, and waited.

He drained the cup.

"Another draft of ale?" I inquired sweetly.

"I might . . ."

I reached for the pottery jug, then held on to it and did not pour. "A slab of cheese, perhaps? A collop of mutton?"

"Well, I might be persuaded. . . ."

"And I might empty this over your head!"

He laughed. "You won't provoke me!"

"But *you* provoke *me*!"

"I'll do it no more." The lines of his face grew stern. "Accept the lifting of the banishment for what it is, Alice."

"Because I won't like what they demand in recompense."

"No. You won't. There are strings well and truly attached. . . ."

My voice caught. "You said they had changed their minds. . . ." Surely he would not hide an even worse outcome from me? No, no. He would not have sat through a meal without telling me. He had said I was free, that we both were. But what had that woman done? How far would Joan's vengeance stretch?

"God's Blood, Will!"

His hands, now unoccupied with knife and bread, took mine. "No, no. Do you think me so cruel? You are free, Alice, as I said. No banishment. You don't get your manors back—you can't expect miracles— but there's no further punishment. But here's the rub." And there was the gleam of friendly mischief back in his eyes. "You are free as long as you live with me, as my wife, and I am willing to keep you and stand surety for your good behavior."

I inhaled sharply. "A prisoner . . ."

"I thought you might see it in that light!"

"So I have to live within your governance."

When he handed me his cup, I gulped the ale inelegantly.

"As would any wife with her husband. And Parliament in its wisdom has decided to leave the judgment against you intact and unrepealed, to hang over your head, undeserving as you are of their compassion. To ensure your future good behavior." His teeth showed in a cold smile.

"So I am not pardoned."

"Yes, you are—but only on their terms—and mine." His expression warmed. "You have of necessity to please me, so that I don't cast you off."

"We cannot live without arguing!" I retorted.

"Oh, I think we can." He stretched his hands across the board again, to pin my restless fingers flat beneath his. "Don't you trust me? After all we've been through? And I thought you liked living with me."

"Yes . . . No! Of course I do! But, oh, Will!" The words were there before I could stop them. "When you didn't come back—I was afraid that you would betray me," I admitted. "I thought you would agree never to see me again, and I would be alone. . . ."

"Foolish girl!" He was completely unmoved by my lack of faith. By now he knew my buried fears well enough. "I will only abandon you and drive you from my door if you are very bad and argue over every juncture."

Turning my hands so that they could grip his, I sighed softly, letting myself respond appropriately to his dry wit. "Then I must be good. I'd better start now!" I reached for the jug again and refilled his cup, one question still remaining. "Why did they do it, Will?"

"That's simple, my love. The situation in France is deteriorating and they need able men."

I stared at him. Of course. It made sense. "You." My heart leaped uncomfortably against my ribs.

"Me, as you say. I think they have in mind a position for me. So they're keeping me, sweet."

"You bargained with them. . . ."

"I did. They've too many issues knocking on their door, not least a child king, to spend time on you and me."

"What did Joan say? Did you see her?"

"Briefly." His mouth twisted with distaste, but there was a flash of enjoyment after all. "Joan kept her opinions to herself in the presence of the young King's counselors. She managed to refrain from cursing you—but from the look in her eye I expect she has set fire to Richard's inherited bed. But for once she made the right decision. She put the good of the realm—my expert offices—before her personal vendetta—you, my love. She needs me." He yawned widely. "Now, since you're legally bound to be an amenable wife, or I may cast you from my door, come and help me remove these boots. . . ."

I removed more than that. Nor was I reluctant.

It was good to have him home.

Windsor was right. What an uncanny nose he had for political intrigue. Within the month he had been offered the eminent position of Governor of the newly acquired port of Cherbourg. His eyes positively gleamed at this new venture, and in them I read that he could not refuse. Nor should he. He was a politician, through blood and bone and sinew.

Ah, well! Loneliness beckoned for me.

"You'll take it," I said, a statement rather than a question.

"I think I will." He slid me a quizzical glance over the official request, heavy with its ink and red seals. "But they'll not get me cheaply. I'll make them pay for my loyalty."

"With what?"

"Aha! Nosy!"

"Tell me!"

"Not I! Or at least, not until I'm sure of my ground."

Not for the first time, his confidence, his damned superiority, rattled me. "Are you so sure you'll find the right bait to hook Parliament?"

"Certainly I am. There are few with my expertise in handling difficult provinces or squeezing money out of a reluctant populace."

He spent the next few days in the parlor, his lawyer and clerk in attendance, the door closed firmly against me. He emerged, so it seemed to me, only to eat and sleep. The work was long and laborious, if the number of ruined quills was anything to go by.

Then, without a word of explanation, we were packed and off to London.

"Why won't you tell me?" I asked.

"It would risk ill luck to air my plans at this stage. It's the Lords I need to convince." He was morose and preoccupied, staring between his horse's ears. Perhaps he was not as confident as he would like me to believe, which made me shiver. Then suddenly he grinned. "But they will have no answer to make against my arguments, so there's no reason for you to be concerned."

Westminster. The memories it stirred up ripped through my careful composure. How is it that dread, even when the reason for it is gone, is easily reawakened? When *I* had appeared before the Lords, Windsor had been refused admission. Would I be forced to wait out the time in an anteroom with pages and servants whilst he put some questionable bargain before the lordships that they could not refuse? I hated the thought, and my powerlessness in the whole proceedings.

I was not even sure why he had insisted that I accompany him.

"Why am I here, Will?" I asked as we stood in that same ill-fated antechamber.

"Are you afraid?" He looked surprised. "Alice, my love. Would I have brought you back here if I had thought you in any danger at all?" He raised my hand in an unexpected grave and formal salute to his lips. "You are here as Lady de Windsor, my excellent wife, under my protection. The law can't hurt you. . . ."

"No, it's not that," I admitted. "I'm just not sure why you need me. . . ."

"Because you are essential to me. Do you think you can manage an air of outraged innocence for the next hour?"

I stared at him.

"Perhaps not. Just don't speak unless spoken to. Keep your eyes down in a wifely, respectful manner. And follow my lead. And here . . ."

Rummaging in the leather purse at his belt, he removed an object that glinted gold. Seizing my left hand, he pushed the ring onto my finger. It was a tight fit. With a grunt of irritation, as if it were my fault, he forced it over my knuckle.

"And make sure it's obvious to every one of them!"

Before I could ask more, Windsor was ushering me into the chamber and I was left to take in the atmosphere. The Lords were expecting an undemanding session to confirm Windsor's promotion. Self-congratulation sat comfortably on them until I entered at Windsor's side, with Windsor brushing aside any objection and addressing the Lords with impressive authority. A little bubble of laughter swelled in my breast. The expression on their collective faces—one of fury—was a blessing to me. Windsor ignored it.

"My lords." His voice and stance captured their attention. "The lady, known to you all, is here at my invitation. She is my wife, my lords. Lady de Windsor. The matter is pertinent to her and so the law makes provision for her attendance. She should not be required to stand. A seat for her, if you please."

An attendant scurried forward with a stool. Windsor led me to it, ignoring the rumble of comment. I sat. I tried to project outraged innocence, my blood humming in expectation, as I turned the gold circle with its ruby stone around my finger. It did not turn easily. What in heaven's name was he about? Gaunt, to my relief, was not present, but I did not think it would have mattered one way or another to Windsor.

Windsor bowed to me, then to the assembled gathering, and began without preamble. "I am honored by your offer of the post of Governor of Cherbourg, my lords."

"We value your experience, Sir William." I watched Northumberland's uncertainty with pleasure.

Windsor bowed again, impressively austere in his courtesy. "I am gratified. However, I find my acceptance of the honor is compromised, and I am undecided. A small matter that you alone can rectify, my lords."

"We will do all we can. . . ."

"It is the status of my wife, my lords."

It was as if every man there held his breath. So did I.

"Indeed, sir?" Northumberland had no documents to help him now. I did not smile. I sat demurely with eyes downcast.

"I request, my lords, a reversal and annulment of all your judgments against her." Windsor's voice filled the chamber. The air was as thick as smoke.

What are you doing, Windsor? They'll never do it.

"The law demands that a man—or woman—be tried in the weighty matters of fraud and treason before the Court of King's Bench. When my wife was summoned by your august selves, she was given judgment by a Commission." He allowed his eyes to roam thoughtfully over the startled faces. "My wife was not given due process before the King's Bench, which is her right. Thus, I hold the judgment against her—of banishment from the realm, and most pertinently the confiscation of her property—to be illegal."

"It was a time of great uncertainty, Sir William," Northumberland stammered.

"It was a time when the law should have been upheld, my lord, as you and I both know." Windsor drove on the attack. "Furthermore, my wife was not permitted to be present during the whole of the deliberations concerning her guilt or innocence. She was asked to leave the chamber. I know because I was cognizant of the whole series of events during your deliberations. This is not lawful, my lords. Do I continue? For I regret that there was yet another serious discrepancy between your conduct and the law of the land."

"Ah . . . ! I am not aware. . . ."

"My wife, my lords, was not given adequate time to locate witnesses and prepare her case."

"But, Sir William . . ."

Oh, how he made them squirm. Oh, how I rejoiced!

"One afternoon and one night, my lords. I know it for a fact, since I was present with my wife at the search for those who might stand for her. It was not sufficient time. It was not *legal*."

There was no response. Northumberland studied the knots in the floor at his feet.

"And finally, my lords. My wife was tried as *femme sole*, a woman alone, and in her own unwed name." How uncompromising his stance before the assembled lords. He did not speak loudly, and yet it seemed to me that his voice rang from the stone arches. Yet the thud of my heart in my ears almost drowned it out.

"That should not have happened, my lords, as you are aware. You chose to take advantage of a woman alone. But Alice de Windsor is my wife and thus not without protection. By law, her property is mine. Whatever the judgment against her, Parliament had no right to confiscate her property, since, to put it simply, my lords, it was no longer hers to be confiscated." I could taste the disdain in his condemnation. "The property is mine, my lords, and I demand its return. Immediately. As I demand a pardon for a judgment against Lady de Windsor that should never have been given."

Oh, it was masterly. But would they bend before such erudition? I saw Windsor's hands tighten infinitesimally on the folds of the hat he held.

"If you will give my arguments due consideration, my lords, and uphold the rights of my wife in this case, I will consider the post you offer me. Otherwise . . ."

The pause lengthened. Windsor made no attempt to fill it. The covert threat hung in the air.

We were asked to wait as they deliberated. Whilst I fretted and fussed, Windsor sat in silent contemplation of some distant scene, his shoulders against the wall, his booted ankles crossed. Only when we were resummoned did he take my hand and squeeze it hard.

And he led me in.

Neither of us sat. Their conclusion was stated within the time it took for the sun's rays to crawl, snail-like, the width of a fingernail across the floor. The Lords, cowards that they were but with ludicrous dignity, deferred any decision on their trampling of the legal niceties of my case until the meeting of the next Parliament. A striking example of how to avoid the issue. I felt my courage draining away again.

You've lost, Will. It's a hopeless cause to get them to recognize my innocence. I admire you for it. I love you for it. But you should never have taken them on. You'll lose your chance of promotion. . . . Oh, Will! Why did you risk it?

"But you do admit to the validity of my arguments," Windsor pressed them, unaware of my premonition of disaster.

"We think that the new Parliament will consider the force of your argument, Sir William," Northumberland intoned.

"Excellent. Then I will *consider* the post of Governor of Cherbourg."

"Ah—we trust you will do more than consider, Sir William. . . ."

"That, Lord Henry, might all depend. . . ."

They understood each other very well.

The audience was at an end.

Windsor waved my doubts away. "I'll get it. And you'll get your pardon."

"They'll keep the banishment hanging over me until the day I take my last breath. . . ."

"They won't, you know."

"And my manors are lost to me forever, most of them, I suspect, in Gaunt's devious hands!"

"I'll be the new Governor of Cherbourg before the month is out. Just for once, Alice, accept that you're wrong!"

"Do you want this back?" I asked crossly, trying to work the ring over my knuckle without success. "Now that there's no further need for me to keep it. If I can get it off! You might have to take a sword blade to it. . . ."

"Keep it!" He watched my efforts with amusement until he closed a hand on mine to stop me. "You played your wifely part magnificently. Besides"—he kissed my palm, and then my much-abused finger joint—"I should have given you this years ago. It's of no great value. It was my mother's. I don't think she would have approved of you, but still . . ."

"I'm not good enough for you, I suppose." I scowled to hide my pleasure at the simple little ring. It was of inestimable value to me.

"No. But she didn't have a very high opinion of me either. . . ."

Was he never serious? I hissed my irritation. Windsor kissed me until I stopped. And he was right, of course.

"Will you really reject the preferment?" I asked. "If you don't get your own way?" Who could know what this complex, enigmatic man might do?

His face was fierce with his achievement. "They'll never know. And nor will you."

Epilogue

Windsor went off to Cherbourg, looking every inch the puissant governor, with his weapons polished, his horse's coat gleaming, and a new tunic and boots to mark the preeminence of the position. A port and fortified town, Cherbourg had been obtained by England on excellent terms from Charles of Navarre, and now promised to be a lucrative as well as a prestigious post for its new official. As I watched his wagons and pack animals plod steadily into the distance, I knew that he would enjoy the challenge of bringing Cherbourg firmly under English dominion, and of raising the revenues from the merchants there. In past days he had positively shimmered with energy. Life had been tedious for him since the end of his Irish sojourn. Windsor was meant for rural isolation as little as I.

As for our domestic bliss together, would we live into our dotage with love embracing us?

Never. The love was true. My heart was healed by it. But we were each too independent to rest entirely on the other.

"Come with me!" he urged, even at the eleventh hour, when the horses were stamping and sidling at the delay. "Pack your bags and come to Cherbourg."

His stare urged me; his tone was imperative. His hands were strong around my wrists. By the Virgin, I was tempted. But . . .

"And do what? Sit in my parlor and stitch altar cloths whilst you play the great man?"

"You could entertain the merchants and their wives, seduce them into tossing gold into English coffers."

I raised my brows.

"You could buy up property in and around Cherbourg."

I shook my head.

"You could dress in silks and emeralds and play Lady de Windsor to your heart's content."

"I have already dressed in silk and emeralds. In another life."

"Other women find it satisfying." Impatient though he was, he pressed his lips hard against my temple, my mouth, and almost seduced me.

"I am not other women."

"No, you are not." His smile was a little twisted. "And I love you for that alone. Then stay and hold my manors for me." He kissed me again, then scooped up Jane and held her high above his head. "Look after your lady mother for me. Don't allow her to become too combative if her position as lady of the manor is undermined."

Jane laughed and squirmed, uncomprehending. Joanne hung back, suddenly shy, behind my skirts. Braveheart joined her.

"Farewell, my Alice."

"Farewell, Will. Keep safe."

And then he was gone.

I wept. In the privacy of my chamber. In the far reaches of the great barn where no one would hear me as I howled out my misery. How could I be capable of shedding so many worthless tears over one ungrateful man? I missed him. Oh, how I missed him. I should have gone with him, I told myself—there would be no hindrance to my living across the Channel. My banishment might still exist before the law, to be enforced at any time—the new Parliament had not met to find its way to reconsider it—but Windsor was certain it would be revoked, and that as long as I lived under his roof no harm would come to me. So what if I had little to do in France other than order the household and ply a needle and gossip with merchants' wives? I would be with Windsor.

He has gone! He has left me! How can I live my life without him? Who will comfort me? What will I do if he forgets me . . . ?

What a miserable excuse for a sensible woman you are!

How will it be if one day I cannot recall his face, the fall of his hair against his neck?

You survived his absence well enough when he was in Ireland. Stop whining!

So I set myself to work, a time-honored distraction. I had made my decision. Much as I enjoyed Windsor's company, much as he had become strangely essential to my happiness, life as the Governor's wife in Cherbourg held no attraction for me, and the pull of my beleaguered property, still under confiscation, was strong. So I remained at Gaines with my two growing girls and Braveheart—gray muzzled now but still prepared to chase the coneys from the orchard—and wrote Windsor long, informative letters. And sometimes, when he had the time, he wrote back.

His visits home were sweet with reconciliation. It was not so difficult a journey for him, but they were rarely frequent enough for me.

"Alice!" He was exuberant as ever. "Come and welcome your lord and master."

"I see no lord and master." I looked askance at him, much as I had when we first met, this time from my superior position on horseback. My heart was thudding so hard I could have fallen at his feet. "Do I know you?"

His growl of laughter stirred my belly to hot desire.

I had ridden home to Gaines, after settling a dispute regarding a boundary between two of Windsor's recalcitrant tenants, to find the usual chaos of arrival. There in the midst of all, directing horses and baggage, was Windsor, now striding toward me. His face was alight with the same saturnine smile that had piqued my curiosity so long ago at Edward's Court.

"I hear you've been wielding a heavy stick for me against my tenants." He held out his arms as I slid down from my horse. "My love, my dear, my impossibly belligerent one."

Not caring that we had an interested audience, I leaned into his embrace. He had returned. His clasp was all-encompassing, his lips warm and gratifyingly familiar on mine. All the futile emptiness in my chest dissolved as his arms tightened around me as if he would never let me go, although I knew he would when the time came.

"How long, Will?" It was the only thing that mattered.

"I can manage a few weeks at least. Cherbourg is well in hand." He released me to search in one of his saddlebags. "First things first. I have this for you."

I found I was smiling foolishly. It was good to see him. I did not greatly care what the gift was—a jewel, a pair of gloves, presumably something small enough to be packed into so confined a space. But it was neither. With a flourish, he produced a letter and presented it to me with a courtly bow.

"This is yours, Lady de Windsor. A meager piece of parchment, and much traveled—but of immeasurable value."

He was somber as I opened the sheet, smoothing out the creases. I glanced up at his stern face, then back down at the directive with its heraldic emblem and red seal.

"They've done it, Will!" I gasped. "They've done it at last!"

There it was: beyond all my hopes. My banishment formally, officially, legally, revoked. A pardon granted to me for my breaking of Parliament's command--the crime that I had never committed.

"Did you doubt it?" Windsor asked, his smile like a shaft of sunlight to pierce my heart.

"Yes. Oh, yes. I doubted it," I replied, light-headed with the joy of it.

"I didn't," he responded with the arrogance I had come to accept. "I'm too valuable to antagonize. They knew I could always rescind my decision, leaving them in the lurch to find a new Governor. Now, don't weep over it!" He took the parchment from me, sliding it into his belt. "It's far too valuable to be blurred by unnecessary tears! You lost Gaunt's original letter—we'll not lose this one."

I covered my face with my hands, my relief beyond words, and the tears continued to flow. Windsor took my wrists in a gentle grip and drew my hands down.

"Does that give your restless soul some contentment?"

"Some." I managed a little laugh. "My thanks, Will."

"And that's not all." He paused until he had my attention. "You'll get your property back, legally acknowledged as yours."

"All of it?" Now, that I could not believe.

He shook his head. "Not the manors in Edward's gift. They'll not do that. But all the lands legally purchased by you and Greseley—they will be restored."

"That's enough. . . ." I could barely utter the words. "It's wonderful! I'll have Pallenswick again. . . ."

"But they are not quite yours. . . ." He was leading me into the house.

I stopped.

"What?"

"They will be restored to *me*—as your husband." His shout of laughter at my shocked expression disturbed the doves roosting on the roof of the stables, sending them up into a white-winged cloud.

"God damn them to hell! I don't agree with that. . . ."

"Did I think you would?"

"But I . . ."

"It's the best you can get, Alice. You know how the law stands. Your possessions are mine. But I'm a very generous husband." He was solemn again, holding my hands strongly, palm-to-palm with his, to prevent my possible retaliation. He still read the fire in my eyes. "I make you free of your manors—I won't interfere in their running. And the income from them is yours to use for yourself and your children."

"How generous!"

"Exceedingly! Does it not satisfy you, Alice?"

I allowed my thoughts to settle. I had never thought it to be in my heart and mind, in my very soul, to be satisfied. Had I not always been restless, striving for the unreachable, driven to make a life that was safe and secure, for my children, for me? I must accept reality. A woman was dependent on a man, however much she might like to deny it, and if I would choose to be dependent on any man, it would be William de Windsor.

There he stood, the sun silvering his hair at the temples, the court-yard brimful of his presence, the smile that remained a constant companion even in his absence. Who'd have thought that the infamous Windsor would have a haunting smile? But he did for me.

"Well?" he asked. "I could do no more for you than this, ungrateful hussy."

"I know. And I am very grateful," I replied. I took his arm and we stepped together inside our home. I smiled. "I am satisfied."

Photo courtesy of Orphans Press

Anne O'Brien taught history in the East Riding of Yorkshire, England, before deciding to fulfill an ambition to write historical fiction. She now lives in an eighteenth-century timbered cottage with her husband in the Welsh Marches in Herefordshire, a wild remote area that provides much inspiration for people and events in medieval times.

CONNECT ONLINE

www.anneobrienbooks.com
facebook.com/anneobrienbooks

THE KING'S CONCUBINE

A NOVEL OF ALICE PERRERS

Anne O'Brien

A CONVERSATION WITH
ANNE O'BRIEN

Q. It's amazing to me that a woman of such obscure origins as Alice could rise so high as to become the King's powerful mistress. Was she just a smart woman who got lucky?

A. Alice was without doubt a smart woman. Her origins are difficult to penetrate. Despite recent research, her ancestry is uncertain and there is no record of her birth. If she knew her family, she never made claims on them or promoted them when she came to power. We know nothing of her education except that she was clearly able to read and write and deal with numbers, quite an achievement for a girl of no social standing. It seems she was married briefly to Janyn Perrers, a Lombardy moneylender living in London.

So how did she achieve her preeminence? Part good fortune: There is no record of why or how she came to the attention of the Queen—thus the role of the novelist to fill in the gaps. As for the rest, Alice took advantage of her situation to line her pockets and ensure a comfortable life for herself and her children in preparation for royal patronage coming to an end. Definitely a smart and intelligent woman who used her talents to the full.

Q. Alice strikes me as being highly adaptable and intuitive, able to suss out a situation and identify where her best interest lies. She's the consummate survivor. Do you agree? What do you see as Alice's greatest strengths and weaknesses?

A. Alice was a survivor. Her greatest strength was her astonishing tenacity in pursuing her ambitions in a man's world. She proved herself to be a remarkable businesswoman in using every method open to her to cushion her future. At the same time, I think she cared deeply for Edward and did all she could to alleviate the loneliness and confusion of his last days. She stayed with him to the end.

Her weakness, if it was a weakness, was her ability to make too many powerful enemies— but given her position at Court and her influence over the King, this was inevitable. Even so, compromise did not exist in Alice's planning. Once she had achieved wealth, she wanted more. The pursuit of power and land, which she did with remarkable success, proved to be her undoing.

Q. Despite the wealth and power Alice gains as Edward's mistress, she strikes me as singularly alone during her time at Court—with no one female friend to confide in, and subject to Edward's waxing and waning interest. Do you think she was deeply lonely?

A. I think that Alice was an isolated figure and probably felt the lack of intimacy of female friendship. In all the voices raised against her, not one was raised in her support. Perhaps this was one of the factors that drove her into her liaison with Windsor, seeing in him a kindred spirit and a reflection of her own ambitions. In the novel I suggest that at one point she regretted her lack of a confidante, but I don't think it troubled her overmuch. I think Alice was a man's woman. Female companionship was of little importance to her.

Q. Plague comes through early in the novel. It's hard for us now to imagine the despair and devastation it wrought as it swept periodically through Europe. Can you tell us a little more about its impact?

A. Plague first struck England in the summer of 1348, with dire results. Arriving in Dorset in the west, it spread rapidly, killing perhaps half the population of England within twelve months. It struck indiscriminately at rich and poor alike—Philippa's daughters were victims of the plague—but mostly it was to be found in town communities, where the disease could spread rapidly in the unhealthy conditions. Clerics who ministered to the sick were particularly badly hit. Recovery was rare, and the suffering great from the buboes that grew in armpit and groin, the plague victims usually succumbing within three days and being buried without record in plague pits. There was no understanding of its cause—the bite of the flea that lived on the black rat. I think we do not fully appreciate the full extent of the death rate. What we do know is that the shortage of laborers helped to bring the end of the servitude of the feudal system. The workers who remained demanded higher wages and more freedom from service. The lords had no choice but to accept.

After this first epidemic, plague returned at regular intervals, never so widespread or for so long, but still enough to fill the medieval mind with fear of death and punishment for wrongdoing. The final appearance was in the reign of Charles II in 1665.

Q. *Except for his last years, Edward III seems to have been an effective ruler. What do you see as his lasting legacy? How does he fit into the grand sweep of English history?*

A. Edward III has been celebrated as the most brilliant of all English monarchs, and there is much justification for it. He was a magnificent figurehead and a chivalrous leader, and he took on the demanding role with great enthusiasm until his decline in his final decades. His achievements were outstanding. Throughout his long reign he preserved peace within England, the stability bringing an increase in trade and prosperity. In international affairs, England became supreme and the center of European politics. As patron of the arts and architecture, Edward supervised the extension and improvements of the great palaces, such as

Windsor. Much of the English love of historical pageantry came from Edward: He loved outward show, and it was he who adopted the Flag of Saint George.

Unfortunately, terrible seeds of disaster for the future were sown in Edward's reign. The European empire became untenable, dragging England into expensive war without hope of success. Perhaps of greater misfortune, Edward's creation of titles and wealth for his sons, given the strain of the minority and the character of Richard II, was eventually to lead to the power struggle and civil war of the Wars of the Roses.

Q. How rare was Edward's devotion to Queen Philippa? Do all your sources suggest he sincerely loved her, or is that your romantic imagination at work?

A. Edward and Philippa were soul mates. Theirs was an arranged marriage, but Edward found in Philippa a stability that had been lacking in his early life, when he had been manipulated by his ambitious mother, Queen Isabella, and her lover, Mortimer. Edward was a superlative knight and a courageous fighter, but he needed support at home.

Philippa stood by him, gave him the benefit of her strong common sense, and encouraged him to seize power for himself. This unity developed into a very deep and abiding love, cemented by their large family. Stories of Edward's adultery early in the marriage are regarded by historians as a product of French propaganda against him. It is generally thought that he had no mistress and was entirely faithful to Philippa until Alice Perrers came to court. Even then he had a care for Philippa, hypocritical as it might appear. Her death broke him, pushing him into the slow deterioration of his final years.

I think I have not exaggerated the strength of feeling between them. They were devoted to each other over a marriage of forty years; it was a very satisfying relationship to explore.

Q. Do we know what ailment Philippa suffered from? Was it something her children inherited?

A. Philippa's final years were full of suffering. A fall from her horse when hunting resulted in severe damage to her shoulder, probably a dislocation, which was never reset adequately. This gave her intense pain. It also seems that she suffered from dropsy, the painful swelling of soft tissue due to the accumulation of fluid in the body, a complaint that could be alleviated today but not then. Her children did not inherit it.

The deaths of her daughters Mary and Margaret from the plague in 1361, and later Lionel, her son, sank her into a depression that made her suffering so much worse.

Q. John of Gaunt comes across as wily and ambitious, and one of Edward's more capable sons after the death of his heir. What happened to John after the end of The King's Concubine—*and will you be writing about him in a future book?*

A. John of Gaunt was considered to be perhaps the most able of Edward's sons: A charismatic man but without significant military talent, he was overshadowed by his father and older brother, the Black Prince. He was accused of having an eye to the Crown for himself, but, in fact, he remained loyal to his young nephew Richard II throughout that troubled reign, being greatly saddened when Richard exiled his son Henry (later to be Henry IV) for ten years and later for life. It was Henry who returned to England and overthrew Richard, but that was after Gaunt's death. He died in 1399.

Gaunt will appear in a later novel as the powerful lover of Katherine Swynford, whose children were to carry royal Plantagenet blood into the Beaufort family and thus to the Tudors. The story of Gaunt and Katherine is the quintessential love story.

Q. Can you tell us more about what happened to Alice's four children? Did she have any others?

A. We are fairly certain that John was Edward's son. There is some debate over Jane, Joanne, and Nicholas, but no certainty. Even their birth dates are unknown. I considered it more likely that they were all Edward's children rather than Windsor's, given their ages, and since Windsor never claimed them as his and left no property to them. We know a little of their history:

John de Southeray was born in 1364. He was knighted in April 1377 and died sometime after 1383. He married Matilda Percy, a daughter of the powerful Percy family in the north.

Nicholas Lytlington died in 1386. He was Abbot of Westminster Abbey and made a name for himself collecting books and manuscripts.

Joan—or Joanna—married Robert Skerne.

Jane married Richard Northland.

Q. How much of Alice's relationship with William de Windsor do you base on fact? What happens to them after the events of your novel?

A. The facts of the relationship between Alice and Windsor are few. We know that they were married, probably in 1373, but that Windsor returned to Ireland. We know they bought property together. The marriage was probably kept secret from Edward, who claimed that he knew nothing of it. When Alice came under attack and was threatened with banishment and loss of her property, Windsor came to her rescue, and it was he who negotiated the lifting of the sentence. It was an unusual marriage: They spent little time together, but Windsor had enough concern for Alice to stand by her when no one else would.

In 1381, after the end of novel, Windsor was recalled from Cherbourg and lived with Alice at Upminster, and was created a baron and so sat in the House of Lords from 1381 to 1384. He died at Greyrigg in Westmoreland in September 1394, leaving his land, interestingly, to his three sisters, not to Alice.

Much litigation followed, of course, with Alice determined to get what she considered to be hers, but without success. She lived on, alone, at Upminster and died there in the summer of 1400, leaving her lands and houses to her two daughters. She was buried in the church in Upminster.

Q. At one point Alice owns or leases fifty-six manor houses and a number of town properties! Wasn't this extraordinary even for a time when wealth was concentrated among the aristocracy?

A. It was an exceptional achievement, and for a woman of no wealth or background, it was almost unknown. Alice became the wealthiest common-born woman in the land. If a man had acquired so much wealth, he would have been entitled to the rank of earl. This, of course, is the reason for the extent of the hostility toward her. Today Alice would be considered to be a remarkable businesswoman; then she was damned as a rapacious and grasping female. The accusations were, of course, made by men.

Q. You live in Hereford, in the land between England and Wales. Can you tell us more about this region, which is not a common tourist destination?

A. Herefordshire, part of the Welsh Marches, has always been an area "on the fringe" and still is today. Once, it was a wild, lawless place, and it remains very isolated. It is served by no major road or rail routes. Towns are small, villages even smaller, and there is no significant industry. It is true to say that many people in Britain are not quite sure whereabouts Herefordshire actually is.

For those who do know, it is a very beautiful area, quite wild and uninhabited in places, a land of small fields and massive oak trees, small houses tucked away down quiet lanes, and Hereford cattle, all dominated by the high ridge of the Black Mountains, which mark the border with Wales. The villages have great charm—often called the "black and white" villages because many of the houses are from the original medieval method of building in wood and plaster. Apples are grown for cider and hops for beer. Buzzards fly overhead.

It is also an area of "history," with visual remnants of the Wars of the Roses and the English Civil War. It was once land owned by the great families of Mortimer and Plantagenet. Today there are ruined castles and battlefields and manor houses that keep the past alive.

I love it. It inspires me. I can think of no better place to live.

Q. Have you traveled much in the United States? What do you think of it? Are there any pieces of our history that you find particularly interesting?

A. In 2011, I traveled for two weeks in the southeast of the USA. I thoroughly enjoyed it, particularly Charleston and Savannah and, of course, New Orleans. I realized how limited my knowledge of U.S. history is, and was particularly drawn to the events of the Civil War, partly through the enthusiasm of our very well-informed guide. I had read *Gone with the Wind*, but otherwise my knowledge was very patchy. I am determined to do something about that!

QUESTIONS
FOR DISCUSSION

1. What do you think of Alice? What appeals to you about her, and what doesn't?

2. Aside from Alice, who is your favorite character in the book and why?

3. Do you understand Alice's need for financial security, which she seeks out by owning or controlling property? Do you see her as greedy or needy, or both? And do you know anyone like her in this way?

4. People call Alice ugly, and she considers herself unattractive. Is it possible that her beauty was simply unconventional for the time? Talk about how our notions of what is beautiful change through history, and from one culture to another.

5. Alice and William de Windsor have an unconventional relationship for the mid–thirteen hundreds. What makes their union so unusual? Does it appeal to you? Do you find their romance satisfying?

6. What do you think of Philippa for indirectly arranging for Alice to become her husband's mistress? If you had a long-term illness or

disability that made lovemaking with your husband painful or impossible, would you want him to take another lover?

7. Discuss the mothers in the book—Alice, Philippa, Joan of Kent, etc. Who do you think is the best mother, and why? Compare child-rearing practices back then and now.

8. Alice lives through a period of plague. Can you imagine how you would react to an incurable disease that strikes as indiscriminately and as swiftly? Would you give up or fight tooth and nail to survive?

9. If Alice were born in the United States today, illegitimate and abandoned, what do you think might happen to her?

10. How does Alice compare to other famous women from British history whom you might have read about?